FATHER'S MUSIC

FATHER'S MUSIC

DERMOT BOLGER

Flamingo
An Imprint of HarperCollinsPublishers

This is a work of fiction and the
characters and events are fictitious
products of the author's imagination.
Any similarities to real people or events
is purely coincidental.

Flamingo
An Imprint of HarperCollins*Publishers*
77–85 Fulham Palace Road,
Hammersmith, London W6 8JB

Published by Flamingo 1997
1 3 5 7 9 8 6 4 2

A catalogue record for this book
is available from the British Library

ISBN 0 00 225471 9 (Hardback)
0 00 225655 X (Trade Paperback)

Set in Garamond 3 by
Rowland Phototypesetting Ltd,
Bury St Edmunds, Suffolk

Printed and bound in Great Britain by
Caledonian International Book Manufacturing Ltd, Glasgow

IN MEMORY

Johnny Doherty, travelling fiddle-player
from Donegal,
Seamus Ennis, Ard-Rí of Irish pipers
from Finglas, North Dublin
and
Seosamh Ó hEanaí (Joe Heaney),
Sean-nós singer from Connemara,
County Galway.

I

LONDON

ONE

MY LOVER LOWERS his headphones over my hair, then enters me. He thrusts stiffly and deep. Irish music swirls into my brain, a bow pressing down across a fiddle, teasing and twisting music from taut strings. My breath comes faster as his hands grip my buttocks, managing to rub his shoulder against the walkman's volume control. The tune rises, filling me up. I close my eyes so that I can no longer see Luke, just feel his penis arching out and in. The set of reels change and quicken. I listen to a gale blowing across a treeless landscape, see a black huddle of slanted rooftops and drenched cows dreaming of shelter. The beat is inside my head from child-hood, imagining an old shoe strike the stone flags and the hush of neighbours gathered in.

Luke pulls my legs higher, positions a pillow under my tensed back. I don't want to ever open my eyes. The music is so loud and quick it seems sweet torture. It courses through me. I can see his old face playing, that capped man with nicotined teeth and tufts of greying hairs in his nostrils. His eyes are half closed, his breathing laboured. He looks so infirm that he could hardly shuffle across the room, yet his hand flicks the bow back and forth without mercy. He squeezes the wild tune loose, an old master in utter control, coaxing out grace-notes and bending them pitilessly to his will, while the wind howls outside along sheep tracks known only to mountain foxes and to him. He is my peddler father, the wandering lone wolf tinker my mother would never speak of, whose restless soul must now be constrained in some isolated graveyard.

3

My lover suddenly cries. I know I have drawn blood with my nails against his back. But Luke's voice is lost beneath the reel spinning faster and faster. And I shout too, no longer caring who hears in that cheap hotel near Edgware Road, with no will left of my own. My voice is just one more note lost in the frenzy of a Donegal gale blowing itself out among the rocks beyond the house where my father once played. Then my scream is suddenly loud, piercing the rush of white noise as the reels halt and I hear my lover come, feeling his final thrusts before I twist the headphones off to look up. The same hairline cracks are on the ceiling. A fly blunders against the damp lampshade, clinging insanely to life in late November.

'Did you come?' Luke asks. That's my own business. I stare back until he looks away.

'Does your wife like you to fuck her like this? Or is she more the country-and-western kind?'

We lie still after that. Why do I always need to hurt Luke? Is it my way of keeping any threat of tenderness at bay? In four weeks' time it will be Christmas, with his youngest son waking him before dawn. He gets his store manager to phone the boy from his tile shop every Christmas Eve. Afterwards the child asks, 'Why does Santa have an Irish accent?' I am not jealous. I have no wish to make silent phone calls to eavesdrop on their puzzled tones. Luke would bring me somewhere better than this hotel if I asked. But it suits our relationship which started in the tacky Irish Centre across the road, with Luke embarrassed by his family over from Dublin, like overdressed extras in a gangster film, and me fag-hagging there by fluke with a black queen. The only point my mother and Gran seemed united on was that I would never marry an Irishman.

I listen to the Asian family being bed-and-breakfasted by the Council in the next room and think of how the envious bitch of a receptionist gawks at us each Sunday. I arrived early last week. 'Your *friend* isn't here yet,' she said. 'He's not my friend.' I eyed her coldly, raising my voice. 'He's my *lover*!'

Luke turns towards me, half asleep as always after he comes. Sometimes I claim that he calls me by his wife's name when he wakes. It frightens him in case he's doing the same with her. I like it when I can frighten Luke, especially as he scares me so easily. Maybe this edge of fear has held us together for all these weeks, because I know our affair cannot last.

I touch the scar below his left nipple. After all those early fights, this is the only mark on his body. *The Canal Wars*, he called them. I looked it up once in a book on Irish history. He laughed when I said I couldn't find it, and spoke of rival gangs of Dublin youths fighting for possession of a canal lock where they could swim among the reeds and rusted prams in their underpants. Luke had been ten, sent out by his big brother Christy to spy on the enemy. A rival gang caught him in a laneway and stripped off his shirt before a ginger haired boy with a deformed hand slashed at Luke's flesh with a bicycle chain. He came home with blood on his clothes. His mother sat with him in the hospital while the stitches were done. Weeks later an uncle struck him across the face in the street for allowing himself to be caught by anyone.

'I was never caught again,' Luke told me once. 'The best lesson I ever learnt. Fifteen years later I glanced up in the jakes of a pub in Birmingham and recognised that deformed hand. The man grinned sheepishly. "Jaysus, they were great oul days all the same, Mr Duggan." You couldn't hate a man who grinned like that. I pulled his jacket over his face so as not to leave scars when I kicked his head in.'

I had liked the way Luke said that, the consideration in his voice. Why bother all those years later, I asked. What could it prove? Luke had shrugged and claimed he'd no choice. It was the least that was expected of him back then. For years Ginger's fate had hung over him because he always knew he would meet one of the Duggans again. The man would have felt slighted if Luke hadn't bothered beating him up.

If they met now, Luke claims he wouldn't touch the man, having escaped from the lure of that family name, but I don't know if I want to believe him or not. I trace my finger across Luke's scar. He has had it so long that the stitch marks have faded into his skin. There's something vaguely delicate about it. His eyes watch me.

'Why are you always fidgeting with that?'

I close my eyes and see Luke diving from the rotting beams of a Dublin canal lock, his thin, eleven year old body splitting the green water apart. He sinks down, eyes opening in the fading green light. Bottles, reeds and a rusted milk churn. Something catches his ankle and he panics from memory, floundering his way to the surface to spit the oily water out. No boys are left to wage war since the accident. His cheap vest flaps alone under a stone like a flag of surrender.

'Tell me about the canal again.'

'No.'

'Go on, Luke.'

He rises on one elbow. Is he angry or scared?

'You're one mad bitch at times,' he says.

'Only at times? Go on, tell me about James Kennedy.'

I know he will tell me and he knows that I know. But not for a while yet. The story must be drawn from him. Thirty years later the memory is still raw. Sixteen months ago I watched my mother die in Harrow, but I had been prepared for it, with nurses discreetly waiting in the background and the cleansing scent of disinfectant. Her death had been so prolonged I had grown almost resentful of her. But what must it have been like at eleven to see your best friend drown?

Before then Luke's brother, Christy, was the gang's natural leader. But, at twelve, Christy was initiating himself into the stronger currencies of adolescence; the webs of factory sky-lights, the nods of silent fences, the expanding limits of pubescent girls allowing themselves to be manoeuvred into alleyways. In that vacuum James Kennedy had become the

6

Canal King, the reigning monarch of their childhood who plotted wars and conquests, with Luke happy as his lieutenant.

Somewhere in Luke's memory it must still be that parched July day, when thirty rival youths were beaten back from the canal lock and James Kennedy's gang danced on the rotten planks in Y-fronted celebration. They dived repeatedly from the wooden gates, raising a constant spray of foam as dogs shook themselves dry on the tow-path and an old tramp hunched down to watch, sucking on a discarded butt. What madness made Luke dive from so high up on the lock, and what choice had James but to climb even higher? The hush began before James' body even broken the water, as each boy counted the seconds, waiting for James' head to re-emerge. Thirteen seconds, fourteen, fifteen. Nobody wanted to admit that something was wrong. Nineteen, twenty, the sudden rush of bodies instinctively diving in.

James was still alive when they gathered around him, his foot caught in the spokes of an old wheel. Lush reeds were twisted round his ankle. Some boys claimed that the reeds were alive, wrapping themselves tightly round James' shin no matter how often they tried to prise them away. The others were forced to surface for air, while James' kid brother, Joe, screamed and wet his trousers on the bank. There was only James and Luke left down there, with James' face turning blue and his eyes curiously calm as if saying; 'you're the new king, kiddo, it's all on your shoulders now'. When the others dived again it was to pull their hands apart and bear Luke up into his new kingdom of barking dogs and sirens under the scorching sun.

Soon Luke will tell me this story again beneath the blankets, his voice cold and emotionless. I'll feel his penis stiffen and know that afterwards he will turn me on my stomach, his hands merciless as he grasps my hips to drag me back and forth. I will raise my hands to pull the blankets tight, drowning under the blackness we are submerged beneath, as I listen

7

to his hard excited breath and think of how his heart will beat, loud and fast as if scared, in the silence after we have spent.

I open my eyes, surprised that I have slept. I can hear the Asians watching a Star Trek movie. The carpet is threadbare and cold against my feet. I find my tights in the street light coming through the gaps in the blinds, hesitate and then pocket his walkman with the tape. Sean Maguire is the fiddler, he says. I think of Luke in jail that ·one time in Dublin, slopping out and being ridiculed for listening to bog music like that, with his family name alone protecting him. Luke claims that he has been a legitimate businessman for years now, but he never tells me why he served time and there are things that even I know not to ask.

The hotel room is freezing. I find my skirt and shoes. Luke hates me leaving without waking him. That's why he has hidden my knickers. He will reach for them beneath the mattress in half an hour's time, fingering them like some obscure consolation as he imagines me sitting on the swaying tube to Angel, being eyed by black youths in baseball hats. My legs will be crossed as I read the ads for fountain pens and office temps, while in my ears his tape will play like a phantom pain, bringing back all the memories I have never told him about.

The child whom I was once in my grandparents' house in Harrow seems like a stranger now. By day she would obey her Gran's clock-work ordinance, but alone at night she would close her eyes to imagine rooftops huddled against a Donegal hillside and neighbours gathering to hear her father play in hamlets and remote glens. I can see her still dancing barefoot, while my mother and Gran argued about her future downstairs. Swaying to tunes she could only imagine and spinning ever faster until, finally, falling on to the bed and gripping the blankets dizzily over her head, she almost believed that his fiddler's hands were swaying in the shadow of the cherry-blossom branches against her window: my dark father secretly making music for the daughter whose existence he had never bothered to acknowledge.

II

TWO

THAT SUMMER BEFORE I had met Luke it seemed to be raining incessantly almost every Sunday when I woke. Drab light pervaded my bedsit as I lay on until noon, stranded between dreams and wakening, before dragging myself under the shower down the hallway.

Later, as winter came in, I would resent Luke for becoming the focus of my Sundays. Before I met him they never dragged in that way. I had taken a slovenly delight in them, only bothering to cook myself a leisurely dinner and eat it in my dressing gown before the television when daylight was already teetering in the sky. The payphone on the landing rarely rang on Sundays and I made certain it never rang for me. I lived my real life away from that house of cheap flats in Islington and I recognised the other tenants only by the tread of their footsteps past my door.

Since moving into that flat after my mother's death, Sunday was the evening when, once a month or so, I allowed men to chat me up. I liked Sunday nights for that and I liked to hunt alone. The weekend was effectively over, with men less on the prowl and less in love with themselves and, on Monday morning, if they were lucky enough (few were and fewer deserved to be) I'd enjoy their predicament in trying to manoeuvre me from their beds in time to make a dash for work. Sometimes, with the more nervous types, I'd sleepily turn over, letting them stew with visions of a ransacked flat on their return and messages scrawled in lipstick for neighbours to read. Once or twice I even stayed on alone, wrapping myself in their bath robes and fingering the details of their lives after they had gone.

I always made sure they had somewhere to go, with proper jobs and nice apartments. I preferred my casual lays to be conventional. Accountants who bleated as they came and grinned uncomfortably when asked if their pure wool pullovers were purchased in Harrods or sheared off their backs by their mammies. *Bitch*, I heard them mutter in their minds. But they were hooked, calculating the odds and afraid to blow it. They'd rush to the bar to buy stronger drinks, hoping to catch their friends' eyes and be rewarded with a wink.

Sex seemed easier with people I'd nothing in common with. Their dull lives were exotic really. Ordered men swallowed any lie you threw at them. They scampered off when I finally allowed them to, desperate to brag confidentially about the former nun from Bishop's Stortford or the Leamington Spa zoologist they had picked up. Perhaps I judged some too harshly. A decent one or two probably bothered to phone the number I gave them and were hurt to find themselves speaking to the answering machine at the Battersea Dogs' Home.

But if I reserved one life for Sundays, it was on Saturdays that I really had my fun back then, with Roxy and Honor. We toured the clubs, trying to stay together as the E took hold and we threw ourselves into the joyous wave of bodies skewed about in the strobe lights and found each other again when we were washed out the other side. Sometimes there were vans that sped for hours along motorways, crammed full of underdressed girls and lank youths with dandruff and socks that could walk home by themselves.

We always had to stop to allow someone to get sick and stood about, arguing with the spaced out driver who swore blind that he wasn't lost. When we finally arrived, the raves were never as good as the expectations built up on those journeys. We would find ourselves in a field at dawn with damp grass and sheep shite trampled underfoot. There was a manic blankness in people's eyes as they danced like their movements were a nervous twitch they couldn't shake off. Even when their eyes closed as if asleep, their legs wouldn't stop moving. Music pulsed inside them like an orgasm they couldn't be released from, the pleasure of which paled and pained but continued on. Finally, when legs shuffled to a halt by themselves, a thirst remained like a purgatory which no Christ in no desert ever endured. By the time the local police arrived, the vans that had brought us there were gone. I hated the journeys where they herded us back to London and I'd finally unlock my flat door, too tired to open a window and release the odour of trapped heat and sour milk.

Those burnt out evenings were to be avoided. That was why Roxy and Honor and I fell out from those dance clubs most Saturday nights before the temptations of vague location maps and offers of lifts were passed around. Sometimes, giggling and swaying about the after-hours streets, we would stumble across a gig in some fire-trap basement club. If the band were inexcusably chronic we'd push our way up to the stage, dancing and screaming our adoration at the acne-scarred singer, puffing him up to more ludicrous posing. We'd cluster at his feet, shouting between songs that we would wait outside for him to take all three of us in the one bed later that night. Rather than fight among ourselves we had decided to share his body.

If the bouncers hadn't already cottoned on to us, we'd point towards the exit and blow kisses at him, before staggering out to laugh and fall against the shop windows, imagining him rushing to finish the gig. We'd play our favourite game of trying to out-stare the mannequins, shrieking over which shop dummy had winked back first. Then we'd order kebabs in some dingy restaurant, taking turns to trip down to the ladies and put our mouths under the tap. We'd sit, trying to cajole a smile from the sullen waitresses. I was happy there, loved by my friends and loving them back. Nothing could ever come between us. My life in Harrow had vanished and my future would have to wait because the present seemed so immaculate.

But eventually, when chairs were being piled onto the formica tables, we were forced on to the streets again. It would be nearly dawn and we'd stumble into Tower Records where serious night owls with horn-rimmed glasses scoured through the back catalogues of Gerry's Left Testicle or other punk bands from Papua New Guinea. We never lasted long there before we were thrown out. But sometimes, as the first ache of sobriety turned my stomach sour, I'd find myself flicking through the Irish section. The foreign names were unpronounceable, crammed with Os and Macs and crooked accents. I'd stare at the high cheekbones and bony elongated fingers of old pipers on sepia covers. There was even a tiny section reserved for sean-nós singing: a solitary, indecipherable wailing without any musical backing at all.

My mother once told me that my father, Frank Sweeney, sang as well as played the fiddle. He had reined in his wanderlust long enough to witness my birth before deserting us to return to Ireland. That was all I knew. I rarely thought about him or cared if he might still be alive. But sometimes during those raids on Tower Records I was glad that Roxy and Honor were goading a nerd as I searched in vain for what my mother once told me was his favourite tune, *Last Night's Joy*. I'd take the earphones from a listening post and select a disc at random. A grainy dawn would have broken with traffic easing off, leaving only black taxis speeding to catch the lights. I'd close my eyes, listening to the ebb of that impenetrable music and think of my mother dying in Northwick Park Hospital a year before. I didn't know what those tunes meant, each one sounding the same, only faster. Even their names gave no clue: *The Frost is All Over*, *Jenny Picking Cockles*, *The Pigeon on the Gate*.

They should have conjured up images of hillsides of barley shaken by the wind, or hares bounding through the winter dark as boots crunched ice on potholes along a lane. Instead

I saw my mother's face on a hospital pillow and thought of how I had never heard her listen to that music which, Grandad told me, my father had played in the back bedroom. My father's music and my mother's pain. Their daughter's futile regrets after the bird had flown. The music gave way to white static and suddenly it was Bessie Smith I wanted to hear, her pain resonating in the heavy pausing as she sang, *Sometimes I feel like a motherless child*.

I should be over her death by now, but too much guilt seemed involved to properly mourn her. I'd listen to the clamour as another reel began, knowing that two hysterical girls were about to grab the headphones and shriek with laughter at what was playing. 'Now that's what I call jungle music,' Honor would mock in her London accent laced with a Jamaican twang. What could I do, except pretend to share their mirth as the guard threw us out and we walked the streets until a taxi was found?

That was how, at six o'clock most Sunday mornings, I'd lean against my bedsit door, knowing the same memories were waiting to entrap me. I would be dejected and hungover, filled with regret for the passing of something I'd never properly known. I'd shut my eyes and see the swings in Cunningham Park in Harrow at dawn that previous August. For once the bowling greens had been without their flock of white-clad pensioners, but a group of teenagers still huddled around a ghetto-blaster, like zombies in a bad B-movie, as I had passed.

I hadn't even found somewhere private to say goodbye to my mother back then. But there had been no special places for the pair of us, no woodlands where mother and daughter had run through a riot of spring flowers or avenues of autumnal leaves. I hadn't even the memory of sharing a garden bench with her some summer night when she might have put names on to the scattered map of the stars. Maybe I had blocked such memories out that morning, because her death left a numb sensation. But, throughout her cremation, all I had kept remembering was a swing creaking in Cunningham Park, and my eight year old voice afraid to repeat the questions about whether I'd once had a daddy and where he might be. I could recall pain lining her face as, distractedly, she pushed me higher into the air than it felt safe to go, and the sense of being punished for saying something wrong.

Those swings were broken last August when I had knelt to scatter her ashes on the grass. She had always liked that view sweeping up to the public school on the hill. There was heavy rain forecast. I remember wondering if the teenagers had sat there all night. They finally lifted their heads indifferently to watch me open the urn. What did I expect to happen? That her ashes might dissolve with the dew or there would be a sign she was finally at peace? I felt foolish kneeling there. I rose and looked down. I had no God to pray to and I knew she couldn't really hear, but inside my head I spoke, if not to her spirit then to the ache she had left behind.

My mother was always crippled with doubt, imprisoned all her life by walls. Not just the walls of Gran's house from which she fled at twenty-two and to which my presence in her womb had forced her to return, or, later on, the walls of mental hospitals with bright day-rooms and discreet gates. It was the invisible walls of Gran's ambitions which corralled her in, the tyranny of Gran's dreams about how our lives should be led. She was their only child and now, with her death, I had been all they had left. But really Gran had abandoned Mammy for me long before she died, almost from the day she arrived home pregnant, in fact. The life they planned for me was plotted in a drawer of gilded photograph frames their own daughter had left blank. Their grandchild in a graduation gown, their grandchild smiling beneath her wedding veil, their great grandchildren playing in the cobbled drive of some house in Gerrards Cross which they had skimped all their lives to pay the deposit on.

Gran would have made careful plans about what to do with

Mammy's ashes, like she made plans for everything. Yet it wasn't for revenge that I had stolen the urn that morning, but from an obscure desire to set my mother free. I had felt nothing except numb indifference towards Gran when I packed my suitcase as they slept, taking whatever cash I could find, and left without leaving a note.

The first trains would be running soon. I had bent down, wanting to touch the ashes but lacking the courage. I climbed the railings at Hindes Road and jumped. I hadn't meant to look back, but when I did a dog was sniffing at the ashes, his owner fifty yards away as he cocked his leg. There was nothing I could do. I watched as he pawed them, then bounded away. Tears only came months later. Just then I had only felt a hollow sense of relief as I pushed the urn into a bin. I grabbed my bag and raced down Roxborough Road, towards the airless warmth of an early morning train and towards this bedsit where I had hoped to start a life I could finally call my own.

THREE

WHAT WAS IT THAT made me agree to accompany Honor's brother, Garth, to that Irish Centre off Edgware Road one Sunday evening in September? I had been his alibi, playing at being a fag-hag as he marauded down from the gay bars of Islington into uncharted territory. Roxy and Honor had rolled four joints before we left and teased him about setting off on mission impossible, claiming that he would never turn the baby-faced singer who was due to croon Irish ballads there. But Garth liked challenges and I liked him so much that I would have agreed to go anywhere.

The Irish Centre was packed when we arrived. We drank sitting at the bar. I watched the singer strut about, awkward in a white shiny suit that was as tight around the bum as a toy sailor's. The boy wasn't even cute. He had no technique and little sense of how to deliver a song, except with the wooden voice of an altar boy. I wondered if Garth could really have seen him peering hesitantly through the doorway of an Islington bar as if the entire clientele were about to devour him? But Garth swore that it was the same face which he had spied by chance on a poster advertising Liam Darcy, '*Drogheda's Own Singing Sensation*', appearing at the Irish Centre.

There had been some sort of football final across in Dublin that day, relayed on a big screen at the bar. The centre was still packed with women and men mingling together in gaudy team colours. The singer's face jerked around like a wind-up doll, trained to make eye contact with every corner of the room. Each time he reached us Garth was waiting to catch his gaze and wink. Grannies wandered up to the stage to leave requests for him. One left a present of a heart shaped tart. The singer had become aware of Garth and now avoided our part of the bar. His head would stop rotating just before it reached us, but each time his cheeks reddened slightly as they jerked back.

'You haven't a hope, Garth,' I laughed. 'Come on, let's get out of this dive and go to a club or something.'

Garth just laughed back. He was a handsome, well built man. I had already felt the envious glances of several women along the bar.

'I'm having a ball,' he replied. 'Sure the kid was as pale as a ghost before we came in. Now look at his cheeks. Here, grab a beer mat and take a request up to him.'

'I will not.'

'Go on,' Garth teased. 'The Nolan Sisters. Weren't they half Irish? Slip up to the stage and tell him Garth wants their old standard, *Let's pull ourselves together.*'

I laughed again and began to peel the back off a beer mat. I remembered the envy I had felt for Honor on the first evening when I'd gone back to her flat and seen Garth teasing her while their mother kept putting on more toast for anyone who casually called in. He looked over my shoulder, joining in my laughter as I wrote.

'Hey,' he said, 'remember that last song he dedicated to everyone present with a little bit of Irish inside them. You tell him to sing the next one for anyone who fancies another little bit of Irish inside them.'

I was drunk enough to bring it up. When I turned a tall Irishman stood right behind us at the bar. I had noticed him already with a large family group who were growing increasingly rowdy. Often men his age made fools of themselves trying to look young, but from his suit I actually thought he was far older until I looked at his face. He was obviously well known at the bar, to which he had been coming up every twenty minutes to buy another round of drinks. He seemed to pay for everything and yet he stood out from the family gathering as much as Garth and I stood out from the ordinary punters at the counter.

'Share the joke,' he said and I stopped laughing.

'What's it to you?' I asked.

'Maybe I could use a laugh.'

'Well, it's private between me and my boy-friend here.'

'I hope your boy-friend's boy-friend doesn't get jealous so.'

Garth stood up. They were shoulder to shoulder, both an inch either side of six foot. If the Irishman was into his forties then he wasn't irredeemably so. Garth would probably be a match for him alone, but not for his family. I was frightened. I had never liked Irish people anyway, because your upbringing doesn't go away. But the stand off between them was so subtle that not even those people beside us seemed aware of it.

'He's cute,' the Irishman said and Garth's eyes flicked briefly towards the stage. 'And you're everything an Irish mother would love her son to bring home: black, six foot tall and male.'

Garth continued staring ever so casually into the Irishman's eyes. There was something boyish about his face, yet also something I didn't quite trust. His voice was so low I could hardly hear it.

'I hear he goes walkabout, our little altar boy. He's a bit of a night bird, inclined to roam about like he doesn't quite know which way to go. Personally I think it's those apple tarts he has to take back to his room. I mean could you sleep, never knowing if some granny with no teeth and a black bra was going to jump out from inside one of them?'

'I've never heard nobody sing with that accent before,' Garth said.

'It's pure Drogheda,' the Irishman said. 'A class of knacker accent. You know knackers . . . cream crackers . . . tinkers? Travellers is the term we're meant to use now. God looks down when a knacker is born and says: "I ordained that this child be born on the side of the road in a freezing trailer that will be burnt out by the locals before Christmas is over, but just in case he survives I'll give him a Drogheda accent as well"'.

'And is he one?' I nodded towards the singer who had started an embarrassing line dancing routine while the crowd cheered. The Irishman laughed and used the opportunity to place his fingers for a second on my shoulder as if I were a child.

'They wouldn't let him through this door if he was,' he said. 'If he sneaked in they'd smash the glass he drank from before anyone here would use it. He's from a wee house in Drogheda.' He nodded to the barman who had assembled the massive round of drinks, then looked at Garth. 'Our singer friend always stays at the Irish Club in Eaton Square. There's an all night coffee shop across from the tube station in Sloane Square. I've come across him there at three in the morning. A man passing might do the same himself.'

'I'll bear that in mind.' Garth's tone was guarded. The barman stood, waiting to be paid.

'Bring lots of whipped cream.' The Irishman reached for his wallet. 'Apple tarts need a little extra something to help them go down.'

He handed a fistful of notes to the barman who began to pass the drinks across. Garth sat back. The Irishman ignored us as he relayed pints and shorts into the willing hands of family members who came forward to help. The table where his family sat was crammed with stacked glasses and crumpled cigarette packets. They were obviously the rump left over from a wedding reception. He rejoined them and bent to say something with his back to us. People laughed and some glanced in our direction. The Irishman didn't look back but I felt nervous. Nobody talked to total strangers like that. Was he winding us up or setting us up? Garth had turned to the bar, nodding at the barman to fetch us two more drinks.

'I hope I'm wrong,' I said quietly, 'but I get this feeling you're going to walk out the door and have your head kicked in.'

'Sweetheart, I have that feeling every morning I go to buy a newspaper,' Garth replied. 'I get that feeling so often that I stopped noticing years ago I ever had it. If you're worried, Tracey, just take your coat and go.'

'Don't be silly. I'm not leaving you.'

'I don't need no babysitting from here on in. The dude seems a bit odd but all right. Still you never can tell.' Garth tossed a fiver on to the counter. 'It's my round, but I've got to shake hands with the unemployed.'

The encounter had left me agitated, but it wasn't just concern about Garth. The man's words made me feel uneasy about myself. If they knew that my father had been a tinker they wouldn't use this glass again. I hated them and their half-assed sentimental music. I'd only come for a laugh but it didn't feel right being here. We were drinking doubles but I got the barman to put an extra vodka into my glass. The Irishman peeled off from his family. I might have been nervous but I wasn't going to show it when he approached again.

'Luke is my name,' he said. 'I've been watching you.'

'So?'

'All evening just watching and sitting there thinking.'

'Thinking what?'

'That if pigs could fly.'

He had eyes which demanded you stare back into them. They were salesman's eyes, I thought, and I wasn't buying.

'Pigs can't,' I said.

'If they could,' he replied, 'your black friend might get an early tube to Sloane Square and leave you sitting here alone.'

'What's it to you if he did?'

'I've been watching ever since you came in. I can't stop. You hate this place more than I do.'

'Why are you here then?'

'Duty, guilt, habit.' He glanced back. 'You know yourself, family life is never easy.'

I followed his glance. It was obviously a rare coming together of relations, animated and yet fitting uneasily together.

'When was the wedding?'

'Yesterday morning,' he said. 'Yesterday evening was the family fight and tonight is the kiss and make up.'

'Do they ever change their clothes?'

'That's tomorrow when they keel over and are carried home,' he said. 'To Dublin mainly, although a few have flung themselves as far as Coventry and Birmingham. The blonde girl in the blue outfit, she's the bride. You'd think she'd feck off on her honeymoon, but there's no fear of her letting us off the hook. She's heading back to America on Tuesday, where she's after getting born again. The first time was because of an accident down a lane off Camden Street. You'd think that second time around she might have got it right.'

The reference to hair wasn't much of a guide because there seemed hardly a woman in his family not bleached blonde. But the bride stood out, beaming with zest and vitamins. She seemed as incapable of being quiet as she was oblivious to the irritation she caused around her.

'She's after getting hitched to some lad from Blackheath she met in Houston and nothing would do her but to be married in London so her new in-laws could meet her old out-laws.' He laughed at his own joke. 'I don't think she informed them in advance that her grandfather Kevin was the biggest thug in the Animal Gang in Dublin.'

There was a family resemblance within some of them. The man who dominated the circle seemed a stockier version of Luke, like a crude police photo-fit. Squeezed into a dress suit, he looked dangerous and comic. He snapped at the bride who went quiet, as if struck. The conversation abated, then resumed

as an older woman took her hand. The man who'd ferried most
of the drinks passed behind the bride to ruffle her hair, coaxing
a smile from her as he made peace all round. He was well into
his thirties yet there was something baby-faced about him. As
he passed us, heading for the gents, I knew he was another
brother. He nodded.

'All right, Luke?'

'Hanging in there, Shane.'

He walked on with a glance at me.

'They're a surly-looking bunch,' I sneered, hoping Luke
would follow his brother.

'Unpredictable too.' He played up the insult. 'Still you can't
swap your family after the January sales. You only get born
with one, you have to love them and get on with it.'

But he showed no interest in rejoining them. I took a sip
of vodka and wished Garth would return. I liked to choose
my Sunday night men, not the other way round. Yet this
Irishman had a come on I'd never encountered before. He
seemed almost anxious to sell himself short. I revised his age
to thirty eight and tried to decide if he was utterly drunk or
sober.

'Seeing as you love your family don't let me detain you
from them,' I snorted, hoping to blow him off.

'Like most families, you'd sooner love them from a distance.'

The way he said it made me laugh. For all his physical
strength and expensive clothes, as he smiled wryly he suddenly
seemed the most miserable trapped son of a bitch I'd seen in
years. He looked like Burt Lancaster staring out in *The Birdman
of Alcatraz*. The thought made me wish I was at home alone,
watching some black and white video and drinking cheap
wine. The Irishman looked like he wouldn't mind being anywhere else either. I told him so and he laughed. Garth returned
and ignored us. The singer finished a big number. A woman
came forward to hand him a rose.

'You don't need to stay for your black friend's sake,' Luke

said. 'It's All Ireland Final night and if anyone's paying him any heed they're only wondering if his granny was Irish and he fancies playing soccer for us. So, say you wanted, you could pick up your coat and walk out of here.'

'I'm sure I could, but I don't. Maybe I fancy the singer too.'

'You don't cradle-snatch.'

'But you do, is it?' Making men feel old normally worked but he refused to be fazed.

'This isn't like me,' he said. 'But all evening I've wondered what you'd do if I asked you to walk out of here with me.'

His voice was calm. I don't know where the image came from, but I could imagine him soothing terrified animals in that tone, leading them tamely into an abattoir. I should have told him to get lost, but I didn't just yet, because something about him intrigued me, although I didn't like myself for responding to it.

'I suppose you're going to tell me you just happen to live in some flash apartment around the corner'

'I live in a boring suburb a long way from here and, besides, my wife wouldn't fancy three of us in the bed. I'm sorry, I was thinking more along the lines of a cheap hotel.'

It seemed the ultimate black joke. For once a single man was chatting me up by pretending to be married. Maybe Luke was bisexual and hoped to rope Garth into the bargain. How many vodkas had I had? I started laughing out loud and he had to point out his wife before I realised with a curious chill that he was serious.

'What does she think you're doing talking to me?'

'Selling wall tiles,' Luke said. 'That's how I make my living. Should you want wall tiles I'm definitely your man. I said to her, "That girl with the black leather queen owns three dance clubs. I'm going to tout for business. Say what you like about dykes but they always have money to burn"'.

It wasn't funny, but Christ how I laughed. I could see some women in his family glancing over. I held the gaze of one of them, a tough-looking black haired girl around nineteen, the only female who wasn't blonde apart from Luke's wife. She looked away self-consciously and when she looked back I winked. I drained my glass. Garth had another round set up. Luke watched me with that half-smile. I shifted his age to forty one and suddenly wondered what he looked like naked.

'Why don't you fuck off before I throw this drink over you,' I said, deciding I'd had enough of him.

He momentarily fingered a wisp of my hair. 'That would look much nicer dyed blonde,' he said. 'You're young, you're lucky, you've still got time for the fairytales men tell you. But I'm being straight. I've watched all night and I've decided I'd give five years of my life for one hour with you. See if you're big enough for a gamble or still just a little girl. There's a doorway beside the shops across the road. I can't leave with you, but wait five minutes and I'll be there.'

Then he was gone before I'd time to tell him what to do with himself. I tried to pay Garth for the drinks but he shook his head, distracted now, weighing hope against disbelief. I noticed the singer glance towards us, taking in Garth's bowed head and I knew Garth would be sitting in that cafe. But I'd no idea if the singer had ever been there. There seemed no reason to trust a word Luke said.

I wondered if I had knowingly slept with a married man. There were occasions where signs pointed to conclusions I hadn't wished to draw. The rotten cheating bastard, I thought, looking at him sitting beside the woman he claimed was his wife, while his family argued above the strains of that country-and-western din. His older brother was locked into a serious argument. But Luke ignored it, as if he'd withdrawn into a world of his own. I knew he was acutely aware of every movement I made.

Those Sunday night men had fed me whatever lies I needed to hear. Was Luke worse for telling the truth? His need seemed raw and uncompromising. Maybe it was the vodkas mixed with the dope and wine in Honor's flat, but suddenly I found that exciting. Just once, what was to stop me doing something truly illicit, something I knew was wrong? Luke had given me the freedom of a role and now I began to play with it, almost seeing myself as that confident, hard-edged club owner. I stared at the black-haired girl in a predatory fashion. If I had been a man she would have blown me away but I sensed her blush instead, then stare back with sudden cold hatred.

That sobered me. I was tired of these games, I wasn't going to be manipulated into feeling emotions that weren't there. It was time to leave if I wanted to get a tube that wasn't crammed with annoying drunks. That was why I was leaving alone I told myself, anything else was too bizarre. I sensed Luke watching. He was clever as well as manipulative. He knew I would say nothing to his wife which might put Garth in danger. A bar full of drunken Irishmen seemed the perfect place for a queer-bashing.

Yet it was his wife I kept watching. For no reason I hated her. Sitting there, plump and content with permed hair and hick clothes that were aeons out of fashion. She was in her late thirties but dressed like someone entering a glamorous granny contest. If Luke's family began to swipe each other with switch-blades, she would simply lift her Pimms and chat away, oblivious to them. But my hatred had nothing to do with her personally, I was uneasy around all happily married couples. If I felt I would become like her, I'd have smashed that vodka glass in the ladies and slashed my wrists.

Screw her anyway, I thought. All my life I'd had that future hammered into me, but I wasn't living by Gran's rules any more. Why not fuck a married man under his family's nose? That would be one for Roxy and Honor, although, even in my drunken state, I knew I'd never tell them. If Luke hadn't attracted me I would never have let him talk for so long. His desire attracted me too, at odds with most men's surface pretence. I wasn't bound by vows I'd no intention of ever getting roped into. Besides, for all his talk, he wouldn't dare. He wanted me here to eyeball. Once I stepped off this stool I would discover him to be all bull-shit, like most men.

I tapped Garth's shoulder and he patted my arm. I didn't look back. Eight vodkas or was it nine? Only when I hit the cold air did I count seriously again. The street was silent before closing time. It was three minutes' walk to the tube. I made a mental note of danger points. But I didn't go that way. Instead I stood in the doorway beside the shuttered shops and fixed my coat, then unbuttoned it again. One minute passed, maybe two. I was going nowhere with Luke but I was curious to see if he dared appear. If he did, I could slip away into the shadows.

Four minutes passed, I couldn't believe I was still there. He hadn't the balls. It was cold. I buttoned my coat again. I found I was excited. How many weeks was it since I'd slept with a man? The air smelt like there would be heavy rain soon. Five minutes turned into six, twice the time it would have taken to walk to the tube. I'd have to hurry now. Luke was just another manipulator, a cheat who ran scared. You could expect no better from the Irish. I remembered Gran repeating the phrase every time there was a bomb on the news. If she saw me now her worst fears would be confirmed, standing like a cheap tart waiting for an Irishman. When would I lose this hatred every time I thought of her, or was hatred a mechanism to keep guilt at bay? In thirteen months I'd never phoned. I should write but what could I say? I had decided to put my past behind me. At that moment I felt removed from everything, consumed by an old ache which I knew neither sex or drink could fill. I felt outside myself, watching this girl who was clearly drunk because she took forever to button her coat. Why had she spent a decade being addicted to crazy notions? I willed myself to move and finally I did so. But I had only walked a dozen paces when I felt Luke take my arm.

'That's the problem with you dykes,' he said quietly. 'Hard-nosed businesswomen always demanding attention now.'

This was when I stopped pretending. The role-playing, the danger of discovery, everything about this situation made me as horny as hell. It was no big deal for a man to feel this way, so why should I be different? I was glad the hotel was only three doors down. I might have felt cheap in reception, except that it felt too much like a game. The bed hadn't been made up, but we didn't get that far. We never even turned the light on. We did it once for Luke, standing up, with sweat on my neck turning cold against the damp wallpaper, and then a second time, more slowly for me, with him sitting on a hard chair. I liked that better, not having to look at him, just rocking back and forth on his knee as I tried to guess at the lives behind curtained windows across the street. I heard muffled calls for an encore at the Irish Centre. Luke withdrew hurriedly before he came and I heard him finish the business with his hand. Even with a condom he was a cautious man. I pulled my dress down between his knees and my buttocks, but it was so soaked with sweat that the sensation remained of naked flesh upon flesh.

Time was against us. They would be clearing the bar in the Irish Centre. But we stayed perfectly still, like children bewitched in a fairytale. There were raised voices below, but the street seemed distant. I heard the condom slip to the floor. Some men often made a joke while others were quiet and tender. Luke did nothing until I felt his cold hands toying with my shoulders.

'Tell me about wall tiles,' I said.

'They're smooth.' His hands moved to my neck. 'You take your time and lay them right until even the joins are smooth. That is unless you make a mistake and they crack.'

There was no force in his hands and nothing in his voice to suggest menace, but I was suddenly scared and he knew it. The room was cheap and my unease made me feel cheap too.

31

Luke must have been crazy to take this risk. How crazy was he and what danger had I placed myself in? I sensed him staring at my neck.

'Shouldn't you head back to your flabby wife?' I wanted to break the spell and control my fear with the insult, but Luke's voice maintained its methodical calm.

'It so happens I love her.'

'Is that meant to be a joke?'

'No. But it doesn't mean I don't enjoy fucking other girls either.' A hint of apology entered his tone. 'You're not just some girl. I don't do this often. Seven times in twenty two years. That's faithful enough as marriages go.'

'That's my age,' I said. 'Twenty two. You must like us young.'

'I've only had one girl younger than you.'

'Flirting with innocence, were you?'

'She was the most deadly of the lot.'

I didn't want a litany. I felt cold and started shivering. Tomorrow I'd wake hungover, trying to convince myself this had never happened. But I'd know that physically it had felt truly good.

'It didn't work, you know,' he said.

'What?'

'Facing away from me. For all your attempts to hide it, I could still tell both times you came.'

I felt vulnerable and wanted to be out of that room. His fingers retreated from my neck to glide slowly along my backbone. When he lifted them away my inability to track their movements made them more menacing. Luke wasn't the first Irishman to touch me. I had fooled myself into thinking I could banish such memories.

'I suppose you're going to say you love me next,' I said.

'No,' he replied. 'I haven't room to love anyone else. But I loved fucking you.' Somehow the inflection he invested in the word stripped it of vulgarity. 'Next Sunday night I can make sure we get this same room. You enjoyed it here, don't say you didn't. Think about it, eh?'

'So much for champagne and flowers,' I mocked.

'I haven't time for that stuff any more and, be honest, you don't want it either. There's a fight brewing out there. I've got to get down. Next Sunday night, around half past nine.'

'Bring a copy of *Penthouse* and a hanky,' I said. 'I'd hate to have you going home frustrated.'

'Half nine,' Luke repeated. 'Ten at the latest. I warn you, I won't wait all night.'

I stood up. My knickers lay a few feet away. I didn't want to put them on with him watching. But when I bent to pick them up he covered them with his foot.

'Pirate's loot,' he said. 'Be a good girl and you'll get them back next week.'

I didn't argue or tell him what to do with those panties alone by himself here next Sunday and every Sunday until he went blind. I held my tongue, sobering up rapidly. I had broken every rule I ever taught myself for protection against this self-destructive urge. I simply wanted to get safely out that door. Only when I had it open did I glance back. Luke was slumped on that chair with his trousers still bunched around his ankles. Something about him, in the light from the hallway, suggested the sight which must greet night porters who enter hotel rooms to find that a murder has occurred. Then he turned his head.

'I couldn't stop looking at you,' he said, as if amazed to find himself there. 'You don't know how desperately I want you to come.'

I ran downstairs, past reception and only stopped when I found myself among the crowds from the Irish Centre. Luke was right, an argument was developing among his family. If his wife saw me leave the hotel she gave no sign, but one or two heads turned when I passed. There was no sign of Garth. The black haired girl stared at me coldly and almost defiantly

33

now. I felt naked as if she had understood Luke's game all along. She could even be his daughter. I pushed my way through the crowd, sensing her eyes still watching me. I felt a chill beneath my skirt as I ran, watching for danger from the shadows. I didn't care now what cranks might be on the train. I was just thankful to have got safely away and to know that I would never see Luke again.

FOUR

IT IS JUST BEFORE my sixth birthday. I remember this because my thoughts are about presents as I rush from school among a flock of children. Now, walking with my mother, I'm anxious to get home to where Gran will have lunch ready and ensure that I finish two glasses of milk before being allowed to watch the children's programmes.

But my mother takes a meandering route as if prolonging our journey. She says nothing to draw me into her brooding world, even when I ask for a story. We reach a footbridge across railway tracks and climb up to look across at wintry back gardens where fluorescent lights shine in kitchens. I tug at her hand, but she waits there. Then the train comes, all noise and slipstream and unwashed roofs of carriages. I'm frightened. I know the train cannot hurt us, thundering beneath our feet. It's my mother I am scared of or scared for. It's the way she watches the train. She wants to leave. That much I understand. She wants to leave Harrow and Gran and Grandad Pete and maybe she wants to leave me.

Or worse, perhaps she wants to bring me with her on those speeding carriages, away from my dolls and Grandad Pete's piggyback to bed, from my shelf of stories and the cherry-blossom petals against my window in springtime. There would only be my mother and I travelling alone, past towns without names, skirting forbidding forests where bears roam. I start crying and finally she looks down. She isn't like mothers in stories or those my classmates have. It's Gran I run to when I hurt my knee. Yet even Gran tells me to call her mother. 'I want to go home,' I say, 'I want my Gran.' I pull at her hand, knowing that if I wait for another train I'll never see her again.

I woke sweating from that dream, the morning after meeting Luke. After sixteen years, my stomach was queasy and I instinctively checked my knickers, remembering how Gran would change the wet sheets while my mother comforted me and I pretended not to remember what my dream was about. How long was it since I had last dreamt of that? Certainly not since my mother's death, even among the myriad dreams I'd had about her after moving into the flat. Dreams where her face hovered among the blouses in my wardrobe, or she stared up from the water in the sink when I bent to wash my hair. In each dream her eyes were the same as during the bedside vigils before she died, disappointed and hinting at unfinished business. My mother's greatest weapons were helplessness and silence. Throughout my childhood, watching her breakdowns re-occur, they had left me feeling perpetually guilty, like I had to compensate for my birth having irrevocably altered her life.

For an hour that morning I stood under the shower, scrubbing at my flesh, but I didn't feel so much soiled by Luke as by myself. I felt caught between conflicting emotions, repulsed by what had happened, yet reliving the excitement of that hotel. I had been so drunk that the memories now held the same dreamlike quality as standing on that railway bridge with my mother.

I honestly believed I'd never see Luke again, or if I did it would be by chance in a glimpse on some crowded escalator. By then he would just be a vaguely familiar face puzzling me until I remembered and turned away. I had been crazy to allow myself to get so drunk. I said nothing to Roxy and Honor and I knew Garth said little about what happened to him.

But Honor claimed he was more withdrawn these days as he came and left at odd hours.

Fragments of Luke's character kept coming back to me during the following week, details which didn't fit together so that it seemed I was remembering two distinct personalities. He'd been a shark certainly, but maybe that was the secret of sharks – not surface confidence but how they manoeuvred you into believing you alone had glimpsed the vulnerablity beneath their cocksure demeanour. Used cars, wall tiles or young women, we were all commodities the same techniques could be adapted to procure or sell. If I hadn't glanced back, leaving the hotel room, I might have convinced myself this was true. But my final picture of Luke was so desolate that what stayed with me most strongly was the sense of an ache within him.

If such pain existed, it was his problem not mine. I stayed in on the following Sunday night, trying to put him out of my mind. I might have felt a grim satisfaction at him waiting in that hotel, but I'd no idea if he would show up. If I had got so drunk, how much further gone must Luke have been to risk such an encounter? There again, was I even sure his family were present? I was certain of nothing, except his first name. He hadn't bothered to ask mine and there was no way he could trace me. Yet later that evening when the hallway was empty, I lifted the receiver off the pay phone so it couldn't ring.

But the meal I cooked tasted lousy and there was no life in the rented film. I felt listless, crossing to the bay window to lean against the glass and gaze past the narrow garden at the street. I wondered if he was waiting, still hoping I might come. I didn't know if I wanted him to be there. I had crept downstairs too often as a teenager to check that the phone was working, after giving my number and trust away, to now feel any qualms about the fake lives I spun for other men.

This was different though. I had made no promises to Luke

and it seemed crazy to contemplate such a risk again. But I was stung by an irrational guilt, even though I remembered his fingers toying with my neck. Luke was too old for me and I didn't mess with married men. I was ashamed of the way I'd looked at his wife. It wasn't her fault if she embodied Gran's dreams. But it was her happiness which I had most resented, for reminding me of how empty my life seemed.

I didn't feel like being alone now, yet I didn't fancy Roxy and Honor's wildness either. I didn't know what I wanted, although I never had and didn't see why I had to. I had sworn that my life would never be black and white or narrowed down to a single job or man. But, as I stepped back to stare at the reflection of myself and the room in the window, my flat looked so shabby and the life I half-led within it utterly shallow. Was this how I really wanted to live? Hungry for two days every week while waiting for the giro, occasionally waitressing or taking temporary jobs in offices I couldn't wait to escape from? Was I living for myself or still playing games? I remembered as a child the thrill of independence I had felt every time I disappointed their expectations. When I'd left home there was nowhere I hadn't planned to visit, a street-wise girl travelling alone with no ties. Thirteen miles in thirteen months was nothing to be proud of. The flat was cold. The rented video fizzled out and now, with a click, began to rewind itself. I decided to return it. I knew it could have waited until tomorrow but it was an excuse to escape from that room.

I kept walking after taking the film back, turning down streets I would normally never take after dark. The pubs were packed with drinkers as rock music blared from upstairs windows. It was almost closing time. Twice I nearly went into a bar and then stopped myself. It wasn't like me to lack the confidence to venture somewhere alone, but tonight I felt unable to adopt a mask. A taxi passed, braking hard to take the corner. There were shops covered by steel shutters except for an Indian restaurant with no customers. I sensed the waiter eyeing me from the lit doorway. I walked quicker to escape his gaze and turned left, intending to circle back towards my flat. But when I got down the street I found it was a cul-de-sac. The last streetlight was a flickering blue as the bulb spluttered out. There was a walled laneway, dividing the street from the high rise flats beyond it.

I knew I should turn back, but I didn't want to admit that I was scared. I was half way down the lane when a youth jumped from the wall. He crouched as he landed, twenty feet from me, then leaned against the wall. That old fear came back from when I was eleven, almost paralysing me, but I managed to walk on. I had never found this area violent, but that was because I knew, with almost a local's instinct, where not to walk. The lane was so narrow I'd have to brush against the youth to get past. He watched me approach, his face betraying nothing. In a few seconds I could be fighting for my life, yet I felt nothing for my would-be attacker. He was as much an anonymous piece of flesh to me as I was to him. At that moment all I felt was anger against myself for being stupid enough to be here. The youth's fingers were clenched, but I couldn't decide if they held anything. I could see his teeth as I drew close. It was like encountering a loose dog, not knowing how he would react. I fought against myself so he wouldn't smell my fear.

I was face to face with him now, not knowing if it was more dangerous to ignore his gaze or stare back. I'd worked the key-ring in my pocket around my knuckle so that when I hit him the keys might rip his cheek. I passed, our jackets briefly touching. I smelt his sour breath and had a sense that I could almost hear his heart. He didn't move a muscle. Then I was beyond him, one yard, two yards, three, still waiting for his arm to grip my neck, trying to prevent myself shaking and restrain my legs from running. I reached the laneway's end. The street ahead was empty. At the top I saw people on the main road as the pubs closed. Still I was afraid to look back. I got half way up the street before allowing myself to run. I couldn't stop the images rushing in on me about what might have happened; the waste ground beyond the wall, a boiler house with its smashed door, the starless triangle of sky I might have glimpsed as my dying vision.

When I reached the main road I kept running, controlling an urge to scream. The youth hadn't raised a finger. He had passively savoured his power to cause terror. I wasn't furious with myself now but with him, the sick prick getting his kicks from fear. For eleven years I had run from such memories. Now I almost wanted him to have given me an excuse to rip his flesh with my key-ring. Yet I couldn't remember his face, though it was only moments since our encounter. It was Luke's face I kept seeing, Luke whom I resented for distracting my judgement until I was like a tourist, floundering about with every scrap of street sense gone.

There were pages of tile shops in the Yellow Pages. I convinced myself that curiosity made me scan them the following Monday, searching for Irish sounding names. The Irish ghettos around Kilburn seemed an obvious place to start. I made a dozen calls, listening to each voice say 'Hello?' before asking if Luke was there. Each one said that no Luke worked there and I hung up disappointed, although if they'd asked me to hold for Luke I would have only waited to hear his voice before putting the phone down. I had nothing to say to him. I just felt that planting a surname and banal workplace on Luke would help diminish him in my mind.

On Tuesday morning I dumped the Yellow Pages in a street bin. I had stood Luke up, yet for the previous two days I'd thought of nothing except him. These were danger signs. If I wasn't careful this obsession could grow. I phoned an employment agency where I sometimes got office work. They had a temporary position, covering for somebody who was sick in

Wilkinson's pharmaceutical importers near Elephant and Castle.

I'd worked there before and had even turned down a permanent job with them. It was a legacy of childhood afternoons in Grandad Pete's chemist shop, watching him twist his tongue around complex generic names while filling prescriptions, before retreating to his alcove to read the *Daily Star* which he binned before going home. By the age of ten I had decided to become a chemist. Grandad even persuaded Gran to cut up one of his white coats for me. In between teaching me intricate names of drugs, he'd staple cardboard boxes together for me to climb into and provide running commentaries of me paddling single-handedly down the Amazon or planting the flag of Harrow and Wealdstone on Jupiter. At home he retreated behind the *Evening Standard*, an inoffensive man who ventured to the club for two pints every evening and whose occasionally animated voice might wake me on his return before Gran's tongue dispatched him to bed.

When I started work on the Wednesday, the girls in Wilkinson's were friendly and we even had a drink after work. But at lunch time and interrupting my journey home on Thursday and Friday, I found myself visiting tile shops and leading the staff on about an order I was hoping to place for the clubs I ran. By Saturday I was an expert on wall tiles. I'd also discovered that tile shop owners were among the drabbest males ever to have been hatched out in the sun.

Saturday night came. I heard Roxy and Honor ring my bell, then wait outside, puzzled by my absence. After they were gone I regretting hiding with the light out. I wasn't in clubbing mood, but I couldn't sit brooding by myself. I called at Honor's flat, though I knew they were gone. Garth was dressing to go out.

'You've missed the girls,' he said.

'They called. I pretended I was out. Was that awful?'

Garth grinned. I'd always liked him more than Honor.

'They're noisy dames,' he said. 'I love Honor as my baby sister but sometimes you need to be in the prime of your health to take her. You want to come for coffee?'

'But you've a date, haven't you?'

He beckoned towards the door. 'It's a late date if he shows at all. These shy young owls are frightened to venture out until the whole wood's asleep.'

'Does this owl hoot like a choir boy?' I teased.

'If he does it's his own business.' Garth was circumspect and I knew I'd intruded into a world he kept private. But I wasn't being nosy, I had just wanted an affirmation that Luke had told the truth in something.

'Listen,' he said, more relaxed as we went down the steps. 'Everyone comes out some time, but occasionally someone does it ten years too late. Do you know who Colonel Parker managed before he got his hands on Elvis? Dancing chickens. He would place chickens on what was actually a hot stove, switch on the music and those chickens danced all night. I never believed in reincarnation, but our friend Liam is so jumpy that in his last life he had to be a dancing chicken way down South.'

The wine bar Garth picked hadn't filled up yet. There would be a jazz session later on with serious buffs clicking their dentures to some piano improv. Garth pressed me about when I'd last eaten, then ordered food. When I took my first sip of wine I knew I had to be careful. Once I started drinking I wouldn't stop.

'Who is he?' Garth asked.

'Who mentioned a man?'

'Come on, Tracey.' Garth grinned. 'I should know the signs.'

'I've only met him once,' I said, with the wine making me realise how hungry I was. 'It was exciting, but we were crazy with the risks we took.'

'Do I know him?'

'We got our roles wrong in the Irish Centre,' I said. 'You should have been my chaperon.'

Garth refilled my glass. 'He wouldn't be my type,' he said. 'I've never liked broody men. They're dangerous, especially when they're married.'

'That's the problem,' I replied. 'He's not my type either.'

Garth laughed in recognition. I wondered about the other part of his life. It was good to talk to someone. The jazz started after the food arrived. It was hard to decide which was worse.

'It's a simple enough cock-up,' I said. 'The chef's obviously playing the piano while the band are locked in the kitchen.'

We finished two bottles of wine, then ventured on to the street where it was raining. Garth waved a taxi down.

'You take it,' I told him, 'you're the man going places.'

He held the door open for me, then climbed in as well.

'You're in a bad way, sister,' he said. 'You'll probably cost me the chance of a mother-in-law in Drogheda but we're going to find out about this Irishman.'

Liam Darcy was waiting in a bar in Kensington. It was twenty minutes to closing time with a stampede of bodies hugging the counter. He saw me with Garth and looked cornered and scared. He rose.

'Who's she? A journalist?'

'Don't be silly,' Garth said. 'Take it easy, Liam.'

'I won't take it easy, I . . .' He lowered his voice as people looked around. 'We agreed.'

'Sit down,' Garth told him. 'The world isn't out to get you and anyway you're safer being seen in public with the likes of her than with me.'

Liam looked at me. 'I can be seen with anyone I like,' he protested. 'Nobody can say that just because I'm having a drink with some . . .'

He stopped, flustered, leaving the word unspoken. It was a long time since I'd seen anyone so nervous. He was twenty-five or six but anxiety made him seem like a teenager on a first date. I could imagine a time when his clothes were fashionable.

They probably still were in Moldova and Uzbekistan. He was good-looking but not in a way that appealed to me.

'You're the least gay looking guy I ever met,' I lied to put him at ease.

'Yeah, but those songs are a dead giveaway,' Garth added.

'What do you mean?' Liam was defensive again.

'They're so corny and sentimental only a man would fall for them.'

It took Liam a moment to realise Garth was having him on. He looked at us, shamefaced. 'I almost said "queer", didn't I?'

'I've been called worse,' Garth replied. 'Names change nothing so take your pick. I'll get us a drink.'

Garth pushed his way through the crowd. I sat in uneasy silence with Liam until he looked across.

'You were in the Irish Centre,' he said. 'I remember your face. I've offended him.'

'That's between you and him.'

'I just panicked. I'm not used to this. I almost didn't turn up tonight.'

'He's a good man, Garth,' I said.

'We're not . . . I mean we haven't.' He looked at me again. 'Do I really not look gay? For years I've tried convincing myself, but you get sick pretending.'

'Why not come out? In the long run it's better.'

'Maybe over here it is,' he said. 'But my manager would kill me. Two years ago I worked in Wavin Pipes in Balbriggan. I'd hardly an arse in my trousers. Now five people make a living out of me. I can't walk away from all that.'

'Would the Irish papers go crazy?'

'They'd love it,' he said. 'I'd be a hero. But papers don't count. They only mock my music anyway. I wouldn't get gigs. The men running this business are fossils who'll never change.'

I saw Garth joke with the barman as he gathered our drinks up. Liam watched him too.

'So you live a lie,' I said.

'What's so wrong with that?' Liam was suddenly angry. 'People think I'm stupid but I'm not. I know those songs are half-arsed but I like them. I like others, sean-nós, traditional stuff you never heard of, blues, rock, all kinds. Maybe my manager's stuck me in one box, but I'll not be stuck straight back in another. The gay country singer. It wouldn't matter what I'd sing. Every bloody question would be about the same thing. I wouldn't be a singer, I'd be a token queer bandied about by everyone for their own use.'

'I'm sorry', I said. 'I'm drunk. I wasn't getting at you.'

Garth put the drinks down and sat back. Liam took a long sip of Jack Daniels and smiled, ruefully.

'I normally have this conversation with myself,' he said. 'My manager says in three years I'll be as big as any of them: Philomena Begley, Daniel O'Donnell, Big Tom. "Leave everything to me," he says and I do. He knows the business. He decides when my albums come out, but I'll decide when I do.'

'That's your business,' Garth said. 'We've more serious things to discuss, like which club to go dancing in.'

It took intense persuading to get Liam to visit a gay club, and he only agreed when Garth repeatedly explained how discreet the one he had chosen was. It was in the taxi that Garth mentioned Luke, asking Liam if he remembered a wedding party in the Irish Centre.

'The place was packed,' Liam replied. 'I play it once a month. I won't know anyone there.'

'There's a guy Tracey wants to know about,' Garth pressed him. 'From Dublin but living here. His name is Luke and he works in tiles. He knew you or a fair amount about you.'

I realised Garth had never told Liam how he came to be in that coffee shop and he was taking a risk for me now.

'What did he claim to know?' Liam was defensive again.

'Where I might meet you, for example.'

Liam lowered the window so that cold air filled the cab. The West Indian driver drove with sullen fury, jerking us about. Liam's good humour had vanished as he digested the news of someone else knowing his movements.

'And that it might be worth your while going there?' Liam asked. Garth said nothing, but Liam leaned back, tense now with the world shrinking in his mind.

'I don't know anyone called Luke,' he said eventually.

I recognised the club when we got there. Garth had taken me there once with Roxy and Honor. I always loved gay clubs. They had the best sounds and least hassle and gay men were great dancers around you. The club was packed. At first Liam made it clear that I was with Garth and he was with Jack Daniels. He downed three of them neat. I could imagine him lying awake, perpetually wondering who knew and who didn't. Now Luke was another name for his list, closer to home than us and therefore more dangerous.

Garth and I danced alone at first and only when Liam was approached by men did we persuade him to join us. He appeared awkward but then, as he relaxed, he took over our part of the floor, slipping into routines which had looked hackneyed in the Irish Centre. Now, though the music was utterly different, they were breath-takingly joyous. Men stopped to watch, infected by his boyish animation. Nobody does Elvis in a gay club, but he did, the younger Elvis, wide-eyed and sexually innocent, before Colonel Parker's gimmicks killed him off. I remembered Garth's story and realised that previously I was watching a dancing chicken. Now I saw the man Garth had always guessed at. The music halted and we returned to the bar for more drinks. Liam took a long sip, his hair damp with sweat.

'You're wrong about something,' I said after Garth went to the gents. 'I do know sean-nós singing.'

Liam looked at me in surprise, struggling to remember his outburst in the pub. 'What does it sound like?'

I tried to recall the unaccompanied drone of an old man's voice through a listening post at dawn.

'Like a sperm-whale clapped out after fucking twenty leagues under the sea.'

Liam laughed, draining his glass. 'Jaysus, you're not far off the mark,' he replied.

'I've only heard it once,' I confessed. 'It's probably an acquired taste, like Jack Daniels.'

'Only words count in sean-nós,' Liam said. 'The voice is an unadorned instrument to get them out. Your friend Luke would know sean-nós singing.'

'You know who he is?'

'I saw him talk to you in the Irish Centre,' Liam replied. 'He's been pointed out to me at traditional sessions over here. He drinks by himself, taking everything in, even me, obviously. He wouldn't be a regular and would only come for the music. I mean he'd have nothing in common with the people you'd meet at a traditional gig.'

'Isn't that music popular in Ireland?' I asked.

'Yes and no,' he replied. 'It won't die out, but country and western is what's big in Ireland. Then there's rock music, U2, Sinead O'Connor, The Cranberries. In Dublin you can't spit without hitting rock stars chilling out. But traditional music has a world of its own. That's why Luke stood out. He's a Duggan, if you know what I mean.'

'I don't,' I said. 'Who are the Duggans?'

A man in a leather jacket asked Liam to dance and he shook his head, watching Garth return. Tomorrow Liam might regret this but now he was drunk and enjoying himself. He wanted to dance again and this time I knew three would be a crowd.

'Traditional music is like a religion in parts of the West or Kerry or Donegal,' Liam said. 'But Luke's types are generally more into James Last. All those lush strings to drown out the noise of knee-caps being broken. Take my word and keep away. The shagging Duggans.' He laughed, heading for the throbbing beat of the dance floor. 'You don't expect to walk into a session and see someone from the biggest shower of thugs in Dublin tapping his feet to the tunes, now do you?'

FIVE

THE FOLLOWING SUNDAY NIGHT I took the tube across London, staring at faces on the platforms and then at my own face reflected back as the train careered through the bowels of the city. People got on and got off, high-heeled girls chattering, lone men with Sunday supplements, everybody rushing somewhere. I might have stayed on the Circle Line all evening, watching the same stations rush back at me. Anywhere was better than a second Sunday alone in that flat.

At Blackfriars the old woman got on. Temple, Embankment, St James's Park. Within minutes I knew she was going nowhere and that she could sense I was faking a destination too. The carriage was empty. I felt her staring. I thought she was lonely and wanted to talk, then I realised her eyes were taunting me. 'I had friends at your age,' she seemed to say, 'I'd a family and a purpose.' Her eyes were bird-bright. She looked like the sort of woman you saw in postcards of Trafalgar Square, with pigeons clouding the air at her shoulders as she tossed broken bread probably soaked with paraquat. I stared back and she held my gaze as if declaring this carriage as her private kingdom.

Even without her eyes taunting me I always knew that eventually I'd get off at Edgware Road. I had simply been delaying the moment, trying to fool myself that I wasn't returning to where I had waited for Luke a fortnight before. It was three minutes' walk from the station, but it seemed longer. Ten minutes would bring me to the splendour of

Marylebone Road, but here the streets seemed more Arabic than English.

It was a strange location for an Irish Centre, surrounded by the scent of spices and taped muzak from cheap restaurants. A notice in a window promised live belly dancing at weekends. I stared at the few diners through the glass. I stood in the doorway opposite the Irish Centre and watched people come from a meeting upstairs. Some left while others drifted towards the bar where rock music was starting. I wanted the street empty like on that night. I closed my eyes but everything felt different.

Loud voices crossed towards me. I walked on so quickly that I was almost past the hotel when I stopped. The lobby was deserted, the receptionist absent from her desk. A stag's head protruded above the unlit fireplace, looking like he'd been strangled by cobwebs. The Irish voices were at my shoulder now. I pushed the door open and stepped into the lobby. Voices chattered down a nearby corridor. I had no excuse if the receptionist came back. I just ran and reached the bend of the stairs before hearing footsteps below and a tray of glasses being set down.

I walked up the final steps and down a dim corridor of trapped smells. Any pretence of glamour ended with the carpet on the stairs. These doors hadn't encountered paint for years. A television blared behind one. I came to what had briefly been our room. There wasn't a sound within. I knocked. If I heard footsteps I was going to run. I just wanted to see inside, to touch the bed we'd never used, the chair and damp wallpaper. I wanted to lay the ghosts of that night to rest.

Down the corridor I heard footsteps. I panicked and tried the handle. The door opened, surprising me. Luke sat in that same chair, facing the window with his back to me. A walkman was over his head and he was absorbed in whatever was playing. His hands were out of sight on his groin. It's a dirty tape, I thought, he's masturbating. I had turned to go when he lifted his hand, which held a small tipped cigar. He took a pull, then slowly released smoke into the air.

Liam Darcy's description came back: the biggest shower of thugs in Dublin. In the taxi home he had been more expansive, detailing the armed robberies for which the most famous of them, Christy Duggan, had become a national figure, after the IRA showed how easily it was done. When robberies became common in Dublin and security tightened, Christy Duggan had orchestrated bank raids which paralysed isolated country towns. The police could never prove anything despite twenty-four-hour surveillance for two years, but, according to Liam, everything about the Duggans was common knowledge. People even knew when Christy's gang were making a hit because he would drive up and down outside police head-quarters. Libel laws meant his name never appeared in the papers, which referred to him as 'The Ice-man'.

I wasn't sure how much of this was the Jack Daniels talking, but Liam had kept us in stitches with the bizarre nicknames by which, he maintained, Dublin criminals were known: *the Wise-cracker, the Commandant, the Cellar-man*. The aliases had turned them into comic book characters, but now, watching Luke, their names and crimes became flesh and blood. He had no idea I was there. I liked the sense of power that gave me. I could watch or leave. If I were his wife I could plunge a scissors into his neck. His jacket lay on the bed. I could steal his credit cards or car keys. Or, if I had any sense, I could turn and run, leaving the door ajar so that he'd suspect someone had stood there, but would never know whether it was me.

There was a click as the tape ended and Luke stirred. This was the moment to slip away. But I stayed there until he turned, slowly as if sensing someone. He seemed neither sur-prised nor pleased to see me. If any emotion showed it was a relief he tried to cloak. Perhaps it was my imagination gone wild, but I got the impression that he had half thought he was about to be shot.

'You're a week late,' he said quietly, drawing the headphones down. A woman's voice, in a language I couldn't understand, drifted along the corridor. Her closeness might have reassured me, only I found I wasn't nervous. 'Still, you're worth the wait.'

The bed was made up this time. A sink in the corner had a cracked mirror above it. I had shared such a room once, running away with my mother.

'How did you know I'd come?'

'I didn't.' He watched me closely. 'Last week I held out some hope, but this week I'd none at all.'

The window pane rattled as a truck passed. There were footsteps on the ceiling and hot-tempered voices.

'Then what are you doing here?'

Luke rose to put his jacket on, slipped the walkman into the pocket, then shrugged and sat on the bed.

'Why shouldn't I be here?' he said. 'It's as good as anywhere else.'

'What's wrong with staying at home?'

He scrutinised me and I stared back, feeling this was a contest of wills. 'That's complex,' he said, 'private.'

'Poor little you.' I tried to mask my elation behind mockery, not wanting to admit to myself how much I had hoped he'd be here.

'We married young,' Luke said, so openly that my jibe sounded cheap. 'A shotgun job, a miscarriage and then a child on top of us before we knew who we were. I kept growing and she didn't. Maybe she'd see it different, but either way there's not much left in common.'

'Where does she think you are now?'

'Stock checking, doing the books. All the things I've no time for during the week.'

'She must think you're a great provider. The businessman who never stops.'

'She wants for nothing and I'll make sure she never does.'

52

Anger entered his tone. I knew he wouldn't be ridiculed. In truth I'd simply been buying time.

'If I hadn't showed up would you have come next Sunday?'

'I don't know.' Luke looked around. 'Last week I found I liked it here. I could hear myself think. It holds good memories, this room.'

Everything looked cheap and worn. Television stations blared through the walls on either side of us.

'Not for many people it doesn't,' I said. 'It's a kip.'

'That depends on who you shared it with.'

'I didn't come for that,' I said sharply. There were footsteps on the stairs. I stepped back into the corridor so I could be seen.

'Don't be frightened,' Luke said.

'I'm not frightened of anyone.'

'We were both very drunk,' he went on. 'I'm afraid I don't even know your name.'

'I know yours,' I said. 'The Duggans are famous.'

He relit his cigar, tipping away dead ash. 'An anonymous fucking hotel,' he said, with quiet resignation. 'You'd think at least here I might be known for myself.'

'That's the problem with infidelity, things always come out.' My defensive mockery was replaced by a relaxed teasing. 'All your family are the same, I hear. Cut-throats, with more nick-names than convictions.'

'We specialise in the white slave trade,' he replied, straight-faced.

'Drugged virgins shipped off in crates of wall tiles.'

'You're in luck,' he said. 'There's an EC moratorium on virgins so we're branching into more experienced types.'

His assertiveness was gone, but a sardonic watchfulness remained. I was surprised by how attracted I felt to him as we toyed with each other. It felt like foreplay, except that I was never going to enter the room. Even when he smiled I sensed his sombreness. The image of him dead in that chair had a prophetic feel. I wondered if I had been an assassin would Luke have greeted me with the same resigned shrug? Yet he gave no impression of being anything other than a small-time businessman. He even seemed to delight in shrinking his world down to two stores in rundown London suburbs. I remembered how he stood out from his family that first time we'd met.

'I want to show you something,' he said.

'What?'

He arose without replying. We walked downstairs. The receptionist was the same age as myself. She lifted her gaze from a magazine to scrutinise us, trying to make Luke feel older.

'She's my daughter,' Luke said, deadpan, returning the key. 'I can never deflate those dolls by myself.'

We reached the street before starting to laugh. Inside his car I asked him to play the tape he had been listening to.

'You won't like it,' he said.

'Try me.'

It was Irish fiddle music from somewhere called Sliabh Luachra, recorded live with bodies moving about and background coughing. Luke had taped it off an Irish radio programme.

'What do the names mean?' I asked. '*The Rambling Pitchfork* or *Boil the Breakfast*. They don't make sense.'

He glanced across, surprised at my knowledge. 'Why should they? Names aren't important. A tune might start in one county and if a travelling fiddler liked it, he'd carry it home with a different name. Only the notes counts.'

'Why do they all sound the same?'

'They don't,' Luke said. 'Listen.' He spoke quietly, showing where each tune slipped effortlessly into the next reel in the set. His enthusiasm made him seem boyish. Yet his suit gave the impression of someone impersonating a Bulgarian trade diplomat. I told him so and he laughed, claiming most people never saw beyond an expensive suit. It was a good way to remain invisible.

'Why do you want to be invisible?'.

'I'm a private man,' he said.

'Enjoying your secrets.'

'Contradictions,' he replied. 'Secrets are dangerous, they self-destruct. Contradictions are different. We're born under the sign of contradiction. Without them we'd still live in the trees.'

'Which am I?'

He looked across and raised the tape. 'You're a bonus,' he said.

'Luke, you're full of shit.' I laughed and he joined in, savouring the joke against himself. I didn't want to talk anymore, I wanted to hear that music. Previously I'd only ever heard snatches, but now it filled me with curious elation. It was seductive. I wondered at how my father's playing had once lured my mother to swap Harrow for the wilderness of Donegal.

I almost told Luke about my father, then remembered his remarks about travellers. I felt a flush of shame not even Gran might have fully understood. For her the problem with my father had been a matter of class, but with Luke it was a matter of caste. Suddenly I felt like an untouchable, an Irish tinker's child.

'You're quiet,' Luke said, watching me. I wanted to strip away that expensive suit and drag him down a peg.

'Your type don't normally like this music.'

'Who are my type?' he replied coolly.

'People from the slums of Dublin.'

'I was born in no slum,' he said. 'Is that what you're after? A bit of rough trade, some peasant Paddy to fuck?'

He seemed about to stop the car, then changed gear and put his foot down.

'I didn't mean to insult . . .'

'You did,' he said, taking a corner at speed before slowing

55

down, his voice more controlled. 'People put you in your box and never let you out. That's why I left Ireland.'

'Is London any freer?'

'It's different at least. You're just another thick Mick to be patronised.'

The tape ended. He turned it over. There was a hiss before music filled the car again.

'What are you after?' Luke said.

'I don't know. I wanted to see who you were. I'm not some . . . I'm not a tart.'

'I know.'

I stared at the passing streets. It might have been better if he had stopped the car and let me out. This evening we were sober and aware of the void between us.

'What are you looking for?' I turned the tables.

'I don't know either.' I felt he was being painfully honest. 'Every morning I brush my teeth but the staleness won't go. I get on with life but it's not me in this suit. I've made myself numb so as not to feel this ache.'

'Why don't you leave?'

'Running away solves nothing,' he said. 'It still leaves tomorrow to face.'

'Is your brother a master criminal?' I asked.

'The Ice-Man?' Luke laughed. 'That sells papers but Christy can hardly tie his shoe-laces. He's no saint, but if he's a gang lord why hasn't he two shillings to rub together? I'm not defending him, but he's your ordinary decent small-time crook. Nobody in the crime world takes him seriously, but he's got a big mouth and papers like that. Two of our uncles were famous hard men. A family is like an area, once it gets a reputation the truth doesn't matter. Real criminals keep their heads down, they like it that way. And they're only trotting behind the the big scams in fraud by accountants. But that's not sexy enough, newspapers need bogeymen with half-arsed nicknames.'

56

He was quiet as a new tune began. '*The Blackbird*,' he said. 'Listen, it's my favourite set dance.'

I was happy not to talk. We'd reached an equilibrium, a wary trust that was as far as we were willing to commit. I closed my eyes, immersed in that lilting tune. It suited the night we drove through, these deserted streets which, in a few hours, would be thronged with every race. We were strangers, separately caught up in the music and wild applause and stamping boots when it finished. Another tune began, with a frighteningly raw sense of abandonment. It was the first time I'd ever felt high on music alone. When I glanced at Luke I felt his sense of isolation.

'Do your children like this music?' I asked.

'It's not their fault,' he said. 'Basically by now they're English. They'd say they're Irish and their pals call them Irish, but in Dublin they're seen as English and rightly so.'

'I'm English,' I said, 'and I like it.'

'But you're not running away from it.'

'How old are they?'

'I've a lad of four,' he said. 'The other two are older, almost your age if you must know.'

'What are they like?'

'Let's say it was different when they were younger.'

'What's your wife's name?'

'Just stop it right fucking there.' Luke pressed the eject button and the tape slid out, filling the car with static. 'Two weeks ago I wanted a ride, not a social worker.'

I stared away, hurt. But maybe it was all he had wanted and all I'd wanted too, or allowed myself to want. Was I not just trying to ease my conscience now? Questions wouldn't change the fact that I'd screwed a married man. We had been a diversion from stale lives. Because that's what my life was, hysterical laughter in clubs only hid its hollowness. I wanted something more, but not a steady job or boy-friend. I wanted excitement. I wanted Luke's brother to be 'The Ice-man'. I wanted to fuck whoever I wanted, with me deciding what was right or wrong.

Luke seemed tense as he parked at a row of shops. No one was about and I grew nervous. Last week I had fled from a youth in a lane, vowing never to walk myself into trouble again. Luke got out, producing keys as he bent to pull a steel shutter up. The shop was called AAAssorted Tiles.

'Do you want marks for spelling and originality?' I asked.

He turned off the alarm and opened the glass door.

'It's first in the Yellow Pages,' he said, 'should you care to look.'

Once inside he pulled the shutter partly down and switched on one set of lights so that half the store lay in shadow. I walked along the display units, fingering tiles and listening to him list the countries they were from. There was something soothing in his tone. There was a beautiful jade tile from India on a shelf. I pocketed it.

'That's stealing,' he said.

'You can't talk.'

Luke smiled, remembering the panties. He walked to the counter and switched the light off. I gripped the tile, wary now. But he just opened the glass door and pulled the shutter up so I could see him clearly in the street light. He turned.

'What you see is what you get,' he said.

'No Godfather, no master criminal.'

'We don't pick our families,' Luke replied. 'We can't give them back either. But we can make lives away from them. Who are your family?'

'I don't have one,' I said.

He stared at my face, as though trying to make me reveal more.

'Everyone has one. In the end that's all we have.'

'My parents are dead,' I said.

'I don't even know your name.'

'Tracey.'

'What you see, Tracey, is what you get. I'm hiding nothing or making no promises I can't keep. But I swear I'll never lie to you. Monday to Saturday I work here for my family. Sunday is my own. Next Sunday I can arrange to get that room. I can't arrange for you to be there. I'll leave you at a tube station now. Don't give me an answer. I just want you to know that I'll be waiting should you decide to come.'

SIX

THE BEST WAY TO HIDE something, according to Luke, was to lay yourself so open that people forgot there was anything to hide. Enter any bar in overalls at closing time and you could walk off with the television, the slot machine or the very seats people sat on. The one place where people never saw things happen was under their noses.

That's why I was wrong at fourteen to hide those initial cuts on my arms. Nobody might have noticed or I could have passed them off as an accident at school. If they hadn't congealed into a secret, the habit might have lapsed and I would never have grown addicted to the sense of control it gave.

Control was something I'd never known in that house. Even Grandad Pete acquiesced to Gran without comment. Only my mother argued and, even then, half-heartedly, knowing she would be brow-beaten. Nothing could deflect Gran from her second chance to rear a success. At sixteen I was to pass my GCSEs and get into Saint David's, the best sixth-form in Harrow. National Savings Certs were waiting to be cashed two years after that, when I would enter university, with every penny calculated so that nothing might distract me from my studies there. When Gran asked would I like to study science it wasn't a question. I had the brains and it was where I might meet a successful prospective husband.

When mother argued that my teachers at Hillside High said I had a gift for English, Gran scoffed at the notion of an Arts degree. That was a catch-all for unambitious people with fuzzy brains and, besides, what would my mother know, having barely scraped through North London Poly before getting herself pregnant. It was a barb used to end all arguments. Mother retreated into silence like a beaten dog and I bent over my homework as if French verbs and equations were a precise world I could lose myself within.

I sometimes wondered about what life my mother might have led if I hadn't been born, although, even then, I understood that it would never have been a stable one. She was too insecure, rearranging the most simple things until they fell apart in her hands. My father would probably have abandoned her anyway, but without the burden of me, she might have found a niche with someone decent who would lend her confidence. She had become attached to fellow patients in hospital, but whenever she was discharged Gran severed the contact, claiming my mother's manic depression couldn't be cured if she was perpetually reminded of it.

Occasionally I saw flushes of devil-may-care mischief in her: out shopping she might drag me into the pictures when we were due home. She'd take my hand and I'd glance at her face, wondering at what life might be like if she could break free of Gran. Only twice had she tried to do so: hitch-hiking around Ireland the summer before I was born and then plotting that disastrous holiday when I was eleven, during which she was blamed for losing me. I never talked about what happened on that trip and they learned not to question me, but for years those memories were still raw, if dormant, for us all.

Even without such tension, fourteen would never have been an easy age. It was a time of half-knowing everything, of self-consciousness, self-questioning and self-hatred. I nicknamed myself Burst Rubber, thrilling in its obscenity. I couldn't stop visualising my own conception, from blue videos seen in friends' houses and the magazines Joan Pitman's brother had, which we found and shrieked with laughter at. There were no faces in the images in my mind, just two torsos – one white-bellied, the other shrouded with greying hair –

61

and the sweating threadbare leather of a car in some Irish bog. The image kept recurring, even in school, a stumpy unwashed penis jutting in and out as the rubber snaps and gathers at the base among ancient curls. Still they rut on, oblivious to my fate passing between them, a fugitive seed meant to have been flung into a ditch, a tadpole struggling upstream to blight that white-bellied Englishwoman's life.

I knew this was a self-loathing fantasy. Frank Sweeney had married my mother in Dublin, so presumably they once imagined some sort of life together. He had even briefly stayed in Harrow. But there was a collective amnesia about any mention of him.

That year I smoked every day after school with the girls in Cunningham Park as we eyed the lads who passed from the swings. Four of us drank a stolen bottle of vodka and myself and a girl called Clare Ashworth vomited into somebody's garden on Devonshire Road. We drank cider in Headstone Cemetery with rough boys from Burnt Oak and Clare and I competed to see who could snog with them the longest in public. We dared each other to steal things we didn't want from shops across from Harrow-on-the-Hill station. We skipped school to party, with curtains drawn and a red bulb in Clare's living room when her parents were at work. Once we ran off in our skimpiest clothes to keep a vigil on a frozen night outside the recording studio where our favourite band was incorrectly rumoured to be and Clare took me home when I became hysterical for no apparent reason as we camped down in the graffiti-covered wall laneway.

One Saturday we had our noses pierced against our parents' consent. On the train home we loudly pretended that our clitoris had been pierced, to embarrass the blushing geek who sat with his legs crossed in the next seat. After he left, we wondered more quietly if it really caused climaxes to last an extra twenty seconds, like Joan Pitman's big sister said, or was she just a cow making it up. Afterwards I walked home with Clare. With the others gone we could stop pretending we weren't scared. I kept a bandage over my nose all evening until Gran grew suspicious. When she pulled it off I broke down in tears.

Outside of home there was no public rebellion I couldn't shame her with, but once inside the front door I was shrunk into being a child again as Gran railed against me wanting to rip my jeans or have my hair cropped. She controlled my appearance as carefully as every other aspect of my life. I was afraid to ask about any secrets they kept from me, and ashamed, in turn, to tell them the secrets which I had buried inside me.

Gran's shame about my origins was bred into me. I told friends I had no idea who my father was. If they pressed, I said that all my mother remembered was that he was strong, white and French – or at least the wine he'd plied her with had been. In truth, all I possessed was his name on my birth certificate and all I knew for certain was that my cauled head and first cries had splintered their unlikely marriage apart. Sweeney had been fifty-nine when he met my mother who was twenty-two. He had abandoned us like Gran always claimed he would, within months of coming to Harrow. Callous, ignorant and selfish, he had been a man who would sooner play music then wash himself. A man who walked away at the first hint of responsibility, leaving his tainted blood coursing through my veins like an infection to be constantly watched.

In my mind I become fourteen again on that sleepless night when the addiction began. I have lain awake for hours, listening to droning voices argue about me downstairs, until I hear my mother's defeated tread and her door close. I feel I can smell cigarette smoke in her room, the first of the dozen butts to be crumpled like spent cartridges in her bedside ashtray by dawn in her one act of defiance. Soon Gran will come up and check for the reassuring flash of the smoke alarm on the landing.

I am marooned by insomnia, almost physically feeling my body curve into new, unwanted shapes. Everything feels strange, except the sense of being a pawn between them. The house settles down with each of us awake, reliving the latest fight over my behaviour. They cannot understand this change. For years my reports were excellent, the perfect bright pupil, frighteningly articulate when not quiet as a doll in class. Now I know Gran is suggesting another school, still convinced that my behaviour is caused by bad influences. Nothing will be said but I'll count the butts by my mother's bedside and know that Gran won.

The radiator contracts with a sullen metallic groan. I am terrified the curtains are not closed properly and I'll wake to find the moon's face prying in on me. I hate myself for such a stupid fear, but even thinking about the moon brings those memories back. I play the game where it happened to someone else, but that doesn't work. I can remember too much, the slanting church roof, the stink of his flesh. I'm a cow for allowing these memories back. My nails dig into my palms. My skin crawls with pent-up tension. Tomorrow my period is due, an unwanted novelty that has worn thin. I turn over, pressing my head into the pillow. My scream is so loud in my mind that I think they will hear. I breathe in the suffocating darkness of the pillow and lift my hands above my head but when I bring them down it is not the roots of my hair they tug at. I know whose hair it is. I have stared at her curls in the photograph on the sitting room wall. That 1960s schoolgirl smiling under her blue beret, surrounded by classmates who've swapped hippy beads for overweight husbands in Northwood and Kensington.

I want to scream that I am not my mother, but I cannot feel any sense of myself. I lie like a crumpled puppet, choked by everyone's need for a second chance. I have felt disembodied once before, after taking pills Clare had found. But the way my body rocks in the bed is more frightening. I twist my head, desperate for comfort, and screw my eyes shut. Other eyes, huge and unblinking, watch from the blurred after-image invading the darkness beyond my eyes: the eyes of the Man in the Moon. They change to those of a fly, triangular legs and twitching limbs tussled in a spider's web. I'm going mad, like my mother. I want to cry for help like a child. But I am fourteen, with buds of breasts and the downiest of hair and the weight of expectations like a skin hardening over mine.

There is a shard of pain as some hair comes loose. I grimace and let go, my knuckles intertwining above my head, fingers clawing against fingers. A fragment of fingernail peels away. It just happens with a sharp incision of pain. I gasp. The nail hangs, jagged and half broken off. I press it across my wrist and squeeze my face into the pillow, too shocked to feel pain or cry out. What I feel is a flush of revenge. I am damaged goods if I could only tell them. Now I am soiling this replica schoolgirl they've tried to create. But suddenly it hurt and aches more as I keep scratching till my arm is a mass of scars.

Then, just as suddenly, it hurts less, as if an amphetamine was unleashed into my bloodstream. The sensation is of giddy exhilaration. If my body is theirs to move about, then these scars are my graffiti scrawled on it. It is no longer myself I'm hurting, but their possession. Without warning, the elixir fades and the brief, startling high is gone. Only a throbbing pain is left, another bewildering layer of guilt, and a fear of discovery which makes me dress next morning with the door locked. I don't know what I have done or why. I'm frightened of what Gran will do if the scars are discovered. I cannot eat with worry. I clench my sleeve under the table before cycling off, waving with my undamaged hand like the dutiful school-girl they all long for.

*   *   *

Now I am twenty-two again and Luke is fucking me. It is the fourth of October, the first of those Sunday evenings we will spend in that hotel. The bedspread is ancient and frayed. It grates against my breasts as I press my face into the pillow. He grips my hips, raising them to meet his thrusts. I can't understand why, since he started touching me, I keep vividly recalling being fourteen again. But the years in between keep disappearing. I feel I'm back in my childhood bedroom. I raise my hands above my head and seem about to stab at my neck before Luke grabs my wrists and pins them down. I am grateful he is withdrawn into his own silent world. I pull my hands free and intertwine the fingers, protecting my neck from him or myself. Luke is suddenly still, watching in the light from the window, with not even his cock moving inside me.

Perhaps he wants to prolong it, anxious not to come too soon. But I feel he can sense this malaise within me. He appears to wait for permission to continue. The pillow is wet. What a kip, I think, even with damp bedclothes. Then I realise I'm crying. I thrust my hips backwards, I want Luke to move, I want to break the spell of uninvited memories. Luke stirs and I try to focus on his hands or cock. But it's like an outer layer of skin has been split open and I am shocked to find my younger self preserved within. I feel robbed of the person I've carefully become and stripped more naked than I ever wish to be again.

These blocked out memories have been swamping me ever since Luke pulled my sweater over my head while undressing me. It is something I have never let any man do before. It reeked too much of being somebody's plaything and was too intimate to be allowed, just like I never permitted some men to kiss my lips. But tonight with Luke it seemed less an act of possession than of boyish wonder.

Tonight he seems less sure of himself, as if surprised at my arrival. There has been bad news, he says, but it doesn't involve him. We are like strangers with little to say, initially as awkward as adolescents. The pretence remains that we are purely here for sex, even if we each suspect there is more to it than that, but are uncertain of what it may be.

There is no sense that we have ever made love before as Luke undresses me. The room is freezing, but he takes his time, starting with my shoes and slowly removing my jeans. I raise my hips, lying back to help and then lean forward, returning his silent smile as I lift my arms to allow him to pull my woollen sweater up. For a second it covers my eyes and, unbidden, the first memory comes. My breath grows faster. I cannot even scream. Luke stops, with the sweater half over my head, disturbed by this sudden tensing of my body.

'What's wrong?' he says.

'Pull the bloody jumper off!'

He does so and I shake my hair free, lying back on the eiderdown with my eyes tightly shut. Luke pauses, unsure of what is happening. Then he begins unbuttoning my blouse. I feel his fingers but am only half aware of them. The memories are so vivid that if I open my eyes I feel I will be back in Gran's kitchen.

I feel my school polo-neck being yanked over my face again so that I'm momentarily blinded. I think I'm suffocating as Mammy holds me down and Gran draws my scarred arms from the sleeves. The kitchen blinds are closed against prying eyes. My flesh is goosepimpled. I feel violated, struggling to extract my head from the polo-neck as Gran fingers the scars. I jerk free from my mother and half fall with the polo-neck caught around my throat. I can't breathe, I'm going to choke. Mammy senses my panic and panics herself, tugging at the twisted garment as Gran shouts at her to pull it off. It comes free and I close my eyes against the questions they keep repeating.

Did a boy inflict these scars? Why had I kept them hidden?

Had a man done anything, a neighbour or a teacher who'd warned me against speaking? Was I in trouble? I sense Gran's fear in this euphemism, her terror of a cycle repeating. Neither of them understand what I need to tell them. I hate them for that as much as I hate myself. A new voice at my ear, a monkey with no face, whispers that I should punish them too.

For three weeks I've hidden these bruised arms away, skipping school to avoid swimming and locking the bathroom when I washed. At night I've only half slept, promising myself I would leave my arms untouched, even counting the hours I managed to stay this itch. But always I know that at some stage the scratching and biting will begin again. Nothing prevents it, silent pacing or meaningless prayers. Behind the radiator I keep a shattered plastic ruler. This ache only stops when I use it to draw blood and creep downstairs for watered whisky to ease the pain. A map of purple bruising stretches up to my shoulders. The addiction feeds on the fear of discovery. Twice I've dreamt my mother has found me in pain and taken me in her arms. Twice I've woken disappointed to fret about hiding the flecks of blood where my arm rested on the pillow.

But now, as they stare at my arms in the kitchen, I am suddenly defiant. They are scared of me for the first time in my life. I have stepped beyond their control. The discovery gives me strength. I sit with half my school uniform torn off. I know I cannot explain these scars but now I don't want to. I hate Mammy for being weak and I'm ashamed of her illness. I hate Gran because I need someone to blame and because no matter how hard I try I can never achieve her dreams heaped on my shoulders.

Even as a baby they had forced me to choose, playing a game where they called from different sides of the playground to see who I'd run to. I remember tottering back and forth until I sat down crying with my arms over my head. Now I stare at their faces, then arch my fingers to scratch my neck with nails I have let grow jagged. I don't notice whose hand grabs my arm. I call out with what sounds like a shriek of pain but is a cry of freedom.

My cry echoes in this hotel room. I open my eyes, surprised by the sound, like someone waking up. Luke has entered me. He stops, his scared eyes looking into mine.

'What's wrong?' he says. 'Have I hurt you?'

'It's nothing to do with you,' I say. 'I didn't ask you to stop.'

'Are you okay?'

'Last week you said you just wanted a fuck,' I tell him. 'This is private. My life is none of your concern.'

I close my eyes, feeling Luke hesitate, then enter me, deep and deeper. Once these memories start they will not stop. I even know the sequence they will follow: the rows as Gran forcibly cut my nails, the dark games where the closer they examined my body the more secretively I hid my scars. Then the doctors and specialists, hours of queueing for professional voices to probe why I was asking for help. The ink dots and idiotic tests, folders crammed with pictures of the moon which I sullenly drew in their offices. And the suspicion that fell about our house, the rumours I could set into motion, making my grandparents live in fear until I controlled their lives for the next three years. Yet, even at the summit of that power, I still lacked courage to speak about the man in the moon and nothing could touch the core of pain within me.

That pain should be banished, now because I am twenty-two, a new person with a new life. I open my eyes. I'm in a hotel bedroom, being fucked – like my mother at that age – by an Irishman. I don't know why the memories have returned, or why my mother seems close, as if watching now. But when I close my eyes an adolescent image returns: dark bogland and sweating leather, grey hairs around a penis jutting out and in.

69

I stretch my arms out, wanting to be held. Can they not see what's happening before their eyes? Can they not even try to understand?

But Luke doesn't understand. I feel him withdraw and his arms turn me over. The bedspread is ancient and frayed. It grates against my breasts. He grips my hips, raising them to meet his thrusts. I press my face into the pillow and the ache is as insatiable as it always was, and the gulf between me and the world is like a scar that can be hidden but never healed.

SEVEN

FOR THE FOLLOWING nine Sundays I made that journey. I saw less and less of Honor and Roxy, despite only being with Luke once a week. But, although I resented him for it, that time had become increasingly central to my life. The job in Wilkinson's finished in late October and I was on social security again. I hated the dark evenings, the rain keeping me isolated in my flat and the secrecy of our relationship.

I know it is irrational, but some Sundays I varied my connection from Angel and changed at Euston instead of King's Cross. I knew no one was following me, but such manoeuvres formed part of a mental foreplay, adding to the illicitness of our encounters. I had done the same after leaving Harrow, convinced my grandparents were searching for me.

At first I had once or twice arrived late, just to let Luke sweat. But recently my anxiety that he mightn't turn up had grown so acute that I hated the uncertainty. We were crazy to cling to this location, where Luke might be spotted, but we seemed unwilling to initiate any change. The temporariness of the hotel suited us, keeping further commitment at bay. Yet this arrangement couldn't be indefinite. Eventually one of us would arrive and instinctively know that the other wasn't late, they had simply ceased coming.

It was early December before we quarrelled. My period wasn't quite over yet. The receptionist eyed us more inquisitively every week and, although I wasn't bothered by her glances, I didn't want her prying at bloodied sheets after we left. Sex had been the reason for our dates and so, although I wanted to see Luke, I almost didn't turn up that week. Perhaps I was afraid of the vacuum its absence might leave, but Luke said that the sex wasn't important, for him at least, and it would be nice to talk for a change.

We did so in bed with the light out, smoking and sharing a bottle of gin. I wanted to roll a joint but Luke was old-fashioned about something as harmless as dope. As always, Luke talked while I probed. Our conversations had become a contest of wills where I tried to needle him into revealing more than he wished to. I told him almost nothing of myself and, although Luke initially appeared open, I soon realised how tightly he defined the world he chose to tell me about.

His talk was mostly about childhood in Dublin, yet the younger self he described seemed removed from the Luke I knew. Silences punctuated his stories so that they made little chronological sense, while nothing was said about the current occupations of his two brothers, who populated every story he told, and his own life in London might not have existed.

'Why did you really come over here?' I asked as we lay, with the bottle half-empty. Somehow the sensation of being in bed without having made love felt more intimate than anything we'd done before.

'You get sick of living in people's shadows,' he replied, taking another slug and staring at the ceiling. 'Over here you're nobody, everyone lives their own life. My neighbour has stupid bloody pillars outside his house with ornate balls on top. Last Christmas I was reversing into my driveway when I knocked into one them. He came running out and it was the first time he'd bothered speaking to me after eight years there.'

'What did he say?'

'How dare you reverse into my balls!' Luke's English accent was perfect. I laughed.

'He did not.'

'No.' Luke agreed. 'Nothing as original as that.'

'What would it be like in Dublin?'

'Different.' The humour drained from his voice.

'Why?'

'It just would be. People think they have your measure there, they point the finger.'

'All the same, would you be happier there?'

'Happy?' he snorted. 'What the fuck has happy got to do with it? I came here tonight to forget that shite, all right.'

I knew by his tone that the conversation had steered out of bounds. Luke turned, his hands sliding down my back and probing into my knickers. But I also knew he didn't really want sex, he just wanted any intimacy kept at bay. It made me feel cheap and I pushed him off.

'We agreed,' I told him, 'so don't start.'

'A few specks of blood never hurt nobody,' he replied. 'Besides, there's more ways than one.'

'Just go and fuck yourself.' I began to climb from the bed, angered by his deliberate mockery. 'Fuck off and play with yourself.'

I started getting dressed, as angry with myself as with him. I had helped set these rules, knowing our relationship couldn't survive beyond these walls. I had never wanted soppy confessions or post-coital angst. But I didn't know what I wanted any more.

'Listen, Tracey.' Luke's tone was conciliatory. 'I didn't mean . . .'

'You did,' I said. 'Be honest, that's all you see me as, a tart, a piece of fluff on the side.'

My back was turned. I had just ripped my skirt in my haste to put it on. I didn't want him looking at me half dressed.

'Is that how you really see yourself?'

I turned, my hand holding closed the blouse I hadn't time to button up. I was trembling.

'You're so clever, aren't you?' I sneered. 'You always know how to shift it back on to me.'

'You should never think of yourself like that.' Luke sounded like a concerned father. He had retreated into his watchful, non-committal self.

'Just how do you think of me?'

'You don't need to ask.'

'No,' I replied. 'It's obvious you're using me. Once you come you'd sooner wave a magic wand and make me vanish.'

'You never wanted lies before.'

'I want the fucking truth.'

'The truth is I'll be here for you next week and every week.' He watched as I managed to do up the last buttons on my blouse. I hated myself for shaking, but who the fuck was Luke anyway? I wasn't asking him to leave his wife, I didn't want more of his precious time, but just that once he might show a shred of affection.

'You're wasted in tiles,' I said, grabbing my coat. 'You should have gone into plastics. You could have simply moulded a likeness of me to blow up.'

I slammed the door. I could imagine the receptionist lifting her head. But when I got downstairs I found that for once I couldn't stare back at her because that was how I felt, a cheap tart, some man's weekend piece of fluff. I kept my head down until I reached the street and ran.

I didn't go back the following Sunday or the Sunday after that. I did nothing, except sit in the flat and smoke roll ups. I stared blankly at titles in the video shop. I splashed out on cheap wine but couldn't even seem to get drunk. Roxy and Honor had stopped calling, perhaps guessing at all the times I was really in with the light out. I could have called for them or taken off by myself like I used to, but I seemed drained of emotion.

There were Christmas lights everywhere, late night shopping and office parties. I considered phoning Harrow, but I didn't want to think of home or Christmas or anything which might drag the past back. One night I dreamt about that old black monkey and woke scared and unsure of where I was. Our affair was over, I told myself. I needed my own life, not some other woman's cast-offs. In Gran's pet phrase, gleaned from years of specialists, I had an addictive personality. Luke was the latest addiction to break.

But Luke was the first encounter to really affect me since my mother's death. Everything else had a second-hand flavour. I wondered if his wife had consented all along. Was that why he had been so open in the Irish Centre? But I knew she didn't know, because wives never do, and I was trying to justify something which had increasingly disturbed me. Every day I told myself it was finished and yet that statement seemed too definite for something as vague as our relationship. Some days I decided I was just playing it cool and letting him sweat for a while. I could break this habit whenever I wanted, but perhaps I should use Luke to get me over the loneliness of Christmas. The problem was that his absence made me realise how empty my life was.

On December the fifteenth I decided to visit his shop. I was on a tube and impulsively stayed on after my stop. I watched the stations flash past, not certain if I'd actually go in or what I expected to happen if Luke was there. Maybe I wanted to haul our relationship out into the wintry light of a Wednesday afternoon and see if anything remained. I just knew I couldn't leave matters as they stood and I couldn't walk back into that hotel any more than I could break away from Luke.

The store was crowded with serious-looking DIY folk beautifying their houses for Christmas. Piped carols were interrupted by special offer announcements. I felt an almost vengeful enjoyment in being there, setting the agenda for once. I moved around the aisles, watching his staff work and wondering if he was here or in the smaller shop a few miles away. The staff were young and well trained, marked out by red company jumpers and enthusiasm. I could hear them repeat the same soothing phrase, 'I'm not trying to sell you this but it might just suit . . ."

A supervisor in a dark suit checked off a stocklist with a visiting sales rep. I passed him twice before I stopped to look back. It was Luke. I watched his eyes flick between the printed order form and the shelves. I felt chilled. I hadn't recognised him and now, when I did, I realised that I didn't know this man and I could never have slept with him. The rep was leaving. Luke called something after him. Even his voice sounded different. I was watching a chameleon. Luke turned to look straight through me for several moments before it occurred to him who I was. His face changed but only slightly. It showed neither encouragement nor surprise. I realised I couldn't talk to him here, I had nothing to say to this man. I backed away, fleeing down a side aisle to escape.

The following Sunday I left it late before deciding to visit the hotel. There were delays with the tube and when it finally came three girls stood by the door laughing hysterically at their own inane comments, as if anxious to antagonise the whole carriage. After Wednesday's visit I had sworn never to go near that hotel again. Yet at King's Cross I raced through the passageways connecting the Northern and Circle lines.

I got stuck behind an old man struggling up the escalator with a suitcase. The case stuck out, blocking the left side where people tried to rush past. They cursed him silently and not so silently as he ignored the log-jam behind him. There was something unnerving in his stillness as he stared up the escalator as though a great fate awaited beyond the ticket barrier, which he had only to haul his battered case across the forecourt to confront.

Honor once told me she believed in angels after seeing one pass her window as a little girl. Momentarily I forgot Luke as I watched the old man, fixated by the notion that he was a soul on its ultimate journey. Perhaps this underground was full of ghosts that nobody noticed as they vanished down tunnels at the end of deserted platforms. I couldn't remember if I had read about such a notion, but, as a child, shabby old men with cases had fascinated me with the unspoken fear that they were my dark father come back.

The suitcase bumped over the rim of the escalator and the old man stumbled, trying to hold it. I pushed past and ran down more stairs just in time to catch the train pulling out on the Circle Line. Yet all the way to Edgware Road I felt an obscure foreboding that I hadn't stopped to help him.

There was no guarantee that Luke would have come or would wait this late. But I felt he would have taken my appearance in the store as a sign that I wanted to talk. If he didn't show up then at least I'd be freed from the illusion that I had found somebody who needed me.

I emerged at Edgware Road into light rain and walked quickly on. Looking back, I realise that if I had paused to help the old man with his case I might have missed my connection and arrived so late that I would have run past the shops opposite the Irish Centre. Instead I slowed to stroll casually past so as not to attract attention. Apart from the restaurant with its bored belly dancer, only the newsagent was open, although even he had one shutter down. I saw him closing up, with a huge rack of foreign newspapers pulled in out of the rain. An Irish Sunday paper was there, incongruous among the mass of Arabic newsprint. I could hardly see the photograph in it and had gone past when the eyes drew me back. I leaned against the glass. It couldn't be Luke, I thought, starting to panic. It was like him, but the face was stockier, the eyes more cold. Ironically it was the suit I recognised first, because, as suits go, Christy Duggan's taste was pretty appalling. The photograph was obviously a family one, taken at a christening or wedding. I banged on the glass. At first I thought the shopkeeper wasn't going to bother opening up. The paper was folded, but I could still make out the headline, *Dublin Gangland Murder*.

I stood outside under a streetlamp, reading the account of his killing over and over until the rain distorted the newsprint. Now I knew that Luke wouldn't be in the hotel. He would have no way of letting me know the news and no way of guessing that I knew. But I walked on anyway, in case there was a message at reception. I wanted there to be a different receptionist, but the same one eyed me coldly, sensing she had the upper hand.

'Is there a letter for me here?' I asked.

'I'm not his messenger,' she retorted. 'Go up and ask him yourself.'

She turned a page of her magazine, deliberately not looking up until I'd gone. I reached the top of the stairs. I hadn't expected this. I must be important if Luke had found time to see me tonight. We had always kept emotions at bay and now I felt ill-equipped to console him. It didn't seem right to walk in on his grief. I knocked twice before he opened the door. If he had been crying it was well hidden. He stepped back to allow me in.

'Luke, I know and I'm sorry,' I said.

He gave a half shrug. 'It was all my fault.'

Even when confronting death he seemed composed. His suit was immaculate although the shirt collar looked scuffed. His manner was more apologetic than mournful.

'You can't blame yourself,' I said. 'I'm just surprised you came tonight.'

'Why?' he asked. 'We can't let setbacks get in our way.'

He took a pull of his cigar and I realised that my suspicions were right all along. He was a total chameleon, a conman who felt nothing for anybody. I remembered his hands on my neck

78

that first night. He could have killed me and thought nothing of it. Luke studied my face, concerned.

'What's wrong, Tracey?' he said. 'I'm here to apologise for the row. I'm sorry about the shop, but we're so busy before Christmas that I was miles away. You were gone before I'd time to say anything.'

He hadn't realised I was talking about Christy. He thought I didn't know what had happened.

'I don't fucking believe this,' I sneered. 'You don't even let death get in the way of a quick fuck!'

I backed away, ready to flee and Luke reached a hand out.

'Don't fucking touch me,' I shouted. Then I looked at his eyes and realised that Luke hadn't heard the news from Dublin.

'Where have you been all day?'

He looked confused by the question. 'I was in Holland since Friday, buying stock from a tile shop closing down over there. I took the van across. It's parked outside still.'

'Oh my God.' I paused but couldn't find a way to soften the words. 'Luke, I'm sorry, but your brother Christy was shot dead in Dublin.'

Only when I held up the sodden newspaper did Luke realise I was serious. His face changed. He took it from me and turned away. I saw his head move as he scanned the blurred columns. Newsprint had stained my hands, the words printed backwards across my fingers. I looked up and realised that Luke was no longer attempting to read. He was silently crying. I went to put my arms around his shoulders, then stopped. Luke had always maintained an emotional distance between us. I could only watch, afraid that any attempt to console him would be rejected.

'Would you like me to go?'

'No. Please.' He walked to the window and put his hands on the pane. I could see him reflected in it and he could see me.

'You were close, weren't you?' I said.

'He could beat the crap out of me, but he'd murder anyone who put a finger near me as well. I was fifteen before I'd clothes of my own. I lived in his hand-me-downs, vests, underpants, even his shoes sometimes.' Luke turned. His face seemed to have aged a decade. 'Even adults were scared of him. He'd take on blokes twice his size and beat them. Yet I was the one always trying to mind him.'

I knew by the way Luke stood that he wanted to be held. I put my arms around him and he buried his face in my hair where I couldn't see him cry. I recalled a story he once told me, set on a factory roof somewhere in Dublin called Rialto. Luke had heard that Christy and an older boy were breaking in there but he knew their plan was inept. The roofs were slippery after rain as he crossed valleys of corrugated iron and hammered glass, searching for them. A watchman's torch flashed below, followed by an alsatian's muffled bark. Then, somewhere among the rooftops, he heard sporadic sobbing. It was too dangerous to call out. Luke waited till the crying resumed, then took a bearing and slid down a gully, where a loose rivet ripped his jeans and flesh. His boots collided with Christy, who rocked back and forth, his crying frightening Luke more than the danger of being caught. Luke stared at the glass below on the concrete floor. The light was bright enough to make the shards sparkle and for Luke to see that the fallen figure lying there had a broken neck.

I stroked Luke's hair, which was thinning and greying at the roots with traces of dandruff. I felt so desperately sorry, but there seemed nothing I could say to console him. I could see those boys in my mind, Luke trying to guide his brother like a blubbering child along the rooftops as he watched for the security guard and unchained dog. Luke had known how to escape. But Christy had seized up, unable to climb down, even after they heard the body being found and knew the police had been called. Luke remained, minding Christy until the firemen raised their ladders, although he knew he would also be charged and sentenced to an Irish industrial school.

Luke raised his head and wiped his eyes.

'You should go home,' I said. 'People will be looking for you.'

'I don't like home,' he replied. 'Before meeting you I thought that what I wanted wasn't important. I put my head down and got on with working for my family. Suits aren't meant to contain feelings. I should go home, there's business to take care of. But fuck it, Tracey, I don't want to ever leave this room.'

'You've no choice,' I said quietly. 'You're needed there.'

'Come with me.'

I thought of his wife and children. 'You know I can't, Luke. But I'll drive with you if you want and see you get safely there.'

'I didn't mean home here,' Luke said. 'It's Dublin I hate. I haven't gone back for years. I'm not sure I can face watching gangsters queue up to shake my hand and knowing one of them set Christy up. Come to Dublin. It would mean so much to know you're there. I need you with me, Tracey. Please.'

III

DUBLIN

EIGHT

LUKE'S WIFE AND CHILDREN would be arriving from London on a later flight. It was a fact Luke simply had to live with, he explained, normally you got hassled by the police at Dublin airport. The family name was enough, it just took one detective trying to get himself a reputation. This was why Luke had deliberately raised his children in England. Now he wanted them kept away from all that. I was discovering that Luke had an excuse for everything, even taking his mistress with him on a flight to Dublin while his wife and children travelled alone.

Security at Dublin Airport was non-existent. The terminal was like a cathedral of homecoming, with Christmas trees and clock-work Santa Clauses in the centre of each luggage conveyor belt. People collected their luggage, then drifted through the blue channel where nobody was on duty. No official paid Luke the slightest heed. Crowds thronged the arrivals hall, greeting returning family members. Luke's younger brother, Shane, had arranged to meet him. I could see him trying to place my face.

'Who's she?' he asked suspiciously as Luke put the bags down.

'Stick around for Carmel and the kids, Shane,' Luke replied, ignoring the question. 'They're on the next plane. We'll get a taxi.'

But Shane still stared at me. He had an open, innocent face. In soft light he would still pass for someone in their twenties. I remembered him acting as a peace-maker in the Irish Centre.

85

'Ah, for Jaysus sake, Luke,' he cottoned on, more exasperated than annoyed.

'Don't worry,' I told him. 'Luke's just some cheap lay I picked up on the flight over.'

Shane threw his eyes to heaven, then picked up the cases and led the way to the car park. Luke's wife could make her own way into Dublin. There was an uneasiness between them, with my presence preventing Shane from discussing family matters. I felt Luke had placed me there like a shield. At the car Luke asked to drive and Shane mumbled about him not being covered by insurance before grudgingly handing the keys over.

Shane sat beside him in silence as we drove on to the motorway. I noticed that Luke didn't turn for Dublin, but drove in the opposite direction to where it petered out into an ordinary road again. The unease I'd known on the flight returned. It had gnawed at me since driving with Luke to the corner of his street in London and watching from the shadows as he reversed past his neighbour's ornate pillars up to his front door where figures rushed out to claim him back.

'Where are we going?' I asked.

'The scenic route,' he replied shortly. We reached a small roundabout and Luke turned left on to a smaller country road which was ploughed up, with pipes and machinery parked on what was once a grass verge. Luke seemed to be trying to track back to Dublin along a network of lanes crisscrossing the countryside between the airport and the city. But there were half finished roads and diversions everywhere. Shane remained silent, slotted into his role as a younger brother, yet I sensed his satisfaction as it became obvious that Luke was lost. I had expected tears at the airport or angry promises of revenge, but instead a web of tension and distrust hung between them. Christy had not yet been mentioned.

'Where the fuck am I?' Luke was forced to mutter at last.

'It's structural funds from Brussels, that Maastricht shite

we got bribed into voting for a couple of years back. You'd know about it if your Government across the water allowed people a say in anything.'

'What do you mean, *my* Government?' Luke said.

'Well, you're not exactly queueing up to vote here.'

'Dublin is still my town and you know it,' Luke said, suddenly bitter.

I thought neither was going to back down, then Shane said quietly: 'I know, but if you want to convince people it might be wiser to come home more than once every five years.'

Luke stared ahead, trying to recognise some landmark.

'I hardly know this way myself,' Shane added, soothingly. 'The Government's gone mad for building roads.'

'So everybody can emigrate quicker.' The bitterness in Luke's voice seemed tempered as he admitted to himself he was lost. 'I wanted to slip in by the back of Ballymun.'

'You're miles away,' Shane said. 'Half the old roads are closed. They're ringing the whole city by a motorway.'

'You could have said something.'

Shane shrugged and Luke pulled in among a line of JCBs and earthmovers parked beside a half constructed flyover. Below us, an encampment of gypsy caravans had already laid claim to an unopened stretch of motorway. Luke got out to change places. The brothers passed each other in the headlights of the car. Shane got back in, but Luke stood for a moment, caught in those lights, staring down at the caravans.

The fields beyond were littered with upturned cars, where men moved about, dismantling vehicles for spare parts in the half light. Cars were pulled in as motorists negotiated deals at the open door of a caravan. Children in ragged coats played hide and seek among the smashed bonnets and rusting car doors. A dog vanished into a pile of tyres. Smoke was rising and although the windows were closed I was convinced I could smell burning rubber. I wondered again what my life would have been like if Mammy hadn't persuaded Frank Sweeney to move to Harrow three months before I was born. I stared at the mucky children careering through the wrecked cars. This was what I had been saved from. As a child I'd had romantic visions about what it might be like, but now it felt as if Gran was beside me, smugly witnessing the justification of everything she had done. What would Luke feel if he knew that his mistress was an Irish tinker's daughter?

'Are you English?' Shane asked quietly.

'Yeah,' I said, looking away from the children.

'Just don't come to the house or the funeral, please.'

There was no animosity in his tone. I didn't know if he saw my nod in reply, but he flicked the lights for Luke to get back in. Instead of sitting next to him, Luke climbed into the back seat beside me. I had never known him to display affection but now he reached for my hand and I sensed Shane tracking the movement in the rear-view mirror. Shane started the car.

'Does Carmel know?' he asked after a moment.

'Neither do you,' was Luke's terse reply. The tension between them was only partly to do with me. Luke stared out at the December twilight and I could only guess at his thoughts. Five minutes later we pulled in at the entrance to an exclusive golf course. Shane cut off the engine and the brothers stared up the long curving driveway.

'The back of McKenna's farm,' Luke said eventually.

'I didn't know if you'd recognise it.'

'I'm not likely to forget the shape of that blasted hill, am I?'

A BMW came down the driveway and accelerated away. Shane watched the tail lights disappear.

'I said it to Christy,' Shane said, 'the week before they shot him. There was no need for all this aggravation for years. He should have just bought McKenna's land and built a golf course. You sit on your arse all day and they queue up to hand their money over.'

It was the first time Christy was mentioned and although

nothing else was said it seemed to ease the reserve between them. Perhaps their shared memories were so engrained that they couldn't speak of them. But, from stories Luke had told me after love-making, I began to understand the need he had felt to drive out here. It was a need Shane must have understood. Soon Luke would be swamped by his extended family, with public rituals and duties to perform. But here in the gathering dark, the space existed to come to terms with death.

On the flight over I had told him for the first time about my mother's death and my visits to Northwick hospital as she grew weaker and more withdrawn until she had just stared back at me. I had grown to hate those visits and to hate myself for resenting the way she used silence like an accusation. I had avoided being there when my grandparents visited, but once I met an old school friend of hers, Jennifer, who called me out into the corridor. 'She's dying,' she said. 'So what are you doing to contact him?' I had stared back, uncomprehendingly. 'Your father,' Jennifer said angrily. 'Surely at least the man has a right to know his wife is dying.'

It was the first time I'd ever had to think of him as flesh and blood. He had been an abstraction before, a shameful bogey-man. Frank Sweeney would be eighty if still alive. But because no one spoke of him, I'd presumed him long dead. I had read in a magazine that the average life-span of Irish travellers was under fifty. Even if he were alive, I had told Jennifer, I could hardly chase around every campsite in Ireland. He'd had twenty years to contact us. Besides, after what he'd done, my mother would hardly want to see him now.

Jennifer had a large house in Belgravia, a husband working in the City, children who passed through private schools and emerged polished as porcelain. All the things Gran had wanted for her daughter. Yet although Gran spoke of Jennifer glowingly, I'd never known her to set foot inside our house. Now she glared at me in the hospital corridor. 'Did you ask her?' she had snapped, momentarily furious. 'You're not a child any more, Tracey. You've caused your mother nothing but grief with your silly games and yet you've never bothered to find out the least thing.'

Jennifer was right and I knew it. At a certain level I had always withdrawn from other people's pain into my interior world. After she left I went back to my mother's ward and asked nothing that might require an awkward response. I had matched her silence with silence and, later, Gran's grief with flight. This was partly why it had felt important to come to Dublin and to just once be there when somebody needed me.

Luke stared up at the lights of the clubhouse and I squeezed his palm. The curved lake, lit by spotlights beside the final green, had to be man-made. I glanced at Luke's face, feeling I was in the way, but also that he wanted me here. I could imagine all three brothers here as boys of twelve, eleven and ten, with those extra years providing a hierarchical chain of command. These roads would have been smaller as they walked out among similar bands of boys at dawn. One night Luke had described McKenna, a burly countryman wrapped in the same greatcoat in all weathers, who would eye up the swarms of boys to decide who might have the honour of filling his baskets with fruit and who would walk the two miles back to the city disappointed.

I remembered how Luke pronouced McKenna's name with quiet contempt, but also a faint echo of childhood awe which I could imagine no adult adversary ever meriting. I couldn't remember the full story, except that it was the first time I'd heard Shane mentioned in detail. He would have been sandwiched between Luke and Christy among the crowd of boys as McKenna made his choice so that all three appeared to be strong, hardened workers. Luke and Christy had covered up for him when his back ached and his hands blistered during the endless day of picking until finally his tally of baskets began to drop. There was a row and Shane had broken down in tears as McKenna threw a handful of coins on the ground and spat on them.

'Was McKenna mean?' I asked Shane.

He snorted. 'As mean as the back of his balls that only ever knew shite.' He glanced back, apologetic for his language. It was thirty years since those events but they still rankled. We eyed each other openly.

'How do I measure up to the others?' I asked him.

'There have been no others.' Shane re-started the car and I believed him and beneath my show of toughness I felt better. Luke ignored our exchange. I wondered what Shane thought of me and was it contempt for his opinion or a bond between brothers which allowed Luke to display his mistress so openly. For the next two days I would have to remain invisible and I sensed that this journey was perhaps Luke's only way to give some acknowledgement to my presence. Shane would never mention me, not even to his own wife. I suspected there were more dangerous secrets locked away in Shane's head that would always stay there with a younger brother's unquestioning loyalty.

We had reached the fringe of the city where back gardens of shabby houses petered out into overgrown fields. Children stood about on corners, with hoods over their heads.

'What happened to McKenna?' I asked.

'He died years ago,' Shane said. 'The last time I saw him he was screaming like a madman up at our house when I was ten. He claimed Christy blinded two of his cattle because he'd cheated me out of a day's pay.'

'How do you mean blinded?'

'The police said it was done with sticks,' Shane replied. 'They cleared us of involvement, but McKenna wouldn't believe it. He was ranting, threatening our Ma who was trying to raise us without a penny the time Da had to go to England for work.'

The thought of such cruelty sickened me. Christy had a

reputation for violence, but this was too extreme even for a twelve year old like him.

'Did Christy do it?' I asked.

'Are you joking?' Shane laughed, coming to a supermarket and turning left. 'Poor Christy go up to the fields by himself in the dark and do the likes of that? He liked animals, Christy did, well dogs and pigeons anyway. Cows gave him the creeps. He was a city kid. He might have done McKenna himself, but cows? No way. That wouldn't have been Christy's style.'

We stopped at traffic lights. Horses stood motionless on a green, tied with lengths of rope. In the darkness beside them dozens of Christmas trees were propped up as if a forest had dropped from the sky. Two boys in over-sized duffel coats hunched down waiting for buyers. The lights changed.

'It was a typical job by your man beside you,' Shane said as he moved off. 'Luke goaded the other kids about being chicken until they went up the fields while the three of us sat at home with alibis watching *The Man from Uncle*.'

Luke laughed and looked at me. 'Don't believe a word that fellow says,' he said, almost absentmindedly. 'It's what Shane does best, wind people up.'

I laughed too, but the problem was that I did believe Shane or, at least, I didn't know whether to believe him or not. True or false, two images stuck in my mind. One was of cows bellowing in agony as blood streamed down their faces and a circle of boys dropped their sticks and ran off with their bravado replaced by a realisation that they had been used. The second image was almost as chilling: an eleven year old calmly standing at his front door during the ad breaks on television where he would be seen by passing neighbours.

As if sensing my unease, Luke took my hand again. Suddenly I wanted to return to my life in London. I felt used as well, manipulated into thinking he needed me here. A suspicion came back even as I tried to dismiss it. Could Luke have known of Christy's death all along, but had come to the hotel for sex anyway, not thinking that I could know? Might he have turned my knowledge to his advantage, sensing a need which he could exploit? Or did my own secretive nature make me suspect him? I wasn't being fully honest with him about my reasons for agreeing to travel to Dublin. I knew nobody here. I would have to walk around alone or wait in some hotel bedroom until Luke found time to come. The unintended irony of the phrase made me feel cheap. I closed my eyes and the image of blinded cattle returned. I wondered again if Luke's wife knew of my existence and, if she discovered I was here, what might be her measure of revenge?

We turned down a side road with a high wall, beyond which I could glimpse the roofs of unlit school buildings. A notice warned of guard dogs, but Shane turned through the gate and across a cattle grid to park with his headlights shining over a panoramic view of streets beyond the dark playing pitches. Luke seemed momentarily disorientated as Shane glanced back, awaiting some response.

'Christy drove by here six months ago and almost crashed,' Shane said.

'I believe it,' Luke said quietly. 'It's thirty years since I've seen that view.'

'The pre-fab was levelled last year,' Shane told him. 'They finally built a permanent extension, out where the sheds used to be. Take a look.'

They both got out, caught up in memories I didn't know, and walked into the glare of the headlights. I watched them bend their heads to talk. Their brother had been one of Dublin's most notorious criminals. I hadn't asked Luke who had killed him or what could happen next. As long as he kept me ignorant I had felt I wasn't involved. Now that we were actually in Dublin I was scared. I didn't know how much of this fear was bound up with Luke or how much stemmed from a terror of confronting ghosts I had spent half my life running from. Yet I knew those spectres had to be banished before I might begin to see some value in myself. It was because I regarded myself so cheaply that I never trusted anyone who reached out to me. Luke's grief in the hotel was real because he had cried like I never could. He wouldn't risk bringing me here unless his need was also genuine.

The two brothers cast out vast shadows in the headlights. I got out to see what they were examining. It was a flat expanse of floor tiles left behind after a pre-fabricated building had been demolished. I could decipher shapes of classrooms from the different styles of tiling. I sensed Luke visualising the building as it had once stood. He climbed up and followed the route of a vanished corridor, retracing his steps to the spot where Christy and he had first shared a desk. We had moved beyond the headlights so that we were now shadows in the dark. If I'd believe in spirits I would have said that Christy's was there at that moment, along with the younger Luke and Shane, hungry for the lives ahead of them.

'If Christy was older why were you in the same class?' I asked, to break the atmosphere. Luke looked back, momentarily drawn into the present.

'Holy communion,' he explained. 'Ma had to put him back a class when he was seven. She couldn't afford the clothes that year.'

He walked to where the classroom wall had once stood and looked across at the lights from neighbouring streets. The main school stood in darkness to our right while there was ugly security fencing around the graceful old building on our left.

'That was a fever convalescent hospital once,' Shane said, motioning me to leave Luke alone. 'When our folks came here first there were still old people in bath chairs coughing up blood under the trees. When TB died out the Christian Brothers opened a school instead. Not for corporation tenants like us, more for the private houses. But the place kept growing until one summer he was home from England, Da got a job sticking this prefab up to cope with the over-crowding.'

Luke had walked further away with his head bowed.

'I can remember being given jam sambos and sent down to watch Da working,' Shane said. 'Ma kept badgering Da to have a word with the Brothers about us getting in here. Luke and Christy were steeped, free secondary education had just arrived. Before then it would have been the Tech or looking for whatever work we could find at fourteen.'

Luke turned. Although it was dark I sensed he'd been crying, or had come as close to tears as he ever would in public. 'You stupid poor bastard, Christy,' he said, almost to himself. He looked at Shane. 'Somebody set him up, didn't they?'

'Somebody did,' Shane agreed carefully, aware of my presence.

'I don't want to know who it was, you understand? Tell your son that. Half-arsed revenge won't bring him back.'

'Al never took any part . . .'

'I know,' Luke said. 'Al's a good kid, so this isn't the time to start.' He looked around. 'I remember trying to drag Christy here every morning. Ma always said it was my job to keep him out of trouble.'

'Christy liked trouble,' Shane replied. Luke walked towards us and Shane put a hand on his shoulder. 'You could have done nothing, Luke.'

'Come on.' Luke replied. 'This place makes me feel old.'

'You are old,' Shane joked, but Luke just grunted and walked towards the car headlights, stepping on all the cracks now, deliberately walking through invisible walls. We followed.

'I didn't want to come,' I told Shane. 'I just felt I couldn't refuse him.'

'Everything will work out fine,' Shane said, more to himself than me.

'How long did Christy last here?'

'Eighteen months of hassle till he got expelled and found

95

a job on the milk floats,' Shane said. 'Luke was different. The Brothers hated him and he hated them. The year he got put away in Saint Raphael's Industrial School they thought they'd seen the back of him, but he came back, put his head down and got first in the school in the Leaving Cert. I think he did it to spite them.'

Back in the car I knew the tour of the past was over. Luke sat beside Shane and they discussed practical arrangements, with Luke rechecking each detail of the funeral. There was something chilling in his tone, as if the business of burying his brother was like another shipment of tiles. I felt in the way. Mentally Luke was back among his family, a different person from the man I'd known in London or even the one who had cried in those school ruins moments before.

He had booked a single room for me in a hotel among a maze of tree-lined streets in Glasnevin. When we pulled up outside it I felt he was anxious to be gone. Shane took my case from the boot. The three of us stood there awkwardly. A handshake would have been ludicrous but I knew Luke wouldn't display any token of affection. It was Shane who reached across to kiss my cheek. He smiled and opened the car door for Luke.

'Don't mind him,' he said. 'Your first time in Dublin, eh? You have a good time, you hear me?'

NINE

BUT ACTUALLY IT WASN'T the first time I'd ever been in Dublin. I remember, one night, watching a programme about the miracle of migration, how the tiniest of birds can instinctively plot a flight path across oceans and continents back to the nondescript cluster of trees where they had pecked their shells asunder. A camera hidden above the nest had shown the chicks with their beaks open, awaiting their mother's return. Their luminous eyes had never ceased gazing up, scanning the constellations and logging the precise configuration of the Plough and Orion and Seven Sisters at that fixed point of their birth, so that no matter how far they scattered, they could perpetually track a course back home.

There had been no stars on the ceiling of that hotel near Dublin's bus station when I was eleven years of age. Instead there had been tributaries and deltas of cracks, pencil-thin veins that clenched themselves up into shapes of staring eyes and demonic heads. I had lain alone beneath them, both longing for and dreading my mother's return. There were footsteps on the ceiling above me, the creaking of a bed gathering meaning and pace. Part of the adjoining room jutted out into ours, a plywood alcove where water sporadically gushed from a tap to cloak the hiss of some man's piss seeping into the sink. The muffled thump of a rock band echoed from the bowels of the shabby building. I had known that my mother was down there, in the dreary lounge overlooking the dangerous street which filled up with shouts, stampeding boots and the shrieks of girls every night at closing time. I was frightened she would meet someone; that perhaps, even now, the creaking bed above me contained her sweating body. I was frightened she would open the hotel door and disappear down those steps into the Dublin night. Most of all, I was scared our money would run out and there would be a scene with other guests staring at us and whispering.

The hotel room made me feel as poor as white trash. An ambulance hustled past with a flicker of blue light. My mother would have finished the three drinks she always allowed herself. I could see her sitting alone among the young couples, nursing the melted ice in her glass as she fretted against the nightly temptation to splash out on a fourth vodka. Soon she would be up. I closed my eyes but the motif of hair-line cracks kept watch above me, staring eyes waiting to catch mine. My stomach was sour with greasy food and anxiety because, after five days, this secret holiday had ceased to be an adventure.

It had seemed exciting when we planned it first, in whispered conversations in the back garden where Grandad Pete had lain down an ornate pond. Fish darted in and out between the perilously balanced rocks, red tails flitting for cover whenever I rippled the surface with my finger. I had never been allowed pets. Now I had spent each June twilight rocking back and forth on a tyre swing suspended from the cherry blossom tree beside the pond, watching in case our neighbour's cat sprang down from the fence where he perched in uncanny stillness.

Mammy had been off work again since the start of May. 'Resting' was the term which Granny taught me to repeat to anyone who asked. For the first fortnight we had visited her in a nursing home with tropical plants and bright windows where people sat like statues. But she was home now. She was better, perpetually smiling and with buoyant words gushing from her. Every evening she began to come out into the garden to push me. I loved to hear her talk like that, after months of withdrawn silence, bubbling away about things I couldn't follow and then breaking easily into laughter at some joke I told her from school. She had a new pet phrase which I heard repeated a dozen times every evening – 'wouldn't it be nice'. At first I think that, even for herself, those words were little more than vague aspirations, but gradually I had sensed a difference in her voice as she homed in on them again and again. 'Wouldn't it be nice if there was just you and me for a change? Wouldn't it be nice if the pair of us visited Ireland?'

Every evening as she laughed and leaned against my shoulder to push me further into the blue air, I felt she was inserting a pause for me to fill in after the words. Even at eleven I knew she would never have the strength to decide any course of action by herself. 'Why don't we just go then?' I said one twilight. She pushed me higher, almost as if buying herself time. I had looked behind as the tyre swung back. Her face was child-like, unable to conceal her delight. I felt suddenly older and protective of her. I kicked the ground and swung the tyre round to stare clandestinely at her, sister to sister. 'Alright then, this is what we do,' she had whispered confidentially, swinging the tyre back round to push me again, as though afraid we were being watched.

In the week that followed we never discussed our plans in the house, even when we were alone there. These secrets were confined to outside with the fish lurking beneath the stones, the branch creaking under the swaying tyre and early summer light succumbing to dark. We were conspirators. Our plans were real and yet, even up to the morning we left, they still had the feel of a child's game. I had packed spare clothes into my school bag, cycled off as usual and even chained my bicycle in the school yard. It was my final week in Northwick Primary school. Class-mates chattered on their way to assembly. I walked back out of the school gates, resisting the urge to run to where my mother was waiting. It felt like being in a film as we hugged each other at the ticket desk and then raced along the platform at Harrow on the Hill station.

We got on the boat train in London. Wales flashed past.

Cars queued for the ferry. I kept waiting for an official to stop us. Finally the ferry sailed. It was hot in the lounges where people sat. Children ran about and screamed, but I felt far older than them. The engine's throb seemed to pass into my stomach. I got sick over the rails, just like my mother told me she had done the first time she made this journey. The water was green on all sides, but it was shaded a colder, soiled grey when it slopped against the side of the boat. I wanted swordfish and porpoises, dolphins to break the spray. Eventually, Ireland slit the horizon, distant, green-capped and mythical. I had the oddest sense of coming home. I asked my mother if I was Irish. 'Well, I suppose in a way you are,' she said. 'Half Irish anyway.' I had never given it much thought before. I tried the description out for size, not sure how it felt. My mother stroked my hair as I let the salty wind blow about my face. She seemed happy and very calm as she watched the coastline slowly approach. I could hear her sing beneath her breath; *'Your hearts are like your mountains, in the homes of Donegal'*.

I didn't think I would find that cheap hotel again, but it was still there on the corner, unchanged on the outside at least. Even the drapes in the lounge window looked as though they hadn't been dry-cleaned in the decade since. I suspected that the ceiling cracks would still be there and the drip in the sink which had tortured my sleep. I was surprised at finding it so soon, having forgotten how small Dublin was, with everything crammed into that tiny city centre.

The tourist brochures in the hotel Luke had chosen puffed the city up, boasting of its rejuvenation. They made it sound as though you'd only to spit over your shoulder on the Liffey's south bank to hit a conceptual artist or a rock star. The brochures squeaked that Dublin was now the nightlife capital of Europe, brimming with Europe's youngest population. Even the typeface swooned into bold italic over these words as if the copywriter had creamed his underpants. I had torn the street map out and binned the rest. The map was so small that I thought the bus station was called Busarse and had to be corrected by the waitress over breakfast that it was 'Busaris'. But I wasn't actually going anywhere, I was just refusing to wait in that hotel for Luke to call. I had finished breakfast and set out to walk in from Glasnevin, cutting dead the ginger-haired youth eyeing me up in reception, even though he looked too cute to be predatory.

Busarse would have been a more suitable name though, because the bus station looked as ugly as I remembered it, like a 1950s office block patched up after shifting during a minor earthquake. Dublin's modernity, which the brochures boasted about, might be evident in the modern office blocks crowding the quays, but here, near the bus station, the streets were as shabby as in my memories of them from eleven years ago. The police station was still beside the morgue, a wrought-iron railway bridge dominated the skyline and the string of cheap hotels on Gardiner Street had their doors open, like on the night I had first arrived in Dublin with my mother.

Gardiner Street was crowded with relaxed Christmas shoppers. Even the crush of bodies into the employment exchange was good-natured, as men emerged, buoyed up by their Christmas money. I found a restaurant up two flights of stairs in Talbot Street, with the work of local cartoonists for sale on the walls, and had a scone and coffee in the bay window looking down on the shoppers. I was the only customer. The morning papers were in a rack and I chose an Irish one. Christy Duggan's face stared out from an inside page, beside a photograph of his parents leaving the funeral home. Luke even got a mention, although not by name. 'The removal of the remains was delayed until this evening to allow Mr Duggan's brother, a businessman in London, and other relatives in America, to return home.'

When I had stood outside the newsagent's off Edgware Road trying to read the Sunday paper, I was too shocked for all the facts to register. Later on, Luke had taken the paper from me. Now, as December sunlight poured through the high restaurant windows, the chronology of Christy Duggan's career in crime was coldly laid out beside his parents' grieving photograph.

His only actual convictions came early on, for petty scams and assaults, starting at fourteen with a spell in Saint Raphael's Industrial School. His last conviction was well over a decade ago, two years before the first in a string of major robberies for which everyone knew he was responsible. Underworld sources said that Christy seemed to change personality around that time. There were no longer any loose ends or loose talk after jobs he had done. Previously, he had been a minor, peripheral figure, noted only for isolated outbursts of extreme violence. He had moved around the fringes of various gangs, occasionally being called upon to slash tyres in some estate where residents objected to a criminal moving in, or being asked to finger uncooperative store owners who remained unconvinced about the benefits of paying protection money.

But basically, according to the paper, Christy had been regarded as a buffoon. This was what made him so deadly. Although not viewed as intelligent enough to carry out major crimes, the details of such jobs were often discussed in his presence. His nickname at the time had been 'The Wallpaper Man', although underworld sources were divided about whether this was because of his respectful silence around senior criminals or because his brother had owned a wallpaper shop in Dublin during that period which had been on the verge of receivership when destroyed by fire.

However, all sources agreed that Christy Duggan was biding his time and studying Dublin's emerging crime scene. His first major heist was a robbery which had been staked out for months in advance by an inner-city crime boss known as Spiderman. Duggan, who sometimes acted as a driver for Spiderman, stole the outline of the plan, modified it to eliminate weaknesses and rounded up several associates of a Coolock criminal nicknamed Bilko to make a pre-emptive strike a week before Spiderman was due to stage the robbery.

That heist was still officially the second biggest in Ireland's history. The biggest occurred just two days later, leading to calls for the resignation of the then Minister for Justice. Christy Duggan was again responsible, this time using four minor associates of Spiderman to carry out a mail robbery, which Bilko had been planning for months, on the Dublin–Belfast express train.

Christy had acted openly in arranging both robberies, knowing that neither Bilko nor Spiderman would believe him capable of carrying out such operations on his own. Both gang-leaders believed Christy to be working for the other. The resulting vendetta had claimed four victims in a week, including Bilko himself, left for dead outside a gay sauna. Christy was rumoured at the time to be in hiding in England. But it was discovered he had been passing himself off as a party worker, volunteering to put up election posters for the Minister for Justice's nephew, who was fighting a by-election in Mayo. By dropping his trousers and allowing himself to be photographed by a tabloid Sunday newspaper up a ladder holding an election poster, Duggan had destroyed the Minister's career, scuttled his Government's chances of winning the by-election and turned himself overnight into an underworld legend and Ireland's best known criminal, with a new nickname of 'The Ice Man'.

Duggan had been held for questioning in the safety of a Garda station. During his detention Spiderman and other, by now, paranoid figures from both gangs were caught in possession of firearms during dawn raids on their homes. It was rumoured that Duggan had tipped the police off about the hiding places of weapons, just as he had tipped off the newspapers about his own whereabouts in Mayo. However the only man known to have publicly made such an allegation to Duggan's face, in an inner city pub, was found dead on wasteground in Blanchardstown a week later. Either way, when Christy Duggan had been released without charge it was to fill a vacuum on Dublin's Northside, along with a new generation of criminals, many of whom had been with him in Saint Raphael's.

These childhood contacts had helped him to maintain his position in recent years when his career in robbery tapered off and he had focused mainly on illegal cigarettes. Therefore there had been surprise in underworld circles in October when 'The Ice-Man' was rumoured to be behind a three quarters of a million pound security van robbery. In a copy-cat of his famous raids, this had allegedly been originally planned by a young gang from the Tallaght/Clondalkin area, known as the Bypass Bombardiers because of the use which they made of the new EC-funded network of motorways to carry out vicious robberies on towns that were suddenly within easy reach of Dublin. If true, then according to the paper, this was a rare miscalculation by someone whom neither the police nor his many enemies had been able to touch until he was gunned down on Saturday.

My coffee had gone cold while I read this account of his life. The restaurant owner came over to offer me a fresh cup. I nodded my thanks and he retreated behind the counter, yet I felt he was watching me. I dismissed it as paranoia, but I kept wondering if anyone had seen me at the airport with Luke. The owner started chalking up a dessert menu on a blackboard. The kitchen staff spilled out to stand around the counter in the lull before the lunch-time rush and joked about local events. I turned over the newspaper, not even wanting to be seen reading about Christy. Luke had never made him sound like this. I felt nervous about returning to the hotel, but I couldn't just buy a cheap ticket to London. The police would be called if I didn't return and my bag searched, containing the airline ticket in my name but booked on Luke's credit card. For the first time we were linked by computer.

It was one thing for Luke to claim in London that he had no links with Christy, but here – a few streets from where Christy was gunned down, and possibly closer to where Christy had caused others to be murdered – I felt I had stumbled into a feud which I couldn't hope to comprehend. I remembered laughing drunkenly with Garth and Liam about the nicknames of Dublin criminals. They didn't sound funny any more. I was out of my depth, but I suspected that by being associated with Luke I could be in danger of being shot, without knowing why or by whom. No cheap gangster film is complete without a scene where the hotel door is kicked in. The criminal's face is briefly glimpsed as he turns from screwing the anonymous girl, but it is her heaving breasts that the camera always lingers on, the token piece of fluff, as they are both riddled by machine guns.

A blind was half pulled up in a window across the street. It was a seedy hotel, occupying the top floor above a row of shops. I couldn't see the young woman's face, just her thin white legs partly covered by a cheap red top as she washed the young boy in the sink. I didn't want to spy on them but found myself staring across, even after they'd moved out of sight and all I could glimpse was the tiny sink and the end of an unmade bed. I felt sick, but wasn't sure if this was caused by nerves or memory. The Dublin restaurants where my mother had sat, over a decade before, had never been as fancy as this, but the hotel room where I had waited for her seemed like a replica of the one opposite me.

The young boy came back to the sink by himself. He was scrawny and small, wearing only a pair of cheap white underpants. He played with plastic models of Batman and the Joker, having them climb on to the taps and fight with each other. Occasionally the Joker fell into the sink and Batman would stand astride the tap in triumph. The boy seemed alternatively bored and then absorbed in the game. The young woman pulled the blind up fully. She was dressed now in a faded track-suit and had his clothes in her hands. She looked tired and stressed. She stared across, meeting my gaze and holding it, before snapping the blind shut. I felt embarrassed, as if caught. Behind me, the staff had returned to the kitchen. The owner was seating the first lunch customers to arrive, part of a boisterous Christmas office party. It was time to leave, yet I couldn't stop myself staring across at that window blind.

I could still recall the weight of the brass hotel key and how I had struggled to turn it in my eleven-year-old hands, knowing that the cleaner was impatient for me to leave so she could do the room. Guests were meant to hand the key in at reception but I was afraid to. For those five summer days in Dublin the room key was the only security I had. I no longer even knew if my mother had enough money to pay the bill. I longed to be invisible. I knew we shouldn't be there, that neither of us was capable of being in control. I would slip out, past the hotel manager whose very silence was a commentary on the sad cases flitting across his lobby.

I always looked for my mother in the cheap cafés off O'Connell Street. When I found her I could estimate by the number of cigarette butts how long she had been sitting over her tea and untouched toast.

'Come on, Mammy,' I'd plead, 'you can't sit here again all day. You promised we'd take a bus to Donegal this morning.'

Sometimes I got her to walk as far as the bus station, but I knew that, even before we reached there, the excuses would start. One route to Donegal went through Northern Ireland, which she was frightened of. The routes through Sligo and Ballyshannon connected different parts of Donegal that she seemed unable to choose between.

'Your Daddy has no proper home, Tracey, do you not under-stand?' she'd say. 'If he's alive at all, he's just wandering around. We could spend months, having doors slammed in our faces and still never track him down.'

It was no good arguing or begging her to take the boat back to London. Even at eleven, I knew she was incapable of making decisions any more. Her gaiety and confidence had vanished into the depths of the Liffey along with the bottle of tablets she had flung from O'Connell Bridge on our first evening there. It was up to me to mind her. Depression had her in its grip again. It was vital she saw a doctor but she so badly wanted to believe herself well that I found myself playing along, desperate to believe it too. Every morning she spent half an hour staring at her face in the tiny mirror like a woman going on a date. All day she kept vanishing into toilets, checking her hair or lipstick. Even the hotel staff recognised that she needed help. Their silent pity made my skin crawl as I stared defiantly back at them over her bowed head.

Three times during that week I stood in call boxes, listening to the phone ring in Harrow. I could almost count Gran's footsteps as she raced from the kitchen to answer it. Once I even let the coin drop and heard her voice call my mother's name, worn-out with worry. But I knew it was me who was really in charge, so that therefore I was to blame. I was too scared to speak as Gran called her daughter's name down the line until the pips came.

On our final day together we spent hours sitting in the church in Berkeley Road where she had been married during the six weeks Frank Sweeney and she had lived together in Dublin. An organist practised in the loft, his gloriously rich music making the church tremble. Occasionally old women lit candles, blessed themselves and knelt to mutter aloud before scurrying out. She told me that there had been no music at her wedding, and almost no people either. It was the only day she ever spent with my father in Ireland when she hadn't heard music played. Previously Sweeney had not set foot in Dublin since before the Second World War.

Yet even at his age he had strong arms that could swing her through the air, my mother told me. He could spin a story for a full hour and never lose one person's attention. In Donegal he walked everywhere, across mountain tracks and tiny roads where no cars passed. She never knew if this was because he was reluctant for people to see them together. People hadn't understood or approved up there. Even when he announced their intention to marry, the women in whose houses they stayed argued that he was almost three times her age and couldn't support a wife anyway. She had never liked this staying in other people's houses, never knowing if she was a guest or was meant to pay. Her own money had run out and she kept putting off phoning Harrow, even when they had taken a bus to Dublin and been married like a pair of fugitives in this empty church. The priest, who was also from Donegal, had to find witnesses. My mother said that Sweeney and he had argued in Gaelic right up to before the service began.

Then my mother stopped talking and I remember how, when the organist ceased playing, it seemed to take an eternity for silence to possess the church again. By bringing me there she had been trying to explain. But I was tired and hungry and didn't bother hiding the disgust in my voice as I scolded her: 'But Mammy, you were only twenty-two. Why did you ever marry such a filthy old tramp?'

For years afterwards Gran used this trip as a weapon against Mammy. My mother carried her guilt silently, but I could never tell her, even when she lay dying, that she hadn't lost me in Dublin, it was me who deliberately lost her. It had been the only way I could bring matters to a head. She was as scared to phone home as I was. If I had started hating Frank Sweeney for what we were being put through, I also found that I was ashamed of my mother. I couldn't cope with being responsible for her any more, I wanted to become a child again.

The incident had occurred on a pedestrianised street where hucksters dodged the Irish police. I could still remember a woman with an enormous deformed lip pushing an ancient pram past, filled with over-ripe fruit. There was a toy display in the window of a department store, with nurses' outfits and tea sets which I had long outgrown. I let go of my mother's hand among the summer crowds and walked a few steps behind her to see if she noticed. She looked pathetic and deranged. I felt that every person was staring at her. I glanced back at the toys, imagining myself playing with them in a warm room, and the perfect miniature worlds I would build with the Lego. I stood at the shop window, counting to fifty before I turned. I could just about see my mother among the crowds who had reached O'Connell Street. People pushed right out into the road, even though cars still had right of way. My mother looked around and put her hand out in panic. I turned away. In the corner of the window there was an old-fashioned doll propped up in a antique pram. Beside it, in the next window display, two window-dressers had stripped a shop dummy. Her bald torso lay on the carpet with plastic breasts exposed. It made me uneasy. I turned around but my mother was nowhere to be seen. I was lost now, no longer having to be in charge. With a giddy thrill I began to run through the crowds, crying like a baby.

I paid for my coffee and went down the steps on to Talbot Street. Bustling Christmas shoppers enveloped me, full of purpose. I was envious of them, with their lists of presents and quarrelling in-laws. I walked a few paces before something made me glance around. I immediately recognised the ginger-haired youth standing inside the doorway of the crowded Pound Shop across the street. He turned to the security guard, as though they were sharing a conversation, but I wasn't fooled. He had been watching me sit in the restaurant window and waiting for me to come down. It was impossible to mistake his bad haircut and those boyish features.

I had put my unease about Christy down to paranoia. But now I was scared. Had the ginger-haired youth followed me from Glasnevin where I'd seen him eye me up in reception? Had he been shadowing me all morning? I walked quickly, trying to lose myself in the crowd. I glanced behind once. Through the jostling bodies I saw that he had left the Pound Shop and stood as if examining a window display. I reached a shopping complex and ducked into a newsagent's, browsing among the magazines and watching the doorway to see if he would follow me in. Five minutes passed with no sign of him. I went out another door and through the arcade of small shops, then found myself out on an open air plaza. A stone charioteer gripped imaginary reins in the centre of a fountain. I ran down steps on to a different street, guessing that I was near the bus station by the railway bridge overhead. I ran towards it, charging across the path of cars as the lights changed. I dodged through the entrance and rushed into the safety of the crowds queuing at the ticket desks.

I felt secure there. Children playing on benches, while countrymen with stained fingers and heavy coats scanned provincial newspapers. It had to be paranoia after all. Returning to Dublin had upset me. I stood beside a haversacked German youth, reading the peeling timetables and amazed by how many of the Donegal placenames I still remembered. Letterkenny, Milford, Rathmelton, Rathmullan, Gweedore, Dunglow. Towns I had never seen, but whose names were implanted in my mind. I focused on them, trying to stifle my fear. Then I became aware of a presence at my shoulder.

'You're not thinking of heading off anywhere?' a voice said.

'What's it to you?' I turned to stare into the youth's face.

He seemed relaxed and friendly, yet his eyes took in every movement around us.

'Somebody we both know might be disappointed, Tracey.'

'I don't know you, pal, and you don't know me either.'

'Don't be frightened,' he said.

'I'm not.' I cursed my voice for betraying me. People tried to push past and read the timetable. I stepped back so that they were between me and the ginger-haired youth. Up close he was older than I had thought, maybe twenty-one or twenty-two. I wanted to run, but I wasn't sure if there were others with him. He side-stepped the people and smiled.

'Don't be nervous, Trace. It's just that you were never in Dublin before. You can get mugged if you don't know where it's safe to walk. He asked me to keep a discreet eye out for you but not get in your way, before I collected you.'

'Who did?'

'My father. Shane. He picked you up at the airport last night.' There was an announcement about a bus to Limerick and people drifted towards a departure gate. Suddenly there was nobody between us. His smile was gone and he looked jaded, like he hadn't slept for a long time. 'Listen, this is a bad time for my family. I've a car parked on double yellow lines outside and the cops would love to bust my arse. You must be tired from the walking. Everything is set up as arranged. Can we go now, please?'

Without waiting for a reply he walked into the crowds. I knew of no arrangement and had no proof that he was who he claimed to be. I could have run but I didn't. I trusted him. Up close, I quite liked the look of him. He seemed the sort of lad I should be going clubbing with, somebody with whom to share a laugh and an uncomplicated relationship. I followed him outside where he had parked right up on the pavement. He held the door open and I got in.

'Did they by any chance give you a name?' I asked.

'No,' he replied, starting the engine with difficulty and

ignoring the bus driver beeping behind him. 'We were much too poor. I had to rob one off a passing sailor. Al.'

'After Al Capone?'

'After Alexander the Great.'

'Where are we going then, Alexander the Great?' I said.

He slowed at the corner and glanced at me, surprised.

'I told you,' he said. 'It's set up like you agreed with Uncle Luke.'

'Yeah, sure.' I nodded as if I understood. To ask more questions would be to look stupid and admit that events had slipped beyond my control. I glanced at Al's face, trying to decide if he was playing along, but he seemed without guile. I had come here because it seemed that, just once, somebody needed me. But this was all Luke thought I was, a sexual toy to be ferried between hotel rooms.

We turned down a street of bricked-up houses where a car had been burnt out. Small children emptied rubbish from a skip. A girl with a soother watched from the centre of the road. She didn't budge, even when Al drove up to her and finally he had to carefully edge his way around. Two shops still stood at the end of the road, a butcher's and what looked like a fortified off-licence. A price list for cider was crudely painted on a square of plywood outside. Al stopped the car. Luke hadn't even bothered with the expense of a hotel. I was furious with him but this street also made me nervous. Al got out. The kids had stopped smashing things to silently watch. I wasn't staying in the car alone and got out too. There was a tacky hairdresser's above the butcher's, with an entrance between the shops. A sign on the door said 'Closed for lunch'. Al rapped three times on the glass panel and footsteps descended. The door was opened by a middle-aged woman who nodded to Al and eyed me. He went up and I followed him, passing the woman who closed the door and stood, as if guarding it.

The place smelt of cigarettes and discount lacquer. The

faded wallpaper had patterns of old china plates. I couldn't believe that even Luke could have brought me here for sex. Al looked back and for the first time it struck me that there was no resemblance to Shane in his face. He could actually be anyone who had tricked me here. He opened the door at the top of the stairs and stepped aside, so that I had to enter first. I was standing in no bedroom, but the saloon itself. There was no sign of Luke. A grey-haired man turned from the window where he had obviously watched me arrive. He studied me quizzically, tapping long glinting scissors against his palm.

'Isn't she just perfect for it,' he addressed the young man who claimed to be Al and who now blocked the doorway. 'Don't worry. I'll make sure not even her own mother would recognise her.'

'Please,' I begged, but I wasn't sure if he could hear me. My throat was so dry the word wouldn't seem to come out. The man took a step closer, then stopped and studied my face.

'It's okay,' he said. 'We know exactly what you're after. I'm just amazed nobody has done it to you before.' He gently twirled a wisp of my hair between his fingers. 'I mean, your hair is so fine, it's just crying out to be dyed blonde.'

I said nothing and never spoke during all the time he worked at my hair, even when they re-opened after lunch and other customers came in. Al stood by the window, keeping an eye on his car. The hairdresser fussed nervously, anxious that a good report would go back to the Duggans.

'You'll want it looking well for the funeral,' he kept whispering. 'I knew your father, Johnny Kavanagh. I remember the day he married Clare Duggan. I know Christy and Johnny haven't spoken in twenty years, but it's great that one of his children came home for the funeral.'

I kept nodding and let him do as instructed. I felt numb and violated. I'd always hated the fantasy of blonde hair, yet I found I couldn't argue because I couldn't explain who I was. He stood back at last, anxious that I approve his work. I stared at myself and wanted to scream. It wasn't just my hair but my whole face which seemed different. I stood up and went to pay him. He shock his head and gripped my hand tight.

'I heard how upset you were at your uncle's murder,' he said. 'Sure you were pale as a ghost when you came in. But a new hair style is a fresh start, eh? You tell the Duggans that Smiley did a good job.'

I walked downstairs with Al and got into the car, still without speaking.

'Is it all right?' he asked. 'I mean is that exactly how you wanted it?' He twisted the rear-view around so that I could stare again at the blonde stranger looking back at me.

'Don't mind Smiley thinking you're Johnny Kavanagh's daughter,' Al said, twisting the mirror around and starting the battered car. 'We knew he'd do it on the spot if he thought you were family, and we could hardly tell him who you really were. But from now on, if anyone asks, you're my girl-friend and I met you in the Pod night-club, okay?'

His words hardly registered as I stared out at the boarded-up houses and the litter blowing against the kerb. Al looked concerned.

'Don't get me wrong,' he said. 'I won't try anything. Anyway, I hardly could with you being who you are. But it was the only way Luke could think of to get you into Christy's house for the funeral. With your new hair no one's going to look too close. But, of course, I know who you really are.'

'Who?'

'Well, I saw you in the Irish Centre in London,' Al said, concerned by the tone of my voice. 'I wasn't sitting with my family, I was trying to chat some girl up and getting the cold shoulder. But I saw you talking to him at the bar. I was surprised when Uncle Luke told me. I know it's hard on you, but it's probably for the best that Auntie Carmel doesn't know. At least not yet. I mean yous have only actually met up fairly recently. Let him drop a few hints first and see if she comes around to the idea.'

'I don't want her to know,' I said. 'Or anyone.'

Al braked at the main road and looked at me. 'Maybe you're right,' he said, treading carefully. 'I mean, how much do you know about him?'

'That's my business,' I said. 'He asked me to come to Dublin. He was upset. I can't believe now that I agreed.'

Two passing youths stared in, eyeing me up in a different way than anyone had ever done before. This was life as a blonde. Al patted my knee very gently.

'You were right to come,' he said. 'Christy was your uncle too. I mean, just because you're illegitimate doesn't mean you're not part of the family. He was always a dark horse, Uncle Luke. I never even knew he had a grown-up daughter.'

I turned away. It should have been the final outrage but instead I had to suppress hysterical nervous laughter. Only someone as utterly devious as Luke could have the audacity to believe he could away get with this. Al drove on, concerned that he had insulted me. I stared out at the derelict streets. I must have been down this way once before with my mother but I recognised nothing. I lowered the window to twist the wing mirror right around but I found that I didn't even recognise myself.

TEN

IT WAS HARD to think of Al as a Duggan. He dressed casually
for a start, as did the three mates who rented a terraced house
with him. I spent the afternoon there, locked in the bathroom
at first, mutely staring at my hair in a mirror. I felt maimed,
as if someone had branded me. I had never chosen my clothes
to impress men. I loved jeans, sweat-shirts, loose jumpers that
kept eyes at bay. This hair belonged to someone else and there
was no way I was letting Luke get away with it. Al came up
to knock on the door, concerned for me and bearing tea and
chocolate biscuits. 'You didn't know about the hairdresser's,
did you?' he asked, except that it wasn't phrased as a question.
I stared into the mirror again. 'Still it suits you,' he said with
such an utter lack of conviction that he made me laugh for
the first time.

The front room of the house was ablaze with dusty Christmas
decorations. I was surprised by such frills until Al explained
that the previous tenant had done a runner the Christmas
before and the lads had never got around to taking the
streamers down when they moved in. The wall to wall bookcase
contained every conceivable type of bottle, all empty and
layered with dust. The only furniture was a battered sofa, two
chairs, a video and a sound system rigged with massive
speakers. Yet I liked it there and, during the afternoon, slowly
learnt to relax with Al. I liked his house-mates too, who drifted
in from work or from being on the doss. They accepted my
presence with a friendly nod, including me in jokes before
they even had their coats off. They slagged Al mercilessly

about where he had produced me from, claiming I must have appeared after he rubbed the dust off an empty Chianti bottle on the shelf.

It was taken for granted that I was travelling with them to the funeral home. Al placed his arm around my shoulder as soon as we entered it. It had originally been a grocery shop, he told me, ruled over by a sour woman with a Welsh accent and a voice to frighten children. Christy, Luke and Shane were often turned away by her and denied tick when their father was looking for work in England. Christy had robbed the shop on the day before the woman retired and stopped the car half a mile down the road to stuff the takings into a church poor-box. Al said it was the only act in Christy's life which had ever been done as a matter of principle.

I couldn't help but like Luke's father. I imagined his face would always wear the same bemused expression, resigned to whatever life threw at him and yet puzzled by how it came to pass. He moved around the funeral home, anxious to make people welcome. He accepted condolences on behalf of the family with a quiet shake of his head, yet I felt that it would never occur to him to think of his own grief. He reminded me of Grandad Pete. I could imagine him later making sand-wiches for neighbours and filling up glasses to ensure that every visitor left with the melancholic bonhomie of a good funeral. Only then, when the house was set to rights, would he allow himself to bow his head and weep.

Al's mates kept up a quiet banter between themselves. They had known Christy and known when to be wary of him. Six men with cropped hair stood apart, circling the top of the open coffin like a colour guard, silently chain-smoking and watching everyone who came and went. Nobody needed to explain their presence to me. They had been a different sort of family to Christy, but a family who seemed just as confident of their place at his funeral. Soon they would join rival gangs. Some might kill or be killed if this feud spilled over. But for now they stood together, defying the world and each other. They were the only people whom Luke's father avoided greeting. He came towards us instead and embraced his grandson with warmth and sadness, smiling as Al kissed his bald forehead.

'You all right there, Al?'

'I'm grand, Grandad.'

'Who's this wee girl with you now?'

'This is an English friend of mine.'

'You're very welcome, love.' Luke's father squeezed my hand, anxious that I feel at home. 'It's a sad day for us. You come back to the house for something to eat afterwards, you hear me now?'

He shook hands with Al's mates as more of the immediate family arrived. I noticed again how blonde hair was standard issue for the Duggan women, with even girls of nine and ten bleached to their roots. Shane arrived with his wife and then the conversation dipped as Luke entered in a mourning coat with one arm around his wife and the other around his daughter who was crying. He glared at the crew-cut men near the coffin, as if claiming back possession of Christy. The room filled with unspoken tension. After a moment the men looked at each other and then, with a shrug, stepped back to lean against a wall and eye Luke up.

The prayers began with Al's mates surprising me by quietly joining in. Luke led the prayers with the throng taking their cue from him. I couldn't stop staring at those lips which had French kissed and nipped and greedily lapped up my body's juices, and were now mouthing the words of some Catholic chant. It was yet another Luke, the head of his family. I noticed how since his arrival his father seemed diminished. Luke was definitely the centre of attention, more so even than Christy's widow and children.

Luke must have been aware that I was there, yet he never glanced in my direction. Neither did his wife or anyone else I recognised from the Irish Centre, except for the black haired girl I had drunkenly eyed up and who had stared at me when I ran from the hotel. Now, from the way people addressed her, I realised she was Christy's daughter. Several times during the prayers she glanced across, trying to place me. I looked away and took Al's hand for security. He glanced down, giving my fingers the slightest squeeze. This was the first role Luke had ever invented which suited me. The funny thing was that, just then, I felt nothing for Luke, not even anger. I watched him out of curiosity, like somebody I'd vaguely heard of. Nothing of our time together seemed real. He looked older than usual and his hair greyer as Al squeezed my hand again, his fingers smooth and warm.

Shane's head was bowed and he also never glanced in my direction. His wife looked as though she spent most of her days turning brown and wrinkled under a sunbed. She wore the sort of hat Jackie Kennedy wore in newsreels and which had been out of fashion even then. Luke's wife stood beside her, the only woman there who didn't look obsessed with her weight or with trying to be something she wasn't. Under a mop of curly black hair she looked chubby and content with middle age. She looked up, taking in my gaze and I had to glance away. I couldn't dislike her. I felt guilty at being here. Maybe this was a torture which Luke had devised to ensure that my self-esteem remained low. I knew I was being hypocritical, but I hated him suddenly for cheating on her.

The prayers finished and Luke took the arm of Christy's widow, helping her to come forward and kiss the body. She looked like a blockier version of Shane's wife, her movements slightly vague as if assisted by tranquillisers. A procession of relatives and friends formed to follow suit, with Luke watching to make sure that the gang members stayed in the background. Al stepped forward. For a moment I thought he was trying to bring me up to the coffin. But he let go my hand and walked across to kiss the corpse as people filed from the room prior to the lid being screwed down. More wreaths were brought in, each one more grandiose and tacky than the last, with cut flowers bent into the shapes of sports cars or arranged to spell PAL or DAD.

It was as if permission had been given for people to cry. The grief inside the room was suddenly naked and so was the anger. During the prayers and rituals, it had been possible to forget that Christy had been shot. Now, as the undertakers waited with the lid, his children left without a father hugged the corpse and had to be helped away. Christy's mother stood at the head of the coffin, beyond tears as she combed his hair over and over with her fingers. I glanced at the huddle of tough-looking men, wondering if one of them had betrayed him. The newspaper had said that Christy's was the fifteenth gangland killing in Dublin this year. Would one of them be next? They watched Luke with undisguised hostility but he stared back, until, eventually and reluctantly, they left, with only one of them pausing to touch the coffin's polished rim.

My mother's funeral had been as subdued and solemn as an inquest. I thought of her again and found that tears, which I had wanted to shed sixteen months ago, were suddenly making everything blurred. Carl, one of Al's house-mates, noticed my distress and thought I was crying for Christy. He put an arm around my shoulder and nodded towards the coffin.

'You didn't know him,' Carl whispered. 'I'll not speak bad of the dead, but Saint Peter better watch his fucking wallet.'

They were dangerous words to say for my sake. I smiled and dried my eyes.

'It's okay,' I lied, 'all funerals do this to me.'

'Listen,' Carl whispered, 'I don't know how long you've known Al, but don't worry, he stays well clear of all this. Hang in there, and we'll go into town afterwards and get seriously drunk.'

Al returned to lead me out into the night air. It was cold with flecks of rain turning amber in the security lights above the doors. Al had warned that there might be a television crew and photographers at the church, but one photographer had got ahead of the posse and was waiting in the driveway. Mourners fanned out on either side of where the hearse waited to receive the coffin. A squad car was parked outside the gates of the funeral home, the policemen inside watching, or gloating, as Al muttered with sudden bitterness. The photographer edged closer until he was at the edge of the waiting crowd where Christy's gang were standing. He looked young and inexperienced. I could sense the tension his presence caused. Luke's parents came out and then Luke appeared, this time with his arms around Christy's widow and daughter. The coffin was being wheeled out behind them.

The photographer stepped forward to kneel with his camera raised. I saw the gang form a shield between him and the squad car. One man turned and with a casual flick of his heel smashed the camera from the photographer's hands and buried his shoe in his face. As the photographer fell back, another man grabbed him by the hair and punched him, with the gang's pent-up fury finding its release. The camera was kicked along the ground, with the high-powered lens falling off and being trodden underfoot.

The squad car doors opened and two policemen charged into the mêlée, followed by a plain clothes detective. Women screamed angrily at the photographer while others shouted for calm. Luke reached the photographer at the same moment as the detective. There was a clash of shoulders as they both stood over him. The photographer was about twenty years of age. He knelt with a space cleared around him. Blood ran down his face which he kept covered. The uniformed policemen looked around, not sure who had committed the actual assault. Even those among the crowd who were disgusted by the attack closed ranks, as the police tried to push their way through and catch sight of the vanishing gang members. I felt suffocated by the crammed bodies, yet curiously part of them, staring back at the police with that collective mute hostility. I sensed movement behind me as a crouching body brushed past and then all was still. Luke knelt beside the photographer and handed him a starched white handkerchief.

'We are not animals,' Luke told him quietly, 'and this is not a circus. Your newspaper helped to set up my brother's murder, printing rumours you could never prove. Go to the church if that's your job, but this is private property. My family are grieving, so keep your distance and let us do so in peace.'

He helped the young man up and pressed the handkerchief against his bloodied nose. 'Hold it like this,' he said, 'and squeeze hard. It's just a spot of blood, it's not broken.'

'Leave him alone,' the detective warned, pushing Luke aside as if trying to provoke him. The photographer looked dazed and angry. For a moment I thought he was about to strike Luke, but Luke continued staring into his face, cutting the detective out. The mood around me was sour, yet I sensed people taking their cue from Luke.

'I'm not touching you, am I?' Luke informed the photographer. 'None of my family touched you. Nobody who was invited here by my family touched you. That's the way it is in Dublin now. You can't trust the police to protect innocent people going about their business. The proof is lying dead in that coffin.'

'Don't be intimidated by anything this scumbag says,' the detective told the photographer. 'You were assaulted. Somebody here can do time for this.'

The young photographer held the handkerchief to his face and stared at Luke, who ignored the detective.

'Not only can you not trust the police to protect you,' Luke continued as people strained to listen, 'sometimes they even set you up. Take a photographer new to the job. He sees a police car outside a funeral home so he asks if it's safe to go in. Walk right up, the police say, we've been trying to pin something on these people for years. The problem is they're clean so nothing sticks. But please, intrude on their grief. See if you can provoke them into breaking your arm or leg while we sit on our arses watching you do our donkey work.'

'That's horsehit,' the detective said in fury. 'Shut the fuck up, Duggan, or we'll have you down the station too.'

'So why exactly did you tell me it was safe to come in?' the photographer asked, suspicious now and silencing the detective.

Luke bent down to pick up the shattered camera. He handed it to the photographer, then reached into his own pocket to produce a compact Kodak.

'Your camera is broken,' Luke said. 'You must have dropped it when you stumbled in the crowd. Have mine as a present. It's not as good, but stand inside the church door and it will get you whatever shots you need. Keep back, though, because it's good manners and, I mean, no matter how you might meet your death we'd respect your widow's privacy at your funeral too.'

The fact that Luke's tone was confiding and friendly made the unspoken threat all the more chilling. The detective pushed Luke aside and gripped the photographer's arm, but the young photographer shook it off.

'Now I know how Christ felt,' he said. 'Strung up between two robbers.'

He ignored the small camera in Luke's hand and turned to walk off.

'You're a scumbag, Duggan,' the detective said.

'You said that before, Mr Brennan,' Luke replied mildly. 'Obviously self-abuse hasn't just stunted your growth but also your vocabulary.'

I hadn't wanted to go back to Christy's house in Howth, but Al said we didn't have to stay long. It was in a tiny estate of fifteen luxury houses crammed together with flat roofs curving into a cul-de-sac. Massive pillars formed an arch at the entrance which looked like it was stolen from a film set. The trees in most of the front gardens had been rigged with Christmas lights, but only one house had these lights actually turned on. The estate seemed deserted, although from an unlit bedroom window I saw two small children stare down at the cars arriving. Christy's daughter angrily got out of the first car and was about to storm across to the house with its Christmas lights on, when Luke put an arm on her shoulder and asked Shane to have a word with them instead. The squad car had followed the cortège and I saw Brennan, the detective, watching as Shane walked across to the offending house.

Christy's house was crammed with knick-knacks and cut glass ornaments. Even the curtains were like something you'd see in a mock Victorian theatre. Carl tried to keep a straight face as he muttered that it was like 'a high-class knacker's caravan'. Al said the decor was modelled on an Irish politician's house which had been featured in a magazine. He claimed that Christy's wife, Margaret, had kept the magazine centrespread pinned up on her wardrobe door, hounding Christy until he produced an exact replica for her.

Children moved about with plates of sandwiches and Carl and the others went off to raid the food available, promising to bring me back a plate. Al left me alone for a moment, pressed into serving drinks. He had returned to pour me what looked like a treble gin when Christy's black-haired daughter angrily grabbed the bottle from his hand.

'Jesus,' she said, 'are you saying my father was mean? People always got a decent measure in this house.' She poured three times the amount into my glass, staring at my face and inquiring, 'Who do we have here?'

'Leave her alone, Christine,' Al butted in. 'I met her down the Pod, she's visiting Dublin. She's with me and my mates.'

Christine turned to glare at Al, shooing him away to serve other people. She looked back, scrutinising my face. Her features were harder than I remembered them in the Irish Centre. Even her mourning clothes were stylishly cut and she reeked of white musk. It was a perfume I associated with teenage girls in high heels and mini-skirts freezing at bus stops. It had the strong musty smell of Gran's bedroom when I used to sneak in as a child to dress up in her scarves and hats. Now the tables were turned from that night in London and I tried not to show my fear.

'I'm a friend of Al's,' I said, holding her gaze.

'Since when?'

'Since recently.'

'I was trying to place your face,' she said. 'But then I forgot, all you English bints look the same. I hate to think of any Duggan falling for an English braser, but don't get too cocky, love, because they always fall back on their own sort, no matter what sort of tricks you do for them in bed.'

She walked off to fill another glass. I saw Al across the room looking concerned, but before he could reach me Luke's father had sat down. He patted my arm and looked at Christine.

'I hope that wee girl didn't upset you,' he said, 'it would be better if she went off and cried, but she has it all bottled inside. She was her Daddy's best girl always. Her boy-friend should be here to comfort her but she never brings him home. Either he's one of the stuck-up types around here who can't stomach us or he's one of us who can't stomach the neighbours here.'

'I'm sorry about your son,' I said.

'I know you are, love.' He patted my hand gently again. 'He was a good lad, Christy, good to everyone. Big fists and a soft heart. People took advantage of him. The dogs in the street wouldn't starve if Christy was around.'

The room was filling up with in-laws, their voices carrying an almost desperate gaiety, although here and there people sat slumped in silence.

'It's a lovely house, isn't it?' he said. 'He did well, Christy, and he'd never let you take a bus home. Taxis to your doorstep. All the same, I don't know what they'll do now. It's mortgaged to the hilt. He could have bought a lovely house, somewhere near his own kind. You could be here till you were a hundred and people still wouldn't give you the time of day. I mean, the neighbours never appreciated Christy. Do you know, there wasn't one burglary on this estate since the day Christy moved in?'

A seven-year-old girl came from the kitchen, with a plate of vol-au-vents. She stood, bewildered by all the people in her living room, until some woman took the plate from her. A man squeezed a ten pound note into her hand, but she stared at him blankly, letting the money fall as she walked off. Luke's father watched her.

'You see wee Jacinta there,' he said. 'Do you know they refused to have prayers for her Daddy in school, like when any other parent died? Only that the other little girls insisted. There's more decency in the kids than in the teachers and all because of the rubbish written in the papers.'

Jacinta ran across to Luke in the other doorway who picked her up. He said nothing but she nestled her head against his chest. Luke's wife joined him and Christine walked over to stroke her young sister's hair. She stared at me until Luke's wife noticed and began to stare too. I wanted to find Carl but Luke's father seemed unable to stop talking. I knew I was going to get his life story, because this torrent of words seemed his only anaesthetic against grief.

He kept touching my hand to emphasise some point as he went through every job he ever had, since starting off at fourteen by sweeping the floor in a barber shop down the markets. Pierrepoint, the last hangman, used to be shaved there, fresh off the boat from England on the morning of an execution. They opened two hours early especially for him. Luke's father showed me how the barber's hand trembled as he worked with the open blade and would finish up by slicking back the hangman's hair with makeshift brilliantine which they concocted from whitewash and other scavenged ingredients in a bathtub hidden in the back room of the shop.

Beyond nodding I found I didn't need to say anything. It was like he was telling these stories to himself, hoping that this time he would understand how he came to be here, decades later, with a son who owned a posh house and was riddled to death. I only really listened when his memories collided with stories Luke had told me. I was more concerned about what Christine knew, or suspected, and how much she might tell Luke's wife. Christine had gone upstairs to look after her mother, but Luke's wife seemed to watch me now every time she entered the room.

'Tell me about Luke,' I asked and his father stopped, surprised.

'I didn't know you knew Luke,' he said.

'I don't. It's just that he handled himself well at the funeral.'

'He did.' Mr Duggan nodded, but it didn't quite seem wholehearted. 'Luke always handled himself well, not like poor Christy. Luke's done well, you couldn't but be proud of him. But he never comes home. I don't like that. I worked anywhere I could find work, but I never lost touch. Luke would put his hand in his pocket for anything you asked him for, but, you see, with Christy you didn't need to ask.' He rose slowly. 'Finish your drink, love. It's the Missus I'm worried for. Christy was always her baby, even though he was her first born.'

He walked towards the kitchen as Luke's wife crossed the room. I knew instinctively she was going to sit beside me and there was nothing I could do. She said nothing but just sighed as if relieved to have the weight off her feet. I don't know how many measures of alcohol Christine had poured me, but I drained them all as I sat in silence beside her. I put the empty glass down and tried to rise, but found that my legs were unsteady. Her arm gripped my elbow. Her grasp was strong. Her nails dug in and hurt.

'Easy does it,' she said casually as I steadied myself, 'even for a young slip like yourself it's sometimes a long way up.'

'Thanks,' I said, 'it's very warm in here.'

'Get a little air and you'll feel better,' she replied. 'Try the back garden. I always say a change is as good as a rest.'

I was steady now but she still didn't let go.

'Your hair is nice,' she said. 'It shows your face off well. It's pretty. Make the most of it while it lasts. My own husband was at me for years to dye my hair blonde.'

'Which one is your husband?' I tried to keep my voice composed. 'I don't think I know him.'

Luke's wife let go my arm, but I could see the imprint of her nails on my skin. She smiled.

'There's few that do, love,' she said confidently. 'Very few ever do.'

I walked away, wanting to run, and opened the sliding doors on to the patio to take great gulps of night air. I slid the door closed, glad to be alone. It seemed an eternity since I had left my hotel to walk into town. There was a child's swing on the lawn and an artificial pond with a miniature fountain worked by a noisy electric pump. Green bulbs created an effect under the water. Trees had been planted against the back wall where a wooden playhouse was built in the shape of a tiny Swiss chalet. Beyond the wall I could see harbour lights in the distance. I was tempted to slip out the side gate and find a taxi, but my disappearance might only create more stir.

Since his arrival Luke hadn't glanced in my direction. The whole day had been an elaborate game of manipulation. I felt vulnerable now and light-headed from drink. I was angry with him, yet I also hoped he would follow me into the garden. I knew it was risky to be seen together, but perhaps I was getting hooked on the danger of this game.

I walked down to the playhouse and had already stooped

128

to enter it when I heard the faint creak of a board and somebody breathing a few inches away. I felt trapped in the darkness of the miniature house. I guessed it was Christine lying in wait after Luke's wife had suggested I come out here. I was too scared to scream or run.

'Trace?'

I recognised Al's whisper and started breathing again. He put a hand out, inadvertently brushing against my breast and then taking my shoulder as he guided me to the seat beside him.

'Are you okay?' he asked. 'I told Carl and the lads to keep on eye on you inside.'

Something made me put my hand up to his face. His cheeks were wet. He sat, letting me wipe them with my fingers.

'I couldn't take any more of it,' he said. 'People in there are almost giddy, like they're in shock. You can see that the kids only half believe it. They think at any moment the door is going to open and Christy will walk in again.'

'Did you like him?' I asked.

'I loved him,' Al replied. 'I helped him assemble this play-house. It cost a fortune. Aunt Margaret saw it in some magazine and had to have it.'

'Aunt Margaret is fond of magazines.'

'Tell me about it,' he said bitterly. 'I mean, who in the name of Jaysus wants to live on top of this bleeding cliff? They're a different fucking breed. Needless to say Aunt Margaret put him up to buying it. That woman was always thick as shite on a blanket. She spent half her life getting pissed in the Berkeley Court Hotel with some stuck-up lush whose granddaddy built chain-stores in England. Creaming her knickers to share a sunbed with a woman who only got mentioned on the gossip pages for drunk driving, and then spending a fortune keeping her pissed in case she discovered that Margaret had once been a scrubber working in the Tayto Crisp factory. All poor oul Christy ever got from Margaret was a string of debts and a few stolen packets of Cheese and Onion.'

'You're all as bad as each other with this poor old Christy business,' I blurted out, with the drink freeing my inhibitions so that I didn't care who I insulted. 'The money for everything here was robbed. I know he was your uncle, but he was still a yob. All the Irish papers say so.'

Al was silent. I couldn't see his face. I had no friends here. It was foolish to antagonise him as well.

'You wouldn't understand, Trace,' he said after a while.

'You mean everything in the papers is lies?'

'No. But things got blown up. Christy didn't mind, he loved the stuff in the papers. He only ever bought the tabloids to see if he was in them. Otherwise he stuck to comics. I remember, when I was twelve, getting really embarrassed over him still talking about Batman and Robin. He loved this Ice Man shit, it made him feel clever. He was always tough and people had reason to fear him but he was never clever. I mean what class of criminal genius marries Aunt Margaret?'

'What paid for all this, then?' I asked.

'I don't really know.' Al looked up at the house where Luke could be seen in the window, pulling the curtains. 'He did the odd stroke and a bit of smuggling here and there, but I often think the big guys paid him to take the rap for jobs and keep the heat off them. There was a time he was public enemy number one. Half of Dublin was able to go on a robbing spree, fecking anything that wasn't nailed down because the entire police force were sitting like monkeys up in the trees here, hoping to provoke Christy into doing something rash.'

'Houses like this don't come cheap,' I argued.

'All Christy ever paid was the deposit,' Al said. 'Everything else is on tick. Some months he had to borrow the mortgage payment off my Da. This last year he's been totally broke. Everyone says he robbed that security van the Bypass Bombardiers were staking out, but I have my suspicions. Last week he was still broke, and not even Christy would be crazy enough to take those lads on unless some bastard set him up. If I ever find out . . .'

There was a noise on the wall above us and Al stopped. The anger in his voice had frightened me. Al looked towards the house where Luke had emerged. He stood, as if looking for someone, then stubbed his cigarette out and began to walk towards the playhouse. I didn't want Luke to find us like this. It looked too suspicious. Al put a hand to my mouth as footsteps thudded on the roof of the playhouse. A man jumped down on to the grass in front of us. My heart was so loud it scared me. Even from the back I recognised him as the thug who had kicked the photographer. Luke let him approach. Al withdrew his hand slowly, warning me to stay still.

'I sort of figured you might surface here,' Luke said.

'We have to talk,' the thug replied. 'The Pig Brennan is out the front. Christy's eldest is running wild, screaming at some neighbour who won't turn his Christmas lights off as a mark of respect. She'll be out with a knife slashing tyres shortly.'

'Christine is a bit wired,' Luke said. 'She's taking her Daddy's death hard.'

'Aren't we all the poorer with Christy gone?' he sneered.

Luke lit another cigarette. 'Not all of us, McGann,' he said. 'Some people may do very nicely from it.'

'Like who?' the thug challenged warily.

'Let's take the residents here.' Luke indicated the rooftops of neighbouring houses beyond the tall hedges. 'I'd say property prices could go up by ten or fifteen per cent when Christy's family are forced to sell. Unless, of course, some of his friends feel obliged to help out.'

'Come off it,' the man said.

'He looked after you when he had money,' Luke said. 'He would have looked after your family too. Christy was like that.'

'Save the sob stories,' the thug said. 'There's money due to us.'

'For what?'

'That was between Christy and us. You just give me a time and place and I'll tell you how much to bring if you don't want trouble.'

'There's nothing left, McGann,' Luke said.

'Where did it all go then?'

'I don't know,' Luke said. 'You tell me how much is missing and where you claim to have got it from. What Christy earned hardly paid for sun-tanning his wife's arse. I know nothing about any other money and neither does anyone else here.'

'Christy was laundering money from a job that he talked us into doing. We'd never have touched it if we'd known. That's all I'll say.'

'Find the money launderer so,' Luke told him.

'I intend to.'

The drapes were pulled back and the sliding door opened. Luke's wife stood in the square of light and called his name. Luke and the man stepped into the shadows at the side of the playhouse, out of sight from her and from us. She called again, then slid the door closed. Only a thin piece of wood separated my head from their voices. I felt Al's hand move across my leg. I thought he was going to try something and in my anger I didn't care about the noise. I let my jacket slip from my shoulders on to the ground and gathered up the zip fastener in my right hand, ready to stab it into his face. Al's fingers skimmed the top of my ski-pants, searching for something, then they found my hand. I realised he was scared and just wanted to hold it. For all his talk of revenge Al was out of his depth here too.

'If you do find him and get paid then you just remember Christy's family,' I heard Luke say. 'They're due his share. That much I do know.'

'And what much else do you know?' the thug asked. 'Like the name of the money launderer, for instance?'

'I stayed out of my brother's business,' Luke told him.

'You fecked off to England, you mean.'

'It's a good country over there.'

'Who are you telling? It's a great country.' The thug laughed. 'I went there in the mid-eighties. Down around Cornwall they hadn't even got protective glass in the banks. The gobshites almost provided footstools so that you could jump over the counter and help yourself.'

'And you're saying you figured out how to jump over it all by yourself?' Luke sneered. There was a rustle and I heard a skull being thrust hard against the playhouse wall. But only when Luke spoke did I realise that it was he who had the thug by the throat.

'I got out years ago,' Luke said. 'I don't want to ever have to come back, but if there's business unfinished I will. You did well out of Christy over the years. If money is floating around then it's not here. The man had eighty seven pounds in the bank.'

'Any withdrawals Christy ever made were with a balaclava.'

The playhouse shook as Luke slammed his skull against it again.

'Don't get fresh, McGann,' Luke said. 'There's a spade in that shed. If you want to dig up the lawn that's your business. How do I know you and Christy even did this job you're talking about? Maybe you're just trying to bully your way into shaking a few bob loose, in case there's money lying around? Well there isn't. Even if money was being laundered Christy never got it back. Whoever has it isn't going to walk up to the front door with an envelope. Death is always messy, it leaves unresolved questions, like which one of you bastards stitched Christy up?'

'It wasn't our fault, honest.' The man seemed hardly able to breathe. 'He was asking for it. Let my throat go, please.'

The sliding door opened again and Luke's wife peered out, anxious now.

'Luke, are you there?' she called. 'The police are trying to arrest Christine. She's after biting Detective Brennan.'

She scanned the darkness suspiciously, then slammed the door shut. There was a rustle as Luke stepped back and I could hear the thug trying to get his breath.

'Christy was different these last few months,' he said. 'He walked us into something we didn't know about and he wouldn't tell us what he was planning next. It had to be something big. Suddenly he was fascinated by boats. He started asking about prices of deals and fixes on the street.'

'Drugs were never Christy's style and you know it,' Luke said.

'I know, but then all of a sudden why was he dropping hints like he was going to swamp the city? Price wars are for supermarkets, it's a delicate fucking market here. Why the fuck was Christy trying to muscle where he had no right and no friends either? All I wanted was my cut from the robbery so that I could run, but no, Christy was holding on to every penny. He knew we were up shit creek, you could see that even he was scared, but he sat on his arse and did nothing. He'd burnt his boats and he was bringing us all down with him.'

'That's horse-shit,' Luke said. 'Christy was frightened of drugs, he hated being around anything the Animal Gang didn't touch back in the 1940s. He had problems with decimal fucking currency.'

'That shows how little you fucking know.'

'I know this, McGann. If there was money it's gone. How Christy blew it is his own business. He'd no life assurance, nothing. He was my big brother and I loved him, but he was never more than a two-bit crook, who collected trash and failures around him. His kids are straight and they stay straight, whatever happens. This house goes up for sale in January. I'll be in England, but I'll keep a watching brief that scum like you stay away. If you and Christy trod on toes then that's your business. But if I hear of you sniffing around again, I'll start asking some serious questions about how my brother wound up as the sacrificial lamb.'

Luke stepped back so that I could first see his feet and then the whole of him in the moonlight.

'What are you going to do?' McGann came into view, as if about to square up to Luke again. 'Hit us with a wall tile? You're not even a player, Duggan.'

'No,' Luke said. 'I'm straight. But that doesn't mean I haven't friends in this city I might call in favours from.'

'Like who?'

'Joe Kennedy for one.'

'Why would he help you?'

'Show your face here again, pal, and you might find out.'

I closed my eyes and James Kennedy's lifeless eyes stared at me through murky canal waters, his story from that hotel room made flesh. Luke once told me that James' kid brother, Joe, had followed him around like a dog for months afterwards and that he often sat in the lane behind the Kennedy house with Joe just allowing the child to cry. I opened my eyes again to the sound of boots scrambling up the wall. There was a thud on the other side and I knew McGann was gone. Luke walked a few paces towards the house so that we could see him clearly as he bent to light another cigarette.

'Are you two coming out?' he asked quietly, 'Or are you auditioning to be gnomes in there?'

Al let go my hand swiftly. 'What about Christine?' he asked.

'Fuck Christine. Let's see whether she or Brennan dies of poisoning first.'

Al climbed out and stood awkwardly on the damp grass. I followed, very sober now.

'Did that bastard set Christy up?' Al asked and Luke shrugged his shoulders. He looked drained as if his toughness had been a front. He produced a hip flask and took a gulp, then held it out for Al.

'I don't know, Al,' he said. 'But no one wins in tit for tat. The right word in the right pub and for a couple of hundred pounds some hit-man will blow anyone you want off the face

135

of the earth. These days it costs about the same as a weekend in Butlins or a ride in a high-class brothel. The only problem is that the man's widow is going to blow the insurance money having the same done to you.'

Al took a slug, then handed the flask to me. Brandy burnt my throat. Now the thug was gone I found my legs were shaking.

'So we do nothing,' Al said, bitterly.

'Christy fucked up bad. We know nothing, we don't want to know nothing. We run away and keep running. I shared a bed with Christy, I wore his clothes. I loved him, do you understand? But even he knew it would always end up like this. You're clean, Al, and your Da is clean. You're not cut out for this, you're not tough enough or stupid enough. If you want to do something, take this daughter of mine into town and show her a good time. All you can do for Christy is bury him, walk away and hope he doesn't come back to haunt us.'

ELEVEN

'WE'LL HAVE TO GET you sorted out,' Carl said and I started laughing as though I was sorted already. I could hear Gran parroting those same words as we leafed through magazines in some doctor's waiting room. I hunched down on a corner beside Carl and his two mates, while Al checked his cash and vanished into the bowels of some basement bar. It was half ten and I had already taken the one acid tab which Carl had offered around to anyone on the journey from Howth. Carl claimed it was meant for Al to improve his driving, but with Christmas check-points Al was taking no chances. The acid was good. It made the whole of Dublin seem like one engulfing throb of music welling up through the surrounding maze of cobbled streets. No DJ could mix sounds as well as the blurred cacophony that seemed to blare through the very walls of the patched-up buildings in this tourist quarter.

'Hey, Lewie, how are they hanging?' Carl called to a friend who passed with two girls dressed in tee-shirts despite the freezing night. The friend turned to fling one of the bottles of water he was carrying across at Carl who caught it.

'Stuff that down your drawers, Carl, and you'll put Mick Jagger to shame.'

Al came back out with three more bottles of water as well as the tabs in his jacket pocket.

'We're sorted,' he said and passed out the extra water. 'Hide this somewhere, for fuck sake, or we'll get in nowhere.'

We reached the riverside and I looked back to where a huge Christmas tree lit up the castle at the end of the street. Along

137

the quays scores of bright flags with childish scribbles flapped above the river walls. The tide was out and the river-bed stank of muck. Coloured spotlights scanned quayside buildings at random. Dancers queued outside a hotel on the far side of the Liffey. A flock of cranes dominated the skyline beyond it, their empty cabs decorated with strings of winking Christmas lights. The cranes reminded me of a black-and-white film they used to play on the ceiling of a dance club in London, about invading aliens who had defeated every human weapon except the common cold virus. I remembered surfing above the dancers there, watching their giant skeletons that were left to mark where they had once straddled a cowered city.

Dublin seemed obsessed with re-building. A hoarding on the corner protected scaffolding around the facade of some roofless old chambers. The night sky was visible through the windows. I stared up, recognising the carved figures in the stone work, and suddenly I knew where I was. I shifted uneasily as the lads walked on. A man in his sixties and a teenage girl leaned against the hoarding, back to back as though unaware of each other. He was pissing openly and blindly, splashing as much urine over his trousers and shoes as on the pavement, while, behind him, the girl vomited up everything that was inside her stomach.

'Say what you like about Christmas,' Carl said, as we manoeuvred past around the narrow corner, 'but it always brings out the best in people.' He walked alongside me as Al and the others moved ahead. 'I saw Christine give you a hard time,' he said quietly. 'Don't mind her. Herself and Al were kissing cousins as kids, but she's moved on to bigger fry since.'

Carl had already rolled numbers for later on during the journey from Christy's house, cursing every bump on the coast road as tobacco and hash scattered over the newspaper on his knee. He lit one of the joints now as we walked towards a sculpture on the quayside, built in the shape of a half buried Viking boat. The others were waiting there. Lasers split the skyline at random, ducking and weaving across rain clouds as Al doled out the Es he had scored in the basement cafe.

We finished the joints sitting on the Viking boat as the lads argued over which club to hit. Carl pointed out a nearby hotel which U2 owned. A single light shone in the penthouse window among grey roof slates. I could imagine Bono up there talking to God, or – if Bono was busy – sending some underling up to talk to God for him. I handed the last joint to Al. He was with us and yet he wasn't. Even when he cracked jokes I could sense a grief consuming him. Tonight he would rave and crowd-surf and drop the Distalgesic in his pocket to aid the hit off the Es. But still it wouldn't give him the oblivion he wanted.

I knew about the search for oblivion. I remembered Roxy and Honor screaming for help in the toilets of some death-trap in Hammersmith where the water had been cut off. That was where they had first found me, three months after my mother died, dehydrated and shivering on the floor, convinced my whole body was swelling up. They could have left me there, but they travelled in the ambulance to sit in casualty and then bring me back to Honor's flat. I still remembered welcoming that sensation of powerlessness within the drug, as it subsumed the grief I couldn't keep at bay.

That seemed the pattern of my life since I was fourteen; perpetually in flight, chasing after any new sensation to bury the sour after-taste of the previous one. My inability to articulate the hurt within me was cloaked by a malaise which others saw as wilful petulance. How often had counsellors or university supervisors said that I could be anything I wanted? But, so often, I just wanted to lose myself inside the beat of dance music and feel nothing except its pulse infused into mine. Yet even at my lowest ebbs, waking among the winos in Soho Square Park at nineteen, I always hauled myself back. A clinical, detached core of my brain observed my deliriums as though they were occurring to somebody else.

I had spent my final year in Saint David's playing truant and still came top of my class in A Levels. I'd had a choice of colleges and took none, until Gran found me a clearance place doing communication studies in what might now be called the University of Westminster, but was still the same North London Poly my mother had crawled through. I only took it because of the room in the hall of residence at Marylebone. I had begun well, but, within weeks, had been unable to cope on my own. I was never schooled for independence. Although Gran had pushed me to study there was always an inference that we were all too stupid to cope without her. Being away from her was liberating and frightening. I hated leaving my mother there and found that I couldn't study or face being alone. I had just danced and partied.

It was my supervisor who told me to take time out to sort my head, so that when Gran thought I was sitting first year exams I was actually earning a pittance scrubbing floors in Burgerland on Tottenham Court Road. Grandad Pete had found me there, stoned, and Gran straightened me out while my mother complained about all her clothes getting too big. They must have known that her cancer was discovered too late, but they never told me as I crawled back to my supervisor and was allowed to start a fresh course in marketing. Yet I doubt if I'd have finished that course, even if my mother hadn't died. My marks were falling again as I spent more time working in the bar at the Forum concert hall or hiding in music shops. I knew those careers weren't for me. Apart from music, I didn't know where my interests lay. Outside that, it always took some element of risk to make me feel alive.

Tonight in Christy's house I had wished to get safely away. But now, sitting with the others, I felt giddy at recalling the danger of speaking to Luke's wife, at Christine's half-knowledge and at eavesdropping on the stand-off between Luke and the thug. I had never outgrown that need for a rush of nervous adrenalin, even though I knew it was dangerous in allowing me to be manipulated beyond myself.

The lads finally decided on a club. Carl and the others rose from the Viking boat. I should have felt cold without the jacket I had forgotten in the playhouse in Christy's garden, but I didn't. I stared across at Al. I had already swallowed an E, but when Al split the last tab I nodded and opened my mouth, letting him drop another half on my tongue.

We left the quays and turned up into Fishamble Street. The name was so bizarre I had never forgotten it, although it looked so different now with modern office blocks towering along the curved street. I knew there was a filthy laneway to the left, with a dilapidated church across from a locked yard where mobile library vans were parked. This was the one place in Dublin I had sworn not to revisit. I prayed we wouldn't turn down it, but the lads walked past up the steep hill. Only at the top did I look back. I shivered. Al put an arm around me.

'Are you okay?' he asked.

'Give me a cigarette.'

The others had walked a few paces on. Al lit my cigarette and I inhaled. I had never tasted tobacco until the night I slept down that lane when I was eleven. There was so little I had tasted or honestly known about before then.

'Did you ever want to get lost, Al?'

'How do you mean?' he asked and then, when I didn't reply, he said: 'Are you really my half-cousin?'

'I am tonight.' It was too complex to explain, but I registered his distrust of Luke.

'Was your mother Irish? Where did she meet Luke?'

'Just leave it out, Al. I don't want to talk about him.' My voice was sharper than it meant to be. I touched his arm. 'How are you?'

'I want to kill someone,' he said. 'I never had that feeling before. There's things happening behind doors but your father shuts me out like I was a kid. I don't even know who's good and who's bad any more.'

'Let's just go dancing, Al,' I said, starting to shiver as I felt the E mix with the earlier acid. 'Let's dance like we're never going to wake up again.'

Why did I think that dance clubs in Dublin were going to be backward? The sounds were as good as anything I'd been at in London. The bouncers knew the lads and we were inside in moments, staring up at the poseurs dangling over the balcony of the VIP area, before we disappeared into the scrum of bodies. Al needn't have scored in advance: girls wandered the floor checking that people were sorted with tabs. Dancers climbed or were lifted on to platforms near each corner, girls barely dressed as they swayed and were caught before falling back into the crowd. We lost the others within minutes. There was just Al and me dancing together and then apart, losing each other as we surfed above the bobbing heads and heaving arms. I fell once, bruising my shoulder, yet I felt nothing as the drugs took hold. Al had made it on to the catwalk above which the DJ was suspended inside a bubble car. He reached down and I grabbed his arm, skimming my knee as I scrambled up. Some girl was massaging his shoulders, then she vanished into the crowd. Al was wild now. I closed my eyes as we danced to the ever increasing tempo of that set. I had an image of Al's heart, like a road-works lamp flashing faster and faster, scorching the skin across his ribcage pink and then red. I was frightened the heat would burn his flesh.

I opened my eyes and he was gone. I looked around but there were just arms reaching out, people moshing me gently, forming a wall of tee-shirts, tops and bras. Banks of TV monitors flickered and changed overhead as lasers flashed like a snake's tongue. I was Cathy suddenly, in the film of *Wuthering Heights*, caught out on the moors in a storm. I was the alien from *War of the Worlds*, towering above everyone on the cat-walk, ready to fall. I was a leaf in a wild-life programme, my life-cycle caught on a speeded-up camera, shooting outwards from the blistering bud to unfold into webbed patterns of delicate veins. Those veins crinkled, turning autumn red within seconds. They became worms, eating the leaf from within, crawling and burrowing through my mother's brain. And I was screaming over the music, falling into space, with my hair being caught and then my sweat-shirt almost being ripped apart as I was steadied, suspended in mid-air and then swung back up on to the platform to stare into Al's scared face.

'Take the worms away,' I screamed. 'Take the worms away.' I knew he couldn't hear over the merciless, throbbing beat. 'It's my heartbeat they're playing with,' I told him. 'Make them stop before they smash it and I die.'

Anonymous hands were helping to lift me down from the platform. Carl was there suddenly, holding water to my lips. It slid like an eel down my throat, coiling up inside my stomach. I wanted to dance and never stop. But the dance wasn't about joy any more but necessity. I needed to be lost inside that beat. I didn't need their music to make me dance. The rhythm was inside me and had always been. I didn't need Al or anyone. I hardly even recognised him now. Trust no-one, that was the rule I had learnt. Just keep dancing, keep running away, keep running.

'How much did she take?' I heard someone ask, a vast distance away. 'What was it cut with?'

'How do I know?' Al sounded scared and defensive. 'It didn't exactly have "made in Hong Kong" stamped on it.'

'It was cut with a knife.' It didn't sound like me talking or my voice alone laughing at the joke.

Doors were opened for me to be carried out, my feet dancing inches above the ground. The night air attacked my face. Even the bouncers sounded worried. The building leaned right back so that I could rest against it, but the pavement heaved and swelled before I found my sealegs. I was eleven years of age now. I wanted dolphins and swordfish. I wanted just to be held. I had to find the mother I'd abandoned in this city. I tried to trace my path back along a map of hairline cracks on a hotel ceiling.

Al left me alone for a second and I jumped overboard, my feet skimming the waves, hearing car horns and brakes as I stumbled against the fender of some car whose brake lights flickered and throbbed like Al's heart. I staggered on, not sure where I was going or what age I was. I tried to sense the ground under my feet but couldn't even hear the echo of my shoes when they slipped on cobbles. I was casting no shadow. If I spread my arms perhaps I might fly. But I hadn't time for games. I was in terrible danger, that's all I knew. I had to find myself before the man in the moon caught me again.

For whole seconds I was lucid and scared for myself, wondering was this the acid or what the E had been mixed with. I tried to control what was happening, but then the logic of dreams overwhelmed me again. I staggered down the tilt of Fishamble Street, genuinely believing I would find my younger self there. I still knew who I was, yet I was also that child I had once been. I ran to save her in time.

It had become that June day again in my mind, after I deserted my mother and ran across O'Connell bridge to stumble into the tinker children begging beside the balustrade. I relived my terror as they surrounded me, sensing easy prey and pushing me back with their jackets across their chests so their arms were free underneath. My knickers were suddenly wet as their vacant faces stared and they jostled and pinched me with so many hands that I had no way to combat the fingers rifling my pockets. My cheap ear-rings were gone. Fingers pulled the comb from my hair. A twelve year old boy pushed through the blur of faces. I only saw a plastic bag at first, then he lifted it away from his mouth and nose and the stench of glue was sickening. His lips loomed towards me as he spat and gave the order to run.

Suddenly I was alone and screaming on the bridge. Adults rushed to my rescue, shouting questions. People called to a policeman across the street. He approached and I pushed through the crowd and ran, just like the tinker boy had said. I could feel his sour spit, as though it had congealed on my face. My head hurt where hair had been pulled away at the roots. I ran like a frightened animal, not even sure why I was running. But I just didn't want to be found. It was too soon. My mother wouldn't have reported me missing yet and the police wouldn't have phoned Harrow. I found a public toilet. I hadn't money to lock the cubicle door. I crouched with my back against it and got sick into the bowl. I held my face under the tap and scrubbed my checks dry with my sleeve but I still felt the boy's spit. Ladies came and went as I hid in the cubicle, until finally one woman got suspicious and pushed the door in.

'Are you okay, child?' she asked, leaning down to where I crouched beside the bowl. 'What are you doing all alone here?'

'My mother ran away,' I sobbed. 'She got a bus to Donegal.'

'You're from England,' the woman said. 'Show me your face. Has somebody beaten you up?'

I walked with her along the quay. It was twilight. I thought of the swing beside the pond in our garden. I imagined my own bed with clean sheets and pop posters on the wall. I wondered was I famous in school? Motorbike radios crackled outside the police station. The woman let go my hand to open the heavy doors. The floor was made of hard patterned stone. Her footsteps were loud. I turned and fled, knowing that my mother would tell them it was me who ran away and I was to blame. Everything was my fault. She was mad, like the girls in school had sneered, and I was old enough to have known not to run away with her.

I raced through darkening streets with her face haunting me until I had no strength left to run. I knew she was searching this city and that strangers would find her soon. Hunger was an ache inside me. I was stumbling along by the river when voices and footsteps charged behind me. A shabby street lay to my left, up a steep hill where almost everything was knocked down. I read the sign for Fishamble Street. The voices came closer and I ran up it, past the last ruined houses and swung left into a small laneway where everything was so dark and silent that my breath sounded loud.

A crooked old church loomed to the left, hinting of ghosts and mice. To the right was a yard with mobile library vans parked behind a wire gate. Two bins stood beside it, crammed with newspapers and rubbish. I crouched between them, wrapping damp newspapers around me. The ground was cold and dirty. I watched the full moon above the church. As a child I had loved to see the face on it. Now it drifted between clouds and emerged brilliantly white to stare down at me. I could make out a man's features, though I knew the lines were only arid canyons and ocean beds. This was what God's face looked like, I thought. The coldness passed right into me and I was too frozen to cry. I decided that my disappearance would have shocked my mother back to sanity. She would find me soon and she would be calm and forgiving, grateful to have me safely back.

Footsteps approached. I was scared. I pulled the newspapers above my face. The footsteps stopped, inches away. I smelt hot chips with salt and vinegar. Somebody was laying them at my feet. Was it her with a peace-offering? But the footsteps were loud, like a man's. My stomach ached for food but I was too scared to make a sound or peep out. Maybe God had heard me and told some man to leave chips down this filthy laneway. Then I heard a zip opening and the splash of urine against the wall. It stopped. Coins jangled as he zipped himself up and I heard a match being struck. The bag of hot chips was picked up off the ground. My stomach was like a hollow cavern. The man might be kind. If I raised my head and begged he might leave me some. But I was too scared to move as the footsteps faded away and only the taunting smell of watered vinegar remained.

Some time afterwards a stray dog came down, nosing in the bins. He pawed at the newspapers and growled, attracted by the scent of my fear. Much later, when the moon had retreated behind clouds, a couple came, whispering together. The girl leaned back against the gate which creaked in rhythm and groaned for oil. I heard their breath quickening and her muffled whisper of 'not inside me'. 'Your hand then,' he said as though in pain. His breath came in one long gasp and then the swaying gate was still. The couple held each other in silence for a long time before their footsteps moved away.

I must have slept then, although I don't know for how long. I dreamt that I was found and I was being tucked back in my own bed. But I couldn't get warm between the sheets because the man in the moon was staring through the window. The sheets were thin as newspapers and he was taking them away. His face was grey and serious and his eyes blinked. Then the feel of his hand caused me to wake fully.

'You all alone?' The man's voice was soft as he bent down between the bins.

'No.' I looked down, away from him.

'Yes you are.'

'No.' My voice was so low I could barely hear the word. I wanted to wake up, even though I knew I was awake.

'I won't hurt you.'

'No.'

'You just be my friend, eh?'

'No.'

'See, my little man's already perking up just to see you.'

'No.'

He tried to lift my face and I stared away, up at the cold moon that had reappeared over the church roof. I wanted him to go away and leave me alone. I wanted someone to find me.

'Just touch it,' he coaxed. 'I bet you've always been curious.'

'Please. No.'

'It won't bite you. It likes little girls to play with it.'

'No.'

'It's just like an ice-pop really.'

'Let go my hair. Please.'

'Do what you're told, you little English tart or I'll make it far worse for you.'

'No. No.'

'You won't choke on it, for Christ's sake. Open your mouth properly, girleen, I know you're on the game.'

My ears were ringing where his fists held them along with fistfuls of my hair. He kept slapping the side of my face until the world grew dark and stank and I couldn't breathe. All night he had been watching and waiting, I thought, up there in the sky above the church roof. It was my fault for being here. Now I was going to choke, I was going to drown. I don't know how long it went on for, before I heard a petrified moan from him as the thud of a boot registered. I twisted my head away, my teeth accidentally biting into his flesh before it popped out. Later, Gran would never understand why I brushed my teeth twenty times a day, but I still wasn't able to shed that taste.

Now I just spat and retched, hunched up into a ball and not even realising at first that it was the tinker children from the bridge who had come along. I crouched down but they ignored me, gathering around the man to kick him from every direction. He flailed out, occasionally catching one of them, but there were always others circling and waiting their chance. Girls scratched at him with their nails, tugging his hair, seeking out his eyes. The twelve year old boy led them, his face animated with hate, his boot slamming into the man's face even when he lay still with blood oozing from his face.

Finally the boy stopped and turned towards me. I was next to be killed, but I was so numb I couldn't even scream. He grabbed me by the jacket and pulled me up out of the way as other children dragged the man into the space between the bins. The boy dumped the rubbish from one bin over him. It covered him so I couldn't see if he really had the face of the man in the moon. But his fly was still open with an inch of flesh protruding, flaccid and bleeding where someone's boots or my teeth had ripped it.

The boy aimed one last kick at him, then gave the order to run. They scattered like a flock of startled birds. I wasn't cold any longer or hungry. I couldn't feel anything. The boy turned back. 'Run,' he shouted again, 'feck you, will you run.' My sleeve had ridden up and I gazed at the white skin on my arm. The man's leg stirred, with an involuntary tremor. I wanted to kick him but I seemed paralysed. Then I looked down again and found that I had scraped my arm. There was a hairline crack and blood came. Still I felt nothing, except a numb ache as though nothing was left inside me. My arm was being tugged. I stumbled forward and stared at the boy who was leading me.

'Come on, for Jaysus sake,' he urged. 'If the cops come they'll crucify us.'

When my hands slammed against the wire gate everything felt so funny that I laughed. The crumbling church had been transformed into what a banner proclaimed was a Viking Adventure Centre. Lights shone in new office blocks on Fish-amble street, while Yuppie pubs and restaurants lit up the far end of the lane. So how could those stinking bins have survived outside this gate when everything else was changed?

I knew who I was now. I was twenty-two and seriously

stoned. I had to get a grip but reality kept shifting away. I still kept thinking I had to find myself in time. I felt my mother stare out through my eyes, frantic to find her daughter. The ground swayed and I staggered against the pebbled wall. I pushed the bins over, kicking at the rubbish dumped there. I stumbled across the road, searching every corner. What if the bastard had got her again? Where was he and why wouldn't he come out to face me?

I lashed at the bins with my feet, I picked one up and flung it against the wire gate. Nobody had ever oiled those hinges. The creak came back from a hundred dreams. But this time I wasn't scared. I would finish him off now and kick him until his bastarding heart was still. I'd smash his teeth with my heels. I would steal my own life back from him. I wouldn't be afraid to squeal any longer. I was finally ready for him if only the pathetic bastard would stop hiding.

'Come out, you fucking coward' I screamed, rattling the gate until my fingers ached.

Then his footsteps came, loud and dragging reality back. They stopped and I turned to face Al and Carl. They looked scared as they panted for breath.

'I don't need you here,' I said, 'I don't need your help this time.'

'Trace, just take it easy, eh?' Al approached cautiously. I saw Carl move to one side, blocking my exit. 'You have us freaked out. It's just a bad trip.'

I knew who Al was. I wanted to be back dancing with him. I hunched down, crying.

'I hate this place.' I said.

'You're stoned, Trace. You were never here in your life. This will be like a bad dream tomorrow.'

Al helped me up. I thought I'd flinch from his touch but I didn't. I wanted him to hold me. I wanted comfort. I put my arms around his shoulder and heard myself laugh, swaying to an inaudible beat.

'I had my doubts,' Al said, 'but now I know you're a Duggan. You're cracked enough. Let's get the hell out of here.'

I must have wandered off on our way to the car because I remember a taxi beeping and some driver cursing as Carl pulled me from its path. I couldn't stop talking out loud to myself. I didn't care what secrets I gave away, although I was so incoherent that I doubt if Al could follow anything I said. Then we were back in his house, although I didn't remember getting there. I wanted glass after glass of water. I kept laughing because the only glasses they had were pint ones stolen from pubs.

'Come outside,' Al said. He draped my arm around his shoulder and staggered under my weight as he forced me to walk up and down the back path. He was stoned himself. I suddenly realised the crazy bastard had driven us home instead of leaving the car in town.

'I want a bath,' I said. 'A long cold bath.'

Carl had disappeared. We had gone inside again and were climbing the stairs. Fingers plucked at my clothes. I felt the shock of freezing enamel against my arse. I lay back, chilled as my naked back touched against it. Water splashed over my face and I opened my mouth to swallow.

'Don't drink this.' Al's voice was clearer, registering more. The jet of water moved from my mouth, cascading over my neck and then down my breasts. It was cold but not quite freezing. I kept blinking as I trained my eyes to focus on the bathroom. Al knelt with his sleeves rolled up, carefully aiming the shower hose over my body. Goose-pimples colonised me. I felt vulnerable and wary and then a protective anger took over. I raised my hand but found that I still had my bra and knickers on. I stared at Al, who moved the shower hose away so that the water drummed on the enamel between my legs.

'You scared the wits out of me,' he said, apologetically. 'I didn't know what else to do. I was frightened you'd fall asleep alone in a bath. I haven't . . . I never touched . . .' He looked at my face. 'I mean, we're half-cousins, aren't we? But I wouldn't take advantage anyway.'

'I know,' I said. 'It's okay. The water feels good, but make it even colder.'

I lay back and closed my eyes, gasping as the jet struck me. I trusted Al, a rare thing with a man. What you saw with him was what you got. Then what was I doing with Luke? My system felt poisoned. The drugs were still coursing through me. I fought against their chemical tricks to get back possession of my own body. I opened my eyes to look at Al.

'How are you doing?' I asked.

'Not too good looking at you,' he confessed. 'If you don't mind maybe I'll use this hose on myself next.'

'We're cousins I'm afraid,' I said. 'That's the way it goes. I wrecked your night, didn't I?'

'You certainly took my mind off other matters.'

I motioned for him to cut off the water. As he put the hose down I took his hand.

'I don't know much about this business with Christy,' I said, 'but it's dangerous. Do nothing stupid, you hear? Leave it to Luke.'

'Why do you always call him Luke and never your father?'

I didn't reply. I reached for a towel to put around me and sat up on the side of the tub. Al lit two cigarettes. I took a long pull. The smoke made me sicker in one way and better in another.

'Luke doesn't live here,' Al said, sourly. 'He just comes home and acts tough like he knows everything.'

'You have a life of your own.'

'With a name like Duggan people don't always let you live it.' He tried to blow a smoke ring, but failed miserably and smiled at his own ineptitude. 'I'd never seen a corpse before.'

'Is it safe for you drive me back to my hotel?'

'You can stay over,' he said. 'I mean in a spare bed.'

'I know,' I told him. 'All the same I'd like to go.'

Al rose and hesitated. 'You said some pretty weird things.' He waited to see if I wanted the conversation to continue.

'I was stoned,' I said. 'I still am, more or less.'

'Yeah. I thought that myself. They made no sense.' He nodded towards the rest of my clothes neatly folded and grinned. 'I'm afraid in terms of dry underwear, you'll have to wait till you get back to your hotel. It's a disgrace in this day and age with five lads sharing the house, but not one of us is a cross-dresser.'

'Hey, Al.' He stopped at the door and turned. I wrapped the towel tighter around me for warmth. 'Al the pal. My minder. Thanks.'

TWELVE

AL WAITED OUTSIDE till the night porter found my key. Only when I noticed the man watching me stagger upstairs did I realise how stoned I still was. I tried to walk straight until I was out of sight. My room was in shadow, lit by a shaving light above the mirror which I must have left on that morning. I stumbled forward and allowed myself to fall across the bed. I could have slept like that, face down and fully dressed except for the wet underwear I had discarded. But, after a few moments – although it could have been longer if I blacked out – I forced myself to rise and sit on the stool before the mirror.

The travel clock told me it was just after four o'clock in the morning. But really it felt as though days had passed since I had left the hotel. I raised my eyes and startled myself. It was like a moment from a dream, seeing somebody else's reflection staring back. I'd forgotten I had been turned blonde. I examined this alien face in the mirror with the whole world asleep. I felt nothing or, at least, I felt the way I sometimes felt in Tower Records, imagining Bessie Smith sing with the dawn.

It was the shoes I noticed first, gleaming dully in the shadows. Then the trouser legs neatly creased. I wasn't scared, merely annoyed at myself for being momentarily surprised. I knew immediately it was Luke. Ever since I had entered the room he'd been watching, a motionless voyeur. Something about my face must have alerted him because he rose from the chair and approached to stare at me staring back at him in the mirror.

'Your hair looks nice,' he said.

'Fuck you.' I was suddenly bitter. 'How did you get in here?'

'Tracey . . .' He fingered the bleached hair.

'Don't touch it!' I picked up a brush and combed where his fingers had touched.' 'You were enjoying it more watching.'

'It wasn't like that, Tracey.' He sat on the bed so that half his face lay in shadow. 'Some of my family have seen you before. If you were going to Christy's removal you had to be made to look different.'

'Who said I had agreed to go to any removal?' I asked. 'You never discussed anything with me. How many lies had I to tell today? Be honest, you just wanted to parade your English mistress in front of your Dublin pals in the know.'

'It was never like that.' He sounded genuinely hurt.

'You never looked at me all evening.' I sounded like a jealous adolescent, but I didn't want Luke intruding on my space here. I wanted to sleep. I closed my eyes, hoping he might be an apparition, one final chemical from the E. But his voice was real, dragging me awake.

'I knew you were there all evening,' he said. 'Within reach and yet out of reach, taking a risk for me. You don't know the strength you gave me by being there.'

'That's just talk.' I forced my eyes open and turned from his reflection to face him. 'I saw you in action, cool as ice. You didn't need me. I doubt if you've needed anyone in your life.'

'Is that how little you know me?'

'Don't twist everything into an accusation.' I was determined not to look away from his staring eyes. 'You wound me round your finger today, you even changed the colour of my hair. Do you know how violated I felt? That's something

155

little wifey always refused to do. So tell me, what else does she refuse to do, or can I guess.'

'It's you who twists everything, always bringing it back to sex.' Luke hadn't raised his voice, but he sounded aggrieved. 'I could get sex off anyone.'

'Then why don't you?'

'Because I care for you,' he replied. 'I care that you stagger in here at four in the morning, pissed or worse. Is this what your life consists of? You almost spent the night conked out, fully dressed on top of that bed.'

'You're not my Daddy,' I snapped back, 'no matter what pack of lies you spin next.'

'I know what I'd do if I were.'

'Just try it!' I was furious now. With Al I had wanted to be hugged, now I wanted to be left alone. Since I was eleven that's what I'd had wanted, for people to stop asking me to be someone I couldn't be any more. I picked up the hair-brush and flung it at him. I thought Luke would duck, but it stuck him above the eye. I was frightened he'd retaliate. It was out of self-defence that I went for him, propelled by an old rage which had nothing to do with him. Luke grabbed my hands tight. I had always hated anyone restraining my hands. I heard the stool being knocked over as we tussled, and then the back of my head hit the bedspread with Luke's face pressed against mine.

'What's got into you? For the love of God, calm down, child.'

I felt his grip loosen. He stared at me, then looked away. I don't know which of us was more shocked by the word 'child'. But it was true, he was twice my age. When my mother first visited Ireland he had already been a lad about town.

'Who are you to lecture me?' I asked, but my anger sounded bogus. I felt jaded and soiled as always after those fits of rage.

'I'm not a bad man,' Luke replied.

'Then what are you doing here?'

156

'I never said I was a good one either.' He let go my hands and lay cautiously beside me. 'People who think they're one thing or the other are liars. Nobody does anything for one reason only.'

'You're saying I'm more than just a cheap lay, eh?'

'I'm not here for sex, Tracey,' he said. 'I'm not just here for your sake, although I worry about you. I'm here for myself as well. If it's selfish, what's so terribly wrong with that? I've done enough for everyone else. There's nobody in that family who don't want a piece of me. Solve this, pay for that. It's been the same all my life. I'm forty-three and I've still got my whole family living in my ear, making candles from the wax.'

He sat up to remove his suit jacket and fold it carefully on the chair. He held his head in his hands as if sick of it all. In the hotel in London I had felt we were inside a bubble that had escaped from the world, but here the world seemed to be crowding in to suffocate us.

'We bury Christy after ten o'clock mass,' he said, lifting his head. 'You'd best stay away from the funeral. I've been waiting here since half past one. I couldn't leave without at least seeing you. You're all that's kept me going today. I just wanted a moment by myself with you.'

'What does your wife want?' It was a low jibe, but his words, and the responses they demanded, made me uncomfortable.

'Not a proper husband any more,' Luke replied. 'She wants some cosy familiar thing to cuddle up to, watching television. She's happy. It's a gift I never had. She has everything she ever wanted. The trouble is that it's not enough for me. I can't accept this is all life has to offer. I need something else.'

'The thrill of a bit on the side.' I drew myself up on to the pillows so the length of the bedspread lay between us.

'Don't mock me or cheapen yourself. Stop running away. You know you mean far more than that.'

'I know nothing,' I said, suddenly honest. 'Not even why I'm here.'

'You're here because you need me too.' Luke reached for my boot. I pulled away at first, then allowed him to place it on his lap. He undid the lace and eased it off. 'You wouldn't have come if you didn't love me. You'd never have allowed your hair to be dyed or risked sitting beside my wife. I love that need in you, because I have it too. I complain that everybody expects me to be Mr Fix-it, but I bring it on my own shoulders. I haven't the confidence to imagine anyone wanting me just for what I am myself.'

'I don't believe you,' I said, feeling him rub my boot gently across my bare sole. 'You've confidence to burn.'

'That's an act learnt by rote. It was never easy being Christy's kid brother. I had to be different, because I was never going to match him for strength. Shane understood that as a baby. He became the clown, the street fool nobody would think of laying a finger on. I became the smart one. It was easy once you gained the reputation. It only took bluff. You let people think that you'd everything sussed and they gave you their scams and their money, desperate for your seal of approval.'

He held my boot as if weighing it, then let it fall.

'All day I've been living out that old lie,' he said. 'But I don't feel clever or tough. I'm like a shell hollow with grief.'

Luke took away his hand that was cradling my foot, but left my bare sole nestling on his crotch. It was my move. I closed my eyes. So often the memories of that laneway suffocated every feeling within me at times like this. Now, almost involuntarily, I fought against it, brushing my toes tentatively against Luke's arm.

'You did well,' I told him. 'The way you handled everything. I was proud of you.'

'I've years of practice clearing up after Christy,' he replied.

'Was Christy really broke when he died?'

'Thugs always make up stories, trying to sniff out if there's money lying about they can pretend they're owed. If there is, Christy took its whereabouts with him.' Luke lifted my other boot and undid the lace. 'There isn't even an insurance policy.'

'How could he get such a big house, if not for cash?' I asked. 'What bank would give him a loan?'

'The house is in my name.' Luke gripped my foot as though I was going to pull away. 'The bank thinks it's my second home. I was the only one with audited accounts to show them. Margaret had her heart set on the place, it was the only way to get Christy's family in there.'

'So you were his landlord. You're actually putting them out.'

'You don't want to understand.' Luke relaxed his grip on my foot, defying me to take it away. 'I simply set up the deal so he could pay the mortgage through my account like a rent. But the house was his in everything but name. I never made a penny from it. Now I haven't the money to keep his family living there any more than Margaret has. But the place has doubled in value. The profit will go to her and the kids to buy a smaller house.'

'What else do you own?'

'Only banks own things.' He eased my shoe off and ran a finger along my calf. 'People like to kid themselves into thinking they do.'

'What do you own on paper then?' I wanted this reckoning to strip away the layers of lies and see who I was really dealing with.

'My house in London,' Luke replied, 'and the two shops there. In Dublin there's Christy's home, a half share of Shane's video store and the lease on some scuttery flower shop I set up for two of my mother's sisters. That's how families are, the webs get tangled. You're lucky, you never need to talk about yours.'

His voice and hand were still, introducing a pause where I might talk. But, although physically there was nothing we hadn't done, or tried to do, in that Edgware hotel room, my past felt too raw to reveal. I needed Luke to keep believing I had come to Dublin for his sake only.

'You're rich,' I said, turning the conversation back to him.

'What does rich mean?' Luke asked. 'Years ago I gave my Da money to buy our family home off the Corporation. It's where we all started and it's still the only building some bank can't foreclose on if I ever stop living off my wits. Everything else is just a house of cards.'

The phrase made me think of big bad wolves. His finger traced a pattern, over and over like a hypnotist, on the sole of my foot. I wanted to lie back and sleep, yet something made me fight against this spell.

'It doesn't add up,' I said. 'The papers say that Christy pulled off the biggest robberies in the state.'

'Newspapers never give the full picture,' Luke explained. 'Their owners wouldn't be comfortable with that. The biggest robberies in Ireland are done by beef barons and accountants burying millions in black holes. They're sentenced to dine for Ireland and serve life sentences in the social columns.' Luke lifted his finger from my sole wearily, sensing I was keeping him at bay. 'Christy's heyday was a decade ago, but let's say someone robs half a million. He can't do it alone. There's a dozen greedy bastards to be paid for their time and silence. Accountants can make money reappear at full value. But, for your small fry, half a million isn't worth a wank till it's laundered. He might get lucky but there could be a glut of cash on the market. Either way, he's at the mercy of some fence and if he's not smart – and, God knows, Christy was dumber than most – not only will the fence clean his money but he'll clean him out as well.'

'Who was Christy's fence?'

'That may be the three quarters of a million pound question.' Luke shrugged. He was tired of talking, his mind already turning to his duties at the funeral in a few hours time. 'There are things any kid finds tough: the fact your parents fuck or your kid brother is smarter than you. It rankled with Christy, he hated coming to me for anything. I never wanted to know his business but he wouldn't tell me anyway. He loved the notion of having the perfect fence nobody else could get to. Whoever he was, he played along, nursing Christy's ego as he fleeced the poor fucker. If Christy was crazy enough to rob that security van, you can be sure some fence who never took a risk in his life is sitting on the money now.'

Luke's fingers were poised inches away from my sole. The withdrawal of physical contact was even more hypnotic. It felt like a foretaste of separation. Decide, his fingers seemed to say, you either want me as I am or you don't. Suddenly I ached to feel his fingers caress me. The only memories of Dublin I wanted were of Luke. I couldn't bear to think of the loneliness without him.

'Walk away while you still can, Luke.' I was surprised at how scared I sounded. 'You've done enough for your family.'

He gripped my foot again, lightly fondling my calf as far as he could reach under the leg of my ski-pants. I wanted to forget everything execpt the feel of his hand. I wanted us to be back in that London hotel.

'All I want is Christy buried and his house sold,' he assured me, 'I'm out of the equation then.'

'No revenge.'

'I walked away from that years ago,' he said. 'When you get older you find that the one thing which never changes is the future. It's boringly predictable. Christy was always going to get killed, just like Margaret will drink the money from the house until she chokes on her own vomit. Christine will go after revenge, taking on whatever cheap crook is rumoured to have plugged her father. I can almost book my next ticket home. She'll be laid out in a coffin in the same funeral home.'

My throat ached and my voice started to slur again. I closed my eyes. The after-image of the room spun like a spider's web. Luke's voice droned on.

'People say it's in the blood, but that's horse-shit. It's how you cope with the lure of a name. My Da's two brothers started it. Ghost cattle-men in the forties, terrorising the docks in the Animal Gang. Their reputation followed us when we moved out from the tenements. It never mattered that my Da had nothing to do with them and worked all his life. We were still Duggans. Break that name up and in some language the letters spell trouble.'

'What about Al?' I forced my eyes open.

'I don't know.' Luke moved up beside me, his hand running down my back to fondle my bottom through the ski-pants. 'He was closer to Christy than I'd have liked. Al's a problem. He's not tough, he doesn't look clever and yet he's nobody's clown.'

'Maybe he's just himself.'

'Then he should get out, because people in Dublin will never let him be.'

I didn't want to worry about Al or anyone any more. I rolled onto my back and Luke's hands found my breasts through the sweat-shirt and paused. I remembered the wet bra I had discarded. His fingers went to slide under my waist band and I stilled his hand. I opened my eyes to find Luke watching me.

'You liked Al, didn't you?' I searched his face for jealousy but it didn't show. 'It's okay. Don't try and hide it. One day you'll outgrow me, I know that, even if you don't. Just promise me this, you'll invite me to your wedding.'

His face was so serious I had to laugh.

'Did I ever tell you that sometimes you're full of shit?' I said.

'I'm serious,' he said. 'Now let's go to bed. I have to be gone before seven.'

'I'm very tired.'

'I never said I was looking for anything,' he replied. 'You sleep if you can. I just want to lie with my arms around you.'

'It won't stop at that.'

'If you want it to, it will.'

I started getting undressed, then stopped. I didn't want him to see I had no knickers on either. I turned my back and slipped my top off and then my ski-pants, sitting on the edge of the bed with the blankets bunched up behind me. I was in the bed before I turned. Luke was still half dressed and watching me.

'Al's a quick worker,' he said.

'It wasn't like that, Luke. Nothing happened.'

Luke didn't reply. He turned off the shaving mirror light and I heard him kick his shoes off, then his trousers being folded across a chair. I could sense the warmth of his body before his hand reached across to take my breast. I wrapped my legs around him. I knew his need was as genuine as mine. Behind our differences we were two of a kind. Black sheep who'd never mastered the whys and wherefores of ordinary life. If I had taken risks for him, then he had also taken risks for my sake. This was the moment I had been hoping for all day.

Luke held me tenderly, demanding nothing, allowing me the option of sleep. I understood why I had mistrusted him and pretended that our relationship was purely for sex. Those memories of Dublin had impeded so much in my life, causing me to mistrust men or to try and use them to get even. They had locked me inside a solitary confinement where I was afraid to allow anyone to get close to me again. Not my mother, even when she lay dying, not my grandparents or the few real friends I'd ever made. But Luke was right, we did nothing for one reason only. I had always known I would return to confront these demons. Now I wasn't sure if being here had helped heal those memories or if it was the effects of the E, but this emotion I was finally allowing myself to experience felt like love. I knew I could tell Luke things I had never been able to tell anyone. I didn't say a word though. It was enough that I had finally found somebody I could trust, if and when I was ready.

I nestled against Luke and planted a deep love bite on his neck which he would be unable to hide at the graveside with his family. He nuzzled back against me with his lips suspended inches from mine, forcing me to take the initiative. He knew me well enough to know that the night wouldn't stop at this.

THIRTEEN

SOMETHING TROUBLED my sleep, a foreboding of danger. The dream I was wrapped within held me for a moment longer, then dissolved into oblivion. I didn't want to wake but an instinct for survival forced me to. Light filtered under the door to sketch the outline of the hotel bedroom. I heard breathing beside me and listened to its unfamiliar rise and fall. I tried to make out the time on the clock, but it took an eternity for its luminous hands to merge into focus. Five past six. I'd only had an hour's sleep. Luke's breathing changed, as if sensing a difference in the room. He seemed asleep still but like a dog on guard with one ear alert.

Our relationship had shifted and everything felt strange and new. There would be difficult commitments to make in London, but this wasn't what had woken me. I turned over, yet my unease wouldn't go away. I thought back through the night, stage by stage, until I remembered and felt stupid. I almost didn't tell Luke, but fear kept me twisting until he woke, suddenly and without fuss, his voice eerily calm in the dark.

'What's wrong?' he whispered.

'It's my jacket. I left it in the playhouse at the end of Christy's garden.'

'I'll get it for you tomorrow evening.'

'That may be too late.'

I couldn't distinguish his features, just the shape of him sitting up.

'My contraceptive pill's in the inside pocket,' I explained.
'I take it after I wake every morning.'

Luke took a deep breath and reached for his shirt. I put out
a hand to touch his shoulder. This was our first night together,
the most intimate moments we had ever known. I didn't want
it to end so abruptly.

'Maybe it will be all right,' I said.

'Having one family is complex enough,' Luke replied
grimly.

'There's the morning-after pill.'

'Even stronger hormones to screw you up. We'll sort it out
now and take no chances.' He switched on the bedside light.
His eyes were ringed with tiredness, the flesh below them
wrinkled. He was already half dressed. 'You sleep on. I'll be
back in forty minutes, but I'll have to leave you then.'

'Wait,' I said. 'I want to go with you.'

We went downstairs together. The night porter had disappeared. On the street outside our footsteps crunched on
wafer-thin ice. The sky was moonless. I looked at Luke under
the amber streetlights, and remembered the story he had told
me about why he married so young. Shortly before his twenty-
first birthday he was skimming through a trolley of books in
a library when a half-used card of contraceptive pills tumbled
out. Luke had never seen the pill before as it was illegal in
Ireland then. He had stared at the cycle of days on the back
and pocketed the card, not understanding how they worked
or wanting to lose face by asking anyone. The following Saturday he told the girl he had started dating that, if she swallowed
the pill marked for Saturday, it would be safe to have sex that
night. Five weeks later, on the night of her debs, Carmel told
him she was pregnant. They were married on her eighteenth
birthday and booked a cheap package holiday to Spain for
their honeymoon. It was their first time flying and Carmel
miscarried on the plane. Luke's whole life could be traced back
to that library book. It was no wonder I never saw him read.

We passed a church set back behind bushes and then a convent wall which made our footsteps echo. Red-brick nineteenth-century houses across the street had the look of flats and, ahead of us, the occasional truck sped past as we reached the airport road. At least Luke's fate had been less painful than Christy's, I thought, remembering Luke's tale about how Christine was conceived in agony in the pigeon-loft in the Duggan garden. Margaret had burst into their kitchen in tears at seventeen, holding up her jeans and blurting out to the entire family: 'Christy's mickey's after getting stuck in my zip and I'm going to get pregnant.' I wondered at what sort of country my mother had visited and how two brothers could have known so little about the world.

A grass verge led down to the airport road. There was a line of old trees with plastic refuse sacks and boxes left out for collection. I glanced at the cardboard boxes, imagining I was going to find children sleeping there. Luke saw me shiver and put his arm around me.

'Are you okay?'

I nodded, but I wasn't. A taxi passed. Luke put his hand out but it went by. I saw a pair of Christmas revellers in the back, curled around each other. Luke cursed and watched the sporadic traffic pass in both directions. I leaned against the railing. I knew Dublin at this hour. It was this time which stood out most from the four days I'd spent among that gang of begging children when I was eleven.

Our nights had been spent sleeping in laneways and abandoned cars. Not that I actually slept, or at least not for more than a few minutes here and there when I may have blacked out. I didn't sleep, mostly I didn't speak and I would have eaten nothing if the traveller boy known as Martin hadn't sat beside me until I learnt not to be afraid, coaxing and sometimes even feeding me by hand. I could still smell the plastic bag he held to my face. I had inhaled not just the sour fumes of glue, but the sticky odour of his unwashed breath. At first I had gagged, then I breathed the glue in again and again, as though I could vanish into that white winter-palace where everything became distant and numb.

Those glue fumes had made the nettles in a derelict plot appear as fantastical as a tropical forest on that first morning when I had lain with my head among rubble, staring at a fireplace implausibly suspended in the exposed chimney breast of the buttressed building next door. I was hardly aware of Martin's vicious fight with some older boy while the others screamed and circled them. If he had lost and they had abandoned me, I would have lain there until I was found or some worse fate befell me. But, after the fight, the others grudgingly accepted me. I was now Martin's woman, although he never touched me, beyond sometimes taking my hand at night. Perhaps he had recognised that we shared the same tinker blood.

I heard Luke's voice call me back into the present and shivered, looking up to see that he had flagged down an ancient-looking taxi. The old driver did a slow U-turn and Luke held the door open for me, before giving him instructions for Howth. The driver looked seventy if he was a day. He had a countryman's peaked cap and spoke with an accent I couldn't always follow.

He pointed out a house where he had been stopped by a Corkman, who asked him to help carry out the contents of his flat and leave him on the Nass dual carriageway where his brother was due to pick him up. The Corkman not only paid in full but gave him a bottle of whiskey for his help. Two days later police had questioned the driver about his cab being spotted at the scene of a burglary where someone's flat was cleaned out. The driver laughed, saying that the Corkman had been a con-man all along.

Luke told a story in return, about two brothers he'd known years ago in Dublin. One would go into pubs in the flat-land off the South Circular Road to sell somebody a colour television for almost nothing. He would even deliver it to the person's flat. The next night the other brother would break in and rob the television back. The flat dweller would be unable to report the robbery without confessing to having knowingly bought a stolen television. The brothers had sold that television twenty times, on one occasion even twice on the same night.

'Dublin's a city of rogues and chancers right enough,' the driver said, nodding. I knew Luke was describing Christy and himself. He mentioned somebody else he'd known, back in the 1970s, who sought out dumb-looking tourists in dodgy pubs to sell them lumps of beef stock cubes as dope. If the tourists said they already had dope, he would flash an official badge, press them against the wall and claim to be from the drug squad. He always let them off with a warning and confiscation. Luke laughed, saying the badge had been a folded dog licence printed in Irish.

I noticed how Luke's voice changed when he spoke with other Irish people. Were these stories of his past being told to entertain the driver or for my benefit? There seemed no end to these myriad Lukes, each one embellished differently when you turned him in the light. Once this trait had seemed threatening, now it felt endearingly childish. The cool dude about town was actually so clueless he didn't even understand how contraceptive pills worked. Tonight was the first time I felt I really knew Luke. Now almost immediately he was trying to blur that honesty with other delinquent versions of himself.

The taxi reached the coast road. Lights of oil terminals lit up the port buildings on the far side of the bay. I looked out and recognised the long wooden bridge leading on to the wild island there and I almost grabbed Luke's shoulder. He glanced at me, then followed the arches out across the dark expanse of mud and water. I wound down the window and breathed in the icy air.

Coldness was the sensation I remembered most from those

days among the children. A numbness within me and a coldness without. The only time I recalled being warm was the night we set fire to the gorse on that island. It had been my turn to scare them. After remaining silent for two days I'd begun screaming along with them as they ran about, plucking up the burning pieces of firelighter with their bare fingers to fling into the bushes. But my scream was different. It wouldn't stop. It was as all pervasive as Martin's bag of glue, a high-pitched wail I tried to vanish inside. I knew if someone had held up a glass it would shatter with the noise. My throat ached, my lungs grew sore, but the scream wouldn't stop. The children ceased charging about and stood, clasping the cider and food they had bought with the goods Martin had taught me how to steal. They watched in silence as I raced between the spreading fires, spinning dizzily and screeching as though my clothes had caught fire and my body was a single mass of blistering flame.

I shivered in the taxi now at that memory. I wound up the window and pressed my palms against the glass. Luke was watching me, just like the children had that night. I heard that scream in my head again and remembered the sensation of being unable to stop it. But I hadn't wanted to stop. I had to keep screaming to expel the pain. Finally Martin had caught me. As soon as his hands grabbed my wrists I clawed at him, trying to bite. He was the strongest in the gang, yet I knocked him over so that his hair almost caught fire. But I wasn't seeing Martin as I fought, I saw that face from the laneway, the same face I would later see in dozens of men. I don't know how Martin got me on to his back. I just remember him staggering through the sand dunes as I kicked and struggled. He fell to his knees once but stumbled on across the strand towards the waves. The water hit me as I fell, shockingly cold and cutting into my bones. I thought I was going to drown, then I realised that Martin was trying to bring me back to my senses.

My screaming had stopped and tears finally came. I looked up and saw how scared Martin was. There were sirens on the causeway as the flames alerted the police and fire service. Martin managed to lift me up in his arms. I was soaked but it wasn't the cold which made me shiver. The others came running, shadows emerging from the billowing smoke and crackling gorse. It was time to flee, like the terrified rabbits and the fox who crossed our path. We raced to the far end of the island where the girls took possession of me, banishing Martin and the boys. They stripped me to the skin, each one proffering an item of their own ragged clothing to keep me warm. Finally I looked like them in every way. Martin returned and I tried to drink cider but it made my stomach heave. I put the bag of glue to my nostrils instead. I no longer cared if my mother was searching for me. We had come to Ireland to find my tinker father. She had failed. Yet here I was among grass and sand dunes, watching the lights of fire-fighters at work, accepted into the very heart of his tribe.

I didn't speak between the island and Howth. Luke's stories had dried up and the driver just drove, humming tiredly to himself. A car had crashed into a cemetery wall at the start of the climb up Howth Head. I could see blood and glass on the roadway. We turned left and halfway up Luke instructed the driver to stop alongside the high wall bordering the cul-de-sac where Christy had lived. The driver glanced back, slightly wary of the location.

'The girl left her jacket in a garden here at a Christmas party,' Luke told him. 'I don't want to disturb anyone in the house at this hour.'

'You wouldn't be going to ask me to meet your brother out along the Nass dual carriageway?' the driver joked, but his eyes checked Luke out. I wondered how often he had been robbed. He seemed too old to be working at this hour.

'I'm not.' Luke got out, then leaned back into the cab. 'And you needn't think she's the bottle of whiskey, either.'

Luke moved along the wall, feeling the bricks as if picking his exact spot. He stepped back and then sprang up to get a grip on the top. He dropped into the garden with surprising speed. The driver watched.

'He's quick on his pins, your Da,' he said.

I held the man's inquisitive gaze in the mirror.

'He's pretty neat in the sack as well,' I replied.

The driver looked away and smiled, beaten at his own game. He lit a cigarette and offered me one. We smoked in silence for a few moments, but Luke was surprisingly long. I sensed the man's unease and asked him about being a taxi driver. He had done it for forty years, he said. People saw the queues at Christmas and thought they were cleaning up, but it didn't matter if a dozen fares were waiting, when you could only take one at a time. Still Christmas was the one time his wife could expect him to knuckle down and arrive home at dawn.

'What would you do the rest of the year?' I glanced back at the deserted road, wishing Luke would re-appear.

The old man laughed. 'Not much at my age.' I didn't think he was going to say any more, but then he muttered that when business was slow he found it hard to sit for hours in some rank. His wife wasn't always happy about his travels, but she accepted that music was in his blood.

I couldn't follow what he said. A car emerged from the estate, testing the road for ice. I asked what music he played and he said he kept an old set of uilleann pipes in the boot. He seemed surprised that someone with my accent knew what they were. When I quizzed him he became reticent. Yet I sensed a fierce pride and knew he was nobody's fool. I remembered finding a book of photographs of Ireland in Harrow library. There was one shot of an old musician at a horse fair, his nicotined fingers playing a cheap tin whistle while his eyes stared with mistrust towards the camera. I'd spent hours staring at it, convinced – though I knew they couldn't be – that it was my father's features I was looking at. Now I gazed at the taxi driver in the same way, equally aware he wasn't my father, but fixated by a world I had to coax him to talk about.

His children were raised now, he said. One lad worked in a nuclear plant in Canada and the other was a doctor in Edinburgh. Times had often been hard, but his house in Whitehall was long paid for and his wife had her friends in the ladies club. On summer nights thirty years ago a dozen musicians often gathered to play in his home with carpets rolled back for set dancing. But music sessions had spread out into pubs now, not like the old days when Dubliners mocked the music. He remembered his sons being bullied on their way home from the Pipers club and an old neighbour who'd served in the British army shouting at them to show him their green tongues. He still drove the taxi to stay out of his wife's way, but when warm weather came, she sometimes knew not to expect him home for three or four days. When his sons were young, she had fought with him over his wandering, but, ironically, now when he had the time he often hadn't the heart for the long drive to Clare.

I glanced out the window but there was still no sign of Luke. I wondered if McGann could be hanging around. The driver was more relaxed and even clicked the meter off. He told me he still wandered off a few times every year. He might deliver a fare to one of the expensive new hotels in Kildare and instead of turning back he would take the sign off the roof and drive on. His friends were older and many were dead. Everything about their lives had changed. Labouring men who had played the bones in his kitchen now often found themselves blinking in the footlights of concert halls in Vienna.

If you weren't careful down the country you'd find a dozen Germans and Danes with video cameras gathered at your feet, he said. Not that he'd hear a word against the young visitors.

They were enthusiastic, amazingly knowledgeable and, God bless their innocence, they believed any story you told them. If it had been left to Irish people alone the music might have died out, although a hard core always existed among certain families, passing tunes on. But now, at times, those men he played with felt like hunted animals. Although they welcomed strangers they often wanted to be left alone. People flocked to pubs in Milltown Malbay and other isolated villages hoping to hear them, but sometimes a quiet word was needed to discover the location of the real session in someone's kitchen.

He wasn't in the same league as those musicians, he said, but he'd been turning up for so long that nobody put any pass on him. Once he found the session, life in Dublin was forgotten. There was magic in the music. You walked in and saw people you knew and others you hadn't seen for a decade, all playing a set together. The music might dip for the slightest half note as they nodded and he'd take his pipes out and wait for a switch between reels to join in. There was no music like it, which could be played by five or twenty-five players. Even a poor player like him could be swept up inside a tune and not sound out of place.

For a moment we had both forgotten about Luke. Now we heard a thud as he jumped from the wall, carrying my jacket. Luke told the driver to return to the hotel in Glasnevin. He placed the jacket on my knee and I checked that the card of pills was there. I didn't want to take it in the car. I took his hand and squeezed it.

'You were a while,' I said.

He nodded and I knew I'd get no more information. The radio had been ripped from the dashboard, but there was a ghetto-blaster on the passenger seat. Luke was silent. I just wanted to go back to bed and not wake up till it was time to take the plane back to London. The driver was quiet too. At the first traffic lights he rooted for a tape which he stuck into the ghetto blaster. Piping filled the car, so low it was hard to hear over the engine. The recording was crackly, made with rudimentary equipment decades ago.

'When the cock crows it is dawn,' Luke announced. I stared at him, not sure who he was talking to, then realised it was the name of the tune. The driver glanced at Luke in the rear-view mirror, surprised, and raised the volume slightly.

'That's Seamus Ennis,' Luke added.

'You're right.' The driver nodded.

'Seamus always said his own father played it far better.'

'He did that,' the driver agreed. 'His father had great fingers for a piper, by all accounts. You knew Seamus?'

'I'd visit him the time he had the mobile home out in the Naul.'

'There's few bothered to visit back then.' The driver shook his head, remembering. 'The High King of Irish Pipers dying by himself in a shabby caravan in some field.'

'That's the way Seamus wanted it,' Luke replied. 'He'd no real will left to live. Many is the time I found him at death's door from drink, willing himself to die.'

'Hundreds of tunes died with Seamus,' the driver said. 'You can't just write down the notes and think the tunes live on.'

We were travelling back along the coast road. It was hard to keep track of their conversation. I closed my eyes and listened to the music as they spoke about some piper and story-teller who died in poverty and another old man who'd been the greatest sean-nós singer ever, yet was forced to earn his living as a bell-hop in a New York apartment block.

Hours earlier I had thought that Dublin's crime world was like a secret society. But now traditional music seemed even more so. The driver questioned Luke about names of players as if suspicious of his accent and background. I remembered Liam Darcy saying how unusual it was for someone like Luke to hang around Irish music. Yet, listening to Luke talk, his journey from being a young hood selling stolen televisions to sitting in the inner circle at sessions made sense, because the cornerstone of his transition were the things closest to any young man's heart – easy money and sex.

Luke explained that at eighteen he had fallen for a girl whose family ran a local hardware shop. Her parents hated Luke and his background, but the girl had dragged him out at weekends to their house at Laytown where musicians from Louth and Cavan gathered for sessions. Luke stood out because of his accent and clothes. He told the taxi driver he hated the music at first, associating it with her parents. But there was one old fiddler, Jamie O'Connor, whose company he enjoyed and who often gave Luke a lift to Dublin. Since his death, O'Connor had been elevated into an icon of the purity of Irish music, but Luke claimed he actually made his living for decades playing in two-bit jazz bands before sensing a change in the wind with the Clancy Brothers and half the country's sheep being stripped for Aran jerseys. The driver laughed, telling Luke how O'Connor had once tried to drive his taxi away, convinced it was his own car.

'That was Jamie for you,' Luke agreed. 'If something as simple as a horse could find its way home he could never understand why something as complex as a car couldn't.'

We were meeting early morning traffic, along a road of old-fashioned houses. Christmas lights lit up bare branches in the long gardens. Luke told the driver about a night when O'Connor drove him back from Laytown. The fiddler pressed his face against the windscreen, complaining of the mist covering the road. Luke had stared out at the beautiful summer's night, before sobering up enough to grab the wheel and make O'Connor stop the car so that Luke could drive.

When they had reached the fiddler's house in Santry at dawn, O'Connor brought Luke into the back garden. The ground had been dug months ago but nothing appeared to be planted. O'Connor had mumbled about Luke earning a fiver by 'digging up the harvest'. Luke had laughed, then realised the fiddler was serious about something being buried there.

An English hitch-hiker had gone missing months before and her body was never traced. The fiddler produced a spade and sat on the doorstep with a pint bottle of stout, giving directions as Luke uneasily set to work.

He wasn't long unearthing the first of ten shallow graves. In each one five cheap German fiddles were buried, the plywood weathered by months in the soil. The fiddler had shaken the dirt off them and loaded up his car boot, before helping Luke to bury another fifty toneless fiddles from the crate in his living room. Luke tried to claim his fiver but O'Connor had cajoled him, with promises of more money, into heading off for the weekend. It grew into a tour of every fair in Ireland. I could imagine Luke, re-invented as Jamie O'Connor's baby-faced grandson, tipping off earnest enthusiasts from Munich and Milwaukee about his grandfather's spare fiddle that had been in the family for seventy years, but which, because of the hard times that were in it, he might be willing to sell privately, without a word to anyone else present.

Luke and the taxi driver were still laughing as we pulled up outside the hotel. I saw the night porter, peering out at the same girl he had let in several hours before. I glanced at Luke, knowing that, for a moment, he had forgotten about Christy's funeral and the quagmire of responsibilities which had settled around him. He glanced at me and, for the first time, I saw envy in his eyes. For half a second it was as if Luke was about to tell the driver to re-start the taxi and head for whatever remote kitchen music was being played in. Then Luke stared at the night porter and his face changed. The driver chuckled away, oblivious to the altered mood.

'These's a queue of men could ring your neck over them blasted fiddles,' he said. 'There were hundreds floating around one time like splinters of the True Cross. I remember Miko Russell saying he couldn't go abroad without seeing some poor unfortunate trying to bang out a tune on one, convinced it was his own clumsiness that made the fiddle sound so bad.'

'That's the funny thing,' Luke said. 'When O'Connor played on them before they were sold he could make them sing.'

'Poor Jamie.' the taxi driver shook his head. 'A harmless oul divil always.'

'The little bastards,' Luke said with quiet fury. 'How can any man be kicked to death and the courts call it manslaughter?'

'Only Jamie would try to help a kid being beaten up on a Ballymun bus,' the driver said. 'Sure those youths didn't know him from a hole in the wall. They waltzed in one door of Mountjoy jail and straight out the other.'

Both were quiet, remembering an event I knew nothing about. It was twenty past seven. Luke was late for his real world. My time was up, as it always would be. A snatched hour here, a furtive night there. The bed would be cold where we had lain, but I would wrap my legs around his pillow, convincing myself his scent was still there. Luke glanced at his watch.

'You kept the music anyway,' the driver said.

'It's infectious,' Luke replied, motioning for me to open the door. 'Jamie was an old fraud but a great bloody fiddler too. The tourists thought he was the real McCoy and the other musicians enjoyed a good con themselves. The only people who objected were the officials at the Fleadh Ceols, trying to run him out of town. That was mainly snobbery because he'd been a tinker and they spent half their lives burning tinkers out of any halting sites within an ass's roar of their own houses.'

I knew from Luke's voice he was waiting for me to get out. The trouble was that suddenly I wasn't ready to go.

'You mean O'Connor was a tinker, a traveller?' I asked, with something about my voice surprising both men.

'That's right,' the driver said.

'Were there many fiddlers who were travellers?'

'A few. Travellers were outsiders, even when I was a boy, but certain families had the music and played it well.'

'Did you ever hear of a traveller called Frank Sweeney?' I asked and the driver shook his head.

'I can't say I have,' he replied. 'Sweeney isn't really a traveller name.'

Luke coughed and I sensed his mood change but this was important. I just wanted him to wait five minutes.

'Frank Sweeney,' I repeated, speaking quickly. 'An old tinker from Donegal. I'm sure he's long dead. A right bastard but he played the fiddle well. You never came across him?'

'Come on, Tracey,' Luke said. 'Stop playing games, I'm dead late. I'll phone the hotel when I can.'

But I wasn't going to be told when to go. Here was my father's world and I wanted to know more.

'I never ventured much into Donegal.' The driver ignored Luke. 'They've their own style of fiddling, more like Scottish music, because that's where they went for work.'

Last Night's Joy,' I said. 'I'm told that's a tune Frank Sweeney especially liked playing.'

'It's a reel I've heard Donegal men play,' the driver said. Luke stared at me, but differently from before. Up to now he had thought I was prevaricating, inventing questions out of pique to delay him. But the name of the reel had flummoxed him. I was his English mistress, slotted into the Sunday night compartment of his life. Now I had revealed part of me which he didn't know about. It was unexpected and therefore I had slipped outside his control.

'Who's this Sweeney fellow?' Luke demanded suspiciously. 'You never mentioned him before. You know there'll be trouble if I don't get to the funeral in time.'

Before I could answer the driver started laughing, unconcerned by Luke's impatience. He gave me confidence. I didn't care if Luke's whole family were waiting, I wasn't a wind-up toy.

Last Night's Joy,' the driver said. 'Sure that and *The Black Fanad Mare* are tunes he's famous for. I never heard him called

Frank Sweeney, but I suppose it's his name. Whoever told you he was a tinker?'

'You know who I'm talking about?' I held my breath. Even Luke sensed the tension in me.

'I think I do,' the driver said, 'but I'm not sure you do.' He looked at Luke. 'Translate it. Frank Sweeney, do you not see? Proinsías Mac Suibhne. I heard him once say that *Last Night's Joy* was the first reel he learnt, from the lilting of a neighbouring woman when he was a boy.'

Luke looked from me to the driver in exasperation. 'You're just paid to drive, pal,' he said. 'This girl wouldn't know Mac Suibhne if he bit her. She's getting it up for me. She was never even in Ireland before.' He glared at me. 'It's half seven. You know I can't be late. What's all this messing for? You've never heard of Proinsías Mac Suibhne, have you?'

'No,' I said. I had never intended things to come out like this. 'The guy I'm talking about was a Donegal traveller. A cheat and a coward who played the fiddle.'

'Mac Suibhne travelled,' the driver explained, 'but he was no traveller. Travellers are never welcome. Even when they mended pots and kettles they were barely tolerated. But Mac Suibhne is like a prince, you understand? You'd be honoured to have him stay in your house. He has his circuit of little places, away from towns. He spends a few days in each and people come to hear him. His whole family were like that for generations. But Proinsías is the best of them. I'd dance from here to Cork if the man came down to play for us.'

I should have felt excitement but instead I had a sense of dread. 'But surely he's dead for years?'

'I never heard that he died?' The driver looked at Luke, then back at me. 'You must be wrong, child. That man will have a cardinal's funeral.'

Luke opened my door and put a hand on my shoulder to push me out. 'You know I have to be gone,' he repeated. 'Get back into the hotel. You said you'd never heard of Mac Suibhne. How could you, when the man spent his life hiding up in the hills? Even locals can't track him down. What's it to you if he's alive or dead?'

It was the force of Luke's hand which caused me to crack. 'He's my father,' I said. Luke stopped pushing and stared as though I was deranged.

'Right, that's it,' he snapped, 'just get the fuck out. I've had enough of your games.'

'Leave the child alone,' the driver warned, with such aggression that I realised Luke had irritated him throughout the journey. 'Can you not see she's crying?'

'She's had a lot to drink,' Luke said. 'She has a colourful imagination.' He lowered his voice to address me like a wayward child. 'Stop stringing the man along. Go on back to your room and get some sleep.'

'What age are you?' the driver asked, over Luke's head.

'Twenty-two.' As I spoke Luke lost patience and physically pushed me from the car. I stumbled on the kerb and he reached out to help me stay upright.

'Leave her alone, you hear?' The driver was angry. I knew he'd be no match for Luke, but he looked willing to give it a go.

'I told you she's drunk and playing games,' Luke snapped. 'She's just some cheap English tart trying to cause a scene and keep me late for my brother's funeral.'

'Lay another finger on Mac Suibhne's girl and I swear to God I'll flatten you.'

Luke snorted as though he had two lunatics to contend with. 'You know Mac Suibhne never left Donegal or looked at a woman for all I know.'

The night porter opened the door, sensing trouble. I saw him as a blurred figure because I was crying. For all of Luke's talk and all my excuses these were words I'd waited for months to hear: *cheap English tart*. That's all I was to him and all I

181

would ever be. It was what my mother had been too, to Sweeney or Mac Suibhne or whatever they called him. I felt naked, as if the porter was staring at Luke's fingerprints brazened on my clothes over my tits and arse. I could imagine him thinking this is the same tart who arrived with another bloke a few hours ago, she must be a cheap foreign whore. I hardly heard what the taxi driver was saying.

'You're a Dublin blow-in, pal. That's all you've ever been. You never heard the rumours over twenty years ago. Mac Suibhne was hiding out in Dublin. I saw him myself once with some girl with long hair and a straw hat. Look at the state of the child. A fool could see she's telling the truth. Now get the fuck out of my taxi and find yourself another one.'

I couldn't bear the thought of Luke being stranded here and me having to deal with him, now or ever again.

'Please,' I pleaded with the driver, 'I don't want him here. Take him away.'

The cab door was still opened. Luke stared out, bewildered by what had happened. He opened his mouth to speak. The driver put his foot down and the door swung shut as he sped away. The porter had come down. I sensed him behind me but when I turned he wasn't looking at me in a sleazy way at all.

'Come inside, love,' he said quietly, 'you'll catch your death. I've the kettle on for the early breakfasts. You'll know you're all right once you're able to sit up and eat an egg.'

I didn't want anything to eat, but five minutes later when I sat crying in bed, holding the pill which had caused all the trouble in my hand, the porter arrived with tea and toast and an egg. He looked so concerned that I had to dry my eyes and try to eat it. He had brought an Irish newspaper to take my mind off things. It was folded on the tray, but I could make out the headline: *Another Dublin Gangland Murder*.

FOURTEEN

IT WAS GRANDAD PETE who had rescued me from Dublin. He had been searching the city for forty-eight hours when I was finally caught shop-lifting. When I disappeared first I might have been a well-dressed English girl, attracting no notice as I concealed items under my coat. But by now I was indistinguishable from the rest of the gang. Henry Street was their morning beat, followed by the amusement arcades and cheap restaurants off Talbot Street. I would never go near the hotel my mother had booked us into. Martin could sense my fear when we approached it and I would run away as he cursed and herded the others after me.

They called me a daft bitch but always followed. If they had accepted me only grudgingly, their loyalty was like the glue holding our lives together. We were outlaws, running the gauntlet of security men with walkie-talkies in shop doorways. Whatever money could be robbed or wheedled from fences was spent that same day. When we could afford to, we ate in a café called Philomena's, in the late morning before other customers might object. Every meal was the same: mounds of white bread already buttered, Coke and Fanta and plates of cold meat and chips. The young waiter shared his cigarettes with us, sitting up on the next table to urge the others to go back to the families they'd run away from or to think about school. Nobody minded him. They knew that he wasn't a real adult and he was our friend. Martin laughed at him, but if we had a pound left over he would leave it as a tip.

The waiter teased me about being the silent one but I never

spoke in his company, terrified he would phone the police if he heard my accent. I knew if I was caught I would be sent away. The others spoke of reformatories and orphanages, with tales of savage nuns and brothers with leather straps. That innocent girl, swinging on a tyre in Harrow, seemed a stranger now. On the third day I saw her photograph on a police notice in a shop doorway. The others crowded round. I realised most of them couldn't read. A well-dressed shopper saw us examining the poster. She stared at me. Suddenly I wanted to be rescued, but her look just contained disgust and suspicion. She tightened the grip on her bag and pushed past as though I was invisible.

That's what I had become. My thoughts were narrowed to finding the next meal and somewhere to sleep or to deciding which lanes were safe to piss in while the girls kept watch. I had no nerves because I'd no identity. I robbed for them, my fingers more adroit than hands which had practised thieving for years. Once, a young brother of Martin's followed us from a doorway where he had been put begging. Martin sent him back, saying he was too young to run away. Their parents would come from the pub soon to collect the money in his shoe box. Martin put enough coins into it to stop them grumbling and gave the child two chocolate bars to hide until their parents had gone back in, warning that he'd be beaten if they thought he had accepted food instead of money. The boy cried as Martin left him. The others had run ahead. Martin said nothing, but when we reached a narrow street by the Pro-Cathedral he kicked every parked car with an alarm until the whole street rang.

Other gangs of children roamed the streets, but they were settled kids from the flats, smashing car windows at traffic lights to snatch bags or being used to courier drugs. They kept their distance, because, even in the underworld, we were still only knackers and tinker gits. They screamed abuse when they were sure of escape routes, singling me out as a pox-bottle braser. Martin had got me pregnant, they shouted, he'd wanked on my leg and let the flies do the rest. We would charge after them, oblivious to shoppers in the way. We wanted their blood, Martin more than most.

On the fourth day Martin almost caught a boy lagging behind his pals. He was four years older, yet when he saw Martin's face he raced straight out into the quayside traffic, dodging between cars until he ran into the path of a truck. Martin tried to pull me away but I wouldn't budge. The boy's skin was unblemished except for a cut above the eye where his head had hit the kerb. There was fluff on his chin but he hadn't yet shaved. Now he never would. Martin tugged at my hair, the pain injecting energy into my legs. We ran past an army barracks and down streets of ruined houses and cheap furniture stores. I kept thinking how easy it was to die and yet how I hadn't got the courage.

We stopped running in Mary Street. The others were gathered there, being eyed from doorways by security men. I remember walking towards O'Connell Street. I stared at myself in some shiny tiles on a wall, but it wasn't me that I saw. I looked more dirty than any child in the gang. I think Martin guessed what I was about to do, but he couldn't stop me walking into the store. I saw the guard raise the walkie-talkie. There was an ambulance siren from the quays. The others suddenly disappeared. I kept walking, even when I heard Martin's urgent hiss. The guard wouldn't see me because I had ceased to exist. I remember lifting silk to my face and thinking how soft it felt, like something I could half-recall.

I didn't bother hiding what I robbed. I filled my pockets and then my arms with useless objects. The security guard walked behind me with the manageress. I saw Martin in the doorway, shaking his head, urging me to drop everything and run. I walked towards him, knowing exactly what I was doing and that he wouldn't flee. He had saved my life in that lane. Without him I would be at peace now like the boy on the quayside. I couldn't forgive him, because I was as dead inside as a stopped clock. I stepped between the security buzzers. The whole street was one alarm triggered off. Martin stood motionless as I piled the stolen goods into his hands. Then his face changed as he realised what I was deliberately doing. Strong arms caught me and I was lifted by the security guard. I knew his face beneath the cap, even though it was twenty years younger. He screamed at the impact of my nails.

It was half-past-ten. I lay in bed in the hotel in Glasnevin, staring at the newspaper headline and the photograph of the latest murder victim. Police didn't directly link his death to Christy's, but were keeping an open mind. I wanted to sleep but I couldn't. I wasn't sure which revelation was disturbing me most – that Luke just saw me as a cheap tart or that some man who might be my father was still alive. The fiddler whom the driver had described, whose name I couldn't even pronounce, bore no relation to the man who had abandoned us. Yet I couldn't dispel my unease at the mention of him being seen with a young woman. I could recall the photographs of my mother in the album she had kept in her wardrobe. They were taken in our garden the summer she finished college. She was confident and laughing in them, with long hair and a straw hat, about to embark on her first solo holiday, hitch-hiking around Ireland.

There was some chance the driver might be mistaken. But Luke's words were unequivocal. I couldn't hide from their callous truth. My mother had returned in disgrace after that summer, made pregnant by an old man who latched on to her and later ran away. I hadn't even been able to find a man of my own. I had made do with another woman's left-overs and now I didn't have a home left to run back to. Throughout my teens I'd tormented my mother by sitting in judgement, wrapped up in the superiority of my own pain. But I had

made as great a mess of my life as she ever made of hers. Gran
had expected more from her than that she would arrive home
secretly married, but I realised that, by the time I had disappeared, Gran would have expected no better from me.

I wanted to phone Grandad Pete, but it was madness to
think that I could after sixteen months away. In my mind I
saw how their house looked at that moment. I knew which
Christmas decorations would be hung where and could even
recall the writing on the cardboard box where the decorations
were kept. Grandad Pete would have purchased the tree on
Saturday, bringing the stand with him in the boot and ensuring the man chopped the base so that it stood straight. There
would be two sets of lights, both ten years old. One flickered
and one did not. I could see him taping the extension cord
along the wall, while Gran sat over her list of cards. The box
of assorted balls and angels would be on the floor beside him.
Arranging them on the branches had been my task for as
long as I remembered. There might be a card for me on the
mantelpiece, with my name on the envelope and a blank space
for the address. Shortly after their eleven o'clock coffee the
post would drop into the hall. Grandad might discreetly check
it before handing the cards to her, but they wouldn't mention
my name.

I couldn't stop this irrational hatred of Gran but I knew
that Grandad Pete could forgive me anything. I remembered
the police station in Dublin eleven years before and the screams
of Martin in another cell being beaten with wet towels. I had
squeezed my knees together with fright as my cell door clanged
open. Grandad Pete had stood there smiling and beckoning
me as he made the problems vanish. There were no charges
pressed. The policewoman had been kind and given me chocolate on the way to the airport. Grandad held my hand on the
plane, showing me cloud canyons out the window. He never
asked a single question, but just said 'You're safe now, Tracey',
and squeezed my hand. My room was exactly as I had left it.

My mother's bed had been turned down, like it was always left when she was in hospital. Even the goldfish had flitted from their rock homes to mouth silent greetings. I was blamed for nothing because I had become a child again. I was secretly pleased to wake up, crying with my bed wet. I had lain between my grandparents in the big front bedroom, remembering the smell of Martin's clothes and the way he would lie curled behind me, never moving although I could feel that stiff part of him touching my back. Months later I overheard them say that he was sent to an Industrial School – the first time I heard that Irish word for a borstal. Ireland itself was never mentioned to me, even when my mother returned, sedated and guilty. They never asked and I never spoke. It had just festered inside me, waiting to seep out through a hundred cuts and wounds.

Finally, at eleven o'clock, I picked up the phone in the hotel room and keyed in the code for London. I even let it ring three times in Harrow before putting it down. The problem was that I was no longer a child and there was no one left to blame. Even Grandad Pete couldn't make this mess disappear and I wouldn't ask him to because the only thing I still owned was my pride.

Lunch-time came, then two o'clock and half past three. I couldn't sleep or find the strength to rise from the bed. Luke had booked the hotel, but I wasn't sure if he had paid in advance. I hadn't enough money to pay the bill myself. My airline ticket was for seven the next morning. Luke had said he wasn't sure if he could travel with me. Now I didn't want to risk meeting him at the airport. I didn't want to see him again. At least I'd never given him my address. I had thirty-nine pounds. If I did a runner from the hotel it might be enough to get me on a cheap coach to London, although with Christmas I didn't know if there would be seats left.

Nobody at reception could be listening but I was afraid to use the phone to inquire about coach tickets. Four o'clock came and then five. I drank from the cold water tap. I wasn't hungry but my throat was raw. I ached for coffee but the shock of Luke's words seemed to have drained the confidence from me to even leave the room. Daylight died beyond the window. There was a remote control beside the bed. I flicked through the channels for light and company. The Irish news came on. I couldn't follow the main stories, so I turned the sound down. A report came on about Christy's funeral. Luke was filmed with his arms around his daughter and his wife. Shane stood behind with Al looking stupid in a suit. Then a police photograph came up and it took me a moment to place the face. I grabbed the remote control to turn the sound up but only caught the end of the sentence: '. . . the second to die in twenty four hours, McGann's body was found in a builder's skip this afternoon.' He had grown fat since the photograph but I still recognised the thug who had challenged Luke in Christy's garden.

The phone rang beside the bed. I shivered and flicked the television off so the room was in darkness. The phone kept ringing but I didn't answer it. Then it stopped and I could hear my heart beating. I felt like a caged animal, a compliant English tart. I should have fled earlier when I had the chance. Footsteps approached down the corridor and there was a soft knock. I lay still, although such pretence was useless. Luke wasn't the type to go away. The knocking came again, louder and more urgent.

'Are you okay in there?'

It took a moment to place the voice. I rose and pulled on a jumper and pair of jeans. I glanced in the mirror in the half light and saw what a mess I looked. I almost didn't open the door, except that the knock came again and the voice was so concerned. It was bright in the corridor. The taxi driver stood there, slightly embarrassed. He had a brown paper bag in his hand.

'I know you're not sick,' he said, 'but I thought flowers

might give the wrong impression. I'm not used to paying visits to young ladies' rooms.'

There were grapes inside the bag and a plastic tag saying *Seedless*. The man looked at my bowed head, not knowing if I was laughing or crying. Grapes were the very thing Grandad Pete would have thought of bringing. Even though it hadn't been his voice, for a second as I opened the door I'd half expected to see my grandfather there.

'I've always hated grapes,' I said, looking up.

'I can't blame you, love,' the man replied. 'I was never gone on them myself.'

I wiped my eyes with the sleeve of my jumper. I was pleased he had called, or at least relieved it wasn't Luke. But I was embarrassed and didn't know what to say.

'I didn't mean to intrude,' he explained. 'I just wanted to check you were okay. I hated seeing you left like that this morning.'

I felt I had to ask him in. He shook his head but I insisted. I turned on the light and saw how dishevelled the room was. I picked up old clothes and drew the curtains. The driver sat on the chair where Luke had watched me and I saw him eye the breakfast tray with the card of contraceptive pills still on it. I pocketed them and pushed the tray under the bed.

'Have you eaten today, child?' he said.

'I'm not a child.'

'I'm sure you're not, but I'm old fashioned and you look like a child to me.'

I sat at the mirror to comb my hair, tugging a brush harshly through the blonde tangles. Then I crossed to the hand basin to splash water over my face.

'I know it's not my business,' he said. 'I hope I haven't offended you by calling?'

I held the towel for a moment over my face. 'I'm okay,' I said. 'I don't need anyone's help.'

'Sure what help would I be?' he replied. 'I'm only an oul

fellow with one foot in the grave. I'm old enough to be your grandfather.' He paused as I lowered the towel and I saw him study my features. 'All the same, I'm younger than your Daddy.'

It was none of his business. I wanted him to step outside so I could get dressed properly. In fact I decided I didn't want him here at all. My father had been dead in my mind for years. I wanted it kept that way. He glanced around the room.

'Your gentleman friend hasn't surfaced since.'

'Luke was stressed out,' I said, 'late for a funeral. We were both tried. You know how it is with families.'

'I do,' he said, but he wasn't fooled. I wanted to scream my fury at Luke, but found myself defending him. It seemed the only way to play down his insult. Our affair had always been private. Now the sympathy in the driver's eyes was too humiliating.

'He's my future uncle-in-law,' I said, 'when he gets angry he makes out I'm not good for his nephew. I mean, who hasn't had a row in a taxi?'

I was amazed by how quickly the lies and justifications came. It could have been Luke himself prompting me.

'I rarely pay any heed to what goes in the back of my car,' the driver said. 'Still I'd hate to think that if it was my daughter . . .'

'I'm not your daughter.'

'I know,' he said. 'I'd just like to think that if you were and, well, if somebody who knew of me came across you, that they'd keep an eye out for you, for my sake if not your own.'

It was the first time I'd ever been viewed as my father's daughter. It felt strange having that abstract figure mentioned as flesh and blood.

'I never heard of this Mac Suibhne guy,' I said. 'Even if he turns out to be my father, you're showing more concern than he ever did. My father left when I was a few months old. I always presumed him dead and he can stay dead, because I want as much to do with him as he ever wanted to do with me.'

'Sweeney is no tinker name,' the driver said. 'If you were Irish I'd think you were making this up. But you really haven't a clue. He's a very great musician, your father. I only heard him play twice, but you'd never forget him. I can still remember the first time, even though it's fifty years ago, at the Oireachtas in Dublin. He brought the house down. He was a striking man, but painfully shy. He kept his back to the crowd for the first two tunes. The crowd wouldn't let him off the stage until the committee finally dropped the curtain down.'

'It doesn't matter how good he was,' I said. 'Nothing gives him the right to walk out on his wife. But weren't you the same yourself, wandering off, leaving your wife to cope? You boasted about it this morning.'

The man nodded. 'I can't deny it. They were different times. Oh, she lacked for nothing, I worked hard when I was here, but . . . a man looked foolish wheeling a pram then. They say it was a man's world and they're right, but we missed out on so much. My son said it to me one time he was home. All he remembered from childhood was sitting in dark pubs, sick from crisps and lemonade, listening to old men play music.' He stood up, awkward now. 'I shouldn't have come. I don't even know your Daddy. But he's an old man. Whatever he did he may regret it now. Your mother . . . ?'

'She's dead.

'I'm sorry. Was it she told you he was a tinker?'

'What you call him doesn't change what he did.'

'He's old, that's all I'll say. He's a solitary man who's spent his life avoiding towns and walking across hills and bogs in the rain with a wooden box on his back. Needles and threads, hairpins and cheap brooches nobody in their right mind would buy. People bought them off him so that he'd have the odd shilling in his pocket. They'd go up to ask for things between sets, and, as often as not, throw them into a ditch on their way home. That was their way of keeping him afloat, you couldn't just put money into his hand. He has a fierce pride. No more than myself, he should be in the grave years ago if the devil wasn't busy elsewhere. But we're not unkillable. If there's any chance he's your Daddy, then you should meet him just once, at least to tell him his wife is dead.'

The driver took out a set of keys. It was hard to think of him ferrying people from discos and clubs out into dangerous suburbs. I knew he was a good man and even though he'd heard the names Luke called me I wasn't ashamed any more. He had turned me from somebody's tart into somebody's daughter. I couldn't reconcile the fiddler he spoke of with the childhood stories I'd heard, but it felt good to see respect in somebody's eyes again.

'Surely there were dozens of Frank Sweeneys,' I said.

'Few were fiddlers,' the taxi man replied, 'and fewer still mastered *Last Night's Joy*. Don't take my word for it. There's a box player who knows Mac Suibhne well, by the name of Jimmy McMahon. Even though it's twenty years ago I often heard Jimmy talk about the time he saw Mac Suibhne in Dublin, walking along Berkeley Road with a young English woman. All kind of rumours flew about back then. I never heard marriage mentioned nor a child, but McMahon will be playing at the session in Hughes pub down the markets tonight. You mightn't want to go there. But whether you're Mac Suibhne's girl or not, please, don't throw your life away on trash washed out from the slums of Dublin.'

He reached out to touch the back of my hand. It was a token of affection and recognition, but for some reason I also felt he was checking the length of my fingers, imagining them holding a bow.

'Thanks for the grapes,' I said.

He paused in the doorway. 'I always wondered what this hotel looked like,' he said. 'The high life, eh? But whatever you say, you're still a child to me and it's a far nicer world out there.'

He walked down the corridor without looking back. I don't know why I did it, but I flicked out the light. I closed the door and dressed myself in the dark where I couldn't see my reflection. I felt confident again and strong. I didn't know where I was going, but I was going out.

There were two parties going on downstairs when I left the hotel at eight o'clock. An elderly committee were bringing their drinks into the restaurant, while younger people made their way through the bar to an office party in the ballroom beyond. I heard a band warming up there. There was nobody at reception as I slipped out. A taxi was leaving people off and I hailed it to bring me into Dublin. The driver knew of Hughes pub but seemed surprised that I was going there alone. He asked why and when I mentioned music he suggested various pubs along the tourist trail. It was rough and ready around Hughes, he explained, and the streets there could be dodgy after dark. It was hard to imagine having this conversation with a London taxi driver. All this concern had started to annoy me with its suggestion that I was incapable of looking after myself.

The area around the pub was ill-lit and deserted though. Some sort of law court stood along the quays, and there were small Victorian terraces overlooked by blocks of modern flats. Trucks were parked up on the pavements of narrow streets leading to the fruit and vegetable markets. There were rows of shuttered warehouses, smashed pallets and the smell of discarded fruit. At first I thought there wasn't going to be music in the pub. There was no platform or lights or microphones. It was early and the place was quiet with just a few older men gathered in one corner with instruments still in their cases. Younger people gradually joined them, including a girl my own age. I sat at the bar, drinking white wine slowly. I wanted to remain sober. Nobody paid me any heed as the bar filled up with a mixture of locals from the markets and people in search of music.

After what seemed an eternity, the musicians took their instruments out to warm up. I only figured out who McMahon was when a man with cropped white hair began to shake notes from a concertina. He nodded and muttered something to the others. The tuning up was suddenly over and, unannounced, the first tune began. The pub didn't go completely quiet but voices were lowered to afford the music respect without undue deference. Similarly, the musicians didn't seem to play for the drinkers gathered in the bar. They were sharing the music with them but still primarily playing amongst themselves. Applause was rare and there were no introductions to songs or sets of reels. The musicians just chatted amongst themselves after a tune and then started again at a nod from McMahon.

Occasionally a man or woman sang, equally without warning or announcement, and there would be silence in the pub, even among the local women in the far corner who had nothing to do with the session. Listening to the unaccompanied singing I understood what the taxi driver meant about certain songs dying out with the death of a singer. Although the words were mostly in Irish, even the ones in English were difficult to comprehend. But their effect was far more than just the words. All the emotion seemed to be carried in the phrasing and spacing, in almost imperceptible lulls and silences between, and often within, individual words. Even the barmen stopped pouring drink as those voices quietly coaxed the song towards its conclusion. The applause that followed was modestly ignored as if singing was an everyday thing, neither deserving or requiring such recognition.

An obvious break came when the musicians began to move about the bar. Sandwiches arrived down with a fresh round of drinks. McMahon had put his concertina carefully back in the box at his feet and was enjoying a cigarette. I picked up my glass and decided to approach, unsure of what I wanted to say.

'You play it well.'

'There's a fine sound in it still,' he replied as though the instrument played itself.

'Are you Jimmy McMahon?'

'That's me,' he agreed, stubbing the cigarette out. 'Why do you ask?'

'Have you ever heard of a musician called Frank Sweeney?'

'I can't say I have. Where would he be from?'

'A fiddle player from Donegal.' I waited to see would he make the same connection between names.

'Donegal, eh? I've known a fair few from there in my time; the Dohertys, James Byrne, Tommy Peoples and the Glackins. But Frank Sweeney? Unless you mean Proinsías Mac Suibhne?'

'Would he ever use the English version of his name?' I asked.

'If it's Proinsías you have in mind he'd never need to,' McMahon explained. 'Where he travels there's nobody who wouldn't know who he is.'

'Say he was introducing himself to an outsider?'

'Mac Suibhne never would,' McMahon said. 'He's the shyest man I know. That is until you put a fiddle into his hand.'

'Where might I find him?'

McMahon laughed and picked up the sandwich. He took a bite and chewed.

'You mightn't,' he said. 'Not easily anyway. He's no tourist attraction. Often you'd find gold or buried weapons in those hills faster. The locals look after him. He's the last of his kind, now that John and Mickie and Simie Doherty are gone. They know if anyone tries to exploit him he won't come back. No doubt he's playing somewhere in Donegal as we speak, but I couldn't begin to tell you where.'

He looked at me more closely, suspicious of my interest.

I wasn't going to blurt everything out like in the taxi. I didn't want another hymn of praise for my father's abilities or more man-made excuses for a man who'd abandoned his family.

'Did he ever play in Dublin?' I asked.

'One time before the war at the Oireachtas, I'm told. He didn't win the gold medal though, Donegal music wasn't regarded as pure Irish then. He was bitterly disappointed. He never entered a competition again.'

'But you yourself saw him in Dublin since then?'

'I don't know who told you that,' he said, with his suspicion renewed. 'I'm just here to play a few tunes. The last time I saw Proinsías was six years ago in a wee village up the Derryveagh Mountains. He was meant to play in the back of a pub that some young fellow was left in charge of, as the owner was away at a funeral. A Belgian film crew bustled their way in, bullying the young lad and sticking up lights and cameras everywhere. Proinsías arrived and took one look before walking out again. The crew wanted to go after him and corner him on the road. God, there were nearly fist fights in the bar before people got rid of them. Some of us went looking for him, but nobody was sure which way he'd gone. There's tracks over those hill known only to Proinsías and the mountain sheep. I found him sheltering in a ditch, like a rabbit escaped from a snare. All the man wants is to be left alone. There's no mystery to him. If he landed on your doorstep you wouldn't recognise what you had on your hands. But because he's wary of cameras you media people want to build him up into some sort of sage, when he's just an old man set in his ways. Now I don't know who you are and what television station you work for, but you'll never get him to record. Any records he made were on old wax discs with Seamus Ennis in the 1950s, playing at house dances at the height of his powers. They're what he wants to be remembered by. He's a proud, lonely old man and he'll join no circus and jump through no hoops for anyone.'

The musicians had gathered back around the table. McMahon's expression made it clear I was in the way.

'I don't work for television,' I said. 'But I believe that my mother knew him over twenty years ago.'

I watched McMahon's face as he carefully studied mine. The musicians were slightly impatient, waiting for him to begin. He saw I was offering no more information.

'Where did she know him?' he asked.

'Firstly in Donegal, then a long way outside it.'

McMahon was quiet for a moment. 'What did she say about him?'

'Nothing and I heard nothing good from anyone else.'

He nodded and pondered. I was certain now that I had discovered my father's identity. McMahon's voice had changed.

'There's few who'd believe Mac Suibhne was ever outside Donegal.'

'Maybe there's lots of things they mightn't believe about him.'

'Did you ever heard his music?'

'No,' I said.

'Has she long hair still, your mother?' he asked.

'She's dead.'

McMahon's eyes studied mine. Part of me wanted to ask how well he remembered seeing her, if she had looked happy and was it on the day she married in Berkeley Street church. But another part of me didn't want to know.

'I hope you find him.'

'I asked where I might find him,' I replied. 'I never said I was going looking.'

I rose and walked back to the bar. I could hear McMahon's voice behind me, raised for the first time.

'There's a reel I'd like to play,' he said, 'although I'm not sure all the musicians here know it. It was given to me by a Donegal fiddler called Proinsías Mac Suibhne who picked it up as a child from the lilting of a woman.' He lowered his voice, obviously addressing the musicians. 'Do any of you know *Last Night's Joy?*'

Some must have nodded, for he began to play and several of the older men joined in. I put my glass down on the counter. He was playing it for me as Frank Sweeney had once played it to please my mother. I found I knew the melody. I could remember my mother humming it to me in bed when she would cuddle into me after reading stories. It was years since I had heard it, but the air had never left my head. I hated McMahon for playing it, I hated its sweet intoxication. The pub was jammed now. I walked to the door and out into the night air without looking back. I walked as fast and as far as I could along those echoing, narrow streets but I still couldn't shake that tune from my head. My father's music and my mother's pain, both trapped inside me. The tune brought back the feel of her arms about me in bed. I cursed all Irishmen and their excuses. No music and no gift gave anyone the right to desert their family. I had always seen him as strong and callous, but the fact that he was as vulnerable as my mother made him no less of a bastard. In fact it was worse. He had not been some raggle-taggle gypsy, seducing and casually forgetting her. He must have understood the torment she went through. He should know that she was dead, but what was the point in going after him? My mother had never wanted revenge for what he had done and I know it was not in my gift to forgive him.

Eventually I stopped in that maze of narrow lanes, with no idea where I was. I hurried on up a side-street littered with smashed pallets. Cardboard boxes were piled in a shop doorway. I was almost past them when a whisper caught my attention. I knew I should keep walking. If it was a man I could be in trouble. But that whisper hadn't been in a man's voice. I approached the boxes which were lined with newspapers and a filthy blanket. The boy who stared aggressively out looked younger than Martin had been. He had his arm protectively around a girl of nine or ten.

'What the fuck do you want?' he demanded.

'Are you not freezing?' I asked, kneeling on the concrete.

'What's it to you?' The girl sounded frozen and suspicious. There was a cut on her arm which could turn septic.

'Have you any money?' the boy asked.

I had a ten and a twenty pound note in my pocket, along with a handful of pound coins. It might just be enough for a cheap coach to London, but I handed him the ten pound note, knowing I was leaving myself stranded. He examined it distrustfully, then watched me stare at the girl's arm.

'What's the story?' he said. 'Are you a bleeding lesbian or what? Lay a finger on my sister and I'll split you.'

'I'm concerned about that cut. It might need a tetanus injection.' The word meant nothing to them, but the girl looked worried.

'I just caught it on some wire,' she said.

'Cuts can be dangerous.'

'Stop scaring her. We can fucking look after ourselves.' The boy was belligerent. I thought he was going to throw the money back at me. There was movement among the papers and, though they tried to prevent it, a third head appeared. This child seemed no more than three or four. She stared, with eyes just opened from sleep. I felt chilled.

'This is crazy,' I pleaded 'There's going to be sharp frost. You can't have her out all night. Where are your parents?'

'Da's always kicking me Ma and he kicks us too,' the girl said, taking strength from her brother. 'Ma's inside, she was caught stealing in Dunnes Stores. We're not going back to me Da and we're not leaving our sister with him.'

She put her arm around the child and pushed her under the

blanket, but she poked her head out again to stare at me with open curiosity.

'It's cold sleeping on the streets,' I said.

'How the fuck would you know?' the boy sneered.

There was no use explaining. They wouldn't believe me.

'Please,' I pleaded with the girl. 'The child shouldn't be out in this weather, none of you should. Let me at least clean the cut on your arm. I'll give you this jacket if you will. You can use it as a blanket for your sister.'

'Take her jacket and she'll want your knickers in return,' the boy snapped aggressively, feeling his authority under-mined. But the girl stared at my jacket and nodded. She held her arm out. I had tissues in my pocket that I had to wet with my own spit to scrub the muck off. The girl winced, but the cut wasn't deep. I was an expert on them from all the times my mother or Gran had cleaned wounds on my arm. I had no antiseptic or cotton wool. I felt helpless.

'You should go home,' I told her. 'Things can happen on the streets that affect you for the rest of your life.'

'Tomo has a knife, he'll look after us,' she said, trying to believe it herself.

The silent child reached beneath the newspapers and pro-duced an empty brown-stained baby's bottle. She sucked on the teat for comfort.

'What was in her bottle?' I asked.

'Coke. She likes coke.'

I took the bottle from her. The child let it go, too scared to cry. One side of her face was bruised. Her eyes told me she expected to be slapped by adults. I stared at the filthy teat. I had never felt so utter despair. I wondered where Martin was now. Probably in jail or with his brain burnt out. I had been his glimpse into a different world and I had let him take all the blame. The children seemed embarrassed by my distress. I felt the boy pat me softly, offering comfort.

'Take it easy, right,' he said.

I handed the empty bottle back to the child and took my jacket off. The girl accepted it without a word and spread it over herself and the child who stared, wide-eyed. She dropped the empty bottle and held her hand out. I reached into my pocket and, taking out three pound coins, placed them in her palm. The child looked at them, then back at me. I realised she had longed for something soft but there was no comfort in the coldness of the coins. I stood up. She clenched her fingers around then and stared after me with silent disappointment.

I walked quickly to a main road and stood, trying to hail a taxi. Every cab was full, everyone in festive mood. I would have walked on except that I had no idea where I was. Finally a cab stopped, the driver surly that I was only travelling a short distance. He never spoke until we had reached the hotel. Cars were parked all along the road and I heard music inside. I searched my pockets for the twenty pound note, but I knew immediately that the boy had pickpocketed it while pretending to comfort me. The driver was impatient to be gone.

'Come on, love,' he said, 'it's a busy night for me.'

A figure stepped from a parked car and seemed to be trying to see who was in the taxi. He had Luke's shape although it was too dark to make him out. If I had money I would have told the driver to move on, but I was trapped without even the fare to pay him.

'I've lost my money,' I said.

'Virginity you lose,' he sneered, 'money you spend. You didn't lose it in here. You knew damn well you'd no money when you hailed my cab. So what are you playing at, how exactly did you plan to pay me?'

The driver leaned back aggressively. The figure outside walked up to the cab window and pulled the door open. It was Al's friend, Carl. He stared at the driver.

'What's your problem, pal?'

'She's no money to pay.'

Carl looked at the meter and counted out the exact amount

from his pocket. He handed it to the driver who accepted it brusquely. Carl helped me from the cab, then leaned in to address the driver.

'You want a tip, pal? Fuck off back to the zoo.'

Carl slammed the door. For a second I thought the driver was going to get out, but the cab just sped off. Carl saw that I was shaken. He put an arm around me.

'Are you all right?' he asked.

'Yeah. Thanks.'

'I was waiting for you.'

'Who sent you?' I pulled slightly away. 'Was it Luke?'

'That cranky oul fuck? It was in me bollox.' He looked more serious. 'I got a phone call from Al. He sounded rough. I didn't know what the stroke is, but he asked me to ask you would you meet him please.'

It was a quarter-of-an-hour's drive before Carl pulled into a massive car park in front of a cinema complex and pleasure dome. An electronic sign announced that breakfast was served twenty-four hours a day. Inside, the noise was deafening. An eight-lane bowling alley was packed, with people cheering and slapping hands at every strike. Lines of video games and poker machines stretched away further than I could see. It was after midnight but people were happily sitting down to full breakfasts. I felt the scene would look exactly the same in five or twenty-five hours' time.

Carl led the way upstairs to where crowds milled around more video games and rows of snooker tables. Rap music was thumping out. It must have been a trick of the light but the pigmentation on people's faces gave the look of a tribe who had forsaken the sensation of daylight. Carl beckoned me up more steel steps to where a laser game was in progress.

Al was among the group of people watching. He turned after a moment, with a hunted look. I noticed that Carl remained in the doorway. Al walked over and I put my hand up to touch his face.

'Are you okay?' I asked. 'What happened?'

'Will you help me, Tracey?' he said. 'I'm in deep shit and you're the only person I can ask.'

FIFTEEN

I HAD FEW ENOUGH clothes to smuggle from the hotel in Glasnevin. In the end I simply wore most of them under my spare coat. The bag was one I had taken from Harrow and I was happy to leave it behind. The night porter was back on duty, but he seemed more concerned with the remnants of the office Christmas party resisting his entreaties to leave. He glanced towards me and smiled, but said nothing. Yesterday I had acquired blonde hair, tonight it looked like I had gained a stone in weight.

I didn't know how much trouble Al was in, or what danger I might put myself in by accompanying him. But, when he had asked, I had immediately agreed to travel to London with him, pretending that I was his girl-friend and we were spending Christmas in my flat if the British police asked. With Christy's death in the papers he felt it would look too suspicious if he simply left the country by himself without any apparent destination. Somebody had put the rumour on the street that he had killed McGann and it was only a matter of time before the police heard it too. He needed to disappear until the business was sorted out. I liked Al and I trusted him but, in my heart, I knew I'd mainly agreed to travel with him because it offered me a chance to avoid meeting Luke on that plane. I was running away every bit as much as Al.

I crossed the road from the hotel and hurried down a side street towards an old schoolhouse with a narrow lane beside it. The street light in the lane was broken. I glanced behind at the deserted road before racing down the lane to scale the iron railway bridge leading across to poorer looking streets on the far side on the tracks. I stopped on the bridge and held my fingers against the wire mesh. Roxy's father, who had been a British Rail driver, once told me that the worst aspect of the job was the suicides. One night a woman had jumped from a bridge to land spreadeagled on the windscreen of an express he was driving. The train's speed had kept her trapped against the glass as though glued to it, staring in at him as he drove on, knowing that once he slowed down the suction would wear off and she would fall to her death. She had wanted instantaneous suicide, instead fate allowed her an audience with her unwilling and unwitting executioner. The train had entered a short tunnel and when it re-emerged she simply wasn't there.

I heard a train approach in the moonlight, with empty trucks rattling as I hurried down the iron steps at the far side. Al had told me there was a laneway to the left, but not that it would be so dark and L-shaped. I ran through it. An isolated terrace of red-brick houses lay beyond, in the shadow of the railway embankment, lit by two amber street lights set into the walls of the terrace itself. This was where Al had promised to wait. Car headlights came on, blinding me as I heard an engine start. I ran towards the lights, praying it was Al as the passenger door swung open.

'You're getting fat,' Al said, eyeing my layers of clothes.

'Get me the hell out of here,' I replied and slammed the door shut.

We turned on to a long road bordering a prison. The car ferry wasn't for six hours yet. Al was tense and I could see that he was just driving aimlessly. Whenever we stopped at traffic lights he put his head down if another car pulled up. He was making me more nervous that I already was. I glanced at him, wondering if perhaps he might have killed McGann. Why was the finger being pointed at him? I remembered his bitterness at Christy's removal and his hints of revenge. Al sensed me watching him.

'I didn't do it,' he said. 'All my life I've stayed out of it and now someone is using me as a scapegoat. I don't know who or why, but it's like a blood-lust out there. Not even Christy would mess with the Bypass Bombardiers. Maybe McGann did the job himself and put the blame on Christy. Christine is convinced McGann set Christy up to try and take the heat off himself, but I swear to God I didn't kill him. I can hardly use a cigarette lighter, never mind a gun. I'd have shot myself in the toe or something. But McGann's mates think I'm gunning for their blood and they have to kill me before I get them.'

'Who killed McGann?'

'How the hell would I know?' Al asked. 'Everyone's at it. There's more guns in this city than hard-ons poking around the blue section in my Da's video store. You're nobody in Dublin now without a trigger. You can smell the taste for blood out there.'

We had crossed the river and turned on to a stretch of motorway bulldozed across a hive of tiny roads. Solitary houses, which had once formed part of terraces, stood shell-shocked on the edge of amputated streets. Al's car chugged along, its engine plotting mutinies. We turned off the motorway to circle through the narrow streets, with Al perpetually checking his mirror. He stopped across from a block of flats. A battered caravan was blocking the entrance with a tricolour painted on the side and a huge sign sprayed on the pavement: NO DRUG PUSHERS HERE. A group of men warmed themselves by an open fire, one of them incongruously dressed in a Santa outfit. I could see a pick-axe handle resting against the open caravan door.

'Drive in there by mistake,' Al said, 'and you'll have some talking to do just to get out with your knee-caps in place. Last week they beat a six-stone junkie to death. It was hardly worth the trouble, the guy could barely walk. They left him dying on the path, screaming at passing girls to stay away because he'd Aids. Even ordinary people are getting in on the act, moving the two-bit pushers and junkies along.'

The men had left the fire to stare at Al's car. Santa Claus reached for the pick-axe handle. Al pulled away as some of them began to cross the road.

'I don't blame them,' he said. 'They see their kids getting strung out and dying. The pushers have people handing out free heroin outside the schools. But all the vigilantes do is move the small fry on to the next estate. There's no fear of them tackling the big barons in their fortified houses.'

'Like Christy,' I said.

'Christy never touched drugs,' Al replied. 'He was old-fashioned. He thought sexual perversion meant the doggie position. Everyone else was making their fortunes from crack and heroin, but Christy was a relic, living off his reputation. Unless you do drugs in Dublin you don't have the muscle to count for nothing any more.'

'Maybe Christy tried to change that,' I said as we reached the deserted motorway. Al turned left, heading back towards town.

'I don't honestly know,' he said. 'I had started going to school before I realised there was anything odd in waking up to find police searching your bedroom. They never found anything but they kept coming back. I'd see it in school, parents whispering to the teacher about having their kids shifted from the desk beside me. I stuck it out and built a life of my own. Now it seems that all someone has to do is whisper and it's snatched away from me again.'

Al slammed on the brakes and pulled in. He stared out, his knuckles white as he gripped the wheel. There was still hours to go before the ferry sailed. He looked across at me.

'This is crazy,' he said, 'we can't drive around all night.

Besides, and don't get me wrong, I really do think you should take some of your clothes off.'

Al parked in the laneway behind his father's video shop, which was in a basement in an old street backing into the quays. He considered the front door too dangerous to approach, but there was a way in through the back, across an overgrown garden filled with rubble. He told me to wait behind a skip as he ran to the back door. He opened it and switched off the alarm, then turned the light on and stood for a moment, as if making himself a target, before beckoning for me to cross the garden. The video shop occupied two rooms. Through a gap in the shutters I could see iron bars protecting the windows. There was a section beside the counter partitioned off with a plywood wall which didn't quite reach the ceiling. A sign on the door read; *Adults Only Admitted.*

Al was afraid to put the main lights on. He rooted behind the counter and took out a red sports bag filled with pirated videos. He dumped them out on to the floor and I read the titles scrawled by hand in red marker: *Anal Girls Three, College Girls Watersports* and *Bizarre in Bucharest.*

'Da gets them by the bucketful from some redneck cop who chases sheep around the bog of Allen,' Al said, matter of factly. 'I don't ask too many questions. I mean, all small shopkeepers need to specialise to compete against the chain stores.'

'You make your living from these things?' I said in disgust and he shrugged.

'You know the joke. A guy walks into a shite café and sees a school-mate working there. "Jaysus, Joe" he says haughtily, "I bet you never thought you'd wind up working in this kip." "I might work here," Joe replies, "but at least I don't eat here."' Al picked the videos off the floor. 'It's just a job, the same as selling CDs or six inch nails. I rent them out, I don't watch them. Well, apart from *Cunnilingus in Clonakilty*. I mean, you'd never think Irish sheep could do that.'

I refused to laugh. Al flicked on the monitor over his head and for a moment I thought he was going to play one. Instead he rewound the security tape. I looked up and saw a tiny camera on the ceiling trained into the adult section. Al found the part he wanted and pressed the play button. The picture quality was poor, with the time and date superimposed on the screen. The adult section was narrow with hardly space for two people to pass and crude shelving on every side. Once or twice for a giggle with Roxy I had run down into the basement of Lovejoys on Tottenham Court Road to jeer at the men standing sheepishly in front of the magazines there, but I had never properly witnessed this male world before. Men were herded into that confined space, brushing against each other but never seeming to speak or acknowledge anyone else's presence as they examined the video cases on the shelves. The grainy quality of the film reminded me of a wildlife programme secretly recording worker bees inside a hive. Men of all ages came and left without comment, intent on their task and on catching nobody else's eye. Two men stood at all times near the door. Every time it opened they glanced out, watching the desk. Al paused the film and pointed to them. I knelt up on to the counter to get a closer look and recognised them as having stood beside McGann at Christy's removal.

'I came in here at eight o'clock last night,' Al said, 'after hearing about McGann on the news. I glanced up at the monitor and saw them just as some punter opened the door. I threw myself down behind the counter and watched the pair of them on the screen staring out, waiting for me. One to plug me, the other to grab the security video. Sheila behind the counter thought I was cracked. I got her to pass me down the phone and called Uncle Luke who told me about the rumour that I had shot McGann.'

I remembered Luke's prediction that nobody in Dublin would allow Al to just be himself.

'All I want is a simple life,' Al said. 'I put in a few hours' work here during the week and at weekends I mess around doing DJ and mixing sounds at parties. I might pop the odd E but I never touched any other shite.' He turned the monitor off. 'I ran out of here as soon as the door into the adult section was closed and I'm running still. I'm scared, Tracey. It doesn't matter if I'm innocent or guilty, they'll get me no matter where I hide in Dublin. Once rumours start they don't stop. That's why I've a bigger favour to ask. You know the cock-and-bull story for the police about me spending Christmas in your flat? Well, I need somewhere in London to crash, away from my family or from anyone they could track down. You don't have to say yes, but if you had a sofa or anything for a few days, you'd be saving my life.'

I wanted to break away from Luke and his family. But I also knew I was returning to London to sit in that cold flat over Christmas and nurse my wounds. I didn't want to be alone, inventing excuses to convince myself I wasn't lonely.

'My flat is poky,' I said. 'There's only a single bed which I share with my teddy. Three would be a crowd, if I make myself clear.'

Al nodded. 'You've a soft heart.'

'I've a bloody hard sofa as well.'

He laughed. 'I can keep an eye on the place for you on Christmas Day when you're with your family.'

'I've no family left,' I told him.

'Just a father.'

I wanted the conversation over. I picked up the empty sports bag and decided to put the rest of my clothes in it. The only place available to change in was the adult section. I closed the door behind me. Girls' faces stared from the shelves in the half moonlight, sucking on erect cocks, imprisoned by chains or pouting as they fondled their own breasts while being taken from behind. I felt suffocated in there with the ghosts of a hundred men. How could Al casually handle these cassettes as a way of life? I stared uncomfortably up at the security camera, with no way of knowing if he had turned it on. I felt grubby. I had never run away from a hotel without paying before. I took out the clean underwear I had stuffed into my pockets. Undressing behind that plywood partition was like a microcosm of my time with Luke in Dublin, having to take everything on trust, never certain of anything or fully in control.

I felt better with less clothes on. I threw everything else into the bag and opened the door quickly, trying to catch Al out. Al stood near the window, peering up through the shutters and checking the street, with the monitor turned off. I knew Luke would have sat at the counter, making no secret of enjoying the show to be had on screen.

'Would you like to get some sleep?' Al asked.

'I think I'm learning how to do without it.'

I walked around the shelves in the main shop and picked an old Spencer Tracy movie. Perhaps it was the fact that we shared a name but I had always loved to watch his films on TV as a child. I had imagined the adult world would be like his films, a place where simple, honest people won through. I sat with Al on the floor and we watched Tracy battle against prejudice with only his integrity and soft voice as weapons. Al fished under the counter for a hidden bit of hash and rolled a number. He put an arm around me, a little uncertainly and I snuggled against his chest.

'You're my favourite cousin, Trace,' he said, 'and I never even knew I had you.'

I remembered Carl's remark about Christine and Al being kissing cousins once and wondered what it meant. I wanted to tell Al the whole truth, but I couldn't. It felt better to seem to be Luke's bastard rather than his cheap English tart. But it also was a way to keep Al's attentions at bay. Not that he would try to force anything, but I suspected he mightn't have to try too hard. It was Al and not Luke I wished I had met in the Irish Centre. He had qualities which part of me felt I would never deserve. Now even though I had decided that my affair with Luke was over, the scars wouldn't easily go away. I felt cheapened and hurt and, no matter how much I liked Al, he would always remind me of Luke.

I must have slept because suddenly I found that Al's shoulder wasn't there, but his jacket was folded under my head. I opened my eyes. Al was hunched down beside me, smiling with a cup of coffee covered by a saucer in his hand.

'I didn't want to wake you, Trace,' he said. 'I was trying to keep it warm.'

I felt he had been studying my face as I slept. The video was turned off. I took the coffee from him and he proffered a packet of biscuits.

'The cheapest of the cheap,' he apologised in advance. 'I hope you don't mind.'

'No, give me E numbers any time,' I said. 'I need all the additives and chemicals I can get.'

It was half-five in the morning. I splashed water on my face in the tiny toilet. I went to flush it but I was afraid of making noise. We left by the same way we had come in, with Al insisting on going a little way in front so that if anyone was waiting they would get him before I appeared. The streets were deserted and coated with thick frost. I thought about the children trying to sleep under my jacket and shivered.

We reached Dun Laoghaire in the dark and joined the queues of cars fanned out into chicanes prior to boarding the ferry. The lines snaked along the concrete wharf, seeming to take forever to crest the ramp which led down into the bowels of the vessel. While we had been on the move Al had managed to cloak his nervousness, but now he looked genuinely terrified. He glanced in his mirror every time the car slowed to a halt. A battered-looking motorbike had begun weaving between the lines of cars. I saw Al watch the motorbike approach, knowing that we were trapped with no space to move in any direction. The bike drew alongside, the motor cyclist casually glancing in at us behind the dark visor of a mud-splattered blue helmet with a dint in the side. Then the bike was past and an official had run out angrily to wave the motor cyclist down and redirect him into line.

Our tickets were checked but nobody bothered asking to see our passports. We parked on board, then walked up on deck. I realised I had come to Dublin twice, once by boat only to return by air and now by that same route in reverse. Only when the boat sailed did Al relax. We watched Dublin shrink and for anyone observing us I knew we looked like any young couple. We shared breakfast in the restaurant while I warned Al about how small my flat was. He asked again if I really had nobody to go home to for Christmas. I told him I had been an only child and all my family were dead. I hoped this would put a halt to his questions but he started asking what my mother had seen in Luke. She never mentioned him much, I said, she had only travelled to Ireland once for a holiday, a long-haired girl in a sun hat with a different life seemingly before her.

'Easy prey for Luke,' Al said, bitterly. 'Get them young and impressionable.'

'He was young himself then.' I wondered why I always seemed to defend him.

Al snorted. 'He's your father and you feel loyal to him but that fellow was never young. He was hatched out middle-aged and with attitude. Give him any challenge and he can never resist it. Give him what he wants and he walks away, bored.'

'Can we leave Luke out of it,' I said, uneasily, wondering if Al was trying to warn me.

'Gladly,' Al replied. 'He's caused nothing but trouble since coming home. I only hope he has the decency to fuck off with himself and leave us alone on the way over at least.'

I put my fork down. The sensation was the same as the night I looked into my hotel mirror to find Luke observing me.

'You mean he's here,' I said, 'on this boat?'

Al looked surprised. 'I thought you knew,' he said. 'He's taking a car which belonged to Christy across to London. He has a buyer for it for ready cash. I mean, it was his idea that I hide in London and ask you if I could stay. When I phoned him from the video shop, he offered to send tickets to the Pleasure Dome by courier. How else could I have got them so late at night?' Al stopped, disturbed by my reaction. 'Are you okay?'

I rose from the table and ran outside. I saw Al through the porthole leave money on his plate and follow me. There was nowhere to run. The sky was overcast and it was cold. The sea was choppy. I felt like a doll being perpetually moved around. I leaned over the rail and my entire breakfast came up. Al found me and held my shoulder.

'Are you okay, Trace?' he asked.

I shook his hand off and stared at him. How much did Al know or was he simply being used as well? That was the problem with lies, they grew to consume you. How could I accuse him of deceit when I had played him along? Since my first trip to Dublin I'd learnt to manipulate the truth as effortlessly as Luke did, concealing scars about my person and lying as convincingly to myself as to anyone else. Now, looking at Al, I was sure he didn't have it in him to cover up for Luke. I also knew I could say nothing without revealing how I had played along with the lies told to him.

'I've no sealegs,' I said, 'this is my first time.'

'That's all right.' Al smiled. 'I'm a virgin too.'

'I won't ask where.'

He grinned and I felt shamed by the honesty on his face. He took my arm and led me up steps to an exposed bench on the upper deck.

'Sit here,' he said, 'your stomach won't feel so bad in the open air.'

Although it was cold, he took his jacket off and insisted I wear it. Even on this boat he was uneasy about his safety. When two men mounted the steps to stare towards us for a moment Al went quiet and I felt him take my hand and squeeze it tight. Yet despite his fear, he seemed more concerned with cheering me up. He sang mock Christmas carols about shepherds washing their socks by night and told elaborate yarns about his night-time misadventures and romantic failings. Even as I sat, with one eye waiting for Luke to appear, Al could still make me laugh.

'Did Luke tell you where I lived?' I asked.

'He didn't seem to know the address.'

'Have you to contact him in London?'

'He said not to, unless I was in trouble.'

'Then you have to promise something,' I told him. 'I don't want to see Luke again. If I let you stay you can't give him my address.'

'Have you two fallen out?'

'Just promise.'

Al nodded. 'When did you find out he was your father?' he asked.

'I don't want to talk about it, okay.'

'You don't need him,' Al said. 'You seem to have got on well enough without any father up to now.'

'Just leave it out, Al.'

He said nothing, silenced by a tone in my voice that I regretted. He looked cold but I couldn't get him to take his jacket back. I stood up for us to go back inside. 'Save a few of your stories,' I said, 'or we'll have nothing to talk about in the flat.'

'Fair enough,' Al agreed, 'but there's one rule I'm laying down. From now on you bathe yourself.'

I punched him playfully and he grabbed my hands. It was

the first time any man had done that when I didn't want to pull away. We stood still, our bodies close, both remembering that shower. I leaned forward and Al lowered his face towards mine. We almost kissed, then we both looked away. Al was confused and slightly embarrassed.

'Let's go in,' he said, matter of factly. 'It's bleeding freezing out here.'

I climbed down the steel steps ahead of him. There was a gust of salt wind and I gripped the handrail. I looked back to see him staring at my blown hair.

'Blonde doesn't suit you,' he said.

If Luke was on board he kept well away. We had coffee inside and only came back out on deck when the coastline of Wales appeared. People started to drift down to their cars and we followed. The ship docked and, after a time, daylight appeared as the bow doors opened. The cars began to move slowly forward in two lanes. The police were there along with customs officers, occasionally stopping vehicles for random checks. We were about forty cars away from the checkpoint when Al's door was pulled open. Luke leaned in, not looking at me.

'Listen,' Luke said, 'the English police are searching for someone. I think they want to question you. I called your father on my mobile before we docked. He said the guards called to your flat last night and then to his house asking about you. If Tracey is with you she'll be taken in for questioning as well. Let's keep her out of this, right.'

Luke still hadn't looked across and I didn't look at him. Everything made sense now. He was expecting me to be forced into his car. But I didn't care if the police detained me, I wasn't going to be tricked into changing vehicles.

'What do I do?' Al asked, so scared that I knew he was being manipulated too.

'Get out of the car before we're seen,' Luke ordered. I ignored his demand and then realised that he was still addressing Al. 'Get into Christy's car with me. I'm used to being hassled, but let's get Tracey safely away.'

Al touched my arm. 'Can you drive?' he asked and I nodded, confused. 'I'm sorry about this.'

'It's okay,' I said, forced to turn towards Al. I saw Luke stare at me, genuinely concerned.

'I'm sorry, Tracey,' Luke said. 'Sometimes things happen beyond your control. I'll make it up to you, I promise.'

I didn't reply. Al reached into the back seat for his luggage and Luke stopped him.

'For Christ's sake,' he said. 'Use your brain for once. How suspicious do you want to look? We'll sort things out later.'

Cars were starting to beep as a space cleared in front of Luke's car in the other lane. Luke and Al ran to climb into it and drive on. Everything had happened so fast. I didn't know what to say if I was stopped or what to do afterwards. I clambered over the gear stick and released the hand brake. The car shot forward and I almost crashed into the transit van in front. My hands were shaking. I hated Luke, yet I would have given anything to have him beside me for one minute to explain what I was meant to do. The other lane was moving faster. I saw their car reach the police officers. It was stopped and waved over to one side. Al and Luke got out and I saw Luke being asked for identification while Al was searched. A policeman took the keys from Luke and opened the boot while another man in overalls lay down to examine under the vehicle. It probably only took two minutes for my car to reach the checkpoint, but it seemed an eternity. Al was being led inside while Luke spoke calmly to the policeman examining his passport. I waited to be stopped too. I could imagine the cells nearby and being strip searched. Luke never looked in my direction as cars beeped behind me. A customs official had to tap on the glass.

'Come on now, madam,' he urged, 'you're holding everyone up.'

I kept driving, following the car in front and not even sure if I was taking the route on to the motorway towards London. I pulled in at the first lay-by and sat there for a whole hour and then another, scanning every car which passed. At the speed they were travelling it was impossible to see if Luke's was among them, but I hoped he would see me and pull in. I had never given Al my address. Now I realised how much I'd been looking forward to bringing him home.

Finally I had to drive on, hoping there was enough petrol to get me to London. I only had a few useless Irish coins. I followed the road signs and counted the miles, watching the petrol gauge dip inexorably down. By the outskirts of London it was already near empty. I coaxed the car on, trying to think of short cuts and cursing the afternoon snarl of Christmas traffic. A warning sign for petrol was flashing on the dashboard by the time I reached the start of my road. I left Al's car in a space several hundred yards from my house. I didn't want it parked any closer.

I took out the sportsbag, then Al's bag as well. There were letters piled on the hall table, mainly Christmas cards for tenants who had long since left. Only two envelopes were addressed to me. One contained my giro and the other a card from Garth. My flat stank from a carton of milk I had forgotten to throw out. I lit the gas fire and opened the bay window. The room looked small and shabby. I was hungry but most of all I wanted to sleep. I wondered if Al was okay and how long I would have been detained by the police if Luke hadn't intervened. I was grateful to him for getting me away. *I'll make it up to you*, he'd said. He never could, but I had to admit that I'd been wrong about him at the ferry port. If he had simply been using me he would never have taken my place.

The drive home had drained me. My legs were shaking. I kept walking nervously around, picking up objects and putting them down, trying to reclaim my own space. I locked the flat door and put the bolt on. I closed the window and drew the curtains. I took a blanket off the bed and spread it over me on the armchair, even though it wasn't cold and I was still fully dressed. It was too late to cash the giro and there was nothing to eat. I sweetened a cup of black coffee with sugar and tried to remember when I last had a proper meal. Even breakfast on the boat had been vomited up. The coffee only made me hungrier. Al's bags were thrown just inside the door. I kept ignoring their presence, avoiding any decisions about what to do with them or his car. I'd only seen Luke's house once from a taxi but it had been in a maze of similar streets on a large estate. I couldn't just turn up there. I wondered if there was an address book inside Al's bag or some English money to buy food that I could replace when I cashed my giro in the morning.

I hated opening his bag, but there seemed no other way forward. Taking his clothes out made me realise how impossible it would have been for Al to stay here. I fingered his shirts, liking the style of them. A white tee-shirt offered girls the chance of being wined, dined and sixty-nined. There was an assortment of odd socks, mainly unwashed and a pile of dance CDs in a plastic bag. Four sets of underpants were neatly folded. They looked cute and far too small for him. I had to laugh, enjoying getting to know him through his clothes. There were two notebooks filled with terrible rap lyrics transplanted to Dublinese with lines crossed out like; *'I'm a Dublin Dude from The Five Lamps, my heart wants to rock but my foot just stamps.'* Underneath them, at the bottom of the bag, a thick woollen jumper felt heavy as I lifted it out. Something slid from inside it. I put my hand out to catch whatever it was and it struck my wrist, causing me to wince in pain. It clattered against the leg of the bed and hit the carpet with a soft thud. I stared at it, hearing my heart beat so violently that it frightened me. My breath reminded me of a woman I once saw having an asthma attack on the Tube. I was in shock. I almost seemed to be outside myself, watching as I reached down and stopped. I didn't want to leave fingerprints. I wrapped a nightdress around my hand and only then did I pick up the gun.

I knew it had been used to kill McGann. Al had deceived me all along. I had fallen totally for his act. I placed the barrel in my mouth and closed my eyes. It brought all the memories back. A cheap English tart. The barrel was cold as I bit against it until my teeth hurt. I wanted to hurt every Irishman I'd ever known. I couldn't believe the ways I imagined making them suffer. Then I stopped, sickened with myself, and flung the gun against the far wall. I clutched the pillow, frightened the collision would set it off. But it clattered to the floor and I couldn't even tell if it was loaded. I didn't bother undressing. I pulled the blanket over my head, curled up into a ball and cried my eyes out until, somehow, I finally slept.

I don't know how long my bell was ringing or what time of night it was. I was so exhausted I must have been nearly impossible to wake, but finally the buzzing invaded my sleep. I stirred slowly, then found myself awake. My first thought was of how the continuous ringing must be disturbing every flat in the house. I stumbled sleepily into the hall to unlock the front door. I didn't even think to put the chain on or ask who it was. My eyes hurt and for a few seconds I didn't recognise Al in the street light. His face was battered and there was blood running from his nose. He had been leaning forward with his head against the door and his hand on the bell. He stumbled into the hall and instinctively I caught him.

'Jesus,' I said, 'is this what the police did to you?'

'No.' It was Luke's voice. I looked back to see him on the bottom step. 'I brought him here to apologise.'

He climbed the steps, grabbed Al by the hair and shoved

him through my open flat door. Al stumbled over his bag and slipped on to the floor. I stood in the hallway, looking out. I could scream for help but how would I explain the presence of a gun in my flat? I was white with anger.

'How did you find me?' I screamed. 'How long have you known my address?'

Luke ignored the question and kicked Al. I ran into the flat to come between them. Luke grabbed my hands in the doorway. I tried to shake him off but he held them tight, pulling me close to him and kicking the flat door shut.

'You found the gun, didn't you?' he said. 'We were half-way to London before the little bastard confessed. Can this stupid family of mine never fucking walk away from trouble? Al says the gun isn't his, it belonged to Christine which means Christy had it hidden about the house. God knows what the ballistics experts could link it to. Christine got upset during the funeral. She was wandering around drunk upstairs back in the house. Al says she started waving the gun and talking about killing McGann. He grabbed it from her, but people who should never have been allowed near the house saw him with it being chased down stairs by Christine. After McGann was shot those people put two and two together.'

Al stirred as if trying to rise and Luke used his foot to send him sprawling back on to the carpet.

'You stupid little bastard,' Luke told him angrily and then looked at me. 'He claims he didn't kill McGann, he just walked around for hours trying to find somewhere safe to dump the gun, before he heard about McGann's murder on the news and went back to the video shop. But I'm not convinced yet.'

Luke knelt to grab Al by the hair, swinging him around so that he was staring up at Luke's face.

'Why didn't you dump the fucking gun if you did nothing?' Luke shouted. 'You used Tracey. You told me you wanted somewhere to stay, but she could have gone to jail for travelling in that car. Do you know what you get for conspiracy? Now tell the truth, did you murder McGann?'

I screamed as Luke raised his fist and struck Al again. I grabbed his shoulder and he let Al fall and turned to me.

'I love you,' he said. 'I was crazy bringing you to Dublin. I thought I could keep you out of this, I thought I could keep my whole family out of it, but Christy's left a mess behind. It spiralled. I'm sorry.'

He put his hand out to touch my face and I flinched.

'Don't you dare,' I said.

'I did this for you.' Luke pointed at Al lying on the carpet. 'I'd do the same to anyone who put you in danger. I don't care who they are. That's how much I think of you.'

'I know what you think of me,' I said. Luke looked hurt and spread his hands out.

'You can't hold that business in the taxi against me,' he said. 'I had to shock you back to your senses. I had to get to that funeral. The church was like an explosion waiting to happen, gougers and hardchaws hanging about. I could smell trouble. You knew our time was up and you started inventing a cock and bull story about some fiddler you never heard of. Now I know I was out of line but so were you. Love bites are one thing, but deliberately sabotaging me getting to the funeral is another. Don't pretend you don't know well I never meant a word I said.'

'A cheap English tart,' I said, 'that's all I ever was to you. Now get out!'

'And bring him as well?'

I went quiet, staring at Al looking up through the only eye he seemed about to open. He said nothing, but I knew that he realised I had been lying to him. Luke's voice was quieter.

'Look at him. Would I do that to my own nephew over some tart?'

This felt like a nightmare. I knelt to touch the blood on

Al's face. He stared at me and still didn't speak. I remembered Luke's suspicion that Al was a fast mover.

'I never asked you to do this,' I said.

'We had something special going in Dublin,' Luke replied. 'Don't say you didn't feel it too. You didn't want to let me go in the taxi. It's why you made up that story to delay me.'

'It was the truth.'

'Don't keep it up,' Luke said. 'Mac Suibhne never left Donegal in his life.'

'He lived in Harrow for six months. I didn't know him by that name, I didn't know him at all. He abandoned us.'

'Are you sure about this?' Luke asked after a moment.

'Yes.'

Luke was quiet for a time, watching me. 'I'm sorry,' he said at last. 'I always thought you were English. I honestly didn't know.'

I ignored him and stared at Al.

'Did you kill McGann?' I asked and I saw his eyes turn to Luke as if asking how to reply. 'Look at me, Al. Did you kill McGann?'

Al shook his head.

'Do you still want to stay here with me?'

'That won't be necessary,' Luke said behind my back.

'Stay out of it,' I almost shouted. 'Look at the state you have him in.'

'For his sake and yours,' Luke replied. 'Somebody had to teach him a lesson. You don't smuggle guns, especially into England. There's Irish people serving forty years here for being in the wrong place at the wrong time. You would have gone down with him just for being in the same car.'

'Do you want to stay here, Al?' I asked again. 'Do you want me to mind you?'

I tried to block his sight-lines but I could see he was scared and taking instructions from Luke. He shook his head, although I couldn't decide what his eyes were trying to say. Luke leaned over me to grab Al by the jumper and pull him up.

'Give me the keys of his car,' he said.

'How can you drive both?'

'Just put them in my pocket.'

I picked them up off the mantelpiece and did as instructed. Luke was holding Al against the wall.

'The gun,' he said, 'take the gun off the floor.'

'What are you going to do with him?'

'He's my nephew, I'll look after him, like I look after all my family. You're one of them for me now too.'

'I don't need looking after, especially from you.'

'Look at the squalid kip you're living in. I'll not see you live like this. Now pick up the gun.'

I bent down to pick up the gun and aimed it at him.

'I don't love you, Luke,' I said.

Maybe it was fear which made him sneer as I approached. 'Daughters always love their Daddy.'

'You're sick.'

'And you look horny with a gun. Put it in my pocket, go on.'

I could see Al watching. My hands shook so badly that if I pulled the trigger I don't know which one I would have hit. I pressed the barrel right against Luke's ear and closed my eyes, seeing his ear lobe curve into the face of the man in the moon. For half-a-second I thought I had the courage to do it, then I lowered the gun down until I found Luke's pocket.

'Next time I'm going to fuck you so hard for that,' Luke said. He reached down to grab Al's bags in one hand and motioned for me to open the door. He leaned Al against his shoulder and walked out into the hall.

'Don't come out,' he said. 'Get your sleep, you look tired. Christine can get herself blown to pieces with whoever she's running around with if she wants. Dublin's finished for us now, do you understand? What matters is that you're safe and Al can begin a new life here. We're going to start again, Tracey. We'll do anything you want, but I promise I'll make this up to you.'

He hit the timer switch in the hall. I heard the front door open and they were gone. The hall light switched itself off. I stood as though paralysed, without even the strength to close my own door. Finally I heard a door open upstairs and somebody setting out for an early shift in work. I closed my door and turned around. I felt violated. The flat didn't seem to belonged to me any more. Yet there was nothing to suggest Luke had ever been here, except a tiny bloodstain on the carpet beside the wall.

IV

LONDON

SIXTEEN

EVENTUALLY I SLEPT and no dreams came. No people came either that following morning which was Christmas Eve. I thought of going home to Harrow but pride prevented me turning up there. But I knew that every Christmas Eve Grandad Peter collected our turkey from a butcher in Wandsworth where he had grown up. For weeks beforehand Gran scolded him, claiming there were better stores in Harrow and it was unhygienic to drag some dead bird around the tube, but I suspected that secretly she would have been disapppointed if he purchased one locally. Maybe that's why it was one of the few times he stood up to her, claiming that if people didn't care much for tradition any more, it wasn't Christmas for him until he drank a large Scotch in Stan Thompson's butcher's shop.

For years I was always brought along to help collect the bird. He seemed a different man away from Gran, not especially chatty but not needing words to convey what he felt. Even during my worst teenage years I loved walking through Wandsworth with him. Possibly this was because he genuinely lacked the vocabulary to understand my condition. Back then, I often imagined my disorder as taking the shape of a monkey digging her claws into my neck and whispering her disgust at me into my ear. Other people circled her anxiously, watching so closely that she clung to my neck. But Grandad ignored her and if his stoicism couldn't make her vanish, then at least it made her relax enough to clamber down and walk alongside us.

Every Christmas the ritual would be the same: a walk from the station to the house where he'd been born, then on to the pub where he drank his first pint and finally down to Stan Thompson who was his best friend in school. Every time there had been fewer shops he recognised and fewer locals stopping him for a chat. Stan and the other men filled me with chocolates and talked about streets levelled by German bombs, trips to Brighton to see jazz bands and afternoons listening to the Goon Show behind the counter there. But they never made me see Grandad Pete as young. He had remained always himself, solid and sensible, old and yet ageless and irreducibly my friend.

So, just before two o'clock, after I had cashed my giro and been to the supermarket, I found myself getting off the train alone at Wandsworth. The station was packed with Christmas shoppers, as was the street outside. I walked past the new chain stores, knowing that soon Grandad Pete would stroll along here, putting old names back on to each one. I had no plans beyond running into him, but I knew he would insist that I return to Harrow, for that night and Christmas Day at least. I didn't wish to stay longer, but I was desperate to escape to some place where Luke couldn't crash in and nobody knew of him. By bumping into Grandad Pete I could return not as some stray but as his invited guest. Wandsworth was neutral ground, populated by memories which refused to allow recriminations. He would understand I had come half-way by meeting him on his own childhood streets.

I stood across from the house where Grandad was born. Years ago I used to badger him about who lived there now and why he never asked to be allowed to see inside it. 'That isn't necessary,' he always replied. The way he pronounced *necessary* made him seem in command of everything. It was six years since I'd last stood here with him. I walked to the corner and noticed that the pub had changed its name. I almost ran to the next corner, convinced Thompson's shop would be transformed into another West Indian supermarket. But the butcher's was exactly as I remembered it. I even glimpsed Stan Thompson leaning into the window, gathering up a turkey. I didn't venture any closer, I wanted to retain the pretence that I was meeting Grandad by fluke.

I walked back towards the station, knowing he might possibly be inside the pub but it was too blatant to enter. Besides, he would only have one quick drink there for memory's sake. I reached the station and examined the flowers on sale outside. He might come by car, but I knew the ritual was important for him and Gran would never let him drink and drive. For the next two hours I devised variations of the route, hoping to bump into him. Three times I stood across from Thompson's shop, until finally it was dusk and the scene through the butcher's window was framed by fluorescent light.

I could see the glass jars of assorted chocolates Stan always placed on the counter on Christmas Eve. The queue of customers tapered off. The boy who worked for him began scrubbing down the display units. Older customers still came in. They were men I recognised but I was shocked by how old they had become. They went behind the counter as Stan poured glasses of Scotch and leaned against the chopping block to drink a toast while his boy wrapped their fowl. I knew Grandad Pete should be among them, these hours were the highlight of his Christmas. But I couldn't go over to ask about him. I watched from a lit doorway, until something in Stan's glance made me realise I'd been spotted. I turned in embarrassment and had reached the pub before Stan caught up with me.

'It's Tracey Evans, isn't it? How are you, pet?'

'I'm fine, Mr Thompson.' I'd no choice but to face him.

'Were you too shy to come in?' he asked. 'I'd hardly recognise you now you're blonde. I have the bird wrapped and all, but could he not come himself?' Something about me disturbed him. 'What is it, Tracey? Is your Grandad not well?'

'He's fine,' I said, 'as far as I know. Did he not tell you I left home over a year ago?'

'He was quieter all right last Christmas but he said nothing. Still you know the way it is back there, old fellows talking guff.'

'I was hoping I might see him here.'

'Come back to the shop,' Stan said. 'There was a time you used to demolish a jar of Quality Street by yourself. He's bound to turn up before six o'clock, the man never missed a year yet.'

I didn't want to go with Stan. Of all my childhood outings this was the one I had loved most. The happiness of those memories stung me now.

'Come on, pet,' Stan coaxed. 'You look twenty-two going on seventy-five. Wait till you hear the whingeing from the shower of old codgers back there and it will give you something to smile about. Your Grandad will turn up soon, don't you worry.'

The old men seemed so delighted to see me that I felt like crying. They vied with each other to tell stories about events during my childhood I had forgotten and assured me that Grandad would arrive at any moment. Six o'clock came but they seemed unwilling to desert me. They asked each other if anyone had seen him since last year. Finally one man spoke up, whose name, Edward Manners, had fascinated me as a child.

'I could be wrong,' Mr Manners said, 'but you know how my Dorothy married an Irishman. Well, about a month ago, one Sunday night he took me to this Irish Centre off the Edgware Road. Now I couldn't be certain, and he looked so out of place that I thought it couldn't be him. But there was a man drinking by himself, well-soused in fact, which isn't like Pete, and shabbily dressed too. But I remember thinking that from a distance he looked the spit of Pete Evans.'

'What was he doing there?' I tried to control the unease in my voice.

'I don't even know if it was him,' Mr Manners replied. 'But he had his eye on the door like he was hoping to meet someone.'

The men didn't put much store on the alleged sighting. For half a century they had treated Manners dismissively. They were of an age to have more friends among the dead than the living, and only my presence prevented them from speculating about Grandad's health. Stan Thompson was paying the boy his Christmas bonus. I finished the Scotch he'd poured me and told the men I would call to Harrow and bring Grandad their greetings. Stan came back out and produced a large turkey which he placed in a bag.

'Bring this out to the old rogue,' he said, 'even if he has finally deserted me for the supermarkets. It will make him come back next Christmas to pay for it.'

I knew that behind Stan's jest he was worried. I offered to pay for the bird, but Stan waved my attempts away. He reached for the half empty jar of Quality Street and placed it on top of the turkey in my arms.

'Don't pretend they're not your favourites.' He walked me to the doorway. 'You call to Harrow,' he said quietly. 'He's laid up with a flu or a bug, nothing serious. He's a good lad, your Grandad. I know your Granny has a sharp tongue, but you'll want to be there over Christmas, especially with your mother. She used to come here on Christmas Eve long before you. I can still see her as a girl, the spit of you. You tell her Stan Thompson sends his love.'

I couldn't reply. I just walked and kept walking. I didn't care if passers-by could see I was in tears and they didn't care either. I wanted to throw the turkey into the nearest bin. Grandad had never bothered telling Stan that my mother was dead. What sort of man was he and what gave them the right to hunt me down? It had to be him in the Irish Centre. Maybe they had even hired a private detective, because how else could they have found out about my affair with Luke? I felt fury and that old claustrophobia about being watched. Even as a grown woman they had treated my mother like a child. They weren't going to do the same with me. I didn't know how much Grandad knew, but just thinking about being stalked made me feel unclean.

I sat on the train, holding that stupid turkey. When I had set out I honestly believed I would be travelling home with him and it was possible for us all to start again as adults. But I could never go home. Even if they didn't mention Luke it would be torture not knowing how much they knew about my new life. It left no room for the lies and evasions that had always been the necessary currency for survival between us. Besides, they already had a turkey. Grandad wasn't sick. Supermarkets were cleaner and less fuss. As with everything else, Gran had finally worn him down in the end.

In the basement of the house opposite my flat a separated woman lived with four children. One of her sons had an illness which made his bones weak. He had fallen off a skateboard once on to the pavement and she had come running out terrified. We had never spoken but I'd seen her this morning in the supermarket, pushing a trolley when a basket would have done. It held the cheapest white bread and fizzy drinks, slices of picnic ham and two frozen chickens. Her shoulders were hunched as she pushed the trolley as if it was the heaviest one in the crowded store. I didn't plan anything in advance, but when I reached my flat I walked across and down the steps to ring her basement bell. A girl of eight opened the door with *I'm Too Sexy for My Shirt* blazoned across her top.

'Give that to your mother,' I said and handed her the bag with the turkey in it. She stood it up against her jeans and stared. I could hear her mother asking her who it was. I smiled at the child but she refused to smile back. I handed her the jar of sweets and she tucked them under her arm indifferently.

I was walking out the gate when her mother appeared and looked into the bag suspiciously.

'Whatever you're asking we can't afford it,' she said aggressively. I shrugged and walked across the road.

'Listen, I don't even have a tray big enough to cook the blasted thing,' she shouted. But her aggression sounded different now, more like a defence mechanism. I took out my key and opened the hall door. I know she was standing there with the child, staring across. I couldn't decide if I had done right or wrong or which hurt the worse, hunger or pride. But even if she had wished to, I suspected she was too battered to have it left inside her to call out 'Thanks' or 'Happy Christmas.'

People often say if they had a choice they would spend Christmas Day alone, doing routine tasks and ignoring the collective frenzy of good-will outside. But Christmas is as penetrative as mustard gas, seeping unsettlingly into the most sealed of rooms. I stayed in bed on Christmas morning, cursing myself for waking early as if from habit on this morning. I listened to the silence on the street and remembered how I used to run downstairs, with my mother following in a haze of cigarette smoke to laugh at my excitement in discovering that Santa had remembered to take the carrots for Rudolph. Now I could imagine Luke doing the same with his youngest child, before bringing his wife up gift-wrapped jewellery on a breakfast tray.

I cursed myself for being unable to banish him, but I couldn't stop imagining every part of his morning. I became convinced he had made love to her at dawn, either to cloak his infidelity or because thinking of me had excited him. I could visualise the position they lay in and the acts he refrained from because she laughed at him and for which he had needed me instead.

The images sickened me. I didn't want to ever see him

235

again. His last appearance had such an element of nightmare that only Al's bloodstain on the carpet made it seem real. But Luke was capable of calling today. Even while playing with his child, his mind could be calculating how long it would take to drive here and cajole his way into my flat with excuses, the length of time that would leave him to talk me back into bed and how often he could do it and still get home in time to slice the turkey. Later on, when his son was carried to bed and the older children were out, he even had the ability to celebrate his coup by taking his wife again in the kitchen or anywhere with an element of mock danger. I could see him with his zip open and a hand casually straying in his pocket to finger my knickers, which he would have pinched as a trophy from his afternoon's conquest.

Last night I had put the carving knife under the bed. If Luke did call I swore I would use it on him. But really I knew nobody would call because Christmas Day was for families. These fantasies were part of my old self-loathing, manifestations of how part of me still felt I deserved to be treated. I thought I had left my monkey behind, yet no matter how far I ran he still lurked in the distance, ready to clamber on to my neck. I remembered one doctor asking how I could expect others to love me if I refused to love myself. It was three years since I last cut my flesh. Because the outward signs had stopped I'd convinced myself I was cured. But on Christmas morning I felt back at the bottom of the well I used to dream about, gazing towards the distant circle of sky where confident people who leaned over didn't even notice me crouched there.

I thought I had recognised some of that insecurity within Al. I wondered where he was and what shape he was in. Maybe he had just wrestled the gun from Christine. The hand-written lyrics in his bag were so inept that I found it hard to imagine him harming anyone. Although he could have had me arrested I still felt he was essentially decent. Maybe that was my problem. Mostly I believed the worst about men, then the rest of the time I believed the worst lies told by them.

I got up when I heard the voices of children playing across the road. I stood under the shower and turned it on to hot and then freezing cold. I flicked through the inanity on all the television stations before turning it off again. Then for some strange reason, I decided to say a prayer for my mother. I didn't believe in God, or at least not fully, but it seemed the correct thing to do that morning.

I had no idea where the nearest church was. I thought that if I went out I could follow older people who looked like worshippers but there was a worshipper deficit in Islington. Finally I found a church but couldn't decipher which religion it was. A woman was going in but it seemed a crazy question to ask. I followed her into the porch. An organ was playing. She opened the door and I could see people inside, standing up and confidently singing. Even the children seemed to know the words. I would have felt such an impostor venturing in. I took my time walking home, counting Christmas trees in windows and the plastic signs in gardens saying *Santa, please stop here*. I reached the corner of my street. The children were playing outside the house opposite. I waited until their mother called them. I understood pride and couldn't have borne it if she had asked me in.

I flicked through the afternoon films, trying to blank my mind out. I had scored some dope yesterday after coming home from Wandsworth. I rolled myself a strong number but it only soured my stomach. The television was turned off and I was sitting in a ball when the doorbell rang. I didn't jump or raise my head, although I felt the weight of that monkey spring on to my neck. My dawn thoughts were correct, Luke had the audacity to come. He could smell vulnerability and wouldn't go away. The doorbell rang repeatedly. He knew I was in here, curled like a badger in her set listening to dogs and spades. I took the bread knife from under the mattress, although I knew I hadn't the courage to use it. He would know it too. The only person I had ever cut was myself and that was done in secret timidity. I put the knife down and stepped into the hallway. The bell rang again, loud and insistent. He wouldn't even have brought flowers. I opened the front door and found Garth on the step.

'I knew you were in there, sister,' he said. 'You look like death warmed up. Did I never tell you men aren't worth it? I should know 'cause I'm one of them.'

I threw my arms around him. Garth laughed as the embrace continued.

'Try all you like,' he joked, 'but even you will never turn me.'

'Garth,' I told him, 'you're the big sister I never had.'

'That's the nicest thing anyone's ever said,' he replied. 'For that I'm even going to let you cheat when we pull our Christmas cracker.'

He would listen to no excuses. A place was already set for me at the table. For years his mother had been praying he'd bring a nice girl home and I couldn't let her down now. He bustled me inside to get my coat. I protested that I had no presents for his parents and wasn't dressed to go anywhere but Garth would brook no arguments. I didn't want him to. I might be in no condition for company but I couldn't bear to sit alone any more. We walked the half-mile to his parents' flat.

'It's that Irishman, isn't it?' Garth said. 'They always scurry back to their wives, you know.'

'Is that the voice of personal experience?'

'In my case it's worse,' Garth replied. 'They run back to their mothers.'

'Liam isn't still on the go?'

Garth nodded. 'It's tough work though. When I used to dream about long-distance love I had a burly truck driver in mind. But I said to Liam, this Christmas you're coming out of the country-and-western-closet. Go back to Drogheda and tell your mother straight out, "Mammy, I'm a punky-fucky-techno-head and I can't live without singing that sun-kissed dubby vibe".'

It felt strange hearing myself laugh again. Garth kept it up, forcing me out of myself. The lifts were broken. Garth claimed that Animal Rights activists had turned the power off to stymie Santa Claus as a protest against his treatment of reindeer. It was a mystery how Santa has survived this long. He even picked his reindeer on the basis of blatant gender discrimination. There was no role whatsoever for does in his herd except to head off into the town nearest the North Pole on Christmas Eve and blow a few bucks.

We reached the third floor and Garth opened the door. Roxy had called over or still hadn't gone home from the night before. Honor and she were miming along to Boney M's *Mary's Boy Child*, which Garth's mother kept insisting on playing. They both screamed and threw their arms around me, demanding to know where I had been hiding. They knew it had to be because of a man and kept trying to coax details from me. Garth fended them off, nicknaming them the hyena twins. Garth's father, Mr Adebayo, insisted I sit in his armchair and poured me a vodka and coke without asking. This is how life should be lived, I told myself, not with deceit and men arriving covered with blood. I hadn't eaten a proper meal for so long I had almost forgotten to be hungry, but after three vodkas I became ravenous. The most beautiful smells wafted from the kitchen. I didn't ask Garth at what time he had decided to call, but I remembered trying to find a church this morning and I sensed that somehow my mother had sent him.

After dinner Honor ran downstairs to visit Roxy's flat. Mr Adebayo shooed me away from the dishes and Garth and I stood out on the balcony, looking at the lights of North London. I told him as much as I felt able to about my trip to Dublin, but he seemed to suspect there was more I was holding back.

'It's the nature of families to squabble,' he said. 'But that doesn't mean they're not a good thing. Friends can try our best but we're no substitute really. Whatever quarrel you have with your grandparents you should make it up, for Boxing Day at least.'

'They suffocate me,' I said. 'They won't treat me as an adult. Even now they spy on me and follow me around.'

Garth laughed and said I was being paranoid so I told him about Grandad Pete being spotted in the Irish Centre.

'It's a free country. Maybe the man likes drinking there.'

'He has his routine,' I replied, 'he's gone out at the same time to the same pub year after year. Gran wouldn't let him take off somewhere else. That woman has him in her fist and she squeezed all the fight out of him years ago. They won't let me go.'

'What are you going to do about it?' Garth asked.

'I'm going to change address.'

'Then you are still a child,' he said. 'Why are you running away? This isn't how an adult leaves home. Your Grandad isn't some heavy breather, the dude is worried for you. Go up to him and say, "I'm a grown woman and I'm doing okay. This is how I want to live my life, so now you've done your bit, you ain't responsible no more and leave me alone please."'

Garth was right. I had grown up thinking life was something you lived in secret. My mother's life had been a pattern of flight. Even Grandad's visits to Wandsworth always had an air of illegality. We seemed to be a family where nothing could be openly discussed. Our problems just festered and broke out as hidden wounds. I remembered as a girl dreaming that blood was seeping like damp through my bedroom wallpaper. Perhaps it had always been like this, even before my mother's secret marriage. I knew nothing of Gran's life before she moved to Harrow. If my father was Proinsías Mac Suibhne then I wondered what he had made of us in that spick-and-span house.

Was it any wonder that I had kept the shame of the laneway locked inside me, when I was reared to keep my mouth shut? This conditioning had made me Luke's perfect mistress. The thought of confronting Grandad Pete frightened me, but Garth was correct. Even if he knew about Luke it was not his concern. I sipped my vodka and watched the cars below us. The cold air felt good. It was time to start rebuilding my life. If I didn't face Grandad Pete I would spend my life running away. If Luke called I would find the strength to confront him too. I was finished hiding in flats and waiting for snatches of life in cheap hotels. Yet venturing into the Irish Centre alone worried me and I told Garth so.

'Let's switch roles,' he said. 'Liam is playing there this Sunday. I'll accompany you. They'll think we're quite an item.'

I laughed, savouring the irony. Roxy and Honor emerged into the forecourt and waved for me to come down.

'How are you really getting on with Liam?' I asked.

'We're getting there slowly,' he said. 'The last time Liam went home he went for a long walk on the beach and came straight out, no holds barred, to tell the family dog he was gay. From small acorns, you know. Go down to the hyenas and God help any reindeers who haven't made it home yet.'

It was one in the morning when I finally left them. Roxy and Honor insisted on walking me to the corner of my street. There was music from the basement of the house across the road. The curtains were open and I could see the children still up, bouncing around the room happily. There was a tiny package lying in my hallway, badly wrapped in Christmas paper which had been used before. It had been dropped through the letter box. I knew it was from the family across the road. I shook it. There was obviously a cassette inside the paper. I remembered seeing the mother buy one in the supermaket: cheap instrumental versions of Beatles' songs played by some orchestra in Mongolia or whatever country dodged paying royalties. The family hadn't known my name to write on the wrapping paper, but the fact of finding it there, as a gift from strangers, made it seem like the nicest Christmas present I'd ever been given.

I opened my flat door, went inside and pulled the wrapping paper off. The cassette was home-made. A hand-written label read: *'Field recording of fiddle playing and singing by Proinsías Mac Suibhne in a kitchen in Gortahork, made by Seamus Ennis, for the "I Roved Out" programme, BBC Radio Archives, 1957. Contents: The Lark on the Strand; The Rights of Man; The Black Fanad Mare (Nine Points of Roguery); The Knight on the Road (an unaccompanied song); George the Fourth/The Ewe with the Crooked Horn/Highland Jenny; Last Night's Joy.'*

There was nothing else written on the package. My hands trembled as I took the tape from its plastic case and walked to the mantelpiece to pick up my walkman and lower the earphones over my head. I closed my eyes, remembering Luke's hands doing the same in that hotel. But Luke hadn't come here tonight looking for sex. It must have been virtually impossible to locate this tape within the BBC on Christmas Eve and have it copied. Strokes had been pulled and favours called in. Cheap tarts were fobbed off with jewellery. This was Luke's way of admitting he had been wrong. But it was also as if he was trying to give me something else, an identity and recogition that I was more than someone's mistress.

I suspected he hadn't rung my bell when delivering this and he wouldn't ring that bell again. It would be left to me to make contact when and if I wished to forgive him. I didn't want to see him again, but the thought behind his present made me feel good. I closed my eyes and pressed the button for play. There was a hiss of static and then a bow slowly started out over fiddle strings like the brow of a tiny boat voyaging across uncharted waves. Those waves grew as the music swelled, but the boat held steady, crashing through them, propelled by a master's hand. Except that it wasn't waves I saw any more, nor some kitchen long ago in Gortahork.

I could see Luke quietly driving away after he had dropped the tape into the hall, that most contradictory and dangerous of men hoping that I might stumble upon it and stand like this, listening to my father play music and his singing voice, before Christmas night was out.

SEVENTEEN

IT WAS HARD TO BELIEVE I had only been inside the Irish Centre once before. Maybe it felt so familiar because of all the Sundays I had slipped past its door, worried in case someone might recognise me or notice Luke disappearing into the hotel. On my way in with Garth I stopped to look across at the hotel. It seemed far longer than two weeks since I had told Luke there that Christy was dead. I wondered if Luke might be there now, hoping that I would still come. That man frightened me. Even when he stood over Al with clenched fists I had sensed an alertness behind his apparent display of rage. Yet part of me felt sorry for him, marooned inside a life where nothing gave him contentment. I shivered, making Garth promise that no matter what happened he would see me into a taxi to bring me straight home.

I stood for a moment after we entered the Irish Centre, convinced that eyes were registering the appearance of Luke Duggan's mistress. I knew it was ridiculous, there were thousands of London Irish. Very few knew Luke and fewer still would know his business. Yet I still felt the guilty flush of embarrassment I always experienced when returning to somewhere I had been totally drunk in.

There was no sign of Grandad Pete. The ceiling was festooned with decorations and streamers, yet every drinker seemed sick of the mention of Christmas. Posters advertised the New Year's Eve party on the following night. The crowd who had turned up for Liam was smaller than the first occasion I had been there, though some of the older women had still brought along small Christmas cakes and puddings they wanted to give him. I joked about it with Garth who explained that, according to Liam, a singer called Daniel O'Donnell started the craze. Before him, young girls burnt their fingers holding up cigarette lighters and screamed at singers, demanding to have their babies. Older women would shower the stage with unworn Marks & Spencer's bras. But now Irish country fans seemed determined to poison off singers with white sugar and self-raising flour.

Garth had phoned Liam to tell him we were coming. Normally he wasn't allowed near Liam's gigs but, given cast-iron guarantees of my presence, Liam had grudgingly consented. Garth said that Liam had sounded worried. Lately his manager wasn't around as much. Liam had thought this was because of an additional hotel he had bought in Dublin and was busy refurbishing with period Edwardian furniture. But, while home over Christmas, Liam had discovered that two new singers, just out of their teens, were signed to do precisely the same material as him.

There were fewer bookings in January than at any time over the previous two years. His manager passed it off as the usual post-Christmas dip, but Garth said that Liam could sense the Irish rumour factory starting up. It wasn't in anything people actually said or any negative publicity. Ironically, it came from the worryingly favourable comments printed by columnists who normally ridiculed his records. On Christmas Eve Liam's manager had thrown a newspaper on the desk in front of him. *'Liam Darcy has brought a new interpretation to Country & Ireland music, reversing tired clichés and gleaning new levels of meaning from jaded lyrical formulae.'* 'What do you make of that claptrap,' he had demanded, 'I know these feckers are high on drugs half the time but if they throw enough of this shite some of it is bound to stick.' What exactly he meant by 'this shite' was something Liam's manager had left unsaid.

Taped music played before the gig began. Liam appeared

and walked around the tables chatting to people. Off stage he was an everyday wonder. Mostly people gave a friendly nod or shared a joke with him, while some others wanted a kiss or their photograph taken. But, watching him tonight, Liam seemed a lonely and uncomfortable figure. He kept away from us, even when a middle-aged woman at the counter beside Garth produced a card and tried to call him over. Liam kept pretending he hadn't seen her, until eventually a man at a table had to point her out. Liam came across, but by now the woman was hurt and her husband belligerent. Liam thanked her for the card and promised to sing her request, yet his anxiety to get safely away to another part of the bar was palpable. The woman mistook it as a reflection on herself. I muttered that we shouldn't have come, but Garth shook his head as if to say that it wasn't us Liam was having problems coping with but himself.

Every time someone entered I glanced anxiously at the door. I wasn't sure which I was dreading more, Luke's possible appearance or my grandfather's. Tonight I determined to face both of them if necessary. The calendar on my wall ended in two days' time. There would be no more mornings to mark off as I waited for my period that should have come on Thursday. It was too early to give in to fear, I told myself. I was simply late. Precautions had been taken and there was no way it could happen. Liam disappeared back stage. The band finished setting up and now the drummer asked people to put their hands together for Ireland's latest singing sensation.

Liam reappeared and took the microphone. Perhaps it was because I wasn't drinking as much or because I knew something about him, but – although Liam sounded shaky at first – I found I enjoyed listening to him. There was something different from last time, a depth of feeling which Liam himself almost seemed frightened of. The audience could sense it too, as if the singing had slipped free from the shackles of three-four time. I remembered how, one Christmas Eve, Edward Manners, after a large Scotch, had started singing *I'm just a Lark in a Gilded Cage*, and, even as a young girl, I had caught a glimpse into a life of intense, constrained loneliness.

There was an orange juice near Liam's feet which he sipped between songs. I'm not sure when I became aware that it was strongly laced with alcohol. It might have been from the way the band glanced at each other. I noticed that Liam didn't communicate with them any more. They each had their playlist and got on with their job. When Liam sang *A True Heart These Days is Hard to Find* he looked towards Garth, smiling blatantly. The woman beside us glanced around. I was concerned, then realised that her curiosity was mistakenly directed towards me.

By ten o'clock there was still no sign of Grandad Pete. I had brought along an old picture which Garth showed to the barman. The barman laughed and showed it to the girl working with him behind the counter.

'Are you the police?' the barman said.

'Why?' Garth asked.

'We don't get many blacks in here.'

'Do I look like the police?'

'Well, if you were the police you'd know that the gobshite was never going to get what he was looking for in here.'

'You have him wrong,' I butted in. 'I know what he was looking for.'

'Do you now, missy?' The way he said *missy* was derisive. He looked me over and I felt sorry for Grandad Pete. Maybe he didn't know as much as I had thought. I could see the fun the Irish must have had with him, an old man drinking alone, telling people he was looking for a young girl.

'He's my grandfather,' I said.

'Then you should take him home out of harm's way,' the barman replied. 'Because there's no fool like an old fool. I don't know who told him he could come here and expect to buy what he's after. Somebody must have been winding him

247

up. I admit we did the same ourselves, all the lads telling him different places he should look. But what do you expect? The guy is asking to get himself locked up.'

'Stop talking like he was some sort of dirty old man,' I said angrily. 'He's a decent, honest person.'

'I thought he was nice at first too,' the girl who had been shown the photograph said. 'But it gave me the shivers when I found out what he was after. I mean it's so bloody racist, eh? Try the Irish.'

'Some of the lads sent him to the Big Top in Cricklewood,' the barman said. 'They told him to hang around near the gents and ask for a man called Big Tom to see if he could fix him up.'

The girl laughed, then saw that we didn't get the joke. 'Big Tom,' she repeated. 'He's an Irish country singer, sixteen stone and sixty years of age, with a big farm in Monaghan. The idea of Big Tom fixing anyone up is gas.'

She laughed again, expecting us to join in, but it only made me more aggravated. I had never heard anyone ridicule Grandad before. He obviously didn't know anything about Luke. Somebody must have told him I was seen here. I remembered spotting a girl from Harrow in a corner on my first visit here. Her mother lived on the far side of Cunningham Park. I had never known my grandparents to be friendly with her but maybe word gets around when someone disappears. I couldn't feel threatened by him looking for me any more. He had always seemed so much in control that the idea of anyone finding him pathetic horrified me. I knew it wasn't possessiveness which had him stalking these bars. It was concern. I wanted him to come in now, not to scold him but to apologise.

'How often did he come here?' I asked the barman, who now seemed bored and uneasy with the conversation.

'He still surfaces now and then like a bad penny,' the barman replied. 'He doesn't talk much any more, he just drinks himself silly. Maybe he likes the music, I don't know, but so long as he bothers no one it's not my problem. I didn't mean to insult you, nobody here meant him any disrespect but you must admit he was pushing his luck.'

The band had stopped for the interval and the counter was suddenly crowded. The barman moved away to pull pints. Garth was watching Liam push his way in to stand beside us. People let him through, surprised that he had not gone backstage with the musicians. Liam nodded to the barman who broke away from serving someone to pour another orange juice and top it up with vodka. Liam nodded again and the barman looked quizzically at him before pouring a second vodka into the glass.

'Isn't there a dressing room where you chill out with the band?' I asked.

'Fuck them.' Liam took a long slug. Garth had turned his back, ignoring him.

'I thought your manager didn't allow you to drink during a gig,' I said. 'Doesn't it ruin the clean-cut image?'

'Fuck him too, then.' Liam giggled dangerously at the unintentioned double meaning. 'Though Jesus, he's such an arsehole it would be like sticking a sausage up O'Connell Street.'

The woman beside me stared at Liam. Her husband half-rose as if objecting to the language. Liam seemed about to say something to him. He looked animated and almost giddy, his eyes glazed with drink. Garth turned and put a hand on his shoulder. The whole bar was watching.

'I think you should get some fresh air,' Garth said. 'Go outside with your girl-friend and sort out whatever's bothering you.'

It was a lie I never thought I'd hear Garth say. Liam stared at him. I stood up and took his hand.

'I'm sorry I gave you a hard time earlier on,' I said, joining in the pretence and leaning forward to kiss Liam. His cheek was shaded like death. People relaxed around us, animated from the thrill of overhearing us. This was a story with legs.

I walked across the bar with Liam and through the lobby on to the street. We crossed the road and stood in the doorway where I had waited for Luke. Liam was shivering. I wanted to put my arms around him but didn't know how he would react.

'All through the set I was gathering courage for Garth's sake,' he said. 'He's always saying I should do it. I was coming out and the man turns around to fucking deny me.'

'Maybe Garth felt this wasn't the place,' I replied, 'Maybe he thought you might regret it tomorrow.'

'He'd be right,' Liam said. 'Why do you think I've been drinking? I'd wake up scared shitless. But who says it wouldn't be better than this half-living?' Liam leaned against the wall, trying to stop his hands trembling. 'On Christmas night I walked up to the Wavin Pipe factory. I used to be happy there. I never wanted to be a singer, at least not a fucking puppet like this. I'm not even allowed a say in how I dress. Who the fuck does Garth think he is to deny me?'

'Maybe he's like the rest of us,' I said. 'He gets scared.'

'Have you a cigarette?'

I gave him one and lit one myself.

'Working in that factory I thought I knew what scared meant,' Liam said, after a drag. 'They'd all kinds of blind alleys, perfect for a queer-bashing. But I wasn't really scared, because I was nobody, I could always vanish. Now there's nowhere left to vanish to. Liam Darcy, the wannabe star. Once you sign up you lose the person that you were, you become the person they all want you to be.'

I thought of my father hiding from tape recorders in the hills of Donegal. Was that the price of being yourself, or was it another kind of trap, his simplicity or – for all I knew – stupidity being mistaken for enigma? How could my grand-parents have understood him? But even if they couldn't grasp who he was and he couldn't become what they had wished him to be, it hadn't given him the right to vanish.

'I've spend my life living out lies,' Liam said quietly, 'and the one time I try to tell the truth the only person I trust lies into my face.'

'We should go back,' I urged, 'the band will be coming out.'

'Lucky fucking band, eh?' Liam laughed, then stopped. 'They're not even my band, my manager made changes. I could feel three pairs of eyes watching me, reporting back to him.'

'Sing a request for me if you know it,' I said, '*The Knight on the Road.*'

Liam looked at me quizzically. 'I know it,' he said, 'I've just never been asked to sing it. Where did you hear it?'

'Someone my mother once knew sang it.'

The drummer came out to stare across at us. Liam stubbed his cigarette out.

'Now I'm definitely sacked,' he joked, 'because it sure as hell isn't on their playlist.'

We went inside. People were watching, wondering what was about to happen. Garth sat quietly facing the bar. He had ordered another drink for me. I took a sip.

'You hurt him,' I said. 'Liam was coming out for you.'

'He was pissed and besides, I never asked him to,' Garth replied. 'Heroic gestures for someone else are too easy. When it goes wrong you've a scapegoat to blame. If Liam wants to come out let him do it for himself, because he's the guy who's going to have to live with it.'

'I never heard you lie before.'

'We all lie to protect those we love,' Garth said. 'That doesn't mean we're proud of it.'

He turned to stare at Liam as the first song ended. The drummer tapped to give the beat for the next tune but Liam stood motionless at the microphone until all noise ceased and even the band were staring at him, uncertain of what he was about to do. Liam closed his eyes and began to sing. His unaccompanied voice, and the eerie picture it drew, instilled total silence throughout the bar.

What brings you here so late? said the knight on the road.
I go to meet my God, said the child as he stood
And he stood and he stood and 'twas well that he stood,
I go to meet my God, said the child as he stood.

How come you go by land? said the knight on the road.
With a good staff in my hand, said the child as he stood,
And he stood and he stood and 'twas well that he stood
With a good staff in my hand, said the child as he stood.

I turned to spot Grandad Pete at the far end of the bar. He must have entered when I was outside. Surely he had seen us arrive back, yet he wasn't looking towards me but at Liam, as if transfixed by those lyrics. I was scared for him, although I wasn't sure why. He had aged so much that it had taken me a moment to recognise him. Mr Manners was right, his clothes were shabby. He had the look of someone who'd been drinking all evening but still hadn't managed to forget whatever pain was causing him to get smashed. I didn't like him staring at Liam that way. The barman's contempt came back. Maybe he hadn't been searching for a girl after all. Could he have lived a secret life for decades? But why come here of all places? Surely he knew there were gay bars.

Methinks I hear a bell, said the knight on the road
And it's ringing you to hell, said the child as he stood,
And he stood and he stood and 'twas well that he stood
And it's ringing you to hell, said the child as he stood.

There was silence for a moment as the song finished. I had no idea what it meant, only that I had never heard anything suit Liam's voice better. I could see him as that solitary, solemn child confronting an evil presence on a lonely road. The bar erupted into tumultuous applause with only the band looking nonplussed and irritated. Grandad immediately lost interest in Liam and I realised it was the song and not the singer that had fascinated him. I wondered whether he had heard it years before, sung by my father?

Before the applause was over the drummer started into the intro for the next song. The guitar and keyboards joined in, ensuring that Liam took off on no more solo runs. He didn't look around at them but smiled towards Garth and myself, savouring his brief independence. Garth nodded back in salute, holding his gaze. I stared again at Grandad, who sensed someone's gaze on him. He looked along the bar, yet his eyes were curiously dead. At first I thought he didn't recognise me because of my blonde hair, then I realised that he was registering his success in finally tracking me down with numb indifference. I stood up and walked towards him. Garth watched me go, realising who it was. Liam started into the song, his voice more confident now, soaring above the backing band. Couples were drifting on to the dance floor. Grandad watched me approach, then turned back to his drink. I stood with my hands against the back of his barstool.

'You tracked me down,' I said. He glanced at me with neither triumph nor warmth in his manner. 'How did you know I was ever in here?'

'I didn't.'

'Then how did you find me?'

He turned back to finish his drink and lift a finger to the barman for another Scotch. I stood awkwardly at his shoulder, feeling like an intruder.

'You've got it wrong, Tracey,' he said. 'It's you who found me. Why should I be looking for you? You made it plain you didn't want us in your life. You're over twenty-one, so that's your choice. You've been saying you're grown up now for bloody well long enough.'

'But you're still my grandfather,' I said, scared by his tone. I had always imagined I was calling the shots in this game, that my bedroom with the cherry blossom branches tapping against the window would still be there for me.

'You walked out on us with your mother barely dead, remember?' He kept his back turned to me. 'The very time a family needs comfort. You stole her ashes. You knew how much that would hurt and you were hurting people who loved you. But that's all you've done for years, wrapped up in your private world. There's no pain like Tracey's pain. Still, you didn't need to sneak out like a thief, no one who would have stopped you. You've made your choice, girl, so stop following me around.'

The barman put his Scotch down and, picking up a five-pound note, cast an eye over me. 'Your granddaughter found you,' he remarked. 'Maybe she can get her hands on what you're after.'

'I doubt it,' Grandad Pete replied sourly, ignoring the man's sarcasm. He watered the Scotch and drank, still not bothering to look at me. The barman placed the change down.

'What are you doing here, Grandad?' I asked.

'I'm drinking. What does it look like?'

'They said you were after something.'

'The little spy,' he christened me mockingly, then shook his head at his own gullibility. 'A stupid mistake . . . your Gran thought somewhere like here would be swimming in them.'

'Does she know you're here?' Everything about him frightened me. He laughed morosely.

'When did you ever give a fig about your Gran?'

'Is she . . . ?' I couldn't say the word. Somehow I had always seen her as indestructible.

'Sorry to disappoint you. She isn't dead yet.'

'I never . . .''

'Come off it, Tracey.' He turned, resigned to the fact I wasn't going away. 'You spent years inventing new ways to punish that woman until you found the ultimate humiliation. You must have known you'd be seen in Cunningham Park. Somebody even fished the urn out of a bin and brought it

254

back. I had to go down and scoop bits of ashes up with a spoon. Dogs had pissed on them, people walked them all over the grass.'

'I did it for Mammy,' I said. 'I wanted her spirit set . . ."

'Her spirit?' He almost spat out the word. 'What spirit? The dead are dead. The only pain that's real is the pain of the living. Everything else is bollocks. Don't deny you've always hated your Gran.'

I'd never heard him curse before. It was more shocking than if he had struck me. He took another slug of Scotch. Coming here I had rehearsed speeches about the right to lead my own life. Now I couldn't think of anything to say. He was waiting for me to go.

'All right,' I confessed. 'She's a bitter woman, hard on us all and hard on you. Admit it yourself, she's no easy woman to love.'

'No,' he said, 'but any fool could love a saint. That's not love, it's too easy. Your Gran has made my life hell. Hundreds of times I've been like a reed about to snap, but I never have because she was hardest of all on herself. I love her still like I've never loved anyone else.'

'You're frightening me, Grandad,' I said. 'Why did you come here the first time?'

He eyed me, deciding if I was worth the bother. Then he snorted, in self-disgust.

'Prejudice, I suppose,' he said. 'Your Gran meant me to try the Irish pubs around Kilburn. A man in one of them played a trick on me. More fool me to believe him, but I got that from your Gran too, always think the worst of Irishmen. He claimed this place was awash with them. All I had to do was tip the barman fifty quid and he'd point out a table where I could hire a gun.'

I wanted to laugh. Grandad always had the driest humour. He must be winding me up. But there was no trace of humour in his eyes as he stared, indifferent to my response.

'What are you talking about, Grandad?' I said. 'What would you want a gun for?'

'Because your Gran was always scared of needles,' he said. 'She'd never let anyone near her with one. Otherwise it would be easy, I've friends who are chemists still. Thirty seconds' struggle with a pillow would probably do it as well, but that seemed so cowardly. It was a gun she always asked for.'

'You're drunk,' I said. 'Look at the state of your shirt and you haven't shaved either. What does Granny say about you going around like this?'

'She says nothing.' He turned back to his drink. 'She can't speak or eat or even move. She was a proud woman always. I know she can't stand the nurses changing her bag, moving her around like a vegetable. She made me promise years ago that I'd have the courage if anything like this happened to her. It's what she wanted. It still is, I know. She used to say; "Don't leave me lying in some hospital for years. Go down to the Irish bars, they're full of thugs and gunmen. If it's the last thing you do for me, Peter Evans, find yourself a gun and blow my brains out."'

My throat was dry. I couldn't bear to look at his bowed head any more. The hair had greyed around the bald patch on top. It made it hard to see the dandruff crusted into his scalp. The floor behind us was crammed with dancers as Liam sang *I Just Want to Dance with You*. I had seen him sing it the first night I was here and remembered him going down on to the floor with the microphone. This time as Liam left the stage I guessed where he was heading. His nervousness was gone. He knew exactly what he was doing and why. Garth could sense the difference too as he stood up, ready to dance if asked. The band glanced at each other, wanting to end the tune. Phone calls would be made to Dublin tonight. But I watched almost indifferently as Liam reached Garth who put his hands on to his shoulders. Nothing felt real. Grandad Pete turned dispassionately to watch Liam and Garth dance.

'Gay as a coot that singer,' he remarked. 'I think that's why the women all want to mother him. He plays here once a month or so. I think the only mystery was whether he knew himself. Still, he's a fool to dance like that. They love their secrets, the Irish, but it's one thing for them to know, it's another when the truth gets flaunted in their faces.'

A small space cleared around Liam and Garth as people hesitated and then self-consciously resumed dancing. After a few moments Liam broke away and sang the chorus again as he moved through the crowd who stopped dancing to watch him climb back up on stage and confront the band. I swallowed hard and forced enough moisture on to my tongue to speak.

'You can't do this to Gran,' I whispered. 'You don't want to.'

'It's not your concern.'

'You're frightening me. What's wrong with her?'

EIGHTEEN

I SMOKED TWO CIGARETTES in the hospital car park, the name of which I had finally forced Grandad to give me, almost grudgingly, indifferent as to whether I visited her or not. All the way home last night and then for hours staring at the darkness above my bed, I had been stung by the invective in his parting words outside the Irish Centre, 'You've done enough to her already'. The sense of guilt I could understand, but why did I feel such grief as well?

I stubbed the second cigarette out and entered the lobby. It was sixteen months since I had been inside any hospital. Inside it was like a minor shopping mall, with rows of flower and gift boutiques, a coffee dock and a brightly coloured play area. A child listened to the hospital radio station on head-phones as she keyed in a request. There was almost a holiday feel about the New Year's Eve visitors, armed with cards and bouquets and fortitude. What could I bring her? Grandad had said the stroke had left her paralysed and incontinent, able to be fed only by a drip tube through her nose. I chose a spray of white and red carnations, though I had never known Gran to have much time for flowers unless important visitors were expected.

Her semi-private room was two floors up. People queued for the lifts but I preferred to walk. It was a habit left over from visiting my mother, using those extra moments alone to brace myself against the pain in her eyes. I had always been sly in choosing visiting times, ensuring that I never had to share her bedside with Gran. Only when she died had we stood together, and even then I had deliberately remained on the opposite side of the bed. I hadn't had any room at the time for Gran's pain. When I had thought of her, it was as a scapegoat to blame for the grief I wasn't able to articulate. Because I had always presumed I would have sufficient time to make amends to my mother for everything which had happened between us and suddenly I had found that time snatched away.

I came to the glass doors leaning on to Gran's corridor, feeling that this chance had been stolen from me again. Often, late at night, I had acted out scenarios about confronting my grandparents in a few years' time. Normally I would have returned from abroad, having proved myself so successful that they were forced to view me afresh. Some nights only the childish thrill of those fantasies had sustained me in that bedsit. Now I followed the ward signs with a sense of dread. Patients queued in the corridor for a card phone. A man walked slowly in a dressing gown, wheeling his drip alongside him. The door to her room was ajar. I could see Grandad Peter seated by the bed. He had shaved this morning but his shirt were the same one as last night. He sat in silence like a soldier keeping vigil. I felt that if I slipped off and returned in several hours time I would find him in that same position.

I wanted to run but I pushed the door open instead. Gran was strapped into a chair on the opposite side of the bed. I could see her incontinence bag. She was stooped low over the bed table where Grandad had opened a magazine for her. But I knew she couldn't read it. It was just so that her eyes were not staring down at the formica table top all day long. I wanted her to lift those eyes and acknowledge I had come, even though I knew she couldn't, unless by some miracle. Grandad took in my presence without a word of greeting. The other bed in the room had been stripped, prior to being made ready for the next patient. I walked in and sat on the bed between them. I put my hand out to touch her hair. I had been a little girl on the last occasion I touched it or allowed her to hug me. Her hair was soft and fine. Somebody must have washed it recently.

'It's me, Gran,' I said, 'Tracey.'

I leaned down to hear what she was murmuring, but those sounds weren't words or at least not words I could comprehend. They weren't addressed to me either. They were part of an ongoing monologue which she had been struggling with before I entered the room and, for all I know, even before Grandad had arrived. I looked at him.

'Does she know that I'm here?'

He rose and walked around to kneel beside her chair.

'It's Tracey,' he said, staring up into her face. 'Tracey. Helen's child.'

Was this what I was reduced to in their eyes, my mother's daughter? Yet his words didn't sound like a deliberate slight to hurt me. His attention was focused purely on his wife's face where the skin was drooped on one side so that her lip hung down. She moaned something, although I didn't know if it was in reply. It sounded like an echo of the sounds she had mumbled before.

'Tracey's come to visit,' Grandad went on. 'We're all here with you now.'

Gran went silent. Grandad turned the page of the magazine for her. It was an issue of *Country Life*, a colour spread on some big house. A resolute middle-aged woman smiled among the daffodils on her lawn, while a great dane lolled obediently beside her. Grandad patted Gran's hands which had been folded on her lap and rose to stare down at her stooped frame.

I tried not to stare at the catheter tube. I felt sickened. I wanted so many things but most of all I wanted her not to make those sounds again. Her mumbling carried such a register of pain. It was like a scream broken down by computers and relayed in the slowest of slow motions. There was nothing human left in her voice, I thought, and then I realised I was totally wrong. All that was left in her voice was essentially human, with only the decorum which we cloaked ourselves in stripped away. It was a cry of pain at its most naked. For years I had harboured resentment of her. I searched inside myself for any shred of triumph, for which I could despise myself now. But I just felt shock and grief and also a sense of unreality as if I was shielding myself from the scene. If I was watching this happen to someone else in a film I would have cried my eyes out. Grandad stared at me. There was no escape from the question he was about to ask.

'What do you think she's saying?'

'I don't know,' I replied, suddenly scared of him.

'Listen.'

He bent down beside her again as if encouraging those terrible utterances. I didn't want to listen.

'Stop,' I said. 'Please.'

'Inside her head the doctors say she understands every single thing that's going on,' he said. 'If there is a God then why couldn't he have the decency to let her go daft? There's women in nursing homes with perfect physical health except that they don't know if they're aged eight or eighty. Yet he comes along to strike your Gran down and leaves her with a brain as sharp as a diamond. What class of a bastard would do that? She'll never recover. They're not even bothering to try speech therapy. They say there's nothing we can do except wait. And she always had a will inside her like an ox. It doesn't matter how terrible the pain is, your Gran can will herself to do anything, except get better or die.'

Gran moaned suddenly and began to mumble. I wanted to run from the room. I had never heard any sound more terrifying. There was a sequence to the garbled mumbling. You couldn't describe it as a phrase or a sentence, but something was being repeated over and over. I could feel the anguish in her desperation to communicate.

'I can't understand a word,' I lied.

261

'Then listen harder!' His voice was terse and raised. I was a child no longer. Footsteps passed along the corridor. People glanced in and then hurried quickly on, trying to block her image from their minds.

'Was it me?' I asked. 'Did my going away cause this?'

'That's right,' Grandad snorted, 'make yourself the centre of everything. This has nothing to do with you. At least she had some peace when you left. I came home four months ago and found her lying in her own dirt. I don't know for how long, she can't say, can she, or we can't understand. The doctors say she could be like this for years. Soon they'll farm her out to a nursing home, with strangers putting nappies on her at night. Your Gran was always proud, proud of your mother, proud of you. When you ran off she wanted to sit and cry. I could see it, but all her life she had to be strong. She reared two brothers when only a child herself. Her blackguard of a father did nothing except drink himself stupid and beat them. I remember him on Sunday mornings shivering outside the pub in Cricklewood in a stained suit, waiting for it to open and spitting like he was back in the arse of whatever Irish bog he crawled from. A stinking, mean bastard. Your Gran wouldn't marry me till he finally died. She couldn't bear the thought of being given away in church by him. She'd find him lying in pools of vomit and patch him up, keeping him alive. Is it any wonder the woman was always ashamed of being half-Irish?'

Gran moaned again, even more high-pitched and distressed. It made my skin crawl. Grandad knelt to take her hands. She had never mentioned her parents once during my childhood or told me a single story about growing up. It had made her seem like someone who had never been young and all the harder for any child to identify with. I realised I didn't even know her maiden name. Surely I must have asked or perhaps I'd never had any sense of her owning a life before us. We were her life, myself and my mother before me, she keeping us healthy and the house spotless. I stared at her stooped head. The grey hair was shaking. Her father had beaten her. Were there more secrets she had never spoken of? What else had that Irishman done, rolling home drunk when she was a girl? I had never been able to tell her about Dublin. I had remained mute in those doctors' waiting rooms, absorbed in my own guilt, when perhaps Gran, of all people, would have understood? I could imagine her suddenly, silhouetted in the doorway the night my mother brought an Irish husband home, and fearing that another cycle was being repeated.

'I never knew Gran was Irish,' I said. 'Did Mammy know?'

'Your Gran was thirty-eight when she walked down the aisle with me,' he replied, his tone softened by memory. 'She took the name Evans. I said to her, "No one will ever look down their nose at you again, girl."'

'She must have hated my father's arrival.'

Grandad stroked her hands and rose stiffly. I had never asked him about my father before. Indeed, until last night we had never had a proper adult conversation. He had just been my grandfather. Now he was someone I wasn't sure of any more.

'Your father was a harmless enough old codger,' he said eventually. 'Though in some ways I think your Gran would have preferred it if he was drunk or violent. She would have understood what she was up against. But nobody knew what he was on about. Your Gran couldn't make head nor tail of him.'

'What was he like?'

Grandad walked to the window, staring at the car park below in the fading daylight. I looked at the flowers on the bed. It seemed a cruel joke to have brought them when Gran couldn't even raise her head.

'He was old.'

'That's no answer. I was always let believe he was a heartless bastard.'

'She was only your age,' Grandad protested, 'and he got her pregnant. Can you imagine going with some man old enough to be your . . .' He stopped, sickened by the thought, but I sensed his unease. 'You never asked before.'

'I'm asking now?'

'He was nearly three times your mother's age,' he replied sharply, then glanced at Gran, before continuing more quietly. 'Age wasn't the real problem. Deep down, himself and your mother were both cut too soft. Your mother was always the same, a lost soul. But if anything your father was worse, sitting up in the bedroom playing that bloody fiddle all evening. It's all he ever did, the same bloody tune over and over, and your mother thinking he was God's gift because of it. The man was older than me and he'd never worked, except picking spuds in Scotland as a boy. He was a peddler, a tinker. I even found his company too old. He thought *Terry and June* the funniest programme ever. He'd laugh his head off at Norman Wisdom like he'd never seen him before. I don't know if he'd ever watched television. He tried to fit in, I'll give him that, he found a job as a postman. Up at dawn, walking for miles. He was the fittest man I ever knew but he'd give you the creeps and that's the truth. The other postmen were never done taking the piss out of him.'

Gran started to moan again. I saw the effect her cry had on Grandad. He had always seemed so self-contained, but I knew he'd be lost without her. The wailing went on, like a blade grating on a blade. I couldn't decide if she was following our talk. But I'd avoided this conversation for years and now I had to finish it, whether Gran could hear or not.

'Why did he disappear?'

Grandad stared at Gran's bowed head. 'Listen to her, Tracey,' he said. 'Tell me what she's saying.'

'Answer my question.'

'Your father went back to where he belonged. It was the best for everyone.'

264

'Who decided it was best for everyone?'

'For God's sake, Tracey,' Grandad snapped as Gran moaned again. 'They might have called it love but he was a dirty old man to me. I could hear them lying in the bedroom next door, listening through the wall for any sound from us. Your Gran made sure they were never alone. It would have been better if your mother had got herself banged up after a dance in Hammersmith. She was bright enough when she put her mind to it. We'd plans for her, she could have done well. That old tramp had done enough damage. If he'd any decency he would have buggered off himself.'

'He wasn't a tramp,' I said angrily. 'I know what he was.'

'Then it's more than we ever did,' Grandad shot back, just as angry. 'What was he? Had he a job or a house? He'd the daftest notions about the three of you tramping back to Donegal in the depths of winter when you were only a few months old. What sort of life did he think we'd allow you to live? The man was daft, stroking your fingers for hours and saying they were made for a fiddle. The long-winded names he tried to give you, like a fucking Welsh railway station. It was bad enough being Irish, your Gran said, without flaunting it. There were bombs going off a few miles down the road and he wanted to take you all off hawking needles and thread and sponging off strangers in the arse of nowhere.'

'What did my mother want?' I said.

'She wanted what your Gran told her to want. We had to drill it into her for your sake. She wanted what any mother should want, a safe home for her child. She wasn't some flighty girl any longer, she was a mother.'

His voice had risen as if to drown the sounds Gran was making. It wasn't her fault, she was in pain, but I wanted to shake her to make the noise stop. I couldn't bear it any longer.

'It was Gran who stopped us going with him, wasn't it?'

'Can you not see you're upsetting her?' he asked.

'Wasn't it?'

265

'Nobody could have stopped your mother if she really wanted to go,' he said. 'And no one would have stopped him if he'd chosen to stay. He'd a job here and all. Your Gran would have cooked for him, like she cooked for her own father. No one kicked him out. It was he who left her.'

Gran stopped moaning suddenly. The silence was as terrible as the noise had been. Grandad walked over to stroke her hair. I saw how distressed he was, like a man on the edge.

'I have to tell Tracey,' he told her, 'while one of us still can.' He put his forehead down to touch her hair and placed his arms around Gran. It was the first time I'd ever seen him close to tears. Very softly Gran repeated that brief jumble of sounds. 'Stop asking me,' he said. 'You know I can't do it.'

I watched them, linked in pain. Even in childhood I had never seen them embrace like this. I walked over but found I couldn't put my hand out to either of them. I had become a stranger. Gran moaned over and over. I knew she would spend all evening like this, until the nurses got her back into bed, and that tomorrow would be the same and the day after. The same monotonous moan, jabbing at the nerves like a scratched record. I forced myself to kneel and listen. This was the woman who had driven my parents apart, who had set standards and expectations which helped to mar my life. I didn't know if I could really decipher her words or if I was just hearing what Grandad had claimed they meant. But he looked at me, coldly and desperately, as if defying me to deny that I could hear her moan; *You promised to shoot me, you promised to shoot me.*

I backed away, my hands shaking. A nurse came in with a tray of drugs. She left it beside the bed and walked out into the corridor. Gran had gone silent. I knew they were about to change her bag. Grandad Pete looked up.

'Every day it's the same,' he said. 'The sound goes on and on. Even in my sleep I hear it. She's haunting me already and she's not even dead yet. The doctors tell me nothing. I can't

266

discuss it with anyone in case they try to stop me. It should be so easy. Look at the state of her. But I can't do it unless I find a gun.'

'I promise I'll get you one,' I heard myself say. I honestly believed that my offer might be enough to break the spell. Last night he had told me he'd once tried to suffocate her but had been unable to bear her body's involuntary struggle. Surely, when it came to it, somebody who loved her this much couldn't put a gun to her head. But all his life he had done her bidding, no matter how he felt inside. Grandad looked at me in despair for a moment before the nurse returned.

'When did you ever keep a promise?' he sneered.

I could still hear Grandad's scorn as I got on the Northern Line. The carriage was packed with sullen people. I wondered how many of them would wind up like Gran and how many – if they knew their fate – would sooner throw themselves under this train. Nobody should have to live like that. I felt sickened, remembering the way her head lolled as one tube fed into her and another tube slopped out. She would never let me out into the garden with food in my hand and had frowned on women smoking in the street. No purgatory for her could be crueller than this.

It was after six o'clock when I reached Luke's shop but I knew AAAsorted Tiles would still be open. You don't put yourself first in the Yellow Pages unless you're the sort of person to hold monster late-closing New Year's Eve sales. The store was crammed with bargain hunters. I walked along the main aisle and spied Luke through the window of the office, talking on the telephone. This time he knew exactly who I was as I approached. I climbed the steps up and pushed open the office door. There were boxes of tiles on the floor and scattered bunches of dockets and invoices on his desk. I leaned on the edge of it and watched him deal methodically with the details of his business call. I had never wanted to see him again, but who else had I to turn to? I'd seen Luke turn violent on Al and, put to the test, scorn me. His family were criminals and he cheated on his wife. Yet, deep down, part of me still felt that I could trust him. Finally he lowered the phone.

'I want you to get a gun.' I knew if I didn't say it straight out I'd lose my nerve.

Luke laughed quietly and stared out at the aisles of shoppers.

'There's such a thing as foreplay,' he said, 'like "hello Luke" or "Happy New Year".'

'Don't mock me,' I said. 'I'm serious. I need a gun.'

'Why?'

'That's private.'

'You don't need a gun, Tracey,' he said. 'Guns settle nothing. Tell me who's annoying you and I'll have a word with them.'

'I don't want you to have a word.' I wanted to scream that the strongest woman in my life was now dribbling shit into a plastic bag. I wanted him to see how shaken I was. I needed somebody strong to put their arms around me and a voice to drown out her moaning in my head. 'I just want a gun, for fuck's sake,' I snapped. 'I've never asked for anything before.'

'Then ask for something now,' Luke replied. 'Ask for anything but this.'

The door opened and a girl entered carrying a sheaf of papers. She paused, trying to gauge the atmosphere. 'It's important,' she announced apologetically.

Luke glanced at her and shook his head. She retreated reluctantly and closed the door. He sat on the desk beside me and I let him take my hand. It felt good just to talk to someone. Anybody glancing up could see us. He was taking the risk deliberately as a gesture. A round of deliveries was going out. Boxes were being loaded from an open bay at the back of the shop into a van. The driver came around to collect the paperwork. He had a large *A–Z* sticking out of his jacket. He never looked up. The bruises on his face had deepened so much in colour that it took me a moment to recognise Al.

'I wasn't sure I'd ever see you again,' Luke said.

'It's finished between us, Luke.' I took a deep breath and watched his reaction. I expected protests, but maybe my words hadn't sunk in yet. 'I want a gun from you and nothing else.'

'If I gave you a gun, it wouldn't be in exchange for anything else.'

'I know that.' I found the quietude of his voice was calming mine. 'Thank you for the tape.'

'I've a friend in the BBC,' Luke said, refusing to make a fuss of it. He stroked the back of my hand.

'Have I fingers that could play the fiddle?' I asked.

'If you're a Mac Suibhne you must have,' he replied. 'All the family played. Mac Suibhne's father was a hard task master. No one living can play like him. His sons divided Donegal between them, never gathering under the same roof after his funeral. You'd be the last of that family, because none of them married.' He gently scraped the nail of my index finger. 'These fingers weren't made to pull a trigger.'

'I won't be the one pulling it,' I replied. 'Please, if you cared for me you'd help.'

'Is it really over?'

'Dublin finished us.'

'Maybe Dublin changed us, brought things to a head.' He paused but I didn't reply. 'Why do you need a gun?'

'To help someone kill the person they love.'

The tone in my voice caused Luke to put his arm around my shoulder and draw me close. In Dublin I had genuinely believed I loved him. I began to cry as I told him about Gran, while he stroked my hair and let me talk.

'Your grandfather doesn't want to kill her,' he said. 'He just thinks he does.'

'You haven't seen her,' I said. 'If Gran was a dog they'd

put her down. All his life he's done what she's told him to. Nobody would want to live like that. Find me a gun they can't trace, Luke. I know you have the contacts. Grandad won't know where it came from and he'd never give me away to the police.'

'If he kills her, he'll probably kill himself,' Luke said. 'Your family is all you have. Do you want to lose them both?'

I hadn't thought about that. I had just seen their pain and reacted. Yet I couldn't shake Gran's agony from my mind or forget Grandad's scorn. He didn't expect me to get a gun or to even bother showing up again. If I did, it would be the first promise to them I had ever kept.

'I have to see this through,' I said.

I lifted my head from his arm and saw Al in the loading bay, staring up at us. He looked scared. He shook his head as if trying to convey something. Luke turned, taking in his presence and Al turned away to load the last boxes into his van.

'Hiring a gun is like sleeping with a stranger,' Luke said. 'You don't know who the trail leads back to if anything goes wrong. I can't believe it's finished between us, but if you want to walk away I won't stop you. Finding a gun is dangerous, but, if that's the last thing you want from me, I'll do it because I love you.'

I sat in the pub down the road from Luke's shop. A gang of grunge heads were in, tanking up for New Year's Eve. They played the poker machines and shouted across the pool table in an alcove. I wanted to be left alone to figure out which had disturbed me most – the phone call Luke had made to arrange a gun for tomorrow or his repeated declaration of love.

When had anyone last said they loved me? My mother and I were unable to use that phrase when she was dying, and I had never heard my grandparents say it to each other. Even Luke had deliberately skirted the words, until the night he punched Al in my flat. He had made them sound dangerous and possessive then. But this evening he seemed so resigned to losing me that I believed him and found the belief disturbing. Why had he never spoken before, when it might have counted? There were many frightening sides to Luke and yet, perhaps he was the only person who did love me.

Sex had never been the sole lure for either of us. I had pushed the physical acts between us to their limit as a barrier to keep emotions at bay. I had moaned and cried out because I was afraid of what I might say in silence. Luke too, with his hands and cock, had tried to swamp any growing emotion. We had been right to do so, because once we started caring for each other we were doomed. Now even if he did care, I told myself it was impossible to sustain our relationship in the real world. Luke would have to get over me, just as I would eventually get over him. What I didn't know yet was whether there might be new life growing inside me in exchange for an old life we were about to terminate.

I finished my second drink and tried not to think of Gran, blocking all feelings out, except horror at her predicament. I told myself that anyone would want to die, caged in such a crippled body. But I still couldn't make killing her feel right. Initially, it had seemed the brave thing to do. Now I suspected it would require greater courage to simply sit with her, that it wasn't grand gestures which were needed but a mundane everyday sharing in her suffering. If I could talk to Grandad then maybe I might make him see that, but I knew he would view it as me shirking out of another promise. He wouldn't believe I had the will-power to visit her daily and I wasn't sure if I had it either.

Tomorrow she would be dead and possibly Grandad as well. I realised I would inherit everything, unless they had changed their will. But I didn't want their money or to be forced to confront their past in drawers and sealed documents. I needed someone strong to talk to, but it was Al whom I kept hoping might walk into the pub after work.

The grunge heads took turns chancing their luck, then grew sour at my lack of response. They wandered out, sneering about frigid bitches. I remained drinking until ten o'clock. I had no idea if Al ever drank there after parking the van, but I couldn't bear the thought of going home.

It was half eleven and I was very drunk when I phoned Grandad Pete from a card phone off Soho Square.

'I've kept my promise,' I said, 'if you still really want to go ahead.'

He was silent and I thought he was coming to his senses. Then I heard his breath being released and sensed the relief in his voice as he questioned me about practical arrangements. He was going through with it and I was hurt that he wasn't shocked at my being able to procure a gun. What sort of person did he think I was now? The distance in his voice made it impossible to argue with him. I agreed a time to meet and we were both silent. Then, as if sensing the hurt in my voice but mistaking it for self-interest, he added; 'Don't worry, I'll keep you well out of this.'

He didn't use my name and there seemed no warmth in his words. I could imagine him repeating the same phrase to an anonymous criminal. Then, as if on cue but at least with some hesitancy, he asked if I was okay financially. 'Yes,' I replied. I couldn't have borne it if he had asked how much he owed me. There was an awkward pause before we hung up. We both baulked at the absurdity of wishing the other a Happy New Year.

I put the phone down and stared at the cards from prostitutes on the kiosk walls. I remained there until someone came along to use the phone. I didn't want to go home yet, but I had nowhere else to go. I followed the crowds towards Trafalgar Square where the fountains had been drained and boarded off.

Policemen on horseback ignored the jeers aimed at them. The crowds shoved good-humouredly as they counted down the New Year. I felt safe there, another anonymous reveller with nothing to link me to plans for murder. At midnight the crowds surged forward and danced. I found my hand being taken by a Danish boy with a crew-cut. I allowed him to kiss me. I led him on and behaved like a total slut. Only a few months before I had coldly chosen men. Why should I feel bound to fidelity with someone who two-timed his wife and whom I had sworn never to sleep with again?

The Dane took my hand and guided it to his pocket. I misunderstood and pulled back, then realised that he was showing me the tabs of E he had there. He shouted the name of the hotel where he was staying near Charing Cross. I fancied his uncomplicated strength and the fact that he looked so dumb. I wanted to fuck him and just get stoned. Let Luke and Grandad both wait in vain for me tomorrow, I didn't have to go through with being a courier for death. I wanted to go on a spree, unencumbered by responsibilities. But I couldn't because whenever I closed my eyes I saw Gran stooped over that table. I could see the feeding tube in her nose and hear her moaning. I pushed my way with the Dane into the very heart of the crowd. It was dangerous there. I got elbowed in the face and almost slipped under the mass of stomping feet. It wasn't fully over with Luke until I knew if I was carrying his child. One minute the Dane was there and the next I had managed to lose him. I pushed my way free and found a taxi even though I knew it would leave me short of money for the week. But somehow it seemed hard to imagine a future beyond half past four on the following afternoon.

NINETEEN

AT TEN PAST FOUR on New Year's Day I met Luke who was sitting on a park bench near the hospital. Visiting time was over in twenty minutes. Grandad would have washed and shaved and worn his best suit before going into hospital early this morning. He would be there now, waiting. A patient was being moved into the other bed this evening, a woman who'd been allowed home into the care of her family for New Year. This was Grandad's last chance of having the room to himself. I wondered if he had spent the morning talking at Gran, going over their life together or if they had passed these final hours in silence.

I stood over Luke, reluctant to sit down, and warned him that Grandad had said not to leave it too late as the nurses came in with the medication trolley just after half past. I asked if he had fixed a silencer on to the gun, like he had promised, and told him that I'd passed on instructions to Grandad about a pillow being wrapped around the barrel and positioned over her skull. I was talking too openly and too much but I couldn't stop. I knew that if I gave myself time to think I'd never go through with this.

'Give me the gun,' I said, 'and let me go.'

'Sit down,' Luke replied.

'We agreed everything. Now I haven't got time.' If I sat down I was frightened my legs wouldn't be able to get up again.

'He still wants to carry this out?' Luke asked. I nodded. Luke kept silent until reluctantly I had to sit down. He took my hand.

'He should never have asked you to arrange this.'

'I offered.'

'It's all the one.' There were children wrapped in coats and scarfs in the playground nearby. Luke watched them and shook his head. 'This is madness,' he said, almost to himself. 'Your Granny doesn't want to die.'

'She does.'

'No one ever does,' Luke said. 'Not when it comes to the crunch. They struggle for every last second of breath.'

'Just stop it, right.'

'What kind of a grandfather would ask you this? If you were my . . .'

'I'm not your anything, do you understand?' Tension made me raise my voice so that heads turned in the playground. 'You're a bit late with this love stuff. When it came to the crunch I was your cheap English tart,' I said, more quietly.

'I was hassled. Maybe I was trying to deny my own feelings. I didn't plan to fall in love.'

'I'm sorry, Luke, I never needed no father figure before and I'm not looking for one now.'

'You already have a father,' Luke said, 'if you bothered to find him.'

'It's a bit late now.'

'It's never too late. This business with your Gran will be messy, there's no two ways about it. Afterwards you should leave London for a while. Go back to Ireland.' He saw that I thought he was joking. 'I'm serious. If you're really Mac Suibhne's daughter then find him. You've said you left it too late to patch things up with your mother. Your father's an old man and you may never get the chance again.'

'I wouldn't know where to look or what to say to him.'

'Neither will he. It doesn't matter if you both just sit in silence. In an hour's time he's all you're going to have.'

Luke opened his jacket to reveal a white plastic bag in his inside pocket. I knew by its shape that it contained a gun. I

275

reached across and felt the warmth of his body through his shirt. I had my fingers around the bag when he caught my hand.

'Years ago I came out of jail and swore I'd never touch a firearm again,' he said. 'I'm helping to kill one of your family. You mightn't grieve now but you will in time. Make it easier for me, let me bring you to Donegal. I've the contacts to find him.'

'I told you, it's finished.'

'Not like this,' Luke said. 'With a stupid row in a taxi and an old woman's blood being spilt. I couldn't bear if that was how you remembered me. I always knew I'd lose you. I'm asking for nothing else, except that at least you'll remember me as the man who found your father.'

'You've shops to run here,' I said, 'and the business with Christy . . .'

Luke squeezed my hand gently until my fingers let go of the gun. It slipped back into his pocket and I could feel sweat on his shirt and sense his heart-beat inches from my fingertips.

'To hell with them all for once,' Luke said. 'If I dropped dead they'd have to cope without me, so they can cope for a while now. I want to do one last thing with you.'

'I have to go,' I pleaded. 'My grandfather's waiting.'

'Promise me.'

'I'll see.'

It was a quarter past four. I'd have promised anything to have this day over. I reached for the gun, but Luke's grip prevented me. I was suddenly afraid.

'I'm not letting you walk in there with a gun,' he said. 'Give me the room number and I'll deliver it to your grandfather myself. There's no need for you to be involved.'

'No,' I said furiously. 'You're cheating.'

'Guns are dangerous, especially with amateurs. I'll not risk anything happening to you.'

For a moment it was tempting to think of getting on a

276

tube and hearing about it on the six o'clock news. But I couldn't run away, I had to be there. I argued furiously but I couldn't get the gun off him. I had only twelve minutes left when I finally agreed to compromise. I would walk ahead and he would follow with the gun from a distance. I left the park and ran across the hospital car park to take the stairs hurriedly, knowing Luke was somewhere behind. Already this business was going wrong. My nerves were raw. I kept hoping the other patient might have arrived early and the room would be full of visitors.

Gran's door was closed. I hesitated and saw Luke appear at the end of the deserted corridor. He had a hat that would block out his features on the security cameras. He had taken gloves from his pocket. I had planned to argue and plead with Grandad, now I knew there wouldn't be time. I pushed the door open and entered. Grandad sat quietly beside Gran who was strapped into that same chair. He looked at me with a silent question. I'd never seen him in so much pain. The door opened behind me and Luke entered.

'Who's he?' Grandad Pete asked suspiciously.

'I'm with Tracey.'

Grandad took in Luke's accent and his age. 'Like mother, like daughter,' he said sourly.

Gran was silent, her face slumped inches from the bed table. There were old family photographs jumbled up in front of her eyes, snaps of Christmas mornings and summer evenings in the garden. I could see myself there as a child and my mother as a girl before me. I knelt to look up into her eyes, trying to convince myself again that this was what she wanted and that it was right. It was as horrifying to see her condition today as yesterday. If our roles were reversed I would wish to die. Luke closed the door and looked at Gran, shocked by her appearance.

'Tracey was right,' he said. 'The woman's a vegetable. Killing her might be a mercy.'

'What are you doing here?' Grandad asked angrily.

'I'm the man with the gun,' Luke said. 'Now I want to know your intentions?' It was the ultimate black joke, hearing my lover ask my grandfather this question.

'What do you mean?' Grandad asked belligerently.

'Are you going to top yourself as well?'

'That's none of your business.' Grandad glared at me, furious at my bringing him here.

'It is, pal. I need to know whose blood is on my conscience. Little people like you get a gun into their hands after fantasising for years. Next thing they're like a kid with an erect cock, pumping it into everything in sight. How do I know you're not going to take your bitterness out all over the hospital so that we have another Dunblane on our hands?'

'Grandad isn't like that,' I said.

'He's just a quiet family man,' Luke sneered 'The very sort to go berserk at one sniff of power. Quiet family men don't murder their wives.'

'It's what she wants,' Grandad retorted. 'Now leave the gun and go. I'll pay whatever money you want.'

'You don't know what she wants,' Luke said. 'She might be singing "Chitty-Chitty-Fucking-Bang-Bang" for all you can tell. If she told you to jump in the Thames would you do it?'

'Yes.'

The brevity of Grandad's reply silenced Luke, who looked at Gran again.

'All right,' he said, 'but let's get Tracey safely out of it. Even you don't want her going down as an accessory.' Luke looked at me. 'You've done your bit, Tracey, go home. There's no cameras on this corridor. You visited your Gran. Your Grandad was alone. He told you nothing, you saw nothing. Go on now.'

'You leave the gun and go with her,' Grandad told him.

'I'll see this through,' Luke said. 'When Tracey goes I'll

give you the gun. With the silencer and the radio playing no one will hear you. There's two bullets. If you want to plug her twice that's your business. I know a back way out of here. Now it's twenty-five past. Decide if you're going to turn her into a stiff or not.'

'Don't tell me what to do with my wife,' I heard Grandad say but I wasn't looking at the men. I kept staring up at Gran's face, hoping she would give some sign.

'She's a vegetable. Now are you going to plug her or not?'

'Don't talk about her like that,' Grandad snapped. Gran blinked and opened her mouth as if about to mumble, but her lips just stayed open, forming an involuntary O. Luke knelt beside me and stroked her face.

'She must have been a fine looking woman, yet you seem certain this is what she wants,' he said. 'Maybe you haven't the balls to do it.'

Grandad stretched his hand out and Luke gave him the plastic bag. I squeezed Granny's hand as Luke took my shoulder and drew me up.

'You've done your bit, Tracey,' he said. 'You don't want to see this. Walk out now and keep walking.'

'I'm going nowhere,' I said, putting my back against the door. 'I'm not leaving you two together.'

Grandad turned the radio on loud and took the gun out. It was smaller than the one in Al's bag and the silencer made it look comic.

'Move away from my wife, mister,' Grandad ordered. Luke stepped back and turned to the window, leaving Grandad to get on with it alone.

'It's what you always said you wanted, Lily,' Grandad said. 'I can't bear seeing you in such pain any longer.'

Gran suddenly began mumbling that phrase over and over, but it wasn't clear to me any longer what it meant. Grandad had taken a pillow and placed it tenderly over her hair. His hands trembled so badly that I wasn't sure if the bullet would miss. Luke turned to watch.

'Hold the pillow firm,' he advised. 'That way there's less chance of her brains being splattered everywhere.'

'Will you shut the fuck up, mister!'

Grandad controlled his shaking enough to point the pistol down on to the pillow, aimed directly into her head. It was three minutes to half-past. Anyone could come in. He closed his eyes and tried to squeeze the trigger. But he couldn't do it and finally the pistol slipped from his grip and clattered onto the ground. His head sank down to rest on the pillow on top of her hair.

'I'm sorry, Lily,' he said in tears, 'I've failed you.'

I knelt to retrieve the gun and looked straight up into Gran's face. She only had that one expression which was impossible to read.

'I tried,' Grandad told her in anguish. 'I haven't got it in me.'

Gran's eyes were suddenly still, her pupils staring into mine. How often had I wished her dead in adolescence, cursing her perpetual humiliation of my mother and her second chance quest for a perfect daughter through me? I tried to recapture my hatred and substitute that bitter, formidable woman for the broken creature in this chair. Surely just for once I could do something right? I tried not to give myself time to think of the consequences. I lifted the gun and aimed. She was slumped forward, chained like a half-dead animal. This wasn't revenge, it was a mercy killing. Nobody should be forced to vegetate like this. Grandad saw what was happening and stepped back, with one palm open wide. I couldn't decipher what he was trying to say. My hands were shaking. I closed my eyes but I couldn't do it either. I felt Luke take the gun from my hands and I was so relieved it was over.

'People think they could kill,' Luke said quietly, 'but it's never easy. Especially with someone you love, no matter how much pain they're in. Such things are better done by a stranger. Somebody has to release her.'

He reached for the pillow and, placing it to her head, aimed the gun firmly into the centre of it. Both Grandad and I screamed at the same time and threw ourselves forward. We clawed at Luke but were too late to prevent him squeezing the trigger. There was a hollow click before Grandad sent him flying against the wall and flung his arms around Gran. I put my arms around the pair of them, shaking and crying with relief that she was safe. A nurse opened the door to look in. Luke had risen to stand with his feet blocking the gun.

'Is everything okay in here?' she said.

No one replied. She walked away but left the door open. Luke knelt to open the gun. He opened it in front of Gran to show her the empty chambers and stroked her face which was wet with someone else's tears.

'You're a very lucky lady,' he told her. 'Not everybody gets to find out how much their family loves them.'

Grandad stared at Luke but said nothing. I stepped back, unsure of whether they wanted me to hug them, but Grandad reached his hand back to find mine and squeezed it. I looked at Luke, not sure of what I felt for him. I couldn't decide if he had played me for a fool. Then he took a hand from his pocket to show me three bullets nestling in his palm. If we still wanted to go ahead, I knew he would have loaded the gun properly for us this time.

How did he seem to always know what people wanted, even when they themselves didn't? Your family is all you have, he had said, and calculated this situation deliberately to bring us to the brink and made us look beyond it. I stared at him.

'Donegal,' he said quietly. 'It's up to you. Phone me when you decide.'

The nurse came back in with the trolley. 'How is Mrs Evans today?' she asked cheerfully.

Grandad raised his eyes again to follow Luke's movements as he walked towards the door, leaving us alone.

'She's just fine,' Grandad replied. 'Now she has her family around her.'

The following day I finally returned to Harrow. Ice had frozen over the pond overlooking Northwick Park hospital. I sat in the coffee shop, in the same seat as on the morning my mother had died. I stood again at the window on the bend of the stairs where I had looked out, numbed by her death, and touched the glass pane as if only now unlocking that grief. I sat in the hospital chapel and cried the tears I had been unable to shed back then. I felt good for crying and younger than I'd felt for years. It was like starting a new life again after the horror of that scene in the hospital.

But maybe it wasn't only a new life for me. I was six days overdue. For the hundredth time I went over that morning in Dublin after Luke pushed me from the taxi. Alone in the hotel and still in tears, I could recall popping the contraceptive pill from its card and holding it in my hand when the night porter arrived unbidden with breakfast. I hadn't wanted to swallow it in front of him. I remembered the feel of it cupped in my palm as the man lingered, anxious that I was all right. Surely I had swallowed it instinctively after he left, but I'd no memory of doing so. I wondered could I have dropped the pill on the tray beside the toast I was too upset to eat? I had felt so cheap after Luke's remark that I even wondered if it could have been my subconscious revenge upon Luke or myself? I was scared now, I had even looked up the numbers of abortion clinics. But I didn't want to think about decisions until I'd had a test done.

I let myself into my grandparents' house with my old key. The place smelt musty and unkept, even though the breakfast dishes had been washed and left to dry. But the oven hadn't been used for weeks and dust and cowbebs had finally conquered the shelves and high corners. The rooms seemed smaller than I remembered. I knew Grandad Pete wouldn't be home from the hospital until six, but I wasn't really sure what I planned to do. The previous evening I had remained in the hospital for a time after Luke left, but neither of us seemed able to mention what had almost occurred. When I rose to leave Grandad had said: 'Thank you, Tracey,' and I realised it was the first time since we met again that he'd used my name. I thought of cooking him a meal, but the kitchen cupboards were almost bare. I sat in the drawing room for a long time before I dialled the number of Luke's store.

'Hello, AAAsorted Tiles,' a .voice at the far end answered.

'Is Luke there?' I asked and there was silence for a moment.

'Trace?' The voice dropped to a whisper I recognised. I almost put the phone down. Just now Al was the last person I wanted to talk to.

'What are you doing working for him?' I asked. 'You said you wanted to get away from your family?'

'What choice had I? I've no money and nowhere else to stay.' The hint of an accusation infuriated me.

'That isn't my fault.' I said. 'I didn't leave you alone in a car with a loaded gun.'

'It wasn't like that.'

'I could have gone to jail because of you.'

'You sound like your "father",' Al sneered.

'I never set out to deceive you. Luke invented a pack of lies and I had to play along.'

'Why?'

'You're over twenty-one, Al. Figure it out for yourself.'

'I just couldn't believe it,' Al said quietly. 'You and Luke. What could you see in that fellow?'

'That's my business.'

'He wants you to go away, doesn't he?'

'I never told him I was going.'

'But you are, aren't you?'

'It's finished between us.'

'Don't kid yourself,' Al said. 'Where's he bringing you?'

'That's my business.' I was hurt by his tone.

'Where?' His voice was taut.

'Donegal.'

'Don't go with him, Trace. Put a stop to it.'

'This is a stop to it,' I replied. 'And I'll go where I like. At least I can trust him to mind me, which is more than you did.'

'He thinks we slept together,' Al said. 'That's why he beat me up.'

'He knows we never slept together. He lost his temper when he found out about the gun. You should have dumped it in the Liffey. I can't trust you any more. I . . .'

There was a click at the far end. I was infuriated, thinking Al had hung up rather than face the truth, but then I wondered if somebody had walked into the office. I didn't want to cause more trouble and decided to wait before phoning back. Al was right, I had decided to go, but I wondered how he knew what Luke was planning. I stared around the drawing room, trying to figure out what was different. Something was missing. Normally there would be a Christmas tree and decorations but it wasn't that. After five minutes I redialled the number and Luke himself answered.

'It's me,' I said.

'How is your grandfather?'

'Shaken. I haven't seen him today.'

'He's a lonely old man, scared of having to cope on his own,' Luke said and paused. 'I would have given him the bullets if that was what he really wanted.'

'I know.' I waited a moment, not wishing to make it sound like a favour in exchange. 'I'll go away with you if you still want.'

'You don't have to.'

'I want to.'

'Then let's go tomorrow,' Luke said. 'We can fly from Stansted at nine in the morning. I know it's soon, but the more notice I give people the more roadblocks they put in my path. They're used to me flying to Europe to buy tiles at short notice.' He paused, uncertain if I was still there. 'Tracey?'

But I was only half-listening. I had just realised what was missing from the dining room: it was me. The photographs of my few achievements were gone. Even the cheap plaques I had won in school races had been thrown out.

'The sooner the better,' I said, 'I'll meet you at the airport.'

I put the phone down and walked into the sitting room to discover it was the same there. All that remained was my absence, hinted at by a succession of slightly less faded squares of wallpaper where picture frames had once been. It made me feel like an intruder. I was hurt. I wanted to leave at once. I checked the rooms for any sign that I had called today. A small porcelain dog stood on the mantelpiece. As a child I had loved the way his head was cocked but I was never allowed to hold it. I picked it up now and stashed it away in my pocket. But I don't think I did it for spite. Either I wanted a keepsake of this place or else I felt a need to leave an absence to match my own on the wall, a token for Grandad to decipher. I had my coat on and was walking down the hall when the front door opened. We stood for a moment observing each other cagily.

'I let myself in,' I said. 'I didn't think you'd mind.'

'No.' Grandad stared at my coat. 'Were you going or staying?'

'I don't know.' I was more embarrassed now than annoyed. 'I had sort of thought that maybe I might cook you something but there's not much in the kitchen.'

'No. The canteen in the hospital isn't bad really. Your Gran never liked me under her feet in the kitchen.'

We were still wary and unsure of each other. But any hostility was gone from his voice. He seemed more like the

285

grandfather I'd grown up with, yet I knew that neither of us were those people any more. I fingered the china dog in my pocket. Why shouldn't they remove my photographs when I had walked out of their lives?

'I could do you scrambled egg on toast,' I offered.

'That would be lovely.' He sounded so grateful that I knew he was pleased I'd come. 'But I don't know how long the eggs have been there.'

'Beans on toast then. Baked beans never go off.'

'No. You could take baked beans to the moon and back.'

He smiled and I remembered afternoons in the alcove in his shop when we would invent imaginary journeys. I saw myself again, in yellow wellington boots, crouched in a cardboard box with a plastic lunch-box on my head as Grandad counted down the seconds to take off before the bell announced a customer's arrival. The shop had been his kingdom. He hadn't wanted to retire except that Granny pushed him to accept the chainstore's offer to buy him out. She had been right, though, if he had refused they would have simply opened a rival store and priced him out of business. He'd received a lump sum for good-will, but had never lost that bemused look since, like the dispossessed monarch of some obscure statelet whose former name nobody could remember how to pronounce.

'I'll set the table for you,' he said, closing the front door as if he would love to bolt it. Normally we ate in the kitchen but I noticed that he was setting the dining room table. He took out the china normally reserved for visitors, but the gesture wasn't meant to make me feel an outsider. It was his way of trying to make the meal special. The bread was stale but it seemed okay toasted. It felt good to cook for somebody else again. I wanted to give him food to match the occasion, but all I could find was an unopened Swiss roll, one tin of skipjack tuna and one of salmon. I choose the tuna, made a pot of tea and brought everything in on a tray.

'Tuna and beans on toast,' I announced, transferring it on to his china plate. We stared at each other and laughed. The scene had that illicit sensation from childhood. We were both thinking what if Gran could see us now, eating tuna and beans on toast off china plates on her best tablecloth.

'This is lovely,' he said. 'Food always tastes nicer at home.' He went into the kitchen and returned with two cans of beer. 'Do you want a glass?' he asked.

'No.'

He opened a can and handed it to me, then opened the other for himself. We laughed again, like children.

'We could have had tinned salmon if you preferred,' I said.

'Don't tell your Gran, but I always hated tinned salmon,' he replied, sharing a secret. 'For some reason she still thought it was posh, but I developed a taste for the real thing as a boy when my Dad worked down the Billingsgate fish markets. Sometimes fish walked out of there under the supervisors' noses, wrapped in old newspapers.'

'Real salmon,' I said.

'So fresh you'd think it was going to start floundering around on the table. But the real treat, though it only happened twice, was when my Dad brought a whole turbot home. A beautiful fish. You rarely see it on sale now.'

'I never heard you talk about your father before,' I said.

'I never thought you'd be interested.' He took a bit off his plate. 'This is lovely. I can taste it. Everything else has tasted like sawdust since your Gran . . .'

He stopped and put the fork down.

'It must be hard alone,' I said.

He looked away, putting his hand to his forehead to disguise his distress.

'I don't know what you must think of me, Tracey,' he confessed. 'Yesterday was a nightmare. But for months that business was like a madness gnawing away . . .'

287

'Stop,' I said, 'please.' I couldn't bear to see his head bowed. 'It's over, Grandad.'

'I know. Your friend burst all our bubbles.' Grandad sat back and I thought of all the evenings he must have spent here alone. He tried to smile. 'I would be lost without that woman.'

'You would, Grandad.'

'I never thought you'd offer to get a gun. What I really wanted was for you or someone else to talk me out of it. But when you offered, I thought it must be the right thing to do if Tracey isn't shocked.'

'I was shocked,' I said. 'I just didn't want to let you down again.'

'We're a pair of fools, girl,' Grandad said. 'But an old fool is always worse.'

'I was never much use to you, was I?'

'You lit up this house as a child.' He began to eat again, as if cloaking his emotions, then looked up. 'They're flexible about visiting time, but I try not to be in the way. She's much the same today as she'll be until she dies.' He took a sip of beer. 'I might have imagined it though, but she seems more content.' Grandad looked towards the drinks cabinet, as if used to having something stronger when he was alone. 'I talk to her a lot. It's the first time in decades I've really been able to talk to her.' He took another swig, then stared at the can. 'Lily wouldn't like us drinking from a can.'

'It's nicer from a glass,' I agreed and he looked relieved. He had spent his life caught in cross-fire.

'You don't mind if I use one?'

'I'd like one too. But there's tea made as well, don't forget.'

I could see he enjoyed being scolded. He came back in and poured our beers into glasses. He leaned slightly forward, then stopped. I suspected he had been about to lift his glass in a toast of 'Welcome home'. We were wary again, neither of us on firm ground.

'Will you go and see her again?' he asked.

'I don't know.' I searched for a softer way to phrase it. 'It's not because we never got on, I just don't know if I can bear seeing her again. I'm such a coward, but it scares me to death thinking about her.'

'Don't be ashamed,' Grandad said quietly. 'She is frightening, with that stare and the way she can't talk back. I see her every day and part of me still wants to run away.'

We ate in silence for a while. I poured him tea and he reached for a piece of Swiss roll.

'Why all the long faces?' he said, trying to cheer me up. 'Lily wouldn't want us gloomy. I always say you can't go wrong with a Swiss roll.'

'Remember you used to tell me that rabbits rolled them in their burrows up in the Alps.'

'I did not,' he said, but I saw his delight that I remembered.

'You did too. And the burrows were so high up that there were no roads and so storks had to carry sackfuls of cakes down in their beaks. You were an awful liar, do you know that?'

'I still am.' He was smiling and then he stopped to stare at me. I realised he was watching me smile. How long was it since he'd seen me smile? Certainly not during that final year when my mother was in and out of hospital and I fell back into missing lectures and drifting through college, hiding the fact that the supervisor had informed me I was on my last chance. I never discovered just how long they had known she was terminally ill before they told me. I could remember Gran's words: 'You seemed to be doing so well that we wanted to wait until you'd finished your exams'. My smile vanished. I saw Grandad glance at my clothes which were clean but faded.

'What are you doing with your life, Tracey?' he asked, more bemused than prying.

'I'm trying to live it.' The old defensiveness crept into my voice.

'Are you studying or working somewhere?' He knew the answer by looking at me. 'It seems a waste. You always had brains to burn. Are you okay for money?'

'I can look after myself.'

He wanted to say something, but stopped. He was an old hand at recognising the buffers I could draw down in front of myself. I glanced at the unfaded squares of wallpaper.

'It didn't take you long to forget me.' I was sniping from instinct, knowing that Gran would have launched a counter attack. But he followed my gaze and shook his head.

'It wasn't meant that way,' he replied. 'Things happen in life and we cope by pretending that time will sort everything out in the end. It never works like that. We weren't forgetting you, we were trying to let you go. I said to your Gran; "Those photographs aren't Tracey any more. We must stop thinking of her as a little girl or we'll fall into the same trap if she ever comes home." They're not thrown out, they're in your old room. Have you been up there?'

'No.'

'Everything is still there. You've got good clothes in the wardrobe that you could . . .' Grandad stopped. He didn't want me to take them away. He wanted me to stay but didn't know how to ask. 'Do you live with your Irish friend?' he asked.

'No.'

'He's married. I could tell. Are you his mistress?'

'That's my business!'

Grandad said nothing. He hadn't been judging me, he was just concerned. But nothing in this house had taught me how to be open. It wasn't easy now.

'I was his mistress,' I said. 'I don't know any more.'

'He's a shrewd man but cold inside. He brought me to my senses yesterday, but I can't say I liked him.'

'I pick my own friends.'

'You're a big girl,' Grandad replied. 'Nobody can pick them for you. But some people know too much for their own good.'

'About what?'

'Everything. I should never have dragged you into this business, but it's hard not to be bitter. You see, Tracey, I'm just no good on my own. I can put up with anything except loneliness. I stay up half the night because there's no one telling me to go to bed. I do stupid things, I've got into fights in pubs. I lie awake with crazy thoughts and they take hold because there's no one to banish them.' He stopped, flustered and repeated the phrase, like he'd said it to himself a thousand times in empty rooms; 'I'm just no good on my own.'

I understood that loneliness, its ache had consumed me on dozens of sleepless nights in my flat. With someone to talk to I wondered if my obsession with Luke would have grown. At some level at first I'd been screwing him for companionship.

'I have my own life now, Grandad,' I said quietly.

'I know.' This conversation was embarrassing him. 'I didn't mean that I wanted you . . . I just meant if you ever felt like calling.'

'I will,' I promised, 'often.'

'Harrow is out of the way.' He was anxious to let me off the hook. 'It's awkward for any young person to get to.'

'I'm going to Donegal tomorrow,' I said. 'My father is still alive. I want to find him.'

'Is your friend bringing you?'

'You don't approve.'

'What difference would it make?' He shrugged, with self-deprecation. 'I knew from the day you were born that you were stuck with your mother's looks and your Granny's bull-headed stubbornness. That was the problem between you both, although neither of you could see it. You were two sides of the one coin.'

The idea sounded so daft that I laughed. 'Me and Gran, are you joking?'

'Once either of you got a notion nobody could never tell you anything.'

'Mammy must have taken after you then.'

I wanted to make him smile, but instead he reached across to open the drinks cabinet and produced a bottle of Scotch.

'That would have been hard.' Grandad poured himself a measure, then poured another on top of it. 'There's something you should know,' he said. 'Don't get me wrong, I was always proud to call her my daughter, but I couldn't have a child of my own, though it wasn't from lack of trying.'

He took a long sip of Scotch. The glass rattled against the side of the plate as he put it down. He watched me, unsure of how I would take this news.

'I don't know what you mean,' I said.

'Perhaps you shouldn't be asked to. I've never known if secrets are better left unsaid. I think it was you that your Gran would have told eventually. Your mother wouldn't have been able for it. Obviously I knew she was someone else's child, I didn't mind that so much, but it was years before Lily told me. It was on a train, a funny place to tell anyone anything. There was one other passenger in the carriage. He got off at Gerrards Cross. We were alone. Your mother was two years old, playing with a doll beside us. Lily told me everything. Then two women got in at Beaconsfield and we couldn't talk any more. We never mentioned it again.'

He took another sip of whisky. His hand was trembling. This man isn't actually my grandfather, I thought, Evans isn't my real name. I remembered how proud he always was of me on those trips in Wandsworth. He started speaking again, but it was hard to focus on what he was saying. It sounded like even he was still struggling to comprehend the words.

'The bastard's brain must have rotted with drink,' Grandad said. 'The thing is, he was old but still strong as an ox. Lily was the only one who bothered with him. She was already a grown woman, even past her prime. For years I'd been hanging on, wanting to marry, telling her to leave her father. She'd the right to a life of her own. She had ambition, brains, she could have . . .'

Grandad took another drink. I didn't want to hear any more but there was no way to stop him.

'She'd hide her wages, but he'd find them, no matter where. He'd sell anything she brought into the house, even her new clothes so that half the time she'd only old dresses to wear. Neighbours would scold her, saying "Your father called. He says you won't feed him. I gave him rashers and sausages to cook myself." Lily would have to show them the uncooked rashers and sausages in the bin and explain that he had been trying to cadge money off them. The bastard stripped away every scrap of pride she had, any chance to hold up her head. I hated him, but I haven't got it in me to believe that he knew it was his own daughter he was attacking. I mean, sometimes he'd be raving like he didn't know if he was in England or Ireland. But even if he's drunk paint stripper, no man deliberately rapes his own daughter. Not when they've given their life to minding him.'

'I don't believe this,' I said, 'I can't believe it.'

Grandad poured himself another Scotch and looked at me with the bottle raised. I could have used a drink badly but, until I had the pregnancy test done, I wasn't sure if I should be drinking.

'Is it any wonder your poor mother was for the birds,' Grandad said. 'I'm not knocking her, I loved the child. It wasn't her fault. But I think that every time your Gran looked at her . . . well, you'd see him come out in little things, the shape of your mother's nose and the way she smiled sometimes. She could have had an abortion, even then they weren't hard to come by. But that was the thing with your Gran, she saw things through. She believed you worked hard, you rose from what you were and you never looked back. If you didn't get the things you deserved, then your children did or their children after them. The way she kept this house, the way she pushed both of you, it seemed like snobbery but it wasn't, or at least it wasn't just that. She was naive. She'd never set foot outside England in her life, but he'd bred it into her, so that at heart she was always still an emigrant with emigrant dreams.'

Grandad stopped talking. The curtains weren't pulled and I could guess at the outline of the garden beyond the window. But it was Gran I saw as I looked into that darkness. I saw the way her eyes had stared at me, strapped into that hospital chair, with her secrets locked away behind her garbled tongue. I'd never seen her cry, even at the height of my illness or when her daughter died. I'd never known her to admit she was tired or betray the slightest sign of self-pity. There were days when I don't think I ever saw her sit down. She had been too busy trying to move us up a social class, towards her promised land of mock Tudor houses in Northwood and white wedding albums.

Behind her steely resolve she had kept her secrets well. But, when I thought about it, the cracks started coming back. At nine I had gone through a phase of questioning her about my father. I never got much information, just innuendo and a sense of what could never be spoken about. I had formed a picture of him as shabby, callous and malevolent. I remembered puzzling over her mumbled phrase, 'bad blood'. But it had been the man who was both her father and my mother's father whom she was hinting about. He was the spur inside her for what I had mistaken for snobbery but was really pain; for that almost despairing pressure on me to succeed. Gran's dreams had come to nothing. I had never seen a wedding photograph in our house, not even her own. Grandad shrugged when I asked if there had been a photographer in the church.

'What church?' he said. 'It was a register office. The woman was six months pregnant. After all the things her father had done, she still refused to marry until he coughed himself to death.'

'I'm sorry,' I said.

'That's history now.' He looked at me. 'Do you really have
to go to Donegal?'

'She was still his wife, even if he left her. Somebody has to
tell him she's dead. I want it finished, Grandad. I can't blame
him in some ways for running away. The man can hardly have
understood what he walked into. Luke says all we have are
our families, and I don't have much family left, do I?'

Even as I spoke I knew I had phrased it badly. Grandad
looked hurt and old. I took his hand. I saw how much telling
me all this had taken out of him.

'I have you still,' I said, 'You're still my grandfather.'

'You're all I have,' he replied.

'There's no one in the world I'd sooner make baked beans
on toast for.'

I smiled until eventually he had to smile back. 'You mind
yourself flying there,' he said. 'Send him my regards, the daft
old bugger playing his fiddle in the back bedroom. Bring him
a video of Norman Wisdom from me.' His smile faded. 'Things
were handled badly when he left and afterwards. It's easy to
look back and see it, but I did what I thought was right at
the time, like your Gran told me. You were so tiny I had to
protect you.' He stopped, reluctant to say more. He seemed
frightened of losing me again. 'I hope you find him. We parted
badly but I'd like to buy the daft bugger a drink one day. He
had a lovely voice.' Grandad closed his eyes and sang;

'Why come you here so late, said the knight on the road,
I go to meet my God said the child as he stood.'

'I never understood that song, Grandad.'

'Your father sang it once and he said — and he was dead
serious — that if you met the Devil on a lonely road and you
stood totally still, the Devil couldn't harm you. He said it
like he meant it.' Grandad looked at me. 'Go alone.'

'You think I'm making the same mistake as my mother.'

'There's no comparison,' Grandad said. 'Your father was far older. He was like your mother, for the birds. And besides, he was a gentleman.'

V

DONEGAL

TWENTY

THE SMALL PLANE flew low over mountains. There was puffy cloud which we passed through but generally I could distinguish every road and crag between the small hillside lakes and the untamed slopes in the cold winter light. Luke pointed out in the far distance a steep mountain of rock which he claimed pilgrims climbed every year before dawn in their bare feet. I imagined a flock of old women cresting the sharp stones in rags like Bosnian refugees but, according to Luke, hundreds of smartly dressed young girls came from all over Ireland to climb it too.

The plane wheeled and I saw Knock airport below, a line of tarmac carved into a mountain side. The passengers on the far aisle switched seats so that all seven of us stared down at the terminal which seemed to have been dropped from outer space. Luke said that a local monsignor had bullied the Irish Government into building it in this village, whose previous claim to fame has been an apparition by the Blessed Virgin, prophesying about the upcoming evils of French kissing and the Wonderbra. Pilgrims had flocked to this wind-swept mountain ever since. In Lourdes you got cured, Luke said, in Knock you got cured and pneumonia.

The plane began its descent and I saw, to the side, a huge basilica with souvenir shops and flags clustered around it. Before the monsignor had built his airport so that multi-nationals could fly in with suitcases of jobs, Luke said that the only industries had been making rosary beads and ham sandwiches for local sale and raising intervention cattle and children for export. The monsignor was determined to change that, despite open hostility from Dublin. Even Christy's cronies were incensed at the prospect of ordinary, decent tax-payers funding a remote airport – although they didn't pay tax and went to work with their wives' stockings over their heads.

The plane landed smoothly while hillside sheep grazed in the distance. We disembarked, but I could see no sign of customs or security. It seemed like a ghost airport until we left the tarmac and entered the terminal building which was absolutely packed. I had the sensation of walking into a wall of grief. At first I thought a funeral was taking place, as families embraced each other and wept. I asked Luke what was happening.

'It's the third of January,' he said, with stoic anger. 'I would have thought people had gone back by now, but obviously some stayed on for a few extra days' holidays at home.'

A girl my age untangled herself from her parents' arms and walked towards the departure gates. Her baby sister ran crying after her. The girl picked the child up and carried her back to their father who took the child in silence, unable to bring himself to kiss his elder daughter goodbye again. A boarding call for London was being announced. There seemed to be no one present between the ages of eighteen and twenty-eight who wasn't returning to jobs and new lives in Britain. These people were strangers, but I felt close to tears for them.

'What about all this monsignor guy's plans?' I asked.

'He tried, the poor fucker,' Luke replied, 'and kept kicking ass till he keeled over and died.'

We walked out into the chilly air where cars were parked haphazardly. Luke found a taxi driver to take us to a local town called Castlebar.

'I should really wait to see if any locals want to share the cab,' the driver said, 'but, feck it anyway, I have to get away. I've been ferrying people back and forth all week. I don't know what's worse, the journey in with the whole family or the journey back with just the parents saying nothing.'

He spoke to Luke about American wakes in his youth and evenings when all the tiny railway stations, that were long since closed down, had been packed with families seeing off young emigrants. The driver looked like he had never left Mayo but he recited the names of American cities where he'd spent thirty years working before coming home. He called out the nationality of the owners of various old houses we passed which were now holiday homes.

I let Luke and himself talk and stared out at the harsh winter landscape, thinking about that bogey man who was both my real grandfather and my great-grandfather and who must have stood on some God-forsaken platform like this. Could he have ever imagined me, three-quarters of a century later, any more than I could imagine him? I hadn't even asked Grandad for his name, I didn't wish to know it. I wanted him banished from my life as much as Gran had tried to write him out of hers. Yet the fear of him was inside me, a terror of inbred genes. All last night I had lain awake, testing the fault-lines of my life for glimpses of insanity. I kept thinking of Gran and how boringly English she had seemed. The Queen's speech on Christmas Day, her sense of absolute propriety and her mistrust of anything foreign as inferior. Looking back, I realised she had always been that tiny bit too English. Her nationality had been pronounced with the self-consciousness of a person carefully speaking a second language.

Luke's hand brushed against my knee in the back seat. 'You're quiet today,' he said. 'Are you okay?'

I nodded and tried to smile. The driver was chain-smoking. I wanted to ask him to stop, but I felt it would draw attention to myself. I told myself it was the bumpy flight which had left me this queasy but I knew it was more than that. I had never been seven days late before. I couldn't stop glancing at Luke and imagining how his features might come out in a child, in her nose perhaps or sometimes in the way she smiled.

We reached Castlebar and I followed Luke into the car hire firm. There had been a smaller one near Knock, but he hadn't seemed keen to use it. The car hire shop doubled as a flower boutique, but that wasn't doing any business either. The girl at the counter chewed gum and listened to hick music on a local station while traffic snarled up the narrow street outside. You could almost smell January. Even the sale in the small department store across the road looked utterly lethargic. The salesman brought the car around to the door.

'That's the top of the range I have,' he said. 'Where are yous heading?'

'Here and there.' Luke was curt and paid in cash. I didn't know exactly where we were going either. We stopped to eat in an old-fashioned hotel, overlooking a mall of railed off grass. The toilet seats were wooden and the chains were brass. I checked myself in there again, praying for a sign of blood. Seven days wasn't irredeemably late, nothing was certain yet. But I knew this uncertainty was mainly the reason I had agreed to travel with Luke.

I wasn't sure if he understood that this was our final encounter or whether he imagined he could rekindle our relationship again. But once I returned to London I intended changing flat and vanishing. I would never tell him about my pregnancy, no matter whether I went into a clinic or decided to have the child. Whatever grew inside me was mine, but Luke couldn't be trusted to see it that way. Yet I still wanted him near me, at least until I was certain of the news, so that he shared in this waiting, unbeknownst to himself.

We left Castlebar and headed towards Sligo. It began to rain. The road was patchy, stretches of modern highway being suddenly coralled again into a narrow looping road. Luke told me that we were booked into a country house a few miles beyond Donegal town. I asked if it was a hotel and he shook his head.

'Nope,' he said. 'They're too posh to use the word "hotel". It's a former archbishop's palace, tarted up for Yuppies and Yanks.'

But I sensed he had chosen it on purpose, to make up for the poverty of that room off Edgware Road. The car was ostentatious and out of character with Luke, and we had lunched in the hotel dining room when bar food would have done just as well.

'How do we find my father?' I asked.

'I've one or two good contacts,' Luke replied. 'Lads working on the trawlers at Killybegs who are into the music.'

'Could you not have phoned them from London?'

'Not these lads. They're either making money out at sea or spending it playing music in some pub down the town. Besides, you don't want your business broadcast. Not everyone is going to believe you, and locals are protective of your father. What's required is a quiet word in the right ear at the right time.'

I sat back and stared at the scenery. It felt good to let someone else take responsibility. I would have enough decisions to make on my own. Finding my father meant a lot to Luke. I could imagine a time, in twenty or thirty years, when the roles might be reversed and I would bring an unknown son to find him.

We passed Sligo town and drove on, skirting the coast at times. I had never seen a landscape like it; the curious slant of Ben Bulben and then, across the wide bay, the first glimpses of the distant hills of Donegal. Seeing them, I even forgot my nervousness about the father I might finally meet there. I could imagine my mother hitch-hiking these roads in the blazing heat of summer. A young Englishwoman, or so she believed herself to be, intoxicated by this foreignness. I wondered how she had stumbled across my father and what they had first said to each other. I watched the Donegal hills disappear as the road swung inwards and wondered if I was doing the right

303

thing in trying to find him? He'd had years to at least write, if he couldn't bring himself to visit. What if he denied my existence? My nervousness returned. Luke slowed as we entered the edge of the next town, where a huge sign announced WELCOME TO BUNDORAN. The whole place seemed closed as it stretched out forever in a straggle of B&Bs, pubs, shuttered amusement arcades and burger huts locked up for the winter. Rain splattered against an incongruous mural which combined slot machines and palm trees. It looked like an Albanian version of Margate.

'What a dump,' I said.

'We thought it was paradise once.'

I glanced at Luke, but he said nothing further. I wasn't sure if he'd taken offence, although he looked out at the shuttered streets himself as if marvelling at their tackiness. A half mile beyond the town he slowed the car, searching for a turn. He swung left down a small road heading towards the coast, then pulled in at the next tiny junction to stare down both narrow lanes before swinging right. A golf course was flanked by bungalows and woodland where afternoon light flickered through trees. I knew he was looking for somewhere or someone.

'Have we arrived?' I asked.

'No.'

There was an even smaller junction to the right, with a tiny triangle of grass in the centre. Gravel skidded under the wheels as Luke swung down it. Weeds laid siege to the centre of the road. Potholes had been filled with loose chippings which were scattered again. I could glimpse empty caravan parks and faded holiday chalets.

'What are we looking for?' I asked.

'A boarding house. It's thirty years since I was here.'

'How often did you come?'

'Twice. It's a mile from the beach. That's the only directions I can remember.'

We passed a junction and then another, a honeycomb of laneways branching down towards the sea. What information I could get about the place had to be prised from Luke. They were the only two holidays his family could ever afford. His memories seemed haphazard but I tried to memorise each one, thinking that one day I might be asked to pass them on. He talked about swarms of insects beneath the trees beside the house where a Ford Anglia was parked and a Cork boy twisted to silent music on the long pebbled driveway. There were the sickening new tastes of tapioca and rice pudding. They were forced to share the huge upstairs room containing six beds with another family. He remembered the feel of sand walked into patterned lino and the sun's warmth at the window as he sat alone after his family went downstairs and listened to crickets in the field behind the house. He recalled dusk through the ornate front door as Christy and Shane called to him from the gravel and a car passed, its headlights illuminating the local children queueing with buckets at the roadside pump beyond the gate.

Luke somehow seemed more naked recounting these memories than at any time in my arms. We were almost past a tiny lane with a church steeple peeping through trees when he swung down it and pulled up on the gravel outside a small, drab two storey house. Yellow paint flaked on the walls, the side entrance had been bricked up and there was a rusted lock on the main gates which led up a short overgrown driveway. Children played in a mobile home in the field opposite while their father talked to an old man leaning across the fence. Luke got out and crossed over to point at the house. I saw the old man nod while the children stopped playing to stare at us. I got out of the car and stood at the locked gate until Luke joined me.

'It's so small it's hard to believe it's the same house,' he said.

'Everything seems big to a kid.'

'Big and grand.'

There was a broken pane in the front window. I could imagine Luke's parents sitting there for dinner, awkward at being served plates of ham and potatoes and turnip. And I felt Luke could still see himself playing on that gravel long after he had been called in, and his mother coming to the doorway again, her voice low as he reluctantly entered the hall.

'The daughter of the family comes from Cork for a few weeks every summer. That's all it's used for now.'

'Do you want to look in?' I asked.

'No.' I knew by his tone that he wanted to be gone.

'For old times' sake,' I urged without really knowing why. 'You've come this far out of our way to see it.'

'Leave it, Tracey, I said no.'

Luke got back into the car. Curiosity or a battle of wills made me climb the gate as the men across the road watched. I knew I was infuriating Luke by walking up the driveway to peer through the windows. But this seemed more than point scoring. We would never live together. I would never open a drawer to finger his socks or stumble upon old letters or train tickets from forgotten journeys. This was the closest I would ever come to intimacy with the father of my child-to-be, standing in this place where he had never brought his wife.

We could just as easily have flown into Belfast, but now I understood why Luke had chosen Knock. I wanted to force him to leave the car in front of the watching men, to climb that gate and just once to come when he was bid. This sudden jealousy disturbed me. Finally I heard his footsteps on the gravel.

'You're making a mockery of me,' he said, but there was no real anger in his voice. I turned to face him.

'I want you to kiss me,' I said.

'Don't be daft.'

But I didn't care how crazy we looked. Luke had denied me when it suited him. The memory of that taxi still rankled. I had sworn never to let him touch me again. We had never discussed sleeping arrangements for this trip, but I was putting down a marker here that whatever we did was on my terms. Luke glanced back at the watching locals, then lowered his lips as bidden. His tongue was hot and wet. It felt juvenile but I held him in my mouth for thirty or forty seconds. Finally he lifted his lips away and looked at me.

'Are you happy now?'

'You should do what you're told more often, Luke.'

The two men were grinning at the fence. I took Luke's hand proprietorially as we walked along by the side of the house. The back yard was overgrown. Luke pointed to the window of what had been his family's bedroom.

'Shane got lost here the summer he was ten,' Luke remembered. 'My parents had to go to the barracks. Some bikers from Derry found him below the cliffs, almost cut off by the tide. He'd lost his sandals and got his feet stung off by nettles. He'd been crying for hours. I remember them bringing him back, with five motor bikes coming up the drive. All my mother could talk about afterwards was the length of their hair. At dinner-time a squad car came to check that he was all right. We'd done nothing wrong but I still remember the air of shame at the police coming to the door.'

'That's a bit ironic,' I said. 'The way things worked out. But even back then your father's family were no saints.'

'Dublin was different. Here we were respectable for one week in a year. Besides, my Da was the brother who played by the rules and this is all he ever got to show for it. Two lousy holidays, all of us packed into one room in this poky hole.'

'It wasn't poky back then.' I tried to soften the memory. 'You said yourself you thought it was paradise.'

'That makes it okay, eh?' The anger in Luke's voice seemed

to surprise even him. 'Don't patronise me with your well-heeled English accent. If we were too poor and backward to know this kip was poky, that only makes it worse. Because we thought we were the kings of the fucking castle here. In Dublin we were never done boasting about the size of this house. All it does is make us ignorant and dirt poor.'

Luke turned to walk down the path. The men had disappeared. I felt shaken, as if he'd struck me. Something had opened inside him which I didn't understand and, instead of the intimacy I'd wanted to create, it only made me more aware of our differences. The car was already started when I climbed over the gate. I had to jump in as loose gravel spun beneath the wheels and Luke flicked the headlights on against the coming winter dusk.

The hotel was twenty miles further on. We were silent on the journey there. I felt Luke should apologise for his outburst, yet at the same time I felt guilty of somehow provoking him. I stared out at the landscape of Donegal which I had imagined so often as a girl. We passed through Ballyshannon, a place-name come to life from those bus timetables. I became jittery again. I'd uncovered so much about my father over these past weeks, yet he still felt more like a childhood phantom than a man of flesh. I wondered if he had ever fantasised about my mother making such a journey to find him, never imagining it would be their daughter with news of her early death.

Beyond Donegal town we got stuck behind a Landrover towing a horse box. A queue of sales reps tried to get past, but their impatient manoeuvrings didn't seem to register with Luke who was immersed in his own thoughts. He found the sign for the Bishop's Palace Retreat and turned left. The house was a mile further on. We turned in through high ornate gates and followed a curving avenue of high shrubs to park in the cobbled enclosure of what had once been stables. A peacock clambered on to a wall near the car and surveyed us before turning his back. A cat came cautiously half way across the stones, paused and then darted through an archway under which I could glimpse a herb garden. Luke opened the boot and took our bags out.

'They probably have porters for that,' I teased.

'Fuck them.' His voice was low as he slung the bags over his shoulders and walked on. I followed him into the hallway where a fire was blazing. Two more cats arched their backs beside the flames before eyeing us and padding over to settle themselves in a basket in the corner. There was a pile of *Country Living* magazines and international hotel listings on the table beside the long sofas. Luke stood in the centre of the reception area, staring around him. A woman emerged from an inner office and hovered, her smile betraying an edge of anxiety as she waited to attain his attention. She tried to offer tea and home-made biscuits as she fussed over us, but Luke just mumbled a curt 'No' as he allowed her to take the bags, which she insisted upon carrying, and to show us up the two flights of stairs to our room.

I felt more embarrassed here than in London by the discrepancy in our ages. I felt the woman glance at me behind Luke's back but she said nothing. She left us and Luke went into the bathroom to splash water on his face. The room was fabulous yet overdone, like something you'd see on afternoon television in *The Homes of the Rich and Famous*. I lay on the fourposter bed, scanning the brochures and fulsome letters of welcome which had been left in a leather folder beside the complimentary fruit and mineral water. The new owners had composed a poem, with mock nineteenth-century cadences, to welcome their guests and praise the beauties of the house and grounds. Luke came out while I was reading it.

'What's wrong?' I asked, looking at him brooding.

'Nothing.' He unzipped his bag and searched for a carton of duty-free cigarettes.

'It says here they disapprove of smoking in the bedrooms as cigarette smoke can linger for days and may be deeply offensive to future guests.'

'I said fuck them.' He broke the plastic wrapper off a packet and opened it, going to the window of the long bedroom to stare out at the dark evening.

'They also disapprove of casual dress for dinner,' I said, feeling totally out of place. 'You never told me we were going somewhere stuck-up like this. All I have is jumpers and jeans. I didn't bring anything I could wear.'

'Just put that shite away, right.'

'Maybe you're used to these kind of places,' I retorted, 'but I'm not, despite my well-heeled English accent. I don't care if it is shite, I'll read what I like.'

Luke lit the cigarette and turned to observe me. 'I'm tired,' he conceded. 'It's been a long drive.'

It was as much of an apology as I was likely to get. I walked into the bathroom. The tub in the corner was circular and large enough for two people. There were full length mirrors on both walls and on the ceiling above it. This suite felt like it was meant for someone else. Its ambience spoke of middle-aged people having limp sex in Ann Summers lingerie which hadn't looked nearly as ridiculous when worn by models half their age in the catalogues. Luke followed me in and stood at the doorway. He seemed to guess my thoughts and shrugged.

'I picked the place,' he said, 'I didn't pick the furnishings.'

'Does this sort of stuff turn you on?' I asked.

'What answer do you want?'

'It's a long way from Bundoran,' I needled, annoyed at having such surroundings landed on me. 'Does it make you feel you've finally arrived?'

'I'm the man I always was,' he answered surlily.

'With the Dublin accent you always had. I could see it written on that snotty bitch's face downstairs. When she wasn't gawking at me she was eyeing you up, afraid you'll stuff the silver spoons in your inside pocket despite your big car and the trophy mistress.'

I wasn't sure what I wanted to provoke Luke into doing. But I needed to break through that calm façade he had retreated behind again and reach the man I had glimpsed outside the boarding house in Bundoran. Because I was edgy alone with him here, something didn't feel right. Maybe I wanted the turmoil of a row which our bodies could make up.

'You're not a trophy,' Luke said.

'I don't belong here. Can't you see I'm scared to go downstairs? I won't know what fork to use, I've nothing to wear.'

'You're with me.' He sounded angry. 'If you're good enough for me, you're good enough for here. I could buy this place in the fucking morning if I wanted to. I've nothing to prove to anyone.'

He tossed the cigarette into the toilet bowl and left. I leaned against the door and pulled down my jeans. The tampon was just damp with sweat. I wasn't sure what to feel any more. Twice this week I'd dreamt about the release of blood and had woken, bitterly disappointed to find myself still caged by uncertainty. I kept trying not to think of it, but that fear was behind everything I did. I couldn't allow myself to think badly of the child. I had to love it, no matter how unwelcome it was. If Gran could love her own father's child, surely I could learn to love Luke's. But to do that, I couldn't think badly of Luke either.

I hunched down and examined the tampon minutely. Stains of blood would free me from Luke. I might even have been tempted to take my bag and hitch alone to search those mountains. But the tampon was unstained and I kicked off my sneakers and removed my jeans. They were crumpled and I'd had no time to wash them before leaving London. I felt uncomfortable here, no matter what Luke said. I heard a match being struck in the bedroom as he lit another cigarette. The taps on the bath transformed into a shower unit. I turned them on and stood under the spray of hot water, wondering if the sound might lure Luke back in.

I dried myself and puzzled at the various reflections of my body in the maze of mirrors. I looked thin and tired. Somebody else mightn't have noticed the traces of scars still on my arms. If I stared too long I would lose my confidence. I took the initiative and walked into the bedroom. Luke had booked a double room, taking my compliance for granted. Or had he? I couldn't feel that this expensive suite was an attempt to buy me. Its opulence made me uncomfortable, but it was a token of appreciation. No matter what private demons lurked within him, it made me feel that I could trust Luke because he genuinely cared.

He was lying on the bed, smoking and gazing up. He turned to watch me approach and I felt cold, consumed by goosepimples. I lay between the sheets and pulled the quilt over me. Luke waited a moment, then leaned over to kiss me quite roughly. He pulled the quilt back. I think he wanted to see me naked, but I pulled him down between the sheets and drew the quilt around us. Luke stubbed his cigarette out against the gilded edge of a lamp stand and I pulled the quilt even higher above our heads so that we were submerged underneath it, back in the tiny bubble of our private world. Luke worked his hand down my back to cup my buttocks and draw them apart, manoeuvring his fingers inwards towards where I was already drenched. Two birds landed on the roof slates near the window. I could hear their claws scrambling and then lifting off again. There was a hoover in the corridor and the muffled sound of footsteps. I unzipped his suit trousers and managed to pull them down far enough to press my nails into his arse.

I remembered the story of Christy's cock getting stuck in Margaret's zip. But at least they had known the moment when their child was conceived. I had always sworn I would never be stupid enough to get pregnant by mistake. When the need came for a child, whether I was married or single, I had planned to savour her conception. Not the physical pleasure of sex but the miraculous sense of life beginning within me. I wanted to cheat and pretend it was happening now. I knew our affair had run its course, even if Luke didn't. For all his feelings towards me it was wrong because I didn't love him. Yet it was for this final act of love-making as much as to find my father that I had agreed to come here.

His breath was coming faster as he took my breast in his mouth. His back stiffened and then arched. I felt his teeth grip and knew he was about to come. I wrapped my legs around his arse and clasped them high up along his back. I wanted his cock as deep as possible inside me. In years to come this would be the moment of conception I'd choose to remember, the frenzy of his teeth and hands and that spurt as his sperm leapt inside me like a shoal of vaulting salmon. I had chosen my journey to echo theirs, returning to this county where I had been conceived. Luke thrust weakly inside me one last time, then ceased moving, his task done. His back was drenched in deltas of sweat, but I sensed that he shared in the after-taste of vague melancholy which pervaded the room. He rolled off me to rest his head on a pillow.

'You were different,' he said.

'In what way?'

'I don't know. Like a queen bee watching.' Luke was still trying to get his breath. 'You used to make me feel young. Suddenly you're making me old.'

'You are old, remember,' I teased, but gently now, almost magnanimously. I felt so much in control that it frightened me. There seemed nothing I couldn't ask him to do.

'Old isn't the right word,' Luke said. 'Maybe it isn't even you, maybe it's me. I feel cut off from everything.'

'Like what?'

He reached for the cigarettes and lit two. I could feel his

stickiness going cold on the sheet between my legs. He pulled the quilt back and walked to the window. His trousers had been pushed off but his shirt was still on. After a moment I realised he was beckoning me. I stood naked beside him and counted the seconds of darkness before the flash of a lighthouse winked out at sea.

'That's Saint John's Point,' Luke said. 'As isolated a spot as you can get. The lighthouse is automated now, so there's no one left on that headland. I spent a year there with Christy.'

'On the lighthouse?'

'No. The only other building was Saint Raphael's Industrial school. It wasn't as big as Daingan or Letterfrack, but it was just as vicious.' His voice was curiously bereft of emotion. 'There was one Christian Brother, I can't even remember what he was meant to teach us. He'd line us against the wall and invent new reasons to beat us. You could see the cock bulging in his robes when he laid in with the leather. First thing every morning he'd eat an orange and throw the peel in the bin, then spend the whole class coughing up phlegm on top of it. When the bastard finally left you'd see a rush of boys, their hands so bruised they couldn't straighten their fingers, fighting each other for scraps of peel covered in his spit.'

'How did you survive?'

'Dumb insolence,' Luke said. 'I kept my distance from him and all those bastards. I played stupid, never retaliating, never opening my mouth to anyone. I just stored up old scores to settle.'

'And did you settle them with him afterwards?'

'I only saw him once again,' Luke said. 'Down the public toilets in Burgh Quay. Boy prostitutes used to hang around them. He was at the urinal pretending to piss. I saw how agitated he was, trying not to attract attention as he waited for one to come in. I stood at his shoulder and stared into his face. For a moment he hoped I was trying to pick him up, then he got scared even though he'd taken his collar off. I don't know how often I'd dreamt of beating him into a pulp. Every boy who went through his hands must have. But the way he looked at me stopped me from doing anything. It wasn't his fear or . . .' Luke drew on the cigarette and stared at the distant lighthouse. 'He didn't recognise me. He'd beaten my hands raw, yet he didn't know me from a hole in the ground. I was a nobody. I walked out of the jakes and it felt like his look had robbed me of those memories, like they'd happened to someone else. The older I get, the more I feel that way about everything. It was someone else it all happened to.'

'You're just older,' I said. 'You've a different life. Look at you staying here.'

'Then why can't I shake my old life off?' Luke drew the heavy drapes to block out the view. 'I can't escape the smell of it, the fear of waking up poor.'

'You're doing well,' I said, 'you've got shops and all that.'

'None of it matters. Two shops or twenty shops will never be enough to make me feel secure. I can't bring myself to spend money and I don't even get pleasure from making it any more.'

Luke looked so lost that I wanted to rock him back and forth. He walked over to switch on the lamp beside the bed. He stripped off his silk shirt so I could see the scar I had so often played with in London. He leaned forward to rest his elbows on his knees and cup his head jadedly in his palms.

'Sometimes if I wake suddenly,' he said, 'for a moment I feel I'm an old man already or this is a premonition of how I'll feel when my children have grown into middle-aged people who visit when their conscience pricks them. I just know that no matter what I do with my life I'm going to wind up in a cheap nursing home, hardly able to lift myself from the bed, penniless and alone.'

'That's nonsense. You're rich and successful. Even I know that.'

'All the money in the world can't take away the taste of orange peel covered in spit.'

'Is that what drove Christy?' I asked.

'Christy was different.'

'Why?'

'He just was.' Luke lifted his head and sat back on the bed. 'Christy never escaped from himself. He was always that same boy standing with the bruised arms against the wall. You could see it in his need for a big house in Howth and the cars and night-clubs. He was acting out that boy's dreams. Most of the others from Saint Raphael's are still at it in Dublin, those who haven't got themselves shot or wiped out with heroin. Christy would have killed the Christian Brother and boasted about it so often that he'd have been caught.'

'What were your dreams back then?' I asked.

Luke lay down against the pillows and beckoned for me to hunch down on his legs. 'Sometimes,' he said, 'a party of us would be sent to this house to do His Grace's garden. I remember thinking it was huge, the woodlands and lawns and walled kitchen garden. We were never allowed into the house itself. We were lucky if someone bothered to bring us out a mug of water. But we could look up at the windows and imagine life in these rooms.'

'Don't tell me you fancied being a bishop,' I said, trying to make him laugh.

'No.' Luke grabbed my hips and pulled me forward until I was sitting astride his chest. 'But I always knew that one day he'd know something I already knew – that there was no God – and that I'd come back to his house and know something he'd have never known.'

'What's that?' I asked.

'What it feels like to have a young girl sit on your face.'

Without warning Luke managed to burrow down in the bed, thrusting my arse forward with his hands so that I had to grab the brass bedstead to prevent myself colliding with the wall. I felt his tongue tunnel into me and slop away. He hadn't shaved and his bristles stung the parted folds of my flesh, but his sudden wantonness made it exciting also. This time it had nothing to do with storing memories. This was sex as I remembered it with Luke in London, rousing, unpredictable and crude. I knew that for him at that moment I could be any woman. But being part of his boyhood fantasy was liberating too, because I didn't have to think of him. Luke pushed me forward suddenly, gagging for breath.

'Go down,' he panted, 'quickly, get me inside you.'

I turned and clambered down his body, facing away from him as I lowered myself onto his cock. I grasped the end of the bed and rode him for my pleasure only, knowing this was a race and determined I wouldn't be cheated. I came before him and knew there wouldn't be a second time. I slumped down exhausted, and let him lift my haunches and pump away into me. He came quickly and I lay like that until I felt his cock slip out. His hand pressed against my hip for me to roll over and release his legs. I lay at the end of the king-sized bed, staring up at the canopy. He nudged at my ear-lobe with his toes.

'I should have been an actor,' he said, pleased with himself.

'Why?'

'My sense of timing is so perfect. Look.'

I raised my head and saw him push his limp cock to one side to reveal the matted bush of pubic hair circling its base which was lightly smeared with traces of menstrual blood.

TWENTY-ONE

I DON'T KNOW how long I stood by the bedroom window, staring at the distant flicker of light. I had my panties on with a tampon in and just a loose jumper thrown over me. I should have felt relief because the last thing I needed was a child, but I felt tricked that my body had deceived me into being here. Luke came out of the bathroom, having changed for dinner.

'You're quiet in yourself,' he observed, searching for a tie in his bag. I imagined his voice to be a shade more abrupt. I felt cold. I wanted to be held but not by him. This onslaught of blood had broken that bond between us. Besides, his mind seemed fixed on other matters now. I turned from the window and crossed my arms to hug myself. I wanted to be allowed to sit there and wait for tomorrow when Luke had promised we would begin our search. But I knew he wouldn't hear of it. He badgered me smoothly into putting on some clothes for dinner. I could imagine him losing his temper with his wife as she kept changing her mind and trawling through her jewellery box and wardrobes full of dresses on a Saturday night. With me he was more circumspect, but perhaps keeping someone late was one of the few privileges given to a mistress. That was all I was again, now the risk of a child had evaporated. I didn't see how you could mourn something you never had, but I knew that child would have become the missing focus of my life.

I changed in the bathroom to be away from Luke. Not only had I not brought anything that was fancy enough, I didn't even own such clothes. But prevarication would only annoy Luke more. I tried on jeans and sweaters, but I couldn't make my mind up because they were all wrong. Finally Luke walked into the bathroom, with his patience up.

'That's absolutely fine.' he announced, barely glancing at my outfit. 'They're only stiffs here anyway. You'll knock them dead.'

He took my hand leaving the room but our fingers separated as we descended the staircase. Luke looked utterly at home. Any trace of the boy who'd laboured in these gardens was gone. Yet it was impossible to decipher what Luke was feeling in this mode. The owner stood in the hallway to welcome us. She was so overdressed and heavily made-up that she appeared like a madam in a brothel. The five other couples had already come down for dinner and were arrayed around a log fire in the library. They sipped sherry and were being encouraged to mix as they gravely studied the leather bound menus.

I wanted to get this meal over with and not be forced to sit among them like a sore thumb. But an elderly American couple smiled and leaned forward to list their travel itinerary for me like a mantra. A rich Englishwoman beside them butted in when they mentioned Mayo and started to extol the natural beauty there as if the place was populated solely by lichens, moss and winter birds. Everyone oohed over the menu, except for one cranky middle-aged Dublin couple so determined to be unimpressed that I found it hard not to laugh. They exchanged loud whispers about how the Waterford crystal lamp hadn't been dusted and how the china dinner service was the same one as they had 'for everyday usage' at home.

Luke said nothing to any of them and hardly spoke to me, except to decode the menu's flowery language. He seemed neither impressed nor unimpressed by anything, but possessed by a vague indifference which suggested enormous wealth to them. If the owner had seemed unsure of him earlier on, she hovered slavishly now, anxious for his approval. During the meal Luke slotted into the role perfectly, sending back his duck and querying the temperature of the wine, until he had won her complete respect by employing a remote disdain. She never actually spoke to me, even when we were ordering. Occasionally she turned her fixed smile towards me, but her eyes would glare down almost maniacally.

'I have to go out later on,' Luke said, after the owner had finally moved off to fawn over another table.

'Why can't I come?' I was alarmed at the thought of being left alone.

'I need to track these lads down in Killybegs and have a casual drink with them,' he replied. 'Give me a couple of hours and I'll have found out everything we need to know. By this time tomorrow we'll have tracked your father down.'

'I still don't see why I can't come?'

'You'd stand out, Tracey. These are rough pubs in the middle of winter with no tourists about. I'll be better able to loosen tongues on my own. Besides . . .' He paused, trying to conjure a gentle way to phrase it. 'The lads I'm looking for are musicians when they're not out fishing. Once or twice when they've played in a session in London I've given them a bed for the night.' His voice dropped even lower. 'They'd know my wife, do you understand?'

I understood. I glanced around the candle-lit room. It was a kind of exclusive cage where I could safely be exhibited. Its very lavishness made me feel bought in a way I'd never felt in that room off Edgware Road, where home was just a Tube journey away. Here I was captive. Luke reached over to pat my hand.

'Tomorrow, I promise you,' he said. 'Now order any drinks you want, but don't bother waiting up, I could be late.'

He left after the desserts, not waiting for the coffee which was being served back in the library. I tried to sneak upstairs but the owner spotted me.

'It's early,' she said, taking my arm. 'Don't run off on us yet.

Guests always tell me that the chat by the log fire afterwards is the highlight of their stay. We do need you to keep us company. You're so spontaneous. Not everybody could carry off those casual clothes but you made the dining room look so relaxed, almost like a home from home.'

I felt her varnished nails dig into my arm as she positioned me on the main sofa. Coffee was brought in on silver trays and everyone started discussing Georgian architecture and how good young people my age actually were, despite what was written about them. Cognacs were served and cigars lit. The men leaned forward into a huddle to compare the merits of various tablets for ulcers. I knew that the Dubliner would turn out to have brought the most expensive one 'for everyday usage'. It felt worse than being trapped with Chelsea skinheads on a tube. But every time I tried to slip away the owner would look at my empty brandy glass and offer to freshen it for me. She had me hemmed in and seemed determined to engage me in conversation. I asked if she had ever heard of a fiddler called Proinsías Mac Suibhne.

'No,' she said. 'I'm not good at that type of thing but I'm sure someone in the kitchens would know of him.'

I found I couldn't stop staring at her eyes, which seemed hard and huge and totally at variance with her smile as she sized me up in a way she would never dare to judge Luke. But I wasn't the one with the gold credit card.

'You were lucky to get a room,' she said. 'Even at this time of the year we're quite booked out.' The tip of her tongue slipped out of her mouth, moistening her lipstick. I felt something, almost like an electric charge from her. I couldn't tell if it was envy or hatred. I noticed there was no sign of her husband being around. 'I just mention the fact,' she continued, 'in case anyone else was thinking of staying here.'

'I don't know what you mean.'

'A young Dublin man phoned this morning,' she said. 'He wanted to check if you were booked in here. He even asked directions, although he didn't give a name and seemed anxious I didn't mention his call. He might be planning a surprise.' Her eyes savoured my discomfort. 'I'm not sure people want surprises in a quiet place like this, when they're escaping from day-to-day domestic considerations.'

She rose to inquire if any guests wanted another night-cap. Her perfume lingered along with the insults. It had to be Al, nobody else was so stupid. The elderly American lady glanced across at me, then whispered loudly to the owner; 'Where exactly has her father gone?'

I picked up my brandy and left the room. I couldn't bear this any more. No matter what else he was, at least Luke commanded respect for me. Without Al's phone call the owner would never have dared say a word. I didn't need minding and all Al had ever done in the past was make things worse. I tried to dismiss the notion that Al might be hanging around outside, but it took hold.

I opened the front door and left it on the snib. Amber spotlights among the shrubs lit up the ivy-clad walls of the house. I walked across the gravel, still holding the brandy glass and gazed at the sky, amazed at how bright and huge the stars were. I walked on as the crunch of gravel gave way to a croquet lawn, crisp with the onset of frost. I was cold and beyond the reach of the house lights. A black configuration of trees loomed before me. Anyone could be lurking there, watching me approach.

'Al,' I called softly and then slightly louder. Something rustled, a fox or whatever rustles in the countryside. I heard paws scurry through the undergrowth and shivered. I called Al's name again, feeling foolish, and had turned to go inside when I heard a footstep. I froze. Surely if it was Al he'd call my name? I turned. It was Al all right, though I could hardly distinguish him in the shadows.

'I watched you earlier,' he whispered. 'You were hard to make out but I saw you standing naked with him in the window. He had his arm around you. You said it was over. I can't believe you're still his mistress.'

It was too complex to explain and I didn't see why I should have to. Al had no right to come here.

'These things happen,' I said.

'I know.' Al was quiet for a moment. He looked so cold. 'That's what I've kept telling myself since I discovered Luke was fucking my mother.' He didn't seem angry, just distressed. 'He fucked Aunt Margaret before that. He would have fucked me too if I was a girl.'

'I don't believe you.'

'He loves us all, That's Uncle Luke's problem. He wants to mind us. We're his family, whether we want to be or not. Christine was the only one ever to stand up to him. She got a kitchen knife and threatened to chop his balls off if he ever tried to put his dick near her again. I don't know why I thought you were different. But God knows, even if you were his natural daughter he'd probably still have fucked you seeing as you're so willing to spread your legs for him.'

It wasn't the slur that made me snap. It was being confronted by truths about Luke which I'd always known but had never wanted to face. I wanted to hurt someone and Luke wasn't to hand. Even if he was, I would be too scared to. I flung the brandy into Al's face. He pushed my hand away and the glass smashed against a tree trunk. I reached down, searching the ground for the jagged stem. Al had come this far just to rub home how cheap I was. I wanted to stab him or maybe to stab myself for what I had become, a dumb blonde tart who let herself be used. I closed my palm over a shard of glass on the ground and felt the sudden wince of pain submerge this other anguish. My veins burned as I cried out. Al could only guess at what I was doing. He unclenched my palm and carefully prised the glass out.

'No,' he said, 'Trace, please.'

I cried uncontrollably as the shock of the cut subsided. It

had changed nothing as usual. Al hauled me away from the broken glass. I struggled and he lay on top of me, holding me still like a startled animal. Pliability and the curve of my arse were all that had attracted Luke from the start.

'I thought he cared,' I sobbed. 'All I wanted was someone who cared.'

'I do, Trace,' Al said. 'I'm scared for you.'

'Why should you be? You said yourself I was a slut.'

'I never said that. Luke has no interest in sluts. He mesmerises people and adopts them. He weaves lies until they no longer know who they are. He turns them into someone else, like he's been doing with himself for years.'

'Why should I believe you? You nearly had me in jail.'

'I didn't pack my bag,' Al said. 'I was stupid too. Luke told me to hide in the Pleasure Dome. He went to my flat and packed a bag himself for Carl to give me.' Al relaxed his grip on my hands, then raised my cut palm to his lips as if he could stem the blood. He took it away. 'Can you not see, Trace? I knew nothing about the gun. He used us both. He knew the police would stop Christy's car coming off the ferry, but you'd be allowed to drive through. That gun killed McGann, I'm certain of it. You were Luke's way of getting it safely to England.'

Al searched for a handkerchief to stop the bleeding. The cut was slight but sore. In the old days the monkey on my shoulder would have taunted that I deserved worse.

'But what about your confession in my flat?'

'I confessed to nothing,' Al replied. 'Luke did the talking. I knew he'd kill me if I opened my mouth. He thought we'd slept together, that's why he beat me up. If you hadn't found the gun he'd have produced it as an excuse, to show what happens to anyone who crosses him. Is your hand sore?'

'No,' I lied. 'It just needs a plaster.'

'He's using you still,' Al whispered. 'I don't know why or how but you're in danger here.'

'He's helping to find my father.'

'I don't believe that.'

'My father's a fiddler caller Proinsías Mac Suibhne. Luke is in Killybegs, tracking him down.'

I had to believe that much, even if Luke had other reasons to be here. He always said that nobody did anything for one reason only.

'The old biddy blabbed about me phoning,' Al said.

'Only to me, not Luke. How did you know where to find us?'

'It was when you said Donegal. The time we were in London for the wedding there was an article about this place. Christy and Luke started talking about digging the bishop's garden. It's the only time I heard them mention Saint Raphael's. Luke joked about booking the master bedroom here and getting some young girl to sit on his face.' I felt Al half-glance towards me, then look away. 'That's the type of thing he said whenever Christine was present.'

'Even in front of her father?' I had showered afterwards but felt unclean down there now.

'Luke had Christy by the balls,' Al said. 'He has us all by the balls. He owns everything, even his brothers' lives. He borrows bits of their past and you know that he actually believes they happened to him. He's spent his whole life inventing himself. At the wedding he started talking about my Da getting lost on the cliffs at Bundoran. I looked at my Da and I could see from his face that it never happened to him.'

We were hunched on the grass, keeping a slight distance between us. I felt frost invade my limbs. Al had come all this way just for me. I was scared for us both. I wrapped the bottom of my sweater around my wrist and realised how freezing he must be. He looked at the lights of the house.

'I don't suppose you could smuggle me out a ham roll or anything?' he asked, forlornly.

'It's a luxury country house,' I said, 'not a bloody buffet.'

'I was only asking.' Al stared across at the winking light on Saint John's Point. 'It was only towards the end of his life that I got Christy to talk, on our own, building the summer-house in his garden. I'd to prise out information about the smallest things, like the fact that it was Luke who was found on the rocks in Bundoran, bawling his eyes out after shitting himself with fright, or about the year they spent in Saint Raphael's. That's why Luke left Ireland, he could never cut it in Dublin afterwards.'

'Why not?' I asked.

'There was a Brother Damian here, your usual run-of-the-mill horny sadistic fuck. You know how bullies always need a teacher's pet. You can't blame Luke in some ways I suppose, Damian was a vicious cunt and Luke wasn't built as tough as the others. In no time Damian has him running messages, doing little favours, until after a few weeks Luke never gets beaten any more, unless the other kids get him on his own. Even then they had to gang up on Christy before getting a dig at Luke. All these years later, you could see that Christy couldn't bring himself to believe Luke was grassing on them the whole time.'

'He and Luke were close,' I said.

'They were thick as thieves once,' Al agreed. 'I'll give Luke that. He was too clever to have been nicked himself. He got caught risking his neck to save Christy.' Al flung a pebble towards the house and shivered with cold. 'What's it like inside?' he asked.

'They're sitting around discussing their ulcers.'

'It wouldn't be my scene.'

'I can't imagine them grooving to "*I'm a Dublin dude from the Five Lamps, my heart wants to rock but my foot just stamps.*"'

'Christ,' he winced, 'you know how to hit a man when he's down.'

I reached across to warm his hands in mine.

'You're like a block of ice. Where will you sleep tonight?'

'I've the car parked beyond the woods,' he answered. 'I'd to feck the petty cash in AAAsorted Tiles for the ticket. What class of gobshite name is that?'

'It's first in the Yellow Pages.'

'Fecking eejit. Doesn't he know people always flick those books from the back?'

'You're not cut out for business, Al.'

'Neither is Luke if you saw how little petty cash there was. Luckily Carl in Dublin donated his sleeping bag and the money he'd saved for the rent and left stuck up the arse of the plastic reindeer on the mantelpiece for safe-keeping.'

'That was nice of him.'

'I hope Carl thinks so too when he finds out. Let's get the hell away, Trace. I've enough petrol to take us to Dublin.'

'No.'

Al withdrew his fingers from mine. 'I'm not trying to compete,' he said. 'I mightn't be able to match posh hotels, but I'm not asking you to sit on my face.'

'Fuck you,' I said, recoiling into myself. 'I'm nobody's whore.'

'Then what's keeping you here?' Al almost shouted. 'You can't love him. The man is using you.'

'What are you doing?' I accused him back. 'How do I know you're not using me to get back at him?'

'If Luke finds me here I'm dead,' Al replied quietly. 'When the crunch comes, family means nothing to him. He has this obsession to keep hoarding and nothing gets in his way. He's had the others under his spell for so long they're convinced they can't tie their shoe-laces without him. Even going to school I was told not to worry about exams, Luke would always fix something up. I was just to keep my head down and my mouth shut. Even when Christine found my mother sucking Luke's cock I kept my mouth shut and didn't even ask my father if he knew. It's the family way. We Duggans stick together because the world is against us. It's against us because Luke says so and he's the brains who's going to see us all right. He fixed Christy all right. I don't want to be fixed up, I want out. That's why I went to London with you. I planned to take off somewhere. But I wind up sleeping in his house, working in his shop, driving his stinking van. So I don't want him fucking up your life as well.'

'Luke won't harm me,' I said. 'I know that.'

Al clambered to his feet, slapping his shoulders to inject some warmth into them.

'You know nothing,' he said. 'Luke's left hand doesn't know what his right is doing. We could be in Dublin by dawn and I'd put you on a boat. I'm asking for nothing else.'

He looked comic standing there, stamping his feet like he was dying for a piss but was too polite to mention it. I remembered how he had showered me that night in Dublin. Few men wouldn't have taken advantage.

'I can't leave,' I said, 'I came with news for my father. After that I had already decided never to see Luke again.'

'I'll wait for you.'

'I don't need waiting for. You're the one in danger. Get away before he comes back.'

Al sat down again on the grass, deflated.

'I appreciate you coming,' I said.

'It wasn't to get at Luke. I didn't care about him any more.'

'I'm not worth the effort, Al.'

He ran his fingers over my cut palm. 'You are,' he replied quietly. We were both silent.

'Where will you sleep?' I asked again.

'I'll drive out there.' He nodded towards the lighthouse. 'Saint Raphael's is a ruin now. There should be a plaque, because it was an academy of crime. They were all there, with short hair and short trousers, farting at night in big dormitories. They came out and divided Dublin between them, living like rock stars, getting night-club bouncers to kneel and kiss their boots. The Wise-cracker, the Commandant, the Cellar-man.'

'And the Ice-man.'

'The Ice-man wouldn't spend Christmas,' Al said, 'sitting in London, counting the pennies, afraid to come home.'

'What do you mean?'

'You know well what I mean,' Al said. 'Christy was a passable lieutenant, but he could never do more than what he was told. The other criminals tolerated him because he was a good bloke. He'd throw money around the clubs. But they knew he was a front for Luke. Christy never had a thought in his life, but once you told him what to do he'd stick his neck on the line.'

'You mean Luke planned everything?'

'His house in London is like a miniature Dublin. Street maps, directories, even Corporation plans of sewers and underground tributaries. You could rebuild the city from what he has. He sits like God, going over every detail, but the little plastic stars he moves around are flesh and blood and they bleed.'

'Surely McGann and the others knew that?'

'If they did they kept their mouths shut,' Al said. 'Christy had a violent streak and liked the status. He paid over the odds. You knew he was buying their silence, bull-shitting about his great fence, when it was all going back into Luke's pocket.' Al looked at me. 'I'm sorry, I should have warned you, but I thought you were his daughter. The man was fond of dipping his wick. I thought you'd just found him and I didn't know what to say. You can't just tell someone their Da is a bastard.'

Luke had the qualities I had once associated with my father: manipulative, ruthless and being only out for himself. The distant lights of a boat broke the dark expanse of water at sea. I knew Al was watching it too.

'If you told Christy he was rich he'd believe it,' Al said, 'but all he ever got back was peanuts. Enough to splash around the clubs and get mentioned in the papers. Luke kept saying there was money for him in various accounts, but the time was never right to collect it. He was a pit pony slaving for Luke, with every penny vanished to London and coming back in contraband cigarettes that Luke bought in bulk in Holland. Luke was clever. The Irish papers keep screaming about heroin but you can make as much smuggling cigarettes without half the bother. AAAsorted Tiles is the perfect cover, because Luke deals with hauliers the whole time. He was cleaning up, you couldn't walk anywhere in Dublin without hawkers flogging you smuggled fags or lads with bagloads of tobacco. Meanwhile all the heat's on the drug pushers. The only hassle was from the Revenue and Christy knew how to lean on them if they investigated too closely.'

'Put your arm around me,' I said. I couldn't stop shivering. A larger boat emerged from behind rocks near the lighthouse. Luke was there on the small boat going to meet the big one, I thought, or controlling everything from the shore.

'The problem was, it was such a good deal that everyone wanted in on the action,' Al said. 'If you don't live in a country you don't know what's happening. Luke thought he had Dublin sussed. You didn't get up other gangs' noses, you tipped the IRA a few grand at Christmas in case they thought of shooting you and the police weren't worth a wank. But it's different now. There's money made from drugs you wouldn't believe. Christy was safe with the Commandant and the Cellar-Man. Even Big Joe Kennedy put up with Christy, although Luke steered clear of him. There were rumours that Luke let Joe's brother drown when they were kids. But Dublin sprawls for ever now. There's places Luke's never heard of, where kids have no mercy for no one. Christy was a joke to lads like the Bypass Bombardiers, muscling in on everything. Suddenly pitches where he sold fags for years were gone. Legs were broken, you can't get cigarette sellers. But Luke keeps squeezing him for money.

'Then in October, a security van is robbed of three quarters of a million pounds. It's years since Luke planned the like of that. But I never even saw Luke come over. He must have got wind the Bypass Bombardiers were tracking it and so he signs his brother's death warrant. You don't mess with these guys. McGann and the others have no idea whose toes they're treading on till it's over. By then the money has vanished. McGann's mates want to run, only they're broke and greedy. They squeeze Christy for their share. And the Bypass Bombardiers put out the word that unless they get half a million Christy is dead. And Christy walks into the video shop and, I'll never forget it, he has to ask for the loan of twenty pounds. The man is skint and whatever deal Luke is doing, he's not giving Christy a penny back. The heat is on Christy. He asked me to go for a drink and walking into the pub I never saw such respect, everybody nodding and keeping their distance. It was respect for the dead, do you understand?'

We froze as a distant voice called 'You-hoo!' I lay flat on the grass beside Al although we couldn't be seen. It was the owner of the house. She stood on the steps, staring around before calling for two waiters to come out. She must have found the door on the snib. She crossed the gravel, calling 'You-hoo!' and carrying something. Her voice was both facetious and menacing. Al edged back towards the trees. I followed and we watched the waiters spread out.

'Come on, Trace,' he whispered. 'Let's get the hell away.'

I looked into the dark woods. I was scared to stay with Luke, but frightened to run away. Flight would suggest that I knew something. Al would never out-drive Luke if he guessed that I was heading for Dublin. Even if I reached London, Luke knew how to locate me.

'Go yourself,' I said. 'I need to find my father.'

'Leave it till another time.'

'No. You've taken enough risks. Go back to London. I'll meet you there.'

'Don't trust him, Trace. I don't know what's happening but I know you're in danger.'

'You-hoo!' The call was getting closer. The woman's eyes were so weird that it wouldn't surprise me if she could see in the dark.

'For God's sake, go,' I said. 'You're putting me in danger hanging around here. I was safer as a brainless tart.'

'You were never that,' Al whispered. 'None of this would have happened if Joe Kennedy had bothered having Luke killed, like he threatened to when Luke was in jail years ago. But as usual the fucker wormed his way out of it.'

'What was Luke jailed for?'

'Assaulting a Christian Brother in a public toilet. He only served three months. I think he thought it would wipe the slate clean with the Commandant and the Cellar-man. But Christy said all they ever did was crack jokes about it until he left Dublin. They said Luke only hit Brother Damian because he'd offered to pay Luke with a bar of Kit-Kat like all the other times.'

The owner stopped in the centre of the croquet lawn and switched on a powerful flashlight. Al hunched down behind a tree and I walked away from him, blinded by the brilliant beam. I put a hand up to shield my eyes and held my other palm out.

'I went for a walk,' I said in my most stupid voice. 'I fell. I cut myself.'

A simple bandage would have done, but the owner wasn't letting me away so easy. She washed the cut over and over, squeezing it for splinters of glass and dabbing it with stinging iodine. She seemed reluctant to release my hand.

'Not everyone gets cut with Waterford crystal glass,' she said. 'Your young friends will be impressed.'

'I'm sorry I broke it,' I told her, 'I needed some air. I slipped.'

'Accidents happen,' she replied, starting to bandage my hand too tightly. 'Especially when people step out of their natural environment.'

'Does your husband run the hotel with you?' I tried not to show she was hurting my hand.

'It's a country house, dear,' she corrected. 'He left me for a less interesting woman.'

'I'm sorry to hear that.' I realised that sympathy was the worst emotion I could show.

'Have you foreign languages?' she asked

'Just A Levels in German and French.'

'I'm fluent in both those and in Italian and Spanish. It's useful with the tourist trade. But of course she could do things with her mouth that one can't learn by Linguaphone.'

We looked up as the front door opened and Luke entered. He stopped, surprised to see us in her office. I could sense the owner's body language change.

'We've had a little accident,' she said, 'but she's as right as rain. Had you a nice evening out?'

'It was fine.' Luke was curt as he eyed me up. I tried not to act differently, but it was only now when he was here that I realised how scared I was. 'You're shaking,' he observed.

'I think I'm in shock,' I replied. 'I cut my hand.'

Luke banished the owner with a glance and brought me upstairs. He examined the bandage and called her a silly bat as he undid it and bound it up again. I found it hard to look directly at him. He decided I needed a brandy and telephoned for two to be brought up. I wanted him to let go of my hand. There was a knock and he took the drinks without a word, then took off his jacket and started on the buttons of his shirt. He looked at me.

'It's late,' he said. 'You should get undressed.'

'I'm cold.'

'It's a big bed. Go on, I'll soon have you warm.'

He walked to the window and undid the drapes, then beckoned me to come over. I could imagine Al out there, shivering in the woods as he looked up. For a moment I wondered if Luke could know.

'Come here,' he urged softly. 'You have to see this. It's beautiful.'

I had already taken my white sweater off. The cuff was stained with blood. It would look too suspicious if I put it back on. Luke was waiting, watching me. Reluctantly I walked to the window in my jeans and bra. He reached for the brandies on the side table and handed me one.

'You are cold,' he said. 'Your back is covered in goose-pimples.'

He put his hand on my neck and began to stroke my back. We were framed in that square of glass. The bigger ship was still out there, near the lighthouse. How much crack or heroin would three quarters of a million pounds buy?

'It's beautiful, isn't it?' Luke said, with awe in his voice. 'What a view.'

But I couldn't see out properly. The light in the room was so strong that our own image was reflected back as Luke drew me closer towards him. His fingertips very lightly brushed my breast. If he knew of Al's presence he was taunting him now, flaunting his possessions. He kissed my neck.

'Goose-pimples,' he laughed. 'They taste different. I don't mind, you know, about your friend coming.' I froze, not knowing what sign to make to warn Al. Luke laughed again. 'I mean it would be worse if your period didn't come. This afternoon was nice but sex isn't why we came here.'

'No.' I couldn't seem to make my voice go above a whisper.

'Aren't you going to ask me?'

'What?'

He put his brandy down and turned me slightly so that he could slide both arms down and tuck them into my jeans where they rested against the tip of my pubic hair. He laughed, delighted with me, and kissed my ear.

'You really are cold,' he said. 'Take off those jeans that were driving every man in the dining room mad and get away to bed. "What?" she asks. How many brandies had you, Tracey? I've found out where your father is, that's what. It cost me a fortune in drink. I'll tell you about it in the morning.'

'Tell me now.'

'It's late, you're befuddled. It will wait till the morning. Away to bed now.'

He removed his hands from my jeans and coaxed me towards the bed with a soft possessive slap on the backside, then laughed again as he drew the curtains shut. I went into the bathroom and put in a clean tampon. I found the longest tee-shirt in my bag to wear in bed. I waited for as long as I could before coming back out. Luke had already turned the light off. I had to grope my way across to find the bed. I lay on the very edge, trying almost not to breathe, pretending that I wasn't really there.

TWENTY-TWO

I WAS TOO FRIGHTENED to sleep. All night I wanted to use the toilet but I was scared of waking him. Luke slept peacefully, his breathing quiet and regular. Dawn took an eternity to come and even then made little impact through the heavy drapes. I heard squalls of rain turn to sleet against the window. My geography of Ireland was poor but with every passing hour I wondered how close to Dublin I might be now if I had risked fleeing with Al. I didn't know if he had driven off to sleep at Saint John's Point or, if after watching us again in the window, he had decided I wasn't worth the risk any more.

Luke slept on his back, with his mouth slightly open. Yesterday I had been nervous of confronting my father, now I knew the stakes were far higher. This sleeping figure beside me had killed McGann when he asked too many questions. Before that he had let his own brother be shot. A week didn't go by without some minor Dublin criminal opening his front door to be greeted by a gun. How many others had Luke set up? A bishop's palace seemed a bizarre place for my life to end if everything went wrong. Yet Donegal was where it had begun. I might have known every twist of these hills if life had worked out differently.

Luke stirred. I rose to get away from him and walked to the window. Cold light filtered through a gap of brightness. I put my eye against it and saw the gravel path and the croquet lawn with trees beyond. After a moment I noticed movement there. It wasn't Al though, but an older man in a dark anorak. Only when he looked up at the house did I recognise him as

Detective Brennan from Dublin. He spoke into a walkie-talkie before disappearing among the trees. The police were on to Luke. I had to stay calm and act natural. If I found an excuse to leave the room I could run across the gravel and into their care. But that would be to admit that I knew something illegal was going on. It was safer to remain a clueless bimbo being deceived.

'What time is it?' I froze at Luke's voice, then turned from the gap in the drapes.

'I don't know,' I said. 'There's a watch beside you.'

Luke leaned across to check the time. 'There's nothing like country air to make you sleep.' He sprang from the bed where he had slept naked. He slapped his chest and rubbed his chin. 'There's silver in the stubble,' he declared. 'Do you know that song?'

'No.'

'Sure how could you? You English have forgotten all your songs.' Luke began to sing a full-throated paean to the glory of middle age. He walked into the bathroom and I heard him slap cold water heartily on his face, then pull the wooden shutters open. His footsteps stopped. I knew he was looking out at the woods. Somewhere in his baggage a gun had to be hidden. He would use me as a hostage if he saw the police. He came back out and stared at me wearing that long tee-shirt.

'I feel like the cat who got the cream,' he laughed, admiringly. 'Put some clothes on, and don't be driving me daft.'

I dressed in my heaviest clothes, even wearing an extra jumper as if for protection. We went downstairs where everything looked normal. Breakfast was being served in a room with curved walls. I ran ahead of Luke to take the chair facing the window. He laughed.

'She loves a nice view in the morning,' he told the owner. 'That's why I'm sitting here.'

He sat in front of me with his back to the window and I spent the meal trying not to stare out above his head. The sleet had cleared and a leaden dullness hung about the dripping trees. I wondered where Al was and if he had stumbled into the police. I knew they hadn't been tipped off by him. There were too many early morning raids in his childhood for Al ever to trust them. Carl had told me about the pair of them once mistaking a squad car for a taxi after taking two girls home and being beaten down the cells. Luke leaned across to pour my tea.

'You haven't touched your breakfast,' he said. 'I know you're nervous but you should eat.'

'I'm not hungry,' I replied. 'I didn't sleep well.'

He studied my face intently. Something moved in the trees and I couldn't prevent my eyes from tracking it. Luke turned to watch a cat jump from a branch and shake itself dry before darting across the lawn. He looked back.

'You're very pale,' he said, concerned. 'I hope I did right bringing you here. We're lucky it's winter and he's older now. Back in the 1950s when Ciaran Mac Nathuna and Breandán Breathnach were trying to track your father down, they often had to chase him through the Derryveagh Mountains and right to the tip of Inishowen.'

'Have we far to go?' I tried to keep the conversation normal.

'We've all day to get there. Michael James Dwyer told me last night that your father played a few nights in Byrne's pub in Carrick before Christmas. He was seen in Glenties at Midnight Mass and these first weeks of January he winters out with John Cunningham's widow who has a pub beyond Glencolumbkille.'

'Can you not just leave me outside the pub right away?' I asked. 'I'd like to go in alone.'

'Early morning is no time to land on an old man,' Luke said. 'Let's take a drive first. It's magical here, Tracey, even in winter, Slieve League falling into the sea and dozens of tiny roads across to Glenties that your father must have walked a thousand times. I'm not defending him, but if he did desert your mother, at least try to see what lured him back here.'

Luke paid the bill in cash, like he'd paid for everything so far, as though not leaving a trail. We drove out the gates and turned left for Killybegs. A car was pulled in a hundred yards further on. The driver kept his head down but I recognised the anorak. The road was relatively quiet. I used my side mirror to try and guess which of the vehicles occasionally appearing behind us were following Luke.

'Listen to this for playing,' Luke said, switching on a tape. 'Johnny Doherty recorded in a cottage in the 1960s. The only power supply they had was the car battery. You can hear the engine left running all night outside in the yard. Doherty often played duets with your father. No one could match the tight playing of the pair of them. The only fiddler alive who'd come close is James Byrne.'

Fiddle music filled the car as Luke tapped his fingers lightly on the wheel. I wondered if he was remembering the night he had first lowered earphones over my head. We passed a tractor and a truck crammed with two tiers of frightened animals bound for slaughter. Their faces stared out from tiny air-vents. I didn't know where Luke was bringing me. I just hoped the police were not too far behind. I closed my eyes and tried to focus on the music. My mother had been seduced by playing like that. Now, years later, it could be leading me to my death.

I opened my eyes as we entered the fishing port of Killybegs. There were pubs opening up and cars and trucks parked on the quayside beside the line of moored boats. Last night Luke must have met one of these skippers. How long had he been planning this trip? Even if I hadn't contacted Luke again I knew he would have found a way to convince me to travel to Donegal. This was what the tape on Christmas night had been about. Luke drove through the town and a mile further on we swung left, away from the main road. This track was narrow and twisty as it bordered the coastline. We climbed a steep hill cutting us off from the mainland. Few cars would pass this way. I knew it couldn't be a route to Glencolumbkille. Luke sensed my nervousness and smiled.

'Isn't it beautiful?' he asked. 'Look to the west and the next dry land is New York. Old women here a hundred years ago cried far less if their sons went to New York instead of Dublin. Dublin was somewhere foreign they couldn't imagine, but New York was directly out there beyond the mist.' He slowed the car and stared out. 'It's like the far end of the earth.'

The words chilled me. We rounded the bend and I saw a blue Hiace van parked beside the ditch, with its paintwork flaked and rusty. I glanced behind but the road was empty. Two men with the look of fishermen got out of the van. Luke stopped twenty feet from them and reached across to pat my knee.

'Wait here a second,' he said soothingly, 'I've a spot of business.'

This was how inconsequential Luke thought I was, too stupid to grasp what was happening before my eyes. All the nights of drugs came back, sharing joints in Harrow, popping Es and micro-drops with Honor and Roxy and those dawn fields where I'd watched people smoke heroin to come down after raves. I'd never thought much about this side of it, the money made and lives lost. I couldn't believe the drugs were stashed in that van. Luke wouldn't risk carrying them himself, unless Christy's death had left gaps in his plan. Then I realised that couriering them to Dublin was probably my job. I'd been successful once before without even noticing. This was the reason I'd been brought here, to be used again.

The older fishermen opened the van to remove some sort of long flat box, wrapped in a black refuse sack. Luke took his wallet out and joked with the other fisherman. The droning was faint at first, smothered by the intervening hill until suddenly it drowned out the sea birds as an Irish army helicopter crested the hill and hovered above us. The fishermen looked up startled as police cars appeared at both bends of the

340

road. Two plain clothes detectives with Uzi machine guns rose from behind gorse on the slope of the hill. One ran to cover Luke while the other screamed at me to get out of the car. I wanted to explain but the man ordered me to turn around, kicked my legs apart and frisked me roughly. He pushed me towards Luke who ignored the guns and squared up to him.

'Leave her alone,' he said, 'she's only an English tourist.'

Local uniformed guards got out of the squad cars. They stood about, resentful at being ignored by the Dublin detectives. A third car drew up behind them and Detective Brennan climbed out. The older fisherman looked at a local guard.

'What in the name of Jaysus is going on, Seamie?' he asked.

'Weren't you the fecking eejit to get involved in this carry on, Michael James?' the policeman replied. 'Don't deny you were taking bales out of the water.'

'Shut the fuck up!' Brennan roared over the drone of the helicopter. He waved an all clear and the pilot moved off out to sea and then rose further into the air.

'What fecking bales?' the fisherman asked, indignant.

'You were told to stay quiet,' Brennan shouted. 'You will be formally charged.'

The fisherman ignored him and offered a cigarette to the policeman called Seamie who shook his head.

'Is that fecker astray in the head?' he asked Seamie. 'The only bale in our nets last night was a bundle of *Reader's Digests* in a plastic bag. There's only three useless things in life; the Pope's prick, a nun's tit and *Reader's Digest.*'

Luke tried to take my hand to reassure me, but I kept my distance. I was scared, and yet I felt a vengeful glee that he had been caught. He stared at Brennan, saying nothing although his face was white with anger or shock. One of the detectives donned plastic gloves and lifted the refuse sack on to the bonnet of a squad car. He removed a thick polystyrene carton sealed with tape and used a knife to open it carefully. It was packed with ice, from which the round, flat body of a

341

large fish spilled out and would have slithered to the ground if he hadn't caught it. Luke managed to keep his voice calm, but I could see his body shake with fury.

'I've just paid for that turbot,' he said. 'It was meant as a surprise for an old man in London, so get your dirty fucking hands off it.'

The detective placed the fish on the bonnet and examined the hollow carton. There was nothing else inside it. I kept staring at the open mouth and flat glossy eyes of the turbot. I felt sick. I could see Grandad Pete as a boy gazing in wonder as his father laid such a fish on the kitchen table. I had told Luke the story on the plane. Only the most sensitive of men would have bought one for me to bring home on the plane tonight. Awkwardly the detective closed over the ice-box again. A local policemen jumped from the back of the van.

'Clean as a whistle,' he said, 'there's nothing in here.'

'For feck's sake,' the fisherman told Seamie, as annoyance overcame his initial shock. 'I'll confess to going poaching once or twice, seeing as you were with me. But that fish was legitimately caught at sea. I know this man from playing music in London. We'd a drink together last night and he asked me to keep him a turbot if one was caught. You'll find it entered as part of the catch. Not even Brussels can object to that.'

'I'll pay you, Michael James,' Luke said, 'but you can throw it back. I'll not ask anyone to eat anything these bastards have handled.'

The detective deliberately knocked against the carton and it burst open on the roadway. I glanced at Luke, not knowing what to believe.

'This has nothing to do with you,' Luke told the fishermen. 'This detective obviously feels he hasn't already done enough for my family.'

'I'm only warming up, Duggan,' Brennan said. 'I know you're up to something.'

'You could never pin anything on my brother, Brennan,'

Luke addressed him for the first time. 'So you hounded him like a judge and jury, pointing the finger over a robbery you knew he hadn't committed until some lunatic plugged him. It's my turn next, is it? I left Ireland because the likes of you never gave me a chance. I'd a teacher the same who gave me a dig every morning. 'That's for what you did," he'd say. 'If you did nothing, it's for what you're bound to do." My brother is barely cold in the clay where you helped put him and now I can't bring a friend on holiday without you hounding me.'

The younger fisherman who had a foxy look eyed me up. 'Is this your one who imagines she's Mac Suibhne's daughter?' he asked.

'She is who she is,' Luke replied sharply.

'Shut the fuck up, the lot of you,' Brennan ordered. 'Get into the cars. You'll be interviewed in Killybegs.'

'This girl has nothing to do with anything,' Luke told him.

'She'll go where she's fucking told,' Brennan snapped and put his face up to Luke. 'I've had enough of dealing with you and the scum you gather around you.'

'I'm going home to my bed,' Michael James said. 'There's foreign factory ships draining the ocean of every scrap of fish while the Irish navy pisses around like blue-arsed flies in our couple of Mickey Mouse patrol vessels. Yet I can't take a shite without you boyos up my arse about quotas. The fish was caught legally. I know nothing about anything else.'

'You'll stay in custody until we've examined everything you landed in your nets,' Brennan said.

'Well, that's fecking it,' Michael James spat as I was pushed into a car with Luke. 'I always knew the special branch were thick, but I never knew you fecking read *Reader's Digest*.'

I could see a line of squad cars on the quayside in Killybegs which had been sealed off. A battered looking fishing boat was being combed by men in white overalls. A policeman deposited a pile of sodden magazines on to the floor of the station. Michael James kicked them as he was led past.

'The sea is like a tip out there,' he said. 'There was a big yacht moored last night with somebody throwing bags of rubbish overboard. A right spring cleaning. Ask any of the skippers, we all fished up something.'

The fishermen were led into a side room while Luke and I were bundled into another one. Brennan sat at the far side of the table, staring into Luke's face. Luke ignored him, carefully choosing a spot high on the wall to gaze at.

'You've the right to phone your solicitor,' Brennan said.

'I don't need a solicitor. I've done nothing wrong.'

Brennan questioned me about how long I had known Luke and why I'd come to Donegal. Seamie entered the room to lean against the back wall. I sensed he didn't like what was going on with the fishermen, though he was powerless to prevent it. Brennan asked him if he had heard of Proinsías Mac Suibhne.

'A fine fiddle-player,' Seamie said.

'The best,' Luke corrected.

'What would you know, Duggan?' Brennan sneered. 'You're more an Abba man yourself.'

'I grew up, Brennan,' Luke said, 'you just grew. I travelled the length of Ireland with Jamie O'Connor when you were still calling your mother up to boast about the size of your poo.'

All I had against Luke was Al's word. Luke had once told me Al was jealous of him. I wondered could he have invented everything from spite and even tipped off the police after all?

Brennan questioned me again about my father and if I could prove I was his daughter. He asked Seamie to organise for Mac Suibhne to be brought to the station to identify me. There were a dozen ways I had fantasised about meeting my father, but never in my worst dreams had it been like this.

'Please, don't do that,' I begged. I broke down and Luke placed his arm around my shoulder. It felt reassuring to have him beside me.

'The girl hasn't seen her father for twenty years,' I heard Luke say. 'Keep me all day if you want, but you can't drag that man down here at his age.'

'Don't tell me what I can do!' Brennan snapped but I knew Luke's words were aimed more towards Seamie. It was the policeman who spoke.

'Taking him in wouldn't be a good idea.' There was an air of quiet mutiny in his voice. 'I don't know who the lassie is, but you'll find no man here willing to put Mac Suibhne into a squad car.'

'The girl's family in London can verify her story,' Luke said and told Brennan about Gran's stroke. He claimed to be a family friend. I lifted my head, chilled by the way he knew the hospital phone number. He gave Brennan the name of the ward and stated how it was my grandfather's habit to visit around this time. Suddenly my entire family had been roped in to give Luke an alibi for being there. I believed Al again. Brennan watched me. To dispute anything Luke said would be to risk meeting my father for the first time in a police cell. I agreed that Grandad Pete would confirm who my father was and that Luke was taking me to find him. I couldn't understand why this was happening but Luke wouldn't have the hospital phone number memorised unless he had orchestrated every-thing. He reached for my hand when Brennan left to make the call.

'You don't deserve this, Tracey,' he said. 'But it's the same whenever I visit Ireland.'

Two more guards joined Seamie in watching over us.

'You stayed in the Bishop's Palace,' one sneered. 'They've lovely four poster beds, I believe.'

I didn't turn around but I sensed three pairs of eyes undressing me. Luke released my limp hand and stroked my neck possessively, with quiet pride. I knew the policemen envied him.

'Did you really know Jamie O'Connor?' Seamie asked and Luke nodded. 'My uncle played with the best of them in his youth. He even recorded for Decca in New York. His son came home from America twenty years ago and managed to buy a fiddle from O'Connor that had been played in his family for generations.'

There wasn't even the flicker of a smile from Luke.

'Your brother died a few weeks back,' another policeman said. 'The Ice-man they called him.'

'It's a gas country,' Luke said quietly. 'You could rob a dozen banks and if your name was John Smith nobody would want to know you. But acquire a nickname and even if you're only a lollipop lady you'll be nationally famous.'

'Come on now, Duggan,' the policeman said, 'you don't get a nickname for nothing.'

'I'm guilty there,' Luke replied. 'When I was seventeen I smuggled a copy of *Playboy* home from England. There was an article on multiple orgasms. It said the best trick was to pop an ice-cube up your girlfriend's arse just as she was coming. Poor Christy was always susceptible to what he read in magazines.'

'Did it work?' the policeman asked.

'Not exactly. The girl's screams woke her parents and half the street and she nearly battered him to death. But it gave Christy a nickname for life.'

The policemen laughed. I glanced behind. One of them checked for any sign of Brennan in the corridor.

'Has it worked since?' he asked, eyeing me up. In London I would have out-stared him till he looked away, all wimpish and embarrassed. But here I just looked down at the table.

'Leave it out, lads,' Luke told them quietly. He patted my hand and said, 'It won't be long now.' I wanted them to find drugs on that yacht or where divers were searching the sea. I wanted Luke hanged, drawn and quartered, but I knew they would find nothing and I couldn't say a word against Luke because everyone understood that I was the blonde mistress who knew nothing, probably not even the name of her real father. I imagined Grandad Pete being called into a room in the hospital and I couldn't bear the thought of having to face him again. Brennan returned and scowled at the two new policemen.

'What's this, a peep-show?' he demanded. 'What the fuck do yous want?'

'All the divers recovered were a load of business magazines and some soft porn novels by the look of the covers, only they're in Dutch. Do you want to bring them home with you?'

'Don't get fucking smart, right!'

'Can we release the fishermen?' Seamie asked. 'They're decent men who've been up all night.'

'Why were they selling fish by the side of the road?'

'Michael James' wife is tighter than a nun's arse when it comes to money,' Seamie said. 'She gets the cheque from the fishery co-op. It's his only chance to make the price of a few pints on the side.'

'Wait till the yacht is searched,' Brennan insisted.

'The navy phoned in. She's clean as a whistle. They've shadowed her for days and all it was was Dutch tourists.'

'Get the fuck out.' The policemen prised themselves from the wall, savouring Brennan's annoyance as they left. He eyed the pair of us. 'You two as well.'

'You owe this girl an apology,' Luke said, still gazing at a spot above Brennan's head. He knew I wanted to be gone, but couldn't seem to resist a last chance to rub Brennan's nose in it. Brennan ignored Luke and observed me.

'Your Grandad sounds a nice man,' he said. 'But he wouldn't be the first one conned by white trash from the Dublin slums.'

He strode from the room before Luke could reply. We must

only have been alone for a few seconds, but it seemed longer before Luke shifted his gaze from the wall.

'I'm sorry this had to happen,' he said and took my hand.

I jerked it away and pushed the chair back. It clattered to the ground. I walked quickly, trying not to look at anyone. Luke's hired car was parked in the station forecourt. I pushed the glass door open and ran.

I slowed to a fast walk as I turned on to the narrow street. It was just after twelve. I heard Luke call and then the sound of his car starting. The pavement was narrow with cars parked tightly against it. I wanted to run again but I knew it would only make Luke drive faster.

'Get into the car, Tracey,' he called through the open window. 'I know you're upset but that's enough now.'

Maybe it was delayed shock which made me start crying again but I couldn't stop. Two women stood in a shop doorway, observing me. I almost fell over a pram but stumbled on. I hated this town with its cluttered pavements and stink of fish. More locals stopped to watch like it was an entertainment. I passed a television repair shop with the legend 'Mac Suibhne' in tacky plastic lettering above the door. It was the first time I'd seen the word printed. I wanted to be back in London or in any city big enough to swallow me up. My father wouldn't want to know me. What had possessed me to think I could come back to somewhere I had never even been? I reached a corner and Luke swung to a halt in front of me. I thought he was about to jump from the car, but he contented himself with calling out the window again.

'Get into the car, Tracey, please.' He sounded concerned and bewildered. 'Why are you doing this to me? You've no money, you know nobody. Another hour's drive and you'll meet your father.'

'I don't want to meet him,' I said, 'leave me alone.'

I turned right and started to run. At first I thought Luke was letting me go, then I realised he was merely staying at a benevolent distance, like an amused adult indulging my tantrum. There was an archway between two shops. I turned down it, thinking Luke couldn't squeeze the car through but he did. It looked like a dead end. He picked up speed, coming towards me. He was going to kill me, I thought, now that I had served whatever purpose it was that I'd had. Then I saw a narrow passageway to the left. I ran down it, hearing the car stop and Luke curse through the window. He hesitated, trying to decide whether to chase me on foot, and then I heard the car reverse.

I came out on to another road, wider this time and lined with narrow houses. A car was parked in front of me with a trailer attached. I dodged past on to the road. A child sat on the pavement, wrapped in a coat and playing with a toy boat in the gutter. It looked so dangerous I wanted to run over and pick him up. It was years since I'd seen a child unattended in London, but the golden rule was never to touch a stranger's child. I looked around, not sure where Luke might come from. The road merged with the one I had left in a V junction to my left. I turned right and started to run when I heard a car emerge from a laneway beside a pub. It was a blue Volkswagen driven by an elderly man who peered out from under a cap. I didn't so much hitch a lift as threw myself at the passenger door. The driver leaned over to open it.

'That's a bloody desperate way to ask anyone for a lift,' he complained. I didn't answer, but just climbed in and crouched in the passenger seat, raising a sleeve to childishly wipe my face. There was shopping in the back seat. 'Where are you heading at all?'

Luke's car paused at the V as he scanned the deserted street. I sank lower in the Volkswagen as Luke drove towards us.

'Can you take me out of Killybegs?' I asked.

'If the bloody car holds up. The garage man never serviced

it at all.' He released the hand-brake as Luke drove past. I couldn't tell if he'd seen me. The driver moved off with a steady speed, occasionally glancing at me as if I was unstable. He was the crankiest man I had ever encountered. The supermarket were desperate robbers, the chemist would turn milk sour, the sun wouldn't shine if you stuck dynamite up its arse. He cursed everyone he'd met in the town, revelling in their faults. It would have broken his heart if I'd been a smiling wholesome hitch-hiker. Luckily I was sullen and silent and would provide him with hours of pleasant complaining.

'I'm heading up to Glenmalin. Will you mind yourself with them thieving robbers in Carrick if I drop you there?'

'I'd sooner go to where you're heading,' I said, wanting to put as much distance as possible between myself and Killybegs. The driver raised his eyes to heaven. I glanced back. Luke's car was a hundred yards behind us.

'Is it far?' I asked.

'We'll get there when we get there,' he said, 'unless the bloody road has been swept out to sea for all them feckers in the County Council do to mend it.'

Luke had to be following us because he would never drive this slowly. There was nothing I could do. I felt safe as long as I was in the car. In whatever village the old man was heading for I'd have to find a crowded pub where Luke would be afraid to grab me. Mentally I counted whatever money I had, knowing it wasn't enough for a flight home. There might be a cheap bus out of here. I should have left with Al last night. I wondered was he okay.

We passed a hamlet, which was no more than a wide bend on the road, then left the coast and climbed inland, following signposts for Carrick. My father had played there before Christmas in Byrne's pub. I tried to imagine that solitary man walking these roads at all hours of the night. Sometimes Luke's car dipped out of sight as if he was playing a game of cat and mouse, daring me to ask the driver to stop so I could slip out

350

and hide. I knew he was picking up speed every few minutes, studying each ditch and bush he passed. He hadn't planned to kill me in that lane in Killybegs. I was still ignorant of everything as far as he was concerned, and just upset after being dragged into a police station. The safest thing would have been to carry on with him until I got back to London, but even there he would never let me go. There would be a web of lies and compromises woven into my life until I came to depend on him. If I changed address he would stalk me; I'd find his car outside my door and learn to recognise his silence on the phone at night.

By running away I was putting myself in danger. Whatever game he was playing, nobody would be allowed to step out of their role. I kept glancing anxiously back at the road, but every time my gaze had to take in the driver as well. I sensed him become more self-conscious, suspicious that I was after something. He had found nothing to complain about for miles until we reached Carrick. I asked him to point out Byrne's pub. He did and asked again if I would not get out. He wanted to be rid of me but the street looked deserted and Luke's car had already crossed the bridge behind us.

'I'll go on to where you're going,' I said. The old man drove on grudgingly and I looked back at the small pub which doubled as an ordinary house and asked, 'Is it true they've music there?'

'Not so much lately,' the driver complained, 'with these new bloody drink driving laws. There's men living up the mountains afraid to come down and meet their neighbours in case they're done. It's lonely enough in winter, and sure the only thing the poor feckers had was a bit of chat and music in the pub. Otherwise they'd not see a soul the whole day through. I was down in Byrne's myself before Christmas to hear an old lad play, but half the pub were sipping fizzy lemonade with bastards of guards lurking outside. That's no life for grown men, but it's the same with all the new laws coming in. I don't care how much money we got, we should never have sold ourselves to Brussels.'

People in Dublin had spoken about my father in terms of genius. But here he was just an old lad, an everyday wonder. It made him more human and I felt closer to him for that. After several miles the driver left the road for Glencolumbkille and swung left along a potholed road where two cars could hardly pass. I was disappointed and then relieved. Luke was lagging behind and wouldn't have seen us turn. I was free. We drove for several more miles in silence. The road twisted its way along and it was hard to see anything behind us. A huge mountain lay to my left, sombre and almost sinister in its sheer bulk. A lake glinted in the distance, feeding a swollen river which gushed down the mountainside. We plummeted downwards, twisting through a maze of sally trees and hedge-rows. I'd never seen anywhere to match this place. I even stopped glancing behind and now it was the driver who looked across at me. He slowed and I was suddenly nervous. Luke wasn't the problem any more. The man was seventy if a day, but he looked strong and there wasn't a house for miles. It was the sort of spot where a body might lie undisturbed for years. There was a laneway to the left, so overgrown with bushes it was almost impassable. The driver pulled up at the entrance to it and looked me up and down. His lip was flecked with white froth.

'Glenmalin,' he announced. 'It's a bloody desperate glen in winter but at least you're dressed for the walk.'

'This is it?' I asked.

He sighed, exasperated. 'I offered twice to leave you in Carrick.'

'What's up the lane?'

'My house and another bachelor's.'

Something about the way he said it suggested I was the predator. I remembered a story of Luke's about a con-man who drove up isolated lanes with a prostitute in a horse box and robbed bachelor's houses as the woman serviced them. The old man had brought me to my destination, now he wanted me to leave the car.

'What's on ahead?' I asked.

'You'll meet the main road again two miles on. Turn right for Glencolumbkille or, if you're daft enough, go left to Malinbeg. It's a dead-end though. Only a fecking lunatic would go there on a day like this.'

A tractor with a trailer of hay came up behind us. We were blocking the road. I got out and watched the old man drive up the lane, with branches whipping against his windscreen, then stood back to let the tractor pass. The driver lifted a finger in casual salute and I saw Luke's car stuck between the trailer and some yokel on a mud-splattered motor bike who was stuck behind him. The tractor went by slowly, leaving wisps of hay on the hedgerows. There was nowhere to run. Luke saw me and pulled into the laneway. The motor bike swerved past and drove on. To my relief, the tractor pulled into a gateway further on and the motor bike stopped too. There seemed something wrong with the way the engine was firing. The yokel turned the engine off and dismounted, kneeling to try and adjust it. The tractor driver called over to him, then glanced back at me. He reached for a sack of sheep nuts and threw them over the iron gate into a field where hungry sheep crowded up, baaing wildly. I felt safer with the men there. Luke got out of the car and looked as me like I was a wayward child.

'What will I do with you, Tracey?' he asked. 'Do you think I've time to chase half way across Donegal? I came here for your sake. Can't you see the hassle I get every time I come home? Now I promised to bring you to your father, if it was the last thing we did, and I'll keep my promise.'

'Stay away from me.' I stepped back. 'There's people watching.'

Luke glanced at the tractor parked with the engine running.

353

The farmer had disappeared into the field. The yokel kick-started his bike but the engine spluttered out again.

'What's got into you, Tracey?' Luke asked, puzzled. 'It's like you're scared of me. You know I'd never harm a hair of your head.'

'Then leave me alone, please.'

'Here in the middle of nowhere? Get into the car. I'm responsible for you. What would your Grandad . . . ?'

'Leave him out of it! Stop dragging him into your games.'

'What games?'

There was the faintest crack in Luke's forbearance. I should have stayed quiet but I couldn't stop my anger coming out.

'How did you know the number of Gran's hospital?' I said.

'I've a friend who's a porter there. I often phone him. What difference does it make?'

'You set this whole business up. The police, everything. You used me as an alibi.'

Luke looked baffled, but watchful too. 'An alibi for what?' He took a step forward, forcing me further down the lane. 'I knew you were unstable from the very start. The Irish police hated Christy. They could prove nothing against him, now they're starting on me.'

'Keep back,' I said, frightened, 'I know about you . . ."

'You know nothing, Tracey,' Luke said more firmly, taking another step. 'You're getting above yourself now. Three months ago you were a nobody living a nothing life until I took you up. You didn't even know how to suck cock properly till I showed you.'

'Luckily you'd such a good teacher in Brother Damian!'

Luke stopped dead. It was the sort of mistake he would never have made. His features looked different than I'd ever seen them before. This is the real Luke, I thought, what he actually looks like. He walked towards me with exaggerated calmness as I backed down the overgrown lane, out of sight of the men. With the noise from the tractor and the motor bike engine occasionally spluttering into life they probably wouldn't hear if I screamed. We had gone twenty yards when I stopped, scared of Luke, yet too scared to venture further away from the road.

'I never mentioned Brother Damian's name,' he said, quietly. 'Luckily I love you, because you're full of surprises. Suddenly you think you know a lot.'

'Let me go, Luke. I'll say nothing to nobody.'

'I'm not holding you,' he said. 'It's you who keeps walking down this lane. Brother Damian, eh? What else do you think you know?'

'Nothing. Please.'

'Could our friend Al have been talking?' Luke asked. 'I thought I kept you apart in London, but I must have been wrong. Like I was wrong to flatter myself that it was me you wanted, when really you couldn't wait to take your knickers off for any Irishman.'

'It was never like that, Luke.'

He took another step forward. The ditch beside us was deep and flooded with plastic sacks of rubbish. The tractor sounded like it was trying to reverse into the field with difficulty. Luke put his hands out, with the palms wide.

'What else did Al tell you?' he asked. 'That all his life he's been a failure? That I had to take him to London and knock some manhood into him?'

'Maybe he didn't want to go.'

'None of my family ever wanted to do anything. Did he tell you about Shane growing up, never wearing a stitch of clothes I hadn't already worn and Christy before me? About the three of us freezing in one bed in winter? Did he tell you what hunger was like? He did not, because he's never known it. Did he tell what it felt like to have the Vincent de Paul call with their stinking charity vouchers while our two uncles swanned about picking up whores in Dolly Fossett's? Or what it was like to have a father labouring in England, too stuck up to accept cash from his brothers? Did he tell you that my whole family would be still dirt poor if it wasn't for me? That I've had to sort out every dogfight and piece of shit they've walked themselves into? That I'm stuck half way up this fucking bog still trying to do just that?'

'Please, Luke,' I said, 'I don't know anything.' I'd never seen him angry before. Beating up Al had been a carefully controlled act. This was different, like he was in pain. Then his manner took on that unearthly calmness again.

'Anyway, it doesn't matter what Al said.' Luke took another step so that I was forced towards the ditch. 'It's rumour and innuendo, useless against a good barrister. I'm sorry, Tracey, but you're still a nobody. What you know is immaterial unless you can prove it. What's real is the power of what we have going between us. You can't honestly believe it's over. There were nights you drenched your knickers just walking into that hotel room.'

The tractor roared at full throttle as it emerged from the field and came into view at the mouth of the lane. I hoped it would try to turn up the lane past Luke's car but it just went past. I was shaking. I grabbed a branch to stop myself falling into the ditch.

'It's over between us, Luke. Let me go.'

He was suddenly desperate. He shook his head. 'I can't,' he said. 'I couldn't bear it if you weren't part of my life.'

'You knew it could never last. Let me go, please.' Luke came closer. I was scared of the way he looked. 'Grandad will report me missing. The police know I'm here with you.'

He smiled. 'Can't you see that I made sure the whole of Ireland knows you're here with me? I would have brought you quietly if you hadn't been unfaithful with Al. You needed to be taught a lesson. But that's behind us now. What's important is that we find your father.' Luke put a hand to my cheek and I flinched. 'You're quite safe, Donegal is swarming with guards. They even have Ireland's excuse for a navy sweeping the coast.'

The pride in his voice gave me the answer. This whole trip was a decoy, the yacht being tracked at sea, Luke slipping in through a remote airport like Knock. Everyone knew that three quarters of a million pounds was missing. Since Christy's funeral all eyes had been on him.

'Where are you really landing the drugs?' I asked.

'That has nothing to do with me,' Luke said. 'I'm just sorting out another family mess. But one of Ireland's joys is the hundreds of miles of remote bays with few natives left to ask questions. What navy could patrol that, particularly when it's camped off Donegal? But it's nothing to do with you or me. I'm happy selling wall tiles and keeping my kids out of Dublin. That city has gone to hell, with little wankers throwing their weight, thinking they're someone because they've an Armalite in one hand and a condom of heroin up their arse. The Duggans never did drugs. We earned respect the hard way before Christy went crazy and signed his own death warrant, taking these young thugs on.'

Luke had already re-written the story of this robbery in his own mind, absolving himself of any blame. He genuinely saw himself as picking up the pieces of other people's mistakes. I thought I had glimpsed every side to him, but now I realised that only somebody half deranged would have ever dared to pick me up like that in the Irish Centre.

'If they want heroin in Dublin, then they deserve all they get,' Luke said. 'It can sell so cheap that babies will crawl from their prams to queue for it. But I want no part of it. Let the place self-destruct with gangs of punks killing each other. But wait and see, before long one of them will employ outside muscle, the Triads or the Russian mafia. Strangers will sweep in to pick the place clean. Any state worth a wank would have these punks behind bars years ago. Now let's find your father and get the hell out of here.'

357

I had closed my eyes. I couldn't bear looking at Luke's face. He still honestly believed we had a future. I opened them again when I heard the motor bike engine start. The yokel had got it working at last. Luke turned in surprise, having forgotten about him too. I dodged past Luke and ran towards the road, shouting for the motor bike to stop. The motor cyclist came into view and turned down the lane. I stopped, recognising him, not from the bike which was different, but from that blue helmet with the dent in its side. The visor was pulled down. I don't know why my father's song came into my mind.

What brings you here so late, said the knight on the road,
I go to meet my God, said the child as he stood.
And he stood and he stood, 'twas well that he stood,
I go to meet my God, said the child as he stood.

I stood perfectly still like the words instructed me. Luke had reached my shoulder. He stopped, puzzled looking, then backed away and began to run, leaving me to face the bike which approached leisurely. The motorcyclist turned to stare into my face, only he had no face. There were just the shapes of bushes reflected in the visor's smoked glass. I realised who he had been searching for as he weaved his way through the cars waiting to board the ferry in Dublin. He passed me in silence and I turned to watch Luke run. He stumbled on a pothole and crashed to the ground. It was ridiculous but I wanted to tell him that if he stayed still the devil couldn't touch him. The bike stopped. Luke looked up and then back at me.

'The girl is just some cheap tart,' he said. 'She knows nothing.'

He didn't look at me again, but stood up and started walking away. This time he didn't run and I realised that he had only done so the first time to draw the motor cyclist towards him and give me a chance to flee. But I couldn't move. I was amazed at how simple it was to die. Luke fell forward when the first bullet tore into his back, but managed to sit up and stare at the motor cyclist who slowly aimed the gun at Luke's groin. Luke's face changed.

'No,' he said. He looked back at me. 'Please.'

It was not clear what he was pleading for, but it wasn't mercy. He ignored the gun as he struggled up again and walked a few paces forward. The motor cyclist raised the pistol to aim the second shot directly through the base of his skull. Luke fell into the ditch and there was no further sign of him. The bike slowly wheeled around and came back towards me. I couldn't stop the singing in my head:

Hark, I hear a bell, said the knight on the road,
And it's ringing you to hell, said the child as he stood.
He stood and he stood, 'twas well that he stood,
It's ringing you to hell, said the child as he stood.

The bike barely seemed to be moving as it drew alongside me. I couldn't move. I watched the motor cyclist hold the gun out, almost in slow motion. It seemed to brush very lightly against the side of my cheek. I had a sense of how hot the barrel was, and the smell of petrol fumes blended in with a scent of lost childhood afternoons. There was a moment's hesitation, then, almost against his will, he was gone past. The engine roared and finally faded away. Luke lay in those bushes. The thought struck me that somehow he might still be alive, but I was too afraid to look. I don't know how long I stood there until I turned to run past his parked car, in total silence except for the scream which I couldn't shake from my head.

TWENTY-THREE

I HAD LOST any sense of time so I don't know how long it took me to reach the main road leading back into Glencolumbkille. The late afternoon was utterly still. Even the breeze had stopped stirring. There wasn't a sound, except for the echo of shots in my head. I kept walking at the same pace, resisting an urge to run because there was nowhere to run to. I told myself that if the motor cyclist wished to kill me he would have done so back in the lane. But I was still certain he would change his mind and return.

Occasionally I'd stop to slap my palm against a gate or a telegraph pole to convince myself I hadn't gone deaf. I knew I was in shock, but I was afraid to look behind in case he was there. I wondered who would find Luke and how long he would lie in that ditch. Everything felt heightened around me. Those drab motionless clouds might be the last ones I would ever see and now their shapes fascinated me. I had never seen moss growing on a stone wall like this or drenched fields of winter grass or ever listened to water purling down from a dozen hillside streams. I would have given so much to have walked through this landscape just once with my mother, to have had the memory of such a place where I could have brought her ashes to scatter. I thought of Gran too and remembered playing in her bedroom one childhood afternoon.

Only twice did a car pass by, splashing me with water from roadside puddles. I chose the turn for Glencolumbkille almost without thinking. After a mile or two I reached a turn and the sea suddenly stretched out to my left towards a huge headland looming across the bay. Below the road as it swung round another bend was a small pier with a few boats pulled up on the slip. It seemed an insular world, fortified by steep mountains and the wild Atlantic. I walked on until eventually and indifferently, I saw the village spread out in a loose scattering of houses before me. I walked for a long time without the village appearing to get any closer and then suddenly I was outside the first building, which had been a schoolhouse once. I could see a plaque dating from 1912.

A girl of eight or nine sat on the step wearing blue wellington boots which were too large for her. I stopped beside the gate and scanned the road behind me for any sign of the motor bike. There was so much I wanted to tell the child, yet I couldn't make sense of my thoughts and felt unsure if I still held the power of speech. She observed me for a moment before calling back into the house; 'Granny, here's another stray lost without a word of English.'

A middle-aged woman emerged in a blue apron to scold the girl good naturedly for wearing her brother's boots. The child pointed towards me and the woman approached, her tone officious now.

'What is it? We're closed for the winter.'

My throat was parched. I tried to swallow but it hurt too much. She observed me more closely, sensing something was wrong.

'What has you out here in January?' Her voice was almost suspicious. 'Are you looking for somewhere to stay? Have you lost your bags?'

'Please,' I heard myself mumble.

The child had risen to walk over to the gate and stare at me. 'I thought she was deaf and dumb,' she said and her granny hushed her.

'Whist, child, she's only English.' The woman looked at me, concerned now. 'Are you in some sort of trouble? Where have you come from? Do you want to stay?' I felt myself nod.

361

'This is an An Oige hostel. Are you a member of the Irish Youth Hostel Federation?'

I shook my head. Concern or curiosity had softened her manner. 'Maybe you're a member of the English Federation?'

I shook my head again and gripped the bar of the gate. I felt my legs were going to give way, yet I didn't want to collapse in front of the child.

'You probably were a member some time,' the woman said.

I shook my head a third time. The woman wiped her hands on the apron. 'Have you never heard of a white lie?' she scolded. 'Maybe you once thought of joining or knew someone who did?'

The child tugged at the woman's apron. 'Let her stay, Nana.'

'We're closed,' the woman said. 'Officially I can't let anyone stay, which means I can damn well let you stay whether you're a member or not.' She opened the gate and had to prise my hand off the bar. 'Look at the state you're in,' she said, worried now, and instructed the child; 'Molly, run in and lift out those clothes drying in the bath.'

With her initial suspicion gone, it was like the woman and child had adopted me. They sat me in the kitchen while she ran a bath. The girl returned to lay a cup and a plate of scones in front of me. The woman filled the teapot and set it down on the table. The radio was on but the station seemed to be in Irish. I tried to lift the teapot but my hand wouldn't stop shaking. Tea splashed over the oilcloth until the woman held my hand and helped me to pour it. She set the teapot down, then took my hand in her own again and sat on the chair beside me. I saw the child linger in the doorway, knowing that if she came any closer she would be banished.

'You're crying,' the woman said, 'and you don't even seem to notice. What's wrong with you, child? Were you robbed above on the hillside, or did someone hurt you? There's a payphone in the hall if you'd like to phone home.'

I shook my head dully. Through the window I saw a squad car speeding up the hill. The woman followed my gaze.

'That sergeant,' she mocked, 'the only time you see him speeding is when he's hurrying home for his tea.' She squeezed my hand again. 'Is there no one I can phone for you? Would you like me to maybe call a doctor or the guards?'

'There's a man . . .' I began. 'A man out there . . .' I couldn't continue. I lowered my head and Luke's face stared at me, with his skull torn asunder in the ditch. After all the acts our bodies had shared, I had left him lying like that. Luke had never claimed to be good or bad, he said nobody did anything for one reason only. Even though he had used me, I was more than just a decoy. Time had been running out for him, everyone knew he had to land those drugs somewhere. But he could have chosen anywhere in Ireland, knowing the police would follow him. Part of him had wanted to bring me to my father, that part which was in perpetual conflict with the Luke who had exploited me. Yet conflict didn't seem the correct word. I doubted if Luke even noticed how effortlessly he acquired different personalities at different times.

The only way I could remember him now was as a dozen photo-fits that never quite matched. How could I tell the woman which Luke it was who lay in that ditch? Somewhere off the Irish coast a small boat had docked by now, but I had no evidence of that and no idea where. Luke must have lain awake, dreaming of this final big payday which he had staked everything on, even his brother's life. Yet no matter how high the stakes, they would never have been enough to quell the dread of poverty I had glimpsed within him.

The woman squeezed my hand again, trying to coax me to talk. 'What man?' she asked. 'Was he your boy-friend? Had you a row? Is he after leaving you out here with no bags or nothing?' I saw her check my arms and face for signs of an assault. 'Or was it a local man. Did anyone . . . ?' She said something in Irish to the girl in the doorway who retreated from sight. 'Do you understand what I'm saying? Are you all right?'

I nodded my head slowly. Every time I closed my eyes I saw the back of Luke's head caving in as he disappeared into the ditch. The woman let go my hand and rose. She touched my hair, unsure of what to make of me.

'I've water run for a bath,' she said. 'You might feel better able to talk then.'

She led me down a corridor where a door led into the hostel. There had to be shower units there, but the woman brought me into her own small bathroom built on to the back of the house. She had put scented salts into the bath and bubbles of foam floated on the surface. There was a child's duck and a plastic toy boat at the side and sea shells with traces of sand on them. I needed a fresh tampon badly and had to ask her for one.

'I'm beyond all that,' she said, 'and the child's mother is away working in Scotland for the winter. I'll have to send Molly down the town.'

I lay in the hot water, awaiting the child's return. I lowered my head so that just my mouth and nose were uncovered. Soon Luke's car would be found and then his body. The police from Killybegs would come looking for me but what would I tell them? Luke had walked away from me deliberately, giving me back the role of cheap tart with his last words. I was a nobody, too stupid to know anything. Luke had understood the safety of ignorance and calculated the best chance for my survival. He had sought and expected no mercy, grasping human nature so well that even a faceless assassin did his bidding. Perhaps he had recognised that Christy's fate would also be his own. Leaving that hotel on the first night, I had looked back and carried away the image of a man found dead. For once Luke had misjudged the odds. He must have known the Bypass Bombardiers were closing in. Death was stalking him, even as he had tried to re-unite me with my father. Now it had found him along the sort of country lane he had once walked before dawn to pick fruit with his brothers.

I lowered my face fully under the water and opened my eyes. I could see the green foam merging above me again. I felt nothing, not even the need to continue breathing. The door must have opened although I hadn't heard it. The child's face leaned over the bath, distorted by the bubbles. She stared down until I broke the surface.

'I got you these.' She handed me the package. I noticed she had swapped her brother's boots for more feminine sneakers. I waited for her to go but she stayed, staring at my body.

'What were you doing under the water?' she asked.

'Bring me a scissors,' I instructed her, 'or a sharp blade.'

'Do I tell Nana?' she asked. I immersed my face beneath the water and closed my eyes to watch Luke's brain explode. I opened them quickly and surfaced but she was gone. I dried myself and put on the only clothes I had. I found my way to the dormitory. It was a spartan room crowded with triple bunk beds with horsehair mattresses and iron frames. Three tall windows let light into what must once have been a classroom. The air smelt of must and cold. The woman had left out sheets for me and two extra blankets. I lay on a low bunk and watched the last light drain from the sky. The dormitories of Saint Raphael's would have been bigger, eighty boys asleep in each room, dreaming of cars, revenge and women. Only Luke's dreams had been of things which could never be realised. Part of him had never grown up, perhaps it was all we ever had in common. But there came a time to grow up or to die.

The ditch would be dark now where he lay, if nobody had found the car yet. When spring came, flowers and berries would grow along the hedgerow as hikers walked past with thick boots and foreign accents. Nothing would ever be said about him. No plaque would mark the spot and nobody would place flowers. This was tourist country where outsiders left no trace and Luke was as much a foreigner here as I was. Only the old bachelors who used the road would ever glance towards the ditch where he had lain.

I must have entered a different stage of shock because the trembling in my hands had stopped and I was curiously calm. I wanted to mourn Luke but didn't know which man to mourn. At his funeral every mourner would remember a different one. Had he ever allowed himself to be himself, even when alone? I closed my eyes and saw him pick himself up after that first shot and stagger forward. His brain burst open and I watched him fall one last time. I couldn't seem to remember his face any more, there was just blackness before my eyes. I looked up and the child stood beside my bunk holding a long pair of sharp scissors.

'What are you going to do?' she asked.

'Go away.'

The child stared at me, then turned and left the room. But she was too young to keep girlish secrets. She must have fetched her granny because after a few minutes the door opened and I heard footsteps run forward. By then, I was crouched in a ball beneath the high windows. The woman grabbed the scissors from my hand, but she was too late. I saw specks of blood on the shining blades as she dropped them into her apron pocket.

'Your beautiful hair,' she said, 'whatever have you done to it?'

I raised my hand. I hadn't felt pain when the scissors grazed my scalp. Clumps of long blonde hair littered the floor with a tint of black at the base of the roots. The woman placed her arms around me and let me cry, rocking me back and forth without a word. She must have said something to the girl because she was gone and some long time afterwards – I didn't know how long – the child returned with a woman in her thirties who knelt down to inspect my scalp.

'You look a mess,' she said. 'I have a salon down the road. Do you want me to shave it all off?'

I nodded and they brought me back out into the kitchen and placed a towel around my shoulders. A boy of twelve was there, whom the woman banished with a few words of Irish. The girl gathered up my hair from the dormitory floor and carried it in.

'But you've lovely hair,' she said, almost in tears. 'I would kill to have blonde hair like that.'

The hairdresser worked gently, shaving my scalp, trying to soothe me down and help me talk.

'Maire tells me it was a man,' she said. 'Did he do something to you? The local guards are all men themselves, but there's a woman guard I know in Donegal town. Would you like me to phone her or else a doctor? We're worried about you.'

'I just wanted rid of this hair,' I said, surprised at how calm my voice sounded. 'It's been driving me daft this past fortnight.'

'You see the men come up from the pub to a dance here,' the hairdresser said, 'half-drunk for courage, eyeing us up like heifers in a mart. Get me the hell away from here, you say to yourself, off to some place with a bit of panache. But they're still the same wherever you go. The clothes might be different or the hair styles and they've fancy ways to hide it, but you're still a heifer in a mart.'

Molly had forgotten about us and retreated into being a child again, absorbed in some make-believe game with the loose strands of hair. The kettle sang and the woman poured a strong measure of whiskey and sugar into a glass which she half filled with boiling water. She added cloves and pressed it into my fingers.

'Drink that up,' she said, 'it will put some heat inside you. I'll get some dinner on. Guests in the hostel cook for themselves, but we're glad of company this time of year. Every young one is away, even my own daughter, having to leave two children behind. Put your head down after dinner and sleep. Sleep is a great healer. I should know.'

The whiskey burnt against my throat. I was drinking too fast but I put it to my lips again. The hairdresser produced a mirror and handed it to me. I didn't recognise myself but it was a long time since I had. Yet my face seemed more like my own with the blonde hair gone. The news was being broadcast on the radio, low in the background. I heard the name Duggan mentioned and asked what was being said. The hairdresser listened and then translated with a dismissive shrug.

'Just another Dublin gangster found shot dead. It says the man's brother was only killed a few weeks ago.'

For all his craving for respectability that is how Luke had ended up, another gangster meriting a few seconds in Irish on the radio. The police would be here soon. If I had sense I should go to them first.

'When did they find the body?'

'Around lunch-time.'

'But he wasn't . . .' I stopped. The hairdresser didn't seem to notice. She was drying her hands with a towel.

'He was driving a van near Waterford,' she said. 'They hijacked it, emptied out whatever was in the back and shot him. It's worse than New York down there, they're animals.'

The boy appeared at the kitchen door and called his sister. She looked up, torn between him and playing with the blonde hair. He called again and she dropped the hair and ran to obey, with the blind loyalty of the youngest in a family.

Seven o'clock came and then eight. I hadn't taken my clothes off as I lay on the bunk, curled up into a ball with the blankets tightly wrapped around me. I had ceased to see Luke's death in my mind, or even to be haunted by the moment when I thought I was going to die; the image of the visor reflecting back the green bushes and my own scared face, and the feel of a gun brushing against my cheek. What perplexed me was the memory of that faint aroma, almost totally swamped by the stink of petrol fumes, and why it had made me think of Gran. I don't know how long the child was standing beside my bunk before I turned and saw her. She wore a long scarf which was obviously her grandmother's. I closed my eyes and suddenly placed that scent. I saw myself at her age sneaking into Gran's room to try on clothes before the mirror and breathing in that reek of musk which had always pervaded her wardrobe.

'He's here,' the girl said. 'I know it's you he's come for.'

I had an image of Luke stumbling down the hillside like Frankenstein's monster, undead and unslayable. But it couldn't be him. The child beckoned. I wondered if a motor bike was parked outside the gate, its engine running as a faceless knight waited to break the spell. Except that the knight was no longer anonymous. Not only had I been played for a fool, but Luke had been played for one too.

The gravel in front of the hostel was lit by light from the kitchen window where the boy was doing his homework. Al stood by the gate, staring at my shaved head. He looked shaken but I couldn't decide if he had heard the news about his father yet. I walked to the gate, but didn't open it. Everything had changed since we hid among the trees last night. Life might have been so different if I had only gone with him to Dublin.

'Thank God you're safe, Trace,' he said. 'I've been so scared for you.'

I should have told him about his father immediately but there were things I needed to know for myself. The girl stayed back in the doorway.

'Did you actually see Luke sleep with your mother?'

Al looked puzzled by the question. 'Christine saw it. She told me.'

'What else did she tell you?'

'I don't know what you mean,' he said. 'How did you get away from him, Trace?'

I studied his face carefully. He appeared to have taken such risks for me, yet there was nothing or nobody I could be sure of any more.

'Why wasn't Christine's boyfriend at her father's funeral?'

'What's that got to do with anything?' Al asked.

'Answer my question.'

'I don't know why. Whoever he is, she never brings him home. Carl saw her in town once with some guy on a motor bike. These days Christine moves in circles I wouldn't want to know about.'

'How did you find me?' I asked.

'This fiddler guy is pretty famous. Everyone in Donegal knows he lodges in Glencolumbkille for January, then goes into some hospital in Letterkenny until the spring comes.'

'Luke said no one knew where he went.'

'Ask Luke for the time and he'll make you think he's the only person on the planet who knows it,' Al said. 'I tried to follow you this morning but you know that car of mine.' He paused, ruefully. 'I ran out of petrol.'

'For the love of God, Al.'

'I know,' he said. 'I'm incompetent on a good day.'

He reached across to take my hand and I took a step back.

'I've bad news,' I said. 'But I don't know how to tell you.'

'Luke's dead, isn't he?' Al replied. 'I saw an ambulance and two squad cars tearing out from Killybegs and followed them into the arse of some glen. His car was sealed off with tape. There was no sign of it having crashed so I guessed he'd been killed. What I couldn't see was how many bodies they were taking out. I was so relieved when you walked safely out that door.'

'They shot him in the head.' I said. 'I saw it happen.'

'That's not possible. They would have killed you as well.'

'I was there.'

'Did anyone else see you?'

'Not at the moment it happened.'

'Then you know nothing until the police tell you,' Al cautioned. 'Tell the police you fought with Luke and ran away. It's important, Trace. They don't leave witnesses.'

I reached for Al's hand. 'That isn't all I have to tell you. Al, I'm sorry, but your father was shot at lunchtime driving a van in Waterford.'

Al didn't speak and his face didn't even register a change of expression. It was like he was frozen.

'This trip to Donegal was just a decoy,' I explained.

'My father was clean,' Al said. 'All he ever fiddled was the VAT. He stayed out of their business and kept me from it too. He was their kid brother, they looked after him. It was the one thing Christy would have killed Luke for if he'd . . .'

Al stopped. His ginger hair was so different from Shane's that it was only now I noticed how similar their features were.

'They took whatever he was carrying in the van.'

'They had no need to kill him,' Al said, almost to himself. 'He wouldn't even have been armed. Da was an amateur. Ringo the Joker. Everyone knew that.' He was silent for a moment. 'How often did they shoot Luke?'

'Twice. In the back and in the head.'

'One for each brother,' he said, bitterly. 'Twice wasn't enough.' He let go my hand. 'For your own sake, tell the police nothing. They know you were just his . . . that you weren't involved.' He stopped. 'Why were you asking about Christine?'

I was scared. This was the moment when I had to decide if I trusted Al. He could have known all along, maybe he was even Christine's partner. Carl had said they were kissing cousins once. Could Luke's beating have changed him or might he be trying to revenge Christy's death? He had seemed so anxious to get me away from Luke last night that maybe I was the bonus he was playing for.

'And why did you ask about my mother and that bastard?' Al was shaking. I sensed the grief he was trying to hold at

371

bay and I felt sure he was innocent. He had travelled here for my sake, understanding even less than I did about what was happening. But now for his sake I couldn't tell him the truth.

Luke was certainly a gangster, as Al claimed. No doubt he had planned major robberies in the past and ran a cigarette racket with Christy. Yet even in this, I suspected he was really minding Christy, knowing his brother could never cope on his own. There probably was money waiting for Christy in some off-shore account, if Luke could have only broken his obsession to hoard and borne to watch Margaret blow it. But Luke would never have hatched such a plan as the robbery on that security van. A proper gambler only bets when the odds are right, and besides, Luke wouldn't have the contacts to steal plans from the Bypass Bombardiers. I didn't know if Christine's boy-friend was a Bombardier member going solo or just some hood who hung around the fringes of crime. But for once Christy had stopped listening to Luke and had listened to his daughter instead.

I stared up at the dark mountains, realising that Luke hadn't been lying. This operation really had nothing to do with him. He was just sorting out another family mess, organising the shipment which Christine had been incapable of setting up, while his niece used him like she had used her own father. I didn't know if Christine had arranged Shane's killing as well, whether she was being double-crossed in this by her boy-friend or if the Bypass Bombardiers had finally caught up with them both. She was Christy's daughter with Christy's brains and a reputation to live up to. I wondered if she might be lying dead in some other ditch by now. Even if she wasn't, Luke had been right in saying that it was only a matter of time before she was laid out in the same funeral home as her father.

'Why won't you answer my questions?' Al almost shouted and we both became aware of the child in the doorway.

'Does Christine always wear White Musk?' I asked.

'My father's dead and you're asking about perfume.' Al was

angry. I could sense the news of his father's death starting to sink in. He looked so out of his depth that I wanted to wrap my arms around him. Al the pal. The sort of friend I had always hoped would be out there for me one day. But now I held back, because I didn't know if Al was strong enough to resist the lure of his family name and I refused to let myself be destroyed alongside him in that underworld.

I should be dead already, I still didn't know why Christine had spared my life as she stared from behind that visor. Then I remembered Luke saying that he'd only ever slept with someone younger than me once: the most experienced of the lot who had seduced him and been impossible to escape from. Maybe even Christine felt that she owed him one favour, or else she was under instructions from her boy-friend. Luke's murder would cause no more stir than the mundane everyday deaths of strung-out young junkies in those Dublin ghettos Al had shown me. But killing a tourist would bring the police and politicians and the newspapers down on their heads. No would-be mafioso wants to draw that attention.

'Your mother was never unfaithful,' I said.

'How the hell would you know?'

'Trust me. I just do.'

'She's alone in Dublin. I have things to sort out there,' Al said. 'Will you be okay?'

'Don't try to sort them out, Al. They'll tear you to pieces.'

'Legitimate things,' he said angrily. 'Funeral details, insurance, the running of the shop.'

'Sell the shop. Don't let your mother follow another coffin in six months' time.'

'What are you saying?' Al asked. 'That I'm a wimp, like everyone claims? My father's dead and I should just forget it.'

'You know who killed him,' I lied. 'Luke used us all. Even his own brothers meant nothing.' Al had come to Donegal to rescue me, now I wanted to do the same for him. 'Luke is dead. Bury your father, then go back to London. There'll be

373

a bed for you in my grandfather's house, if you come in the next few days.'

Al was quiet for a moment. 'What would I do there?'

'Find a job.'

'But I'm a Duggan,' he said, almost scared. 'I wouldn't know how. I've no skills, nothing. Luke always arranged everything.'

'I'm going back to college in the spring,' I said. 'You could probably do the same somewhere.'

'Do you think so?' His voice was full of self-doubt. 'There's things I would still need to sort out first. They might take a while. Can I call to your flat?'

'I won't be there after next weekend.'

'Where would I find you?'

I said nothing. Luke would have tracked me down, but Al never could. I wouldn't stay in Harrow for ever, but maybe with Grandad and myself there Gran could come home some weekend. It was like Luke's death had spurred me to start living again. I didn't know yet what I wanted to do with my life, but it was time to find out.

'I'm not sure how long things will take in Dublin,' Al said. 'I'll try.' He leaned across the gate to put his arms around me. The last person to kiss me was dead. I had no way of knowing if Al would follow him. He stepped back.

'If you're going you should go,' I said.

Al nodded. He didn't want to leave now.

'Your flat then,' he said.

'I won't wait for ever.'

Al got into the car and started the engine. The girl came out of the hostel doorway to watch the car lights disappear.

'Is he your boy-friend?' she asked.

'What do you think, Molly? Should I let him be?'

The road was in darkness again, but we saw the lights appear at a bend further up the hillside.

'He's all right, I suppose,' she said. 'But wouldn't you prefer someone a bit more rugged?'

'I don't know if I would.'

'My Daddy was rugged,' she said, 'frightened of nothing. They say he drowned. Bits of the fishing boat were washed up and two other bodies, but I know he's out there.'

I looked down. She was staring solemnly out at the dark waves.

'There's every class of foreign boats out there that don't even have phones. With a life belt you'd float for days. If you were strong enough it wouldn't matter how bad the storm was, would it?'

I didn't reply. I don't think she wanted me too. I took her hand and we walked back across the gravel.

TWENTY-FOUR

IT WAS NINE O'CLOCK when I reached Cunningham's pub. If I was going to be picked up for questioning then I decided it would be better there, rather than with Molly watching me being put into a squad car from her bedroom window at the hostel. The pub looked like any other old house on the street, except that it was slightly larger and had the name *Cunningham* painted on the grey stone above the door. Once it would have stood at the very edge of the village, but now further on, beyond the final streetlamp, I could discern the shapes of modern bungalows lighting up the dark. A car passed and returned the street to silence. I entered the pub, although I wasn't sure if the fiddler was really going to play here, without a poster or anything.

Fewer than twenty people were gathered in the bar, most of them elderly men togged out in dark nondescript clothing. I could spot the car drivers among them reluctantly sipping lemonade. Only one or two people nodded, but my presence had been taken in by them all. A cluster of men at the far end of the bar discussed the purchase of land or cattle, while a local ancient in a peaked tweed cap sat alone, slowly nursing a whiskey a few stools away from them. Two married couples on stools talked to the woman behind the counter, whom I guessed was Mrs Cunningham. She detached herself from their company and approached as I took a free stool beside the old man. She eyed my face and then my shaved head so carefully that I thought I was about to be barred.

'You're the girl from the hostel,' she said. 'Noeleen, the hairdresser, mentioned you when she was in earlier.'

I ordered a vodka and tonic and she went to fetch it. A hard-backed chair had been set out a few feet from the wall at the far end of the room. It reminded me of the one Luke had sat on during our first encounter in London. There were no lights or microphones but I knew why it was there.

'Is there going to be music?' I asked the ancient beside me.

'Aye. Maybe later.' The reply was soft spoken but it felt like drawing blood from a stone. You could spot the unmarried men like him by a solitariness in their manner. I could only guess at their lives alone on the surrounding mountains, listening to sheep and the wind and voices in their heads. Mrs Cunningham returned with my drink and seemed about to say something. She contented herself, however, with rejoining the married couples who kept glancing at me as suspiciously as the woman in the hostel had first eyed me up.

I sat in the corner to avoid them all and waited for the police to arrive. Luke would soon be laid naked on a slab. I could imagine every detail of his body, his scar, the silver in the stubble which kept growing for a period after death, the slightly twisted shape of his knees. But it wasn't Luke I saw in my mind as the pub filled up: it was my mother as I had never known her. That girl with long hair and a sun hat in a badly printed photograph. This pub looked unchanged for years. She must have sat in one like it, idly curious about the music to be heard and never imagining that her life was about to be irrevocably changed.

Within the space of ten minutes the pub had become crowded with maybe forty customers now and a quiet sense of anticipation. Mrs Cunningham walked over to a half-open door which led back into her kitchen. I waited for her to open it fully and herald the entrance of the fiddler, but instead she closed it over to block out the noise of a television there. She took a fiddle down which had been hanging behind the bar and handed it to the old man at the counter to whom I had already spoken. He walked over to the chair and sat down, running the bow across the strings and making minor adjustments.

'You'd want superglue to keep that tuned, Proinsías,' someone said and there was a quiet laugh at what was obviously an old joke. I stared dully at my father. Somehow I had imagined our first meeting would be a moment of blinding perception. Yet I was already in his presence for twenty minutes and we had even spoken without either of us recognising each other. Suddenly I felt I should never have set out on this disastrous journey. If I had wanted to tell him about his wife, I could have contacted the Irish police from London. There was a terrible sense of deflation. I already had a family I had only ever hurt.

Through a tiny gap between his socks and grey trousers I could see a pair of faded long-johns. He looked so old that my childhood feelings of disgust came back at the thought of my mother coupling with him. I was the result of that mismatch but I wanted to leave because I knew we could have nothing to say to each other. Then he began to sing:

> One night I was tipsy from drinking strong whiskey,
> The bumpers were passed right merrily round,
> The toasts they were listed and no one resisted
> And Terry his fiddle did cheerfully sound . . .

He raised the fiddle and as he began to play the room was silent. His chin and his eyes were the only still parts of him. It seemed impossible for any old man to play so fast and so strong. I sensed every customer watching his bow hand drawing grace-notes and the tiniest ornamentations from the spaces between notes. The sound was so rich that it seemed more than one fiddle had to be playing, with three and four notes existing at the one time. I had never heard playing like it,

378

not even from the crackling field recording Luke had given me. The applause was loud but also restrained as if out of respect. The fiddler put his head to one side and closed his eyes. Every muscle in his face seemed animated now. If I had gone out and come back in, I wouldn't have recognised him as the man I had spoken to at the counter. His foot tapped on the floor in a rhythm which only he heard until he began to sing again;

> *Good luck to you all now, barring the cat*
> *That sits in the corner there smelling a rat,*
> *O wheesht your philandering girls and behave*
> *And saving your presence, I'll chant you a stave*

He had opened his eyes and they were staring straight at me, with none of the shyness he had displayed at the bar.

> *I come from the land where the pritties grow big*
> *And the boys neat and handy can swirl in a jig*
> *And the girls they would charm your heart for to see*
> *Those darling colleens around Tandragee*

Some of the older men sitting at the bar joined in the chorus.

> *So here's to the boys who are happy and gay*
> *Singing and dancing and tearing away*
> *Rollicksome, frolicsome, frisky and free*
> *We're the rollicking boys around Tandragee.*

I could imagine my mother in such a pub, relishing the abandon in those songs after the strictures of that house in Harrow. His voice was cracked now and older, but it had a lilt which could still carry anyone away. He moved straight from the song into another set of tunes on the fiddle, growing ever faster and more furious. I remembered a story about him which Luke had told me on the plane.

When his father was dying in some public hospital Mac Suibhne had gone to visit him, thinking music might cheer his spirits. He was said to have played his father's favourite tune as well as he thought he had ever played it, but the old man rose from the bed to snatch the fiddle in annoyance and launch into the tune himself, playing it with a frenzy Mac Suibhne had never heard before. His father finished the tune, handed the fiddle to his son and laid his head back to die. At that same moment a fiddle in the family home fell from a nail on the wall and burst asunder. Before now I couldn't imagine the story being true, but, watching him, suddenly I would not have been surprised if the fiddle burst into flames in his hands.

He finished and held the bow still, as though the applause was an intrusion, before starting to play a slow set, filled with an almost unbearable sense of grief. I looked around at the listening faces and wondered what they heard. Maybe they knew each tune and what it meant, or maybe the notes drew out some private loss within themselves. Luke would have loved to hear this lament. I thought of the police and the ambulance up on the hill and Luke being zipped up inside a body-bag. I saw the photograph of my mother again, laughing under a sun hat. I saw Gran strapped into a hospital bed and drugged for the night. And Grandad alone in Harrow waiting for the call from the hospital that would finally come. Only when I lifted my hand to my face did I realise that I was crying for all those lives caught up in the notes of that slow tune. Nobody seemed to notice my tears. The fiddler stopped at last and there was silence for ten or fifteen seconds before the clapping began. People took the chance to drift to the bar, ordering drink in low voices.

'Give us a story, Proinsías,' a man as old as himself asked. The fiddler raised his bow as though he hadn't heard him. He played a few bars, bending them as if to disguise the notes before asking if anyone recognised the tune.

'*Casadh an tSúgáin*,' an old woman close to me said and the fiddler nodded, lowering the bow.

'The Twisting of the Rope, it's called in English.' He lowered the fiddle so that it rested on his knee, his back straight on the hard chair as he looked around. 'And it's not many miles from here that the tune was written by a wandering fiddler on a night as wild as this.'

He paused as the till rang but I heard Mrs Cunningham use her hand to stop it springing open. There was the sound of a glass being placed down and then the room lapsed into silence.

'One time a fiddler was crossing these hills towards dark after playing at a house party in the glen,' the old man began. 'It was a lonesome night with storms coming in and the man was feared to travel on. Only one light did he see and when he made for it he found a girl herding animals in from the storm. And when he told her he'd have more courage to journey on in the morning if there might be a bed of straw somewhere, she promised to ask her mother, for she spied the fiddle inside his great coat and she had a liking for music always.'

The fiddler's eyes travelled the room but seemed to keep coming back to me.

'So pleased was she at the thought of music that she forgot her mother's fear of neighbours whispering. Because the women lived alone, the father being off in Scotland working. When her mother saw her lead the fiddler to the house, and the cut of his clothes and his age she was for running him from the door. The fiddler could sense her black eyes, but if he hadn't felt tired before, then his legs grew weary as he saw the fire lit and the shining house.

'The girl's legs were itching to dance. But the old hag was having none of it and no bad talk brought down by a man staying in the house. Well, she tried every trick to coax him out into the rain, but says he; 'It wasn't you invited me here. I'm a God-fearing man and I'll give my word I'll do you no harm to either of yous this side of morning.'

'The mother saw there was no shifting him, but she was a crafty old one. "Is fiddling all you're good for," says she, "or would you know an honest hour's work?" He told her he was no slacker and she sent the daughter to fetch armfuls of hay, saying; "There's a long grass rope needed in this house". So didn't the fiddler take up the trawhook and set to twisting away at the straw the daughter held, being hell bent on showing how his arms were still strong, for he'd taken as much a liking to the daughter as she had to himself. Soon he had a rope twisted the length of the room, but the old hag was after more and she held the door open for him to work on. Out he went into the yard, twisting the finest straw rope until he fell back with a jerk, for hadn't she cut the rope with a knife, half way between him and the girl before slamming the door in his face. Well, he picked himself up and catching hold of his fiddle this is the tune he made.'

As the laughter died down he picked up the fiddle from his lap and raised it to his chin.

'You never told the story that way before,' the woman said.

'Well, if I told it different before, it wasn't a lie then either. *Casadh an tSúgáin*,' he announced and began to play with his eyes still watching me. I felt angry suddenly. Our lives couldn't be explained away by a simple folk tale, which made no reference to the girl being left with a child. No matter what disgust the girl's mother felt, the fiddler had no right to compose his tune and simply wander off to sing about his rollicksome, frolicsome boys, until somebody had to track the man down to tell him about his bride's death.

I decided that I had seen my father and I had seen enough. I would write from London and tell him he was a widower in crisp impersonal sentences. I wanted to be back in that city now, but I had to go through the charade of having Detective

382

Brennan find me first. I would know nothing. Luke and I had quarrelled and I had run away from him, shaken. I had heard no assassin and seen no motor bike.

I stood up to leave but the lady beside me thought I was looking for the toilet and pointed towards a door at the end of the room. My movements were attracting attention and people were making space for me in that direction, so that I felt too awkward to head for the front door instead. I passed close to the fiddler who didn't look up, and then lifted the latch to go out into the back yard. I hoped there might be a way to escape without being forced to go back to the bar again. A light high up on the back wall lit the gravel yard. A dog rose and padded over to lick my hand. I rubbed his neck and he wagged his tail, acknowledging the attention before retreating back to his corner. A sign saying *Ladies* was pinned to the door of what had once been a sort of cow-byre. There was a stream coming off the hillside which seemed to disappear beneath the shed.

I remembered being cuddled in bed as a child and how my mother had laughed about a pub somewhere where the ladies toilet was just a plank with a hole in it across an open stream. The toilet door was open and I could see that the floor was concreted and a modern toilet was there, perfectly plumbed with a wash-basin and towel. But I knew this had to be the same place, with the stream now piped underground. An open gate at the end of the yard led out to an unploughed field with a low stone wall, where only thistles seemed to grow. I saw lights from bungalows at the end of it and knew that I could flee back on to the road. I'm not sure how long I was being watched until I turned to find Mrs Cunningham standing there.

'It is Tracey, isn't it?' she said. 'It seems strange calling you that after him having his own name for you always.'

'How do you know my name?' I was frightened by her presence.

'Trish, he wanted to call you, for Patricia. They changed it to Tracey. They thought it was a nicer name, I suppose.'

'What are you talking about?' I felt trapped. 'You don't know me.'

'Not at first, I didn't. The shaved head is very different. It's only when you were sitting down that I placed you. You've still got your mother's features. I know Trish was only a pet name but it's hard to think of you as anything else. It's what he called you sometimes late at night.'

'He knows I'm here, doesn't he?'

'Don't be too harsh on him.'

'He hasn't written or shown his face in over twenty years. We're the flesh and blood he left behind for his ramblings.'

'I know,' she said, 'and he knows that too, although he doesn't say it. When he gets out of that chair he rarely says anything. But I know there isn't a day goes by when he doesn't think of you.'

'Thoughts are no use,' I said. 'He would have come to London if he really cared.'

'God knows, he cared,' she said. 'He doted on you. He cared too much, but he didn't know how to mind you, no matter how hard he tried.'

'For six lousy months in London,' I retorted.

'And six terrible weeks here,' she replied.

'I don't know what you mean.'

'They never told you?'

'Told me what?'

Mrs Cunningham glanced up at the unlit bedroom above her head. 'It was madness,' she said. 'Proinsías knew it himself afterwards. He was ashamed of what he did but your mother's family, well, they treated him like a beggar. I think they just didn't understand. Proinsías never talked about it but I could see it in your grandfather's face when he came here.'

'My Grandad was never here in his life,' I said. Then I

remembered Grandad Pete going to say something in Harrow and how he had stopped, as if afraid to lose me again.

'I'm not saying a word against your grandfather,' she said. 'He seemed a nice man. A less patient one would have called the police in, but he traipsed around Donegal till he finally tracked your father down. It wasn't easy. Proinsías was scared because of what he'd done, staying only in the most remote places. There weren't that many phones back then and it was all little local exchanges. He could have vanished for months, but he had to come down here to me in the end. You see, all that time he'd been hoping your mother would follow him back here. Proinsías was never practical. He thought life could go on for the three of yous, just as it had for him. I don't blame your grandparents for being scared of him. He was old and even here locals looked bad on the marriage. But what he did to you was never kidnapping. I suppose they were worried he'd do something crazy again, but they were wrong to threaten him with jail if he ever set foot in England. All the man wanted was to bring you home.'

I looked back up the dark hillside where the wind was blowing. There was no way I could have remembered it, but I could see the pair of us in my mind crossing a dark expanse of bog leading down to an unlit mountain road by the sea. My father wore a long greatcoat with a fiddle hung inside it and I was cradled against his chest strapped in a baby harness. He had a large peddler's pack on his back and he was stumbling under the weight of it, and from tiredness and fear.

'He ran away with me?' I said. 'Are you saying I slept here?'

'For four nights in that room up there.' She pointed to the unlit window above our heads. 'You had nappy rash, I remember. I fed you myself. You loved the sound of his music, I remember that too. It was better than any soother for you. You must have slept in half a dozen houses like this in Donegal, places where there were women your father could trust to mind you. I'm surprised they never said, but maybe they thought it would frighten you as a girl.'

Some man opened the door and stood for a moment looking back at my father playing.

'Why has he never made a proper record?' I asked.

'I suppose nobody cared for the music when he was at his peak,' she said. 'It's only in recent years that Irish people stopped being ashamed of their own music. He says he isn't good enough any more, that he can't play like when he was a young man. But I think he wants it all to die with him. He has no one left here to pass it on to.'

The men at the doorway turned and walked out past us with a nod, making for the gents in the corner. I looked back through the open door and saw the room spell-bound by his playing.

'Do you think he could teach me to play?'

'I don't know, but you have the hands for it,' Mrs Cunningham said. She looked through the doorway. 'He knows you're out here. I can hear it in the way he's playing. He can't seem to stop. That's nerves. He doesn't know whether you're gone out this door for good or if you're coming back inside to him.'

'I didn't know myself.'

'Does your mother know you're here?'

'She died sixteen months ago,' I said. 'That's all I came to tell him. Would you do it for me?'

'I'm desperately sorry to hear that news, child,' Mrs Cunningham said. 'Your mother lit up this place like a flame the time she came. They met in this pub. None of us knew what was going on, except that Proinsías had never stayed so long. She kept putting off going home. They'd walk for miles out of the glen before meeting up. They were as silly as each other, thinking nobody would spy them. But, God knows, she made Proinsías smile like I've never seen before or since.'

She stopped and listened to his playing. 'It was cruel, the

way his father beat the music into him till his fingers bled
from the strings. He taught him little of the world beyond
highlands and reels, because music was all the Mac Suibhnes
had. Your father told me that even when he had to stand in
Letterkenny at twelve, and hire himself out to some farmer
who hit him and fed him nothing but sour milk and salty
spuds, he'd still spend hours practising with a stick, imagining
he could hear the tunes. Any time there was trouble that's
what he'd do, vanish into a world of his own. Your mother
was the only woman to take him out of himself. It was like
a cloud lifting, the pair of them whispering and laughing as
he tried to show her how to hold a bow. They were the oddest
couple and yet I never saw a pair as well matched.' She looked
through the doorway again. 'Proinsías always hoped she'd come
back, even just to visit. I told him often to go across to London,
there was no law stopping him. But they had made him
feel like a tramp and all you Mac Suibhnes were proud and
stubborn always.'

He stopped playing and put the fiddle down. He ignored
the applause and looking right out to where the pair of us
were framed in the light.

'He's stuck in that chair,' Mrs Cunningham said. 'He doesn't
know what to do. You've come this far to tell him your news
and you've more than that to say to him. I know there's so
much he wants to tell you. Will you not talk to him
now?'

I nodded, not to her but slowly towards him. After a
moment he rose. I could hear voices in the bar talking among
themselves, thinking he was taking a break. He seemed very
slow on his feet and careful how he walked. He put his hand
on the door frame for support as he stepped on to the gravel,
cradling the fiddle in the crick of his elbow. These words were
not going to be without pain. He waited until I took a step
towards him, then let go the door frame and grasped the arm
I held out. His fingers were strong and warm and longer than

any that I had ever seen. I touched them with a child's silent curiosity, then looked up and returned his silent smile. We both went to speak at the same time, neither of us knowing what we would say.

The author is indebted to three excellent books: Sean O Boyle's *The Irish Song Tradition* which provided the text of 'The Knight on the Road'; Paddy Tunney's *The Stone Fiddle* which provided the text of 'The Rollicking Boys Around Tandragee' (written by his uncle Michael, a shoemaker in the townland of Tunnyoran) and which also provides a far longer and more accurate account of the story of 'Casadh an tSúgáin' (as narrated to him by the travelling fiddle-player, Mickie Doherty), along with his own superb translation of the original song. Caoimhín MacAoidh's *Between the Jigs and the Reels: The Donegal Fiddle Tradition* (also containing details of the Dohertys' version of 'Casadh an tSúgáin)' proved as invaluable a written source on Donegal as Mr Anthony Glavin (of Glencolmcille and Dublin) proved to be an oral one.

The author especially wishes to thank those who provided the rooms and space within which this book was written.